VARIORUM COLLECTED STUDIES SERIES

Studies in English Church Music, 1550–1900

Nicholas Temperley

Nicholas Temperley

Studies in English Church Music, 1550–1900

This edition © 2009 by Nicholas Temperley

Nicholas Temperley has asserted his moral right under the Copyright, Designs and Patents Act, 1988, to be identified as the author of this work.

Published in the Variorum Collected Studies Series by

Ashgate Publishing Limited
Wey Court East
Union Road
Farnham, Surrey
GU9 7PT
England

Ashgate Publishing Company
Suite 420
101 Cherry Street
Burlington, VT 05401–4405
USA

Ashgate website: http://www.ashgate.com

ISBN 978–0–7546–5998–3

British Library Cataloguing in Publication Data
Temperley, Nicholas
  Studies in English church music, 1550–1900.
  – (Variorum collected studies series)
  1. Church music – England – 16th century 2. Church music – England – 17th century 3. Church music – England – 18th century 4. Church music – England – 19th century
  I. Title
  781.7'1'00942

  ISBN 978–0–7546–5998–3

Library of Congress Cataloging-in-Publication Data
Temperley, Nicholas.
  Studies in English church music, 1550–1900 / Nicholas Temperley.
  p. cm. – (Variorum collected studies series)
  Includes bibliographical references and index.
  ISBN 978–0–7546–5998–3 (hardcover : alk. paper)
  1. Church music – England.
  I. Title.
  ML2931.T46 2009
  781.71'300942 – dc22
                                          2008055069

VARIORUM COLLECTED STUDIES SERIES CS926

CONTENTS

PUBLISHER'S NOTE

The original page numbers of the articles in this volume have been retained along with a new continuous pagination, to facilitate their use where these same studies have been referred to elsewhere. The exceptions are articles I, IX and XIII, which have been re-set for the purposes of this volume.

Asterisks in the margins are to alert readers to additional information supplied in the Addenda and Corrigenda section.

INTRODUCTION

In about 1967 I decided to make English church music one of my main areas of specialization in musicology. Ten years of daily chapel at school, followed by seven years as a student at King's College, Cambridge, had given me not only a strong emotional bond with the Church of England but a detailed knowledge of its music and liturgy. But I felt at a disadvantage compared with contemporaries who had known the cathedral repertoire inside out from their time as choristers.

It turned out that the history of English cathedral music had been thoroughly treated by many knowledgeable writers; so had the music of religious revivals, such as Wesleyan Methodism and the Oxford Movement. But the ordinary music of the parish church had been almost completely neglected. So that was where I concentrated my attention. It led to two main offerings, *The Music of the English Parish Church* (2 vols, Cambridge University Press, 1979, reprinted 2005) and *The Hymn Tune Index: A Census of English-Language Hymn Tunes in Printed Sources from 1535 to 1820* (4 vols, Oxford: Clarendon Press, 1998) (*HTI*). The latter was compiled with the assistance of Charles G. Manns and Joseph Herl, and was placed online in 2001; it is available to the public at http://hymntune. library.illinois.edu/.

Not surprisingly, there were a number of offshoots of this research that appeared in diverse publications, and in course of time they tended to get buried in sets of bound periodicals housed on library shelves. Some of them dealt with special topics in more detail than my two main publications could accommodate; others linked parish-church music to broader topics. Thanks to Ashgate Publishing and the encouragement of John Smedley, I have been able to unearth these and bring them together in a single volume. Most of them have been directly reproduced by photographic methods, which allow for the correction of misprints and minor errors; three essays (I, IX, and XIII) had to be reset because the original formats were unsuitable for reproduction here. In every case the original publisher or copyright owner generously allowed us to republish the article without charge.

Naturally these essays do not add up to a comprehensive history or expound a single theme. But they do group themselves into two broad topics, which I have called 'vernacular' and 'artistic' church music.

Part One, 'Vernacular Church Music', covers the first two centuries after the Reformation, when the music of the parish church was largely left to the people, while the church authorities concerned themselves with limiting the texts sung (to those taken directly from the Bible), and to discouraging organs and choirs. Hence the music heard in the churches was mostly unaccompanied congregational singing of metrical psalms. This is the core subject of Part One. Essays I to III cover both the development and the limitations of the music to which these psalms were sung, exploring the printed books that both enabled and regulated the practice of psalm singing. No. IV shows how the common people, freed from the control of these books, turned the singing into a bizarre and now largely unfamiliar kind of ritual. No. V chronicles the survival of the Anglican communion hymn, despite the prevailing culture of psalms, and No. VI shows how self-appointed choirs, still without professional supervision, began to strive towards artistic musical forms.

Part Two, 'Artistic Church Music', is about the gradual involvement of professional musicians in parochial church music, beginning in the Restoration period. At first this was accomplished primarily through the introduction of organs (VII, VIII) and the training of charity school children (IX). The part played by hymn singing in London charities founded in the 18th century is followed up in Nos. X and XI, and the growing interest in hymns and in psalm chanting in No. XII. In course of time both cathedral music and secular art music had their influence on the parochial scene. No. XIII covers the period of the whole book in a brief survey of organ settings of psalm tunes. Finally, No. XIV reassesses the work of a prominent Victorian cathedral musician, whose music was nevertheless promulgated chiefly in the parish churches.

Inevitably, there is some duplication of material between one essay and another, and between them and the two published books. Cross-references between essays will be found from time to time. The 'Addenda and Corrigenda' section reports on discoveries and reassessments made since the original publication of the essays. Finally, a full index helps to draw the separate essays together.

NICHOLAS TEMPERLEY

Urbana, Illinois
March 2009

ACKNOWLEDGEMENTS

Grateful acknowledgement is made to the following institutions and publishers for their kind permission to reproduce the articles included in this volume: the Folger Shakespeare Library, Washington, DC (for Chapter I); the Bibliographical Society of the University of Virginia, Charlottesville, VA (II); the American Musicological Society, Brunswick, ME, and the University of California Press, Berkeley, CA (III, IV); the Hymn Society of America, Inc., Springfield, OH (V); the Royal Musical Association, London (VI); Laaber-Verlag, Buren, Netherlands (VII); Positif Press, Oxford (VIII); The Musical Times Publications Ltd, London (IX, XIII); Chester Music and Novello & Co. Ltd, London (music supplement to IX); the Board of Trustees of the University of Illinois, Urbana-Champaign, IL (X); Oxford University Press, Oxford (XI); Borthwick Publications, Borthwick Institute for Archives, University of York (XII). For the illustration of St Michael le Belfrey in Chapter XII, I would like to thank the York Museums Trust (York Art Gallery).

I

'If any of you be mery let hym synge psalmes': The Culture of Psalms in Church and Home

The psalms of David loomed large in the consciousness of the English for two centuries after the Reformation. That was the time when phrases from the psalms entered everyday speech: 'from strength to strength' (84:7), 'at their wits' end' (107: 27), 'the apple of [my] eye' (17:8), 'my cup runneth over' (23: 5), and many more. The psalms were favored by all classes of society; as literature, as song, and as liturgy; for public worship and for private contemplation.

The medieval church had required the chanting of certain Latin psalms in the Office by priest and choir. It had also encouraged the use of a group of psalms to assist private meditation: these found their way into many primers and manuals in English prose translation. Especially popular were the 'Seven Penitential Psalms' (6, 32, 38, 51, 102, 130, 143) and the 'Fifteen Psalms' (120–134), also largely penitential or admonitory.[1] What was new in the reformed churches was the idea that psalms are the ideal vehicle for the people's praise of God. This principle was embraced by Jean Calvin, who did not share Luther's fondness for the Latin liturgical hymns or the *geistliche Gesänge* of German tradition, yet saw the value of public expressions of praise: 'Look where we may, we will never find songs better, nor more suited to the purpose, than the psalms of David: which the Holy Ghost himself composed. And so, when we sing them, we are certain that God puts the words in our mouth, as if he himself sang in us to magnify his praise'.[2] Notice that Calvin did not expressly exclude non-scriptural hymns. But he used his growing influence to encourage the singing of psalms, and his views prevailed in the non-Lutheran strands of Protestantism, including those now called Anglicans, Puritans, and Presbyterians.

A text that was frequently cited in support of this position was James 5:13. The Great Bible version of 1539 reads, 'If any of you be vexed let him praye.

---

[1] See Francis Procter, *A History of the Book of Common Prayer* (London and Cambridge, 1864), 12–15.

[2] Jean Calvin, 'La forme des prieres et chants ecclesiastiques'. In *Pseaumes octantetrois de David, mis en rime Francoise . . . par Clement Marot . . . Et trentequatre par Theodore de Besze* (Geneva: Jean Crespin, 1551), A7r–7v; translation mine.

If any of you be mery, let him synge psalmes'. Though the apostle James may not have had any particular songs in mind, the literalism of the reformers took the verse as a specific reference to the 150 canonical psalms. And the injunction encouraged the use of psalms in private as well as in church. Another verse, Colossians 3:16, seemed to allow a wider choice of texts: 'Psalmes and Hymnes, & spiritual songes'. Finally Psalm 148:12 established the important point that all should join the singing: 'Yonge men and maydens/olde men and children, prayse the name of the Lorde'.

The *Book of Common Prayer*, published in 1549 and prescribed for worship by the Act of Uniformity of the same year, was very largely made up of translations of portions of the Latin mass and office. But it contained a unique 'Table for The Ordre of the Psalmes, to be sayed at Matins and Evensong', which divided up all 150 psalms among the days of the month. This was justified in the preface by pointing out that 'of late tyme a fewe of them have been dailye sayed (and ofte repeated) and the rest utterly omitted'.[3]

The 1539 Great Bible translation, principally composed by Miles Coverdale, was adopted as the standard prose psalter and later (1662) incorporated in the *Book of Common Prayer*. It was not displaced by the King James version of the Bible; most people from 1611 onwards had two different prose translations of the psalms ready to hand, and undoubtedly, they were widely read in private, both silently and aloud in family prayers, as well as being heard in church as part of Morning and Evening Prayer. In ordinary churches they were spoken, verse by verse, in alternation by priest and people, though in course of time the people's part dwindled into silence and was left to the parish clerk. In cathedrals and other well-endowed sanctuaries they were chanted daily by the choir to the Gregorian psalm tones, either in unison or harmony, accompanied on the organ. The practice has continued from 1549 to the present, with brief interruptions in 1553–58 and 1645–60. It was not until the late seventeenth century that the composition of new specimens, now called 'Anglican chants', developed.

But the reformers' desire for the psalms to become the universal song of the people came up against the awkward fact that they are in prose. The only kind of song that untutored people could be expected to sing was the kind they knew already: the rhymed strophic ballad, repeating the same music for each stanza. For this reason Calvin had adopted *metrical* psalms as the basis of church song, accepting the resulting departures from literal translation in the interest of having all join in the singing. The core of his metrical psalter was the work of Clément Marot, a court poet who had turned to the versification of some of the psalms in about 1532. After Marot's death in 1544, Calvin commissioned

---

[3]   *The First and Second Prayer Books of King Edward the Sixth* (London and Toronto, 1910), 4.

Theodore de Bèze to finish the task of translating all 150 psalms. The complete French psalter was published at Geneva in 1562, with a splendid set of tunes.

Similarly, the more ardent of the English reformers took the versified 'court' psalms of Thomas Sternhold, groom of the robes to Henry VIII and Edward VI, as the basis for their own metrical psalter. Sternhold, in the preface to his first publication of *Certayne Psalmes Chosen out of the Psalter of Dauid, and Drawen into English Metre* (c1549), had dedicated them to Edward VI, 'trustyng that as your grace taketh pleasure to hear them song sometimes of me, so ye wyll also delyghte not onlye to see and reade them your selfe, but also to commande them to be song to you of others'. After Sternhold's death in 1549, a complete edition of his twenty-seven psalm versions was published by John Hopkins, a country clergyman, who added a further seven of his own.

Queen Mary I (Mary Tudor) restored the Catholic liturgy in 1554. In anticipation of this, a stream of several thousand Protestants left to find a home on the Continent where they would be free to worship as they pleased. Frankfurt was the main center, until a dispute arose between the 'prayer book' party that wished to follow the *Book of Common Prayer* and those who sought a more radical reform. The latter group – the Puritans – moved to Geneva under their leaders John Knox and William Whittingham. There they naturally came under the close influence of Calvin, whose sister Whittingham married. It was in Geneva that the first musical edition of Sternhold and Hopkins's psalms was published, as an appendage to the new service book: *One and Fiftie Psalmes of David in Englishe Metre, whereof .37. were made by Thomas Sterneholde: and the rest by others*. The imprint is 1556 and the preface dated 10 February 1556 (1557 new style). The seven new psalms were the work of Whittingham, who also revised Sternhold's versions: 'Conferred with the Hebrewe, and in certeyn places corrected as the text and sens of the Prophete required'. The service book specified two psalms for particular uses: 103 at communion and 128 after the marriage service. There were fifty-two tunes, three of them adapted from the French Genevan psalter. A second edition of 1558 added more versions and tunes.

The new tunes in these books are mostly bland, unshapely, and unmemorable by comparison with those of the French psalter. Whittingham, unlike Calvin, could not call on some of the best musicians of his country but had to make do with whatever talent was available in the small band of exiles. There is much to suggest that the tunes, though original, derived from a tradition of courtly songs, deprived of their accompaniment (since the Puritans would not allow organs or choirs in the service) and thus tending to lose their rhythmic vitality. A very similar type of tune is found in John Hall's Court of Vertue [1565], which is known to be a moralistic parody of *The Court of Venus*: the tunes may be those to which the original verses had been sung. Considering that an important part of the designed function of metrical psalms was to replace 'amorous and obscene songs' in the affections of the people, the Puritans may have welcomed the adaptation to moral texts of tunes or types of tune associated with erotic secular ballads. The title page of John Day's harmonized psalm book of 1563 says that the psalms might be 'song to al Musical instruments' and were now 'set forth for the encrease of vertue: and aboleshyng of other vayne and triflyng ballades'.

When Queen Elizabeth I decided to pursue a moderately Protestant church polity, she sought a compromise between the two parties in the reformed church, 'some declaring for Geneva, and some for Frankfurt'.[4] In her *Injunctions* of 1559, following the reintroduction of the prayer book, she showed characteristic subtlety. She did not explicitly countenance metrical psalms, but she allowed that 'in the beginning, or in the ende of Common Prayers, either at Morning or Evening prayers, there may be song an Himne, or suchlike Song, to the praise of almightie God in the best sort of Musicke that maye be conveniently devised, having respect that the sentence [sense] of the Himne may be understanded and perceived'.[5] This was taken to authorize both anthems in choral service and metrical psalms in congregational worship, yet it did not quite make either of them a part of the official liturgy.

The queen also granted a joint monopoly in the publishing of metrical psalms to two leading printers, William Seres and John Day. Seres made little use of his privilege, but Day began the series of psalm books that would soon become universal. It is now generally known as the 'Old Version' (or 'Sternhold and Hopkins') to distinguish it from Tate and Brady's New Version of the Psalms (1696). Day took the Geneva books as the starting point, adding more psalm versifications by Hopkins and several other authors. He also used material from a psalm book without tunes published at Wesel in about 1557, which represented the Frankfurt or 'prayer book' party. In particular he included metrical canticles, creeds, and hymns, to which Puritans might have objected, and placed them before and after the 150 canonical psalms.

When all the psalms had been versified, Day published the result in 1562 as *The Whole Booke of Psalmes, Collected into Englysh Metre by T. Starnhold I. Hopkins & others: Conferred with the Ebrue, with apt notes to synge them withal, faithfully perused and alowed according to thordre appointed in the quenes maiesties Injunctions.* It was surpassed in the number of its editions only by the Bible and prayer book (with which it was often bound up). The plan of the book illustrates once again the political

4   H. Robinson, ed., *Zurich Letters*, Parker Society Publications vol. 2 (Cambridge, 1842–45), 17.
5   Church of England, *Injunctions* (1559: *STC* 10110), ff. C4ʳ, C4ᵛ.

compromise inherent in the Elizabethan settlement of religion. It begins with a pedagogical device intended to ensure that all the people sang the psalms, rather than leaving them to trained choirs – a Puritan goal. But the first two songs in the book are a translated Latin Office hymn and an original hymn, neither of which could claim biblical authority.

The combination of Day's printing privilege, the citation of the queen's *Injunctions* on the title page, and the binding-up with the prayer book soon created a widespread impression that the psalm versions and hymns of the Old Version were the only ones authorized for use in church. (This fiction was not legally challenged until 1820.) It is certain that it soon became the only book in normal use, and that weekly singing in church soon made many of its texts and tunes as familiar a part of the culture as the bible itself. Congregations relished the chance to sing. The Puritan associations of the psalms were forgotten as they became a national possession – indeed the only form of organized singing in most people's lives. Church psalmody was nominally led by the parish clerk, solitary survivor of the small musical staff of chantry priests and clerks that had existed in many parish churches in Henry VIII's time. But in the absence of effective professional direction or accompaniment, it soon became a self-regulating crowd performance not unlike that of a stadium of football fans. Over the generations it tended to slow down, while complexities in the tunes were gradually lost.[6]

The tunes printed in the psalm book, with a few exceptions such as Psalm 100 (now called Old 100th), soon fell out of use, especially those of irregular meter derived from the French Genevan psalter. They were replaced by a set of sturdy four-line tunes, of unknown origin but certainly beginning to come in before 1580. By 1592 Thomas East, in publishing a harmonized edition of the Old Version, set the great majority of the psalms to these new tunes, and in 1594 he would state that a mere four of them were used for the psalms 'in most churches of this Realme'.

It is unlikely that four-part harmony such as East provided was within the reach of parish churches, where choirs were unknown in his time. Cathedrals and endowed choral foundations could have used them, but hardly in sufficient quantity to justify publication. East's book belongs, instead, to a series of books primarily intended for domestic use in affluent homes. Day's 1563 collection has already been mentioned. John Cosyn and William Damon also preceded East, while Richard Allison and Thomas Ravenscroft followed him. These compilers presented the psalm settings as substitutes for secular songs, which

---

[6] For a full account of church psalmody in this period, see Nicholas Temperley, *The Music of the English Parish Church* (Cambridge, 1979), especially chapters 2–5.

they characterized with varying degrees of disapproval. Allison's arrangements (1599) were 'to be sung or plaide upon the lute, orpharyon, citterne or base violle'.

But East and Ravenscroft differed from the others in important respects. As well as providing harmonized tunes underlaid with the first verse of a psalm, they printed all the other verses of the psalm below and repeated some tunes for many psalms, so that their books can be regarded as harmonized editions of the Old Version. Perhaps East hoped his book might be used in church as well, though he was too prudent to mention this in title page or preface, as it might have been seen as pushing the pace of reform. Ravenscroft followed suit; but he also dedicated his book to the archbishop of Canterbury and named most of the tunes after cathedrals and choral foundations.

Whereas Cosyn and Allison printed their own harmonizations, East and Ravenscroft commissioned leading musicians of the time, though not those who held leading church positions. East's roster consisted of Allison, Blancks, Cavendish, Cobbold, Dowland, Farmer, Farnaby, Hooper, and Kirby; Ravenscroft added another eleven names, including his own. Unlike the others, these two books entered the permanent repertory. East's was three times revised and reprinted, and Ravenscroft's was a revision of East's. On 27 December 1664, Samuel Pepys took part in a sing-through of 'Ravenscroft's four-part psalms, most admirable music', with two other men and a boy. The New England 'Bay Psalm Book' of 1640 also referred to Ravenscroft's tunes. In the 1670s John Playford 'was much importuned by some persons in the West Country to set out a new edition of Mr Ravenscroft's Psalms'.[7]

If formal harmonization of the psalm tunes was rarely heard in church, there is evidence of a practice of improvised harmonization, perhaps a survival of faburden – the fifteenth-century practice of improvising largely parallel counterpoints to chants. When a well-known tune was sung, one or two skilled singers might add a descant above it, generally moving to the nearest available consonance, with an occasional cadence suspension. In course of time the descant was perceived as the main melody and became separated from its mother tune. One tune, usually known as OXFORD, was specially prone to this practice. It may be itself a derivative of one of the ancient psalm tones, which had regularly been chanted in faburden. No less than three four-line tunes that were popular in the seventeenth century fit perfectly as descants to OXFORD. The other two cases were pointed out by Charles Butler, who said that the mean and tenor of OXFORD had been 'made two several tunes, (under the names of

    [7]   John Playford, *The Whole Book of Psalms . . . Compos'd in Three Parts* (London: W. Godbid for the Company of Stationers, 1677), preface.

Glassenburie and Kentish tunes) with other parts set unto them', though his example confused the tunes concerned.[8]

By the time of the Civil War, metrical psalms could be recruited by both sides, as eye-witnesses reported. In November 1640 the House of Commons attended church at St. Margaret's, Westminster, according to custom; but during the communion service, which was no doubt conducted in Laudian style by that time, some members 'began to sing some of Hopkins's metre, and disturbed the office . . . The Commons, it seems, had a mind to acquaint the people with part of their design'.[9] But during the siege of York in 1644, when those loyal to the king took refuge in the Minster, the whole congregation sang a psalm in the customary manner, led by the choir and 'a most Excellent-large-plump-lusty-full-speaking-Organ'.[10]

Psalms continued to be favored in educated circles, where there was growing discontent with the perceived crudity of the Old Version. George Sandys, a poet who dedicated each of his published works to Charles I, brought out a new set of paraphrases of the psalms and other biblical lyrics in 1636, and selections were set to music by the Lawes brothers, leading musicians of the court. Henry Lawes's *Choice Psalmes Put Into Musick, for Three Voices* was also dedicated to the king. Rather than arrange the common tunes Lawes composed entirely original settings and added some by his deceased brother William. Perhaps for this reason they had little impact on general practice.

In 1645 parliament abolished the *Book of Common Prayer* and substituted a Presbyterian order of service that called for metrical psalms. But neither of the new versions of psalms adopted by parliament (those of William Barton and Francis Rous) made much headway in the churches, even when the practice of lining out[11] was adopted. The people, by and large, went on singing the psalms and tunes they knew, in a slower and slower tempo and in a manner that approached heterophony. The practice continued with little change after the Restoration. But it was a case of survival rather than progress. Only two new psalm tunes were printed in England between 1644 and 1671.[12]

---

[8] Charles Butler, *The Principles of Musik* (London: John Haviland, for the author, 1636), 44; see also Temperley, *Music of the English Parish Church*, I:74.

[9] J. Collier, *An Ecclesiastical History of Great Britain*, ed. F. Barnham, 9 vols (London, 1841), 8:194.

[10] Thomas Mace, *Musick's Monument* (London: T. Ratcliffe and N. Thompson for the author, 1676), 19.

[11] The reading aloud of each line of text by a precentor or parish clerk, before the line was sung by the congregation.

[12] See Temperley, *The Hymn Tune Index*, 4 vols (Oxford and New York, 1998), 3:192–3, tunes 536, 537. The tunes in the census are numbered in chronological order of first printing.

8

The leading reformer of the period was John Playford, stationer, musician, royalist, and clerk to the Temple Church. Sensing a steady decline in standards, he embarked on a campaign to preserve and improve the singing of the old psalms, with their tunes correctly sung and, if possible, with harmony. During the Commonwealth he had to offer the tunes ostensibly for domestic recreation, since the authorities did not approve of rehearsed or accompanied singing in worship. He first included nine Old Version psalms with monophonic tunes in *A Booke of New Lessons for the Cithern and Gittern* (1652). Six years later he placed some of the common psalm tunes, with basses, in a new edition of his *Introduction to Music*, with some guidance to parish clerks as to how to choose the appropriate tune for a given psalm and how to set the pitch.

When the king came into his own again in 1660, the Company of Stationers, which had held the monopoly in psalm printing since 1603, allowed Playford to revise the Old Version in a conservative direction, and he prepared a grand folio edition for parish clerks (1661) in the now archaic black-letter type. It paid special attention to the appropriate matching of tunes and words. He also issued a single leaf of organ settings of psalm tunes for the benefit of cathedrals and the few parish churches that had acquired instruments. [13]

Playford's most ambitious project was *Psalms & Hymns in Solemn Musick*, published in 1671. Here again he was prudently combining church and home use. He recommended accompaniment by organ, lute, or viol. But the settings are for four-part male choir, and it is clear from the preface that he yearned for the choral solemnity that he believed had once infused the singing of the psalms in church. Indeed he presented a number of copies of the book to the Company of Parish Clerks of London, and supervised their weekly practices; the Company had his settings copied out in manuscript partbooks (no longer extant). [14] There was little hope that such singing could be introduced in parish churches, even in London; choirs were as yet unknown, and there was only one clerk in each parish. The enterprise was doomed to failure, and the book was never reprinted.

Playford learned his lesson, and his next effort was a complete edition of the Old Version, *The Whole Book of Psalms . . . Compos'd in Three Parts* (1677). Even this was a little ahead of its time, and it was not widely used before Playford's death in 1686/7. But when voluntary choirs began to form in the 1690s, Playford's son Henry obtained the Company of Stationers' leave to print

---

[13]   Inserted in some copies of Playford's *Musick's Hand-maid* (London: for J. Playford, 1678): see N. Temperley, 'John Playford and the Metrical Psalms', *Journal of the American Musicological Society* 25 (1972): 353–5. [No. III in this volume.]

[14]   Temperley, 'John Playford and the Metrical Psalms': 357. [No. III in this volume.]

a second edition, and others followed in close succession, extending eventually to the twentieth in 1757. The straightforward three-voice settings, set out so that they could also be used with keyboard accompaniment, turned out to be just the right thing for the new reform movement based on a choir leading the congregation. They were also an early example of a uniquely English invention: the ambiguous G clef, designed for trebles and tenors alike.

Of the two domains of psalm singing in the early modern period, the private one was beginning to decline, though devotional settings are still occasionally found through the eighteenth century. Psalm singing in public worship, on the other hand, was about to enter a vigorous revival, after a long sleep for much of the seventeenth century. Poets, musicians, and clergy joined forces to raise psalmody once more to an acceptable level.

From *'Noyses, sounds, and sweet aires': Music in Early Modern England*, ed. J.A. Owens (2006). Reproduced by permission of the Folger Shakespeare Library, Washington, DC.

II

MIDDLEBURG PSALMS

FROM TIME TO TIME, in the seventeenth century, the records of the London Stationers' Company mention 'Middleburg Psalms' (the spelling varies). Thus on 17 February 1623 we find a list of various formats and styles of Sternhold and Hopkins's *Whole Book of Psalms*, for binding up with George Wither's *Hymns and Songs of the Church*. Among others the following are listed.[1]

sixteene Middleborough	octavo Middleborough
sixteene common	octavo Nonparel
	octavo common

Again, on 7 September 1635 the Court of Assistants of the Company rebuked William Stansby for incompetent printing of an edition of the metrical psalms; the Minute[2] continues: "And whereas the said Mr. Stansby hath the Middleborough Psalmes to print It is ordered he shall not go forward with them." The earliest surviving Stock Books, containing inventories of the books in the Treasurer's Warehouse, begin on 1 March 1663.[3] In them we find 'Middleburg psalms', 8vo and 16mo, included in the annual inventory, each year until the destruction of the entire stock by the Great Fire of September 1666. After that we meet with the term no more.

It seems then that Middleburg Psalms were a *kind* of psalm book, distinguished in some feature from others of the same format. What did the term mean? Middelburg, of course, was the town in Holland from which a great deal of English Puritan literature had been printed and distributed illegally in England and Scotland, notably by Richard Schilders between 1579 and 1616.[4] Schilders did print metrical psalms (see Table 1). But the term cannot mean 'Psalms printed at Middelburg', because it was used for editions printed in London on behalf of the Stationers. Among the products of the Schilders press were several editions of the Scottish psalms. William Jackson therefore conjectured that 'Middleburg Psalms' were

1. E. Arber (ed.), *A Transcript of the Registers of the Company of Stationers of London, 1554-1640 A.D.* (1875-77), IV, 13-14.

2. William A. Jackson (ed.), *Records of the Court of the Stationers' Company, 1602 to 1640* (1957), p. 271.

3 Stationers' Company Records, English Stock Book. I am grateful to the Worshipful Company of Stationers and Newspaper Makers for allowing me access to their records.

4. J. Dover Wilson, 'Richard Schilders and the English Puritans', *Trans. Bibliogr. Soc.*, 9 (1909-11), 65-134.

Scottish psalms.[5] But that will not quite make sense either. Scottish psalms were normally published in Scotland, invariably so after 1605. They were not carried by the English Stock of the Stationers' Company, and it is most unlikely that they would have been bound up with Wither's *Hymns*. A possible clue lies in a Court Minute of 7 September 1600:[6]

Mr. Hooke declareth unto A Court holden this day: that he Receaved from m[r] Eldridge A m[er]chant xij books of psalters & psalmes printed At Myddlebourgh by Ric' Skilders. Whereof m[r] Eldridge Receaved ix. back againe bound and thother iij are brought to the hall.

What are 'books of psalters and psalms'? It hardly makes sense in modern idiom. But among booksellers and printers at the time 'psalter' was commonly used for the prose psalms and 'psalms' for those in metre. Mr Hooke was describing books, printed at Middelburg, that combined the two. The following year, for the first time, an edition of the English psalm book appeared 'both in prose and meeter', published in London by 'P[eter] S[hort] for the assignes of W. Seres and R. Day' (STC 2505) —in other words, by the Stationers' Company in all but name.[7] The prose version was that of the Geneva Bible, and it was printed in small type in the margins of the metrical psalms. This was a typically Puritan notion—bringing the word of God home to the singer, so that he might 'sing with understanding'; and it recalled the marginal glosses that had been a popular feature of the Geneva Bible itself. It was also a new way of attacking Anglicans, because the Genevan translation of the psalms was not the one authorised for use in church. More editions 'both in prose and metre' came out in the years that followed, the last in 1649; and it would seem natural enough that they should have been called 'Middelburg Psalms', since the original copy on which they were based had come from there. The three copies brought to Stationers' Hall were doubtless used for printers' copy. The Company had every right to take over an edition that was itself an infringement of the privilege it controlled.

The connection between this prose-and-metre style and Middelburg is placed beyond doubt by an entry in the Register of the Privy Seal of Scotland, dated 31 July 1599, which is described and quoted by William Cowan. It contains

a license granted by the King to John Gibsoun to import a psalm book which he had caused to be printed at Middelburg. The entry bears that 'Iohne Gibsoun his hienes buik binder has upoun his awin grit charges . . . causit imprent within Middilburgh in Flanderis ane new psalme buik in litill volume contening baith the Psalmes in verse as lykwayis the samyn in prose upoun the margine thairof in ane forme nevir practizit nor devisit in any heirtofir.' The name of the actual

5. Jackson, p. 271 n.2.

6. W. W. Greg and E. Boswell (eds.), *Records of the Court of the Stationers' Company, 1576-1602* (1930), p. 79.

7. See Cyprian Blagden, 'The English Stock of the Stationers' Company', *The Library*, 5th ser., 10 (1955), 163-185: especially p. 174.

164

printer is not given, and no edition has yet been discovered bearing the name of John Gibsoun.[8]

Cowan goes on to identify a copy without title page at Aberdeen University[9] as being, in all probability, a copy of this edition. Another, also lacking title page, has been discovered at Dundee Public Library.[10]

But it cannot well have been this edition that was brought to the London Stationers' attention in 1600. Such a book would have been called 'Scotch psalms': to the Stationers, plain 'psalms' meant Sternhold and Hopkins, English version. The two national collections, though both tracing their origins back to the psalm book published by the Geneva exiles in 1556, had diverged considerably. They were not interchangeable, nor were their texts subject to casual alteration.[11] A more likely supposition, therefore, is that Schilders printed up the 'English' psalms in the same way, and distributed them through his normal outlets in London; Mr. Eldridge bought twelve copies and sold them to Mr. Hooke, who informed the Company, and gave them three which they quickly made use of.

A book of precisely this description has survived:

The psalmes of David in meeter, with the prose. For use of the English church in Middelburgh. Middleburgh: R. Schilders, 1599 (STC 2499.5; copies at the British Library and New York Public Library).

Like the Scottish book ordered by Gibsoun, it is 'in litill volume'—16mo in 8's. It contains all 150 psalms in the metrical versions in use in the Church of England (but without the six alternative versions customarily included), with, in smaller type, the Geneva Bible prose version alongside. At the end are the 24 additional psalms, hymns, and canticles normally included in the common psalm book, without marginal prose. There are 81 tunes in type, a larger number than any English edition of Sternhold and Hopkins had contained up to that time. The book was obviously used as copy for the 1601 edition by Peter Short, which has the same general appearance and format, identical verbal content in both metre and prose, and very nearly the same layout page by page. The only significant differences are in the tunes; these will be described later.

It seems clear that the term 'Middleburg Psalms' referred to any edition

8. William Cowan, 'A Bibliography of the Book of Common Order and Psalm Book of the Church of Scotland: 1556-1644', Edin. Bibliogr. Soc. Pub., x (1913), 83.

9. Cowan 24; STC 16587.

10. I am grateful to Katharine Pantzer for kindly placing at my disposal her draft of the forthcoming revised Short Title Catalogue. In addition, Miss Pantzer has

been good enough to verify my conclusions below concerning Schilders's reimposition of standing type. I also wish to thank Donald Krummel, Hugh Macdonald, Frederick Nash, and Oliver Neighbour for help in the preparation of this article.

11. See John Julian, A Dictionary of Hymnology (2nd ed., 1907, repr. 1957), 856-866, 1021-22; Maurice Frost, English and Scottish Psalm and Hymn Tunes c. 1543-1677 (1953), 3-50.

of the English version of metrical psalms with prose psalms in the margin: and we may use it in that sense. It is not appropriate for the Scottish psalms. There is no reason to suppose the term was ever current in Scotland. There was no need for it there, since the prose-and-metre format became the normal one in Scotland, and was adopted for the great harmonized edition of 1635.[12] It was copied, also, for several other popular Puritan psalm books, including Henry Ainsworth's (Amsterdam, 1612). In England, only a minority of editions had the prose psalms in the margin, and it was for these that the term 'Middleburg Psalms' came to be used in the printing trade. But before tracing the history of these English editions, we may take a closer look at Schilders's prototypes.

As a model for his remarkably popular innovation, Schilders looked to certain editions of the French metrical psalter. As early as 1561 a Paris edition of Marot and de Bèze's version had appeared with marginal prose; the title page explained:

nous avons mis a l'opposite de la rime, les vers en prose, de la traduction de feu M. Lois Bude: correspondant l'un a l'autre selon les nombres, verset pour verset.[13]

Several later editions appeared 'avec la prose en marge'. Before 1594 Schilders's liturgical books in English had been for the Brownists and other separatists living on the Continent. In 1594 he had printed an edition of metrical psalms for the Scottish church, containing some innovations. Now, in 1599, he tried to penetrate the far more lucrative English market.

The two 1599 editions, one for Scotland, the other ostensibly 'for the use of the English church in Middelburgh', are quite similar in appearance, and on closer inspection it emerges that many parts of them are actually identical. Schilders in fact reimposed those parts of the type that could be used for both books. For example the whole of quires A, B and C (excluding the title page from consideration), and the first five leaves of quire D, are the same in both books apart from minor details; there are dozens of other complete pages that are the same, and many others again in which some part of the page has been reimposed. The metrical psalm texts, however, have been very carefully revised in otherwise identical sections of type. Slight textual variants, differences between Scottish and English spelling (*gude/good*, *quhilk/which* and so on) have been preserved, while the English custom of dividing up the longer psalms with subheadings (*The second part*, etc.) has been followed in the 'English' edition only. Evidently the versions had become so hallowed by constant use in each country that it would have been fatal to try to change either of them. The prose version,

12. STC 16599. See Neil Livingston, *The Scottish Psalter of 1635* (1864).

13. O. Douen, *Clément Marot et le Psautier Hugenot* (Paris, 1879, repr. 1967), ii, 521, no. 87.

14

on the other hand, is the same in both books, with 'English' spellings reflecting the popularity of the Geneva Bible in both countries. But it is not always printed from the same typesetting, since the differing lengths of some of the metrical versions necessitated different placing of the prose on the page.

Which edition came first? Or were they, from the beginning, planned as a joint production? John Gibsoun claims to have commissioned the 'Scottish' book, and this would tend to indicate primacy for that edition. He might have been merely trying to claim credit for an invention that was not really his own, after paying Schilders to adapt the 'English' edition to Scottish purposes. But there is strong internal evidence that the 'Scottish' edition came first. It is to be found in the selection of tunes. Schilders had already published two editions of the Scottish psalm book, in 1594 and 1596 (STC 16584, 2701); they were substantially copied from early Scottish editions, with the important addition of eight hymns and canticles (besides the two already in use) taken from the English psalm book, and with three psalm tunes not found in earlier Scottish editions. In his 1599 'Scottish' edition, we find the same traditional texts and the same ten hymns; but, presumably as a measure of economy, the number of tunes printed with the psalms is reduced from 121 to 78. All the tunes printed except one are as in the 1594 book. We can say, therefore, that Schilders's 'Scottish' psalm book of 1599 follows the Scottish tradition, in its tunes as well as its metrical texts.

The 'English' edition, however, is a very different story. Here we find that although the texts are carefully copied from the standard English psalm book, many of the tunes are foreign to that book. Twenty-eight of the psalm tunes, and all the tunes for the hymns, would be familiar to English singers—but the majority of these belong to the Scottish tradition as well. Thirty-two of the psalm tunes, however, had never appeared in an English edition with the psalms with which they were now printed. In three cases[14] they actually displaced English tunes; in eighteen cases,[15] the tune chosen was the one that appeared with the same psalm in the 'Scottish' edition. Thus Schilders evidently hoped that he could cut his costs by using some of the Scottish tunes in the 'English' edition. Despite the title page we may discount the possibility that the book was designed purely for the English congregation at Middelburg. The Separatists, who were in rebellion against the Established Church, would have had no reason to be fussy about adherence to the exact forms of the metrical psalm texts used in England. Schilders must have had the English market in mind from the first. Comparison of the type in the reimposed sections tends to confirm that the 'Scottish' edition was printed first.

When Peter Short, no doubt at the behest of the Stationers' Company,

14. Ps. 1, 21, 141.   15. Ps. 1, 2, 7, 8, 9, 10, 15, 16, 19, 20, 21, 23, 28, 33, 34, 66, 87.

brought out the first edition of the 'Middleburg Psalms' in 1601, he based it very closely on Schilders's prototype in format, layout, and texts. But he cast out all but one of the intruding Scotch tunes, and most of the other new tunes introduced by Schilders. He was naturally better informed than any Dutch printer about current English practice. Thomas East, in his harmonized psalm book of 1592,[16] had set most of the psalms to short tunes of a popular type, not to be found in the standard psalm books; and in the second edition (1594) East had written of the four most common of these tunes: 'The Psalmes are song to these 4 tunes in most churches of this Realme.' Short now substituted these tunes, and others from East's psalter, for the novelties of Schilders, and produced a book which would go into more than a dozen editions during the next forty years.

But Schilders made another effort to capture the prose-and-metre market. In 1602 he printed another pair of editions, one for Scottish, the other for English use:[17] and as before, he made them as similar as possible, reimposing sections of type whever he could. Having failed to foist unfamiliar Scottish tunes on English singers, he now attempted the reverse. This time he printed the 'English' edition first, as inspection of the type shows. Taking his cue from Short's edition, he consulted the work of his old master, Thomas East. In the 'English' edition, every one of the 93 tunes was the same that East had allocated to the corresponding psalm.[18] In all other respects the book was very similar to the 1599 edition, but without the hymns. This time he made no pretence that it was for the use of the English church at Middelburg. For the parallel 'Scottish' edition of 1602, the Scottish traditional tune was in 29 cases replaced by the East tune, printed from the same type as in the 'English' edition. In 28 cases the Scottish tune was dropped and no tune substituted. Thus a Scotsman who purchased the book would find that nearly half the familiar tunes were missing.

This time Schilders's drastic alterations to the tunes had some effect in both Scotland and England. At least one subsequent edition printed in Scotland was largely based on Schilders's edition of 1602,[19] while in editions that otherwise returned to the standard tunes (STC 2704 [1610], 16592 [1615]), two of his tunes from England (Ps. 2, 76) were retained, as well as the marginal prose version, which became a permanent feature. The hymns introduced by Schilders in his 'Scottish' editions of 1594, 1599 and 1602 also remained part of the Scottish psalm book in most editions up to 1633. More significant is the fact that three of the twelve 'common tunes', printed separately for the first time in a Scottish edition of 1615 and destined to

16. *The whole booke of psalmes: with their wonted tunes*, STC 2482.

17. STC 16589 (Cowan 27; Frost, p. 31; copies, British Library and elsewhere); STC 2507.5 (copy, British Library).

18. Schilders followed the 1592 edition of East, not that of 1594.

19. STC 16591 (Edinurgh: A. Hart, 1611).

168

play a central role in Scottish psalmody from then until the present, reached the Scottish tradition through Schilders. They were three of the four tunes singled out as most popular by East in 1594, and printed many times over in Schilders's 1602 psalm books.[20]

In England the tunes as well as the texts of Schilders's 1602 book were largely adopted for the first octavo edition of 'Middleburgh psalms', published by the Stationers' Company in 1605. Four psalm tunes of traditional English use, and the hymns with their tunes, were added. This edition, like its 16mo companion, was several times reprinted; but the two formats continued to exist independently, without any effort to resolve the very substantial differences in their musical content.

The history of the English 'Middleburg Psalms' is relatively uncomplicated. It lasts for about fifty years. Table 2 lists all known editions. Several (perhaps all) of the editions were issued in two forms—one complete with alternative versions, 24 hymns, prayers and index, the other lacking the final gatherings containing these items. In the 16mo from 1613 onwards, all six of the alternative psalm versions from the ordinary psalm book were included. From 1625, a number of the tunes were replaced with new tunes derived from Thomas Ravenscroft's harmonized psalter of 1621. (This was also true of many ordinary editions of Sternhold and Hopkins from 1622 onwards.)

Two interesting innovations were made in the later stages. In 1635 an octavo edition appeared in which the prose version was that of the Book of Common Prayer—obviously because of the Laudian influence of the time. A High Church 'Middleburg' psalm book may seem contradictory, but its object must have been quite different from that of the first 'Middleburg' editions. Instead of helping the people to understand the metrical psalms, it was designed to familiarize them with the prose psalms, which had for many years been entirely neglected by parish congregations and left to the dreary alternation of parson and clerk. The church authorities at this time certainly hoped for congregational participation in the liturgy, including the prose psalms, and this was one way to encourage it. At the head of the prose columns was printed 'The i. Day. Morning Prayer', etc. to show the liturgical order of the psalms in Morning and Evening Prayer throughout the month, as in the prayer book. The colon in the middle of each verse was also retained, as an aid to chanting. At the same time the tunes for the metrical psalms were altogether omitted. The 16mo edition of the same

20. The three tunes are Frost 19 ('Low Dutch' in England, 'English' in Scotland); Frost 42 ('Cambridge' in England, 'London' in Scotland); and Frost 121 ('Oxford' in England, 'Old Common' in Scotland). The last had appeared in Scottish psalm books since 1564, but only as a 'proper' tune to Psalm 108; its position as a 'common' tune seems to have been established in England and recognized by East, who also originated the custom of allocating place names to common tunes.

year also had the Prayer Book prose version with liturgical headings, but retained the tunes.

In 1644 the Book of Common Prayer was outlawed by parliamentary ordinance. The last edition of 'Middleburg' Psalms, published in 1649, effected a compromise by substituting the Authorized Version of 1611 (then known as the 'New Translation'), while the metrical texts remained unchanged. Curiously, the liturgical column headings were retained, but not the colons for chanting.

At the Stationers' Company, the English Stock inventory of 1 March 1663 shows 25 octavo 'Middleburg' Psalms in stock and 94 16mo. The latter entry remained unaltered at each stocktaking until 1666, after which it disappeared. Presumably therefore no copies were sold, perhaps because the 16mo edition available still had the now obsolete Geneva Bible translation. The octavo edition, however, was still in demand. Fifty-one copies were sold between March 1663 and March 1666. To keep enough copies in stock, fifty more were brought in by the Treasurer on 11 August 1663 and another fifty on 12 March 1666. Very probably these were reprints of the 1649 edition. After the Fire, however, it was evidently not thought worth while to put an edition together again. The demand was relatively very small: ordinary 12mo psalters were selling at ten or twenty thousand copies a year at this time.[21] The Puritan wing of the clergy had been driven out of the Church by the Act of Uniformity (1662). For the post-Restoration Church, the association of the metrical psalms with the inspired word of God was perhaps less important than the association of Sternhold and Hopkins's translation with the establishment of Church and State. Hence the Middleburg format was no longer apt. As for the dissenters, they had little use for Sternhold and Hopkins; several other translations were available to them. Psalm singing had become a tedious duty, lacking in vitality, no longer embodying the fervent spirit of the early reformers. So it would remain until the rise of the voluntary parish choir at the end of the century.[22]

21. Statistics compiled from the English Stock Book, Stationers' Company records.

22. See my article 'John Playford and the Metrical Psalms', *Journal of the American Musicological Society*, 25 (1972), 331-378.

Table 1. Editions of English metrical psalms printed at Middleburg by Richard Schilders

Date	STC	Bibliographic description	Metrical version	Prose	Additional texts	Musical contents
1594	16584	(Cowan 19) 8vo, T-Zz^8, &-&&&^{8}, &&&&^{10} (part of the Book of Common Order)	Scottish	--	10 hymns	111 psalm tunes, 108 from Scot. edns.(1577, etc.); 10 hymn tunes, 2 from Scot. edns., 8 from Eng. edns.
1596	2701	(Cowan 22) 8vo, A-I^8	Scottish	--	as 16584	as 16584
1599	16587	(Cowan 24) 16mo, A-Co^8 (part of the Book of Common Order)	Scottish	Geneva	as 16584	78 tunes, 77 from 16584
1599	2499.9	16mo, A-Be^8	English	Geneva	24 hymns, 2 prayers	81 tunes, 51 as 16587
1602	2507.5	8vo, A-Ee^8	English	Geneva	--	93 tunes, all from East's Psalmes (1592), STC 2482
1602	16589	(Cowan 27) 8vo, A-Ff^8, Gg^4	Scottish	Geneva	as 16584	89 tunes, 53 as 2507.5

The STC numbers are from the forthcoming revised edition edited by Katharine Pantzer; those after 1640 are from the revised edition of Wing's Short Title Catalogue 1641-1700. The number of tunes in the last column refers to the number printed with different psalm or hymn texts; it does not imply that all the tunes were different.

Table 2. Editions of metrical psalms with the prose in the margin printed in London ("Middleburg Psalms")

Date	STC	Imprint	Bibliographic description	Prose	Additional texts	Musical contents
1601	2505	P. S[hort] for assignes of W. Seres and R. Day	16mo, A-Ee^8	Geneva	--	80 tunes, 55 from East (1594), STC 2488
1603	2511	as 2505	16mo, as 2505 . . .			
1603	2511.5	E. S[hort] for ditto	16mo, A-Ee^8	Geneva	2 alternate versions	78 tunes, 77 as 2505
1605	2518	CS	8vo, A-Ii^8	Geneva	--	115 tunes, 93 as 2507.5
1608	2527.5	CS	16mo, as 2505 . . .			
1610	2535.3	CS	16mo, as 2505 . . .			
1612	2544	CS	16mo, as 2505 . . .			

1617	2559	CS	16mo, as 2505 . . .		
1618	2561.5	CS	8vo, as 2546 . . .		
1619	2567.3	CS	16mo, as 2505 . . .		
1621	2573.5	CS	16mo, as 2505 . . .		
1623	2583	CS	8vo, as 2546 . . .		
1625	2593	CS	16mo, A-Kk^8	Geneva	6 alternate versions	78 tunes, 66 from Ravenscroft's Psalmes (1621), STC 2575
1628	2607	CS	16mo, as 2593 . . .		
1629	2615	CS	8vo, as 2546 . . .		
1631	2630	W. S[tansby] for CS	16mo, as 2593 . . .		
1633	2644	W. S[tansby] for CS	8vo, A-Ii^8 (same content as 2546, cramped)		
1635	2659	F. K[ingston] for CS	8vo, A-Dd^8, Ee^4	PB	as 2546, with liturgical headings	None
1635	2661	T. C[otes] for CS	16mo, as 2593 . . .	PB	liturgical headings	as 2593
1641	Wing B2384	CS	8vo, as 2659 . . .		
1643	Wing B2395	R. C[otes] for CS	16mo, as 2661 . . .		
1649	Wing B2436	CS	8vo, as 2659	AV	as 2659	None

All editions in this table contained, at the end, a supplement of 24 hymns, 2 prayers and index, but several were issued in a second form lacking these items. See also the footnote to Table 1.

CS - Company of Stationers; PB - Prayer Book version; AV - Authorized ("King James") version.

III

John Playford and the Metrical Psalms

IT IS COMMON KNOWLEDGE that John Playford was the leading English music publisher of the later 17th century—indeed for much of his lifetime the only one of any importance.[1] His publications ranged from cathedral music to instrumental tutors. They included the famous *Introduction to the Skill of Music*, which remained the standard English text on the rudiments for more than a century.[2] His *Dancing Master* was the first description of the country dance ever printed and remains one of the principal sources for English folk music.[3]

He did equally important work in the field of parish church music— or, in other words, of metrical psalms. Here his role has been misunderstood and undervalued. He has been accused of debasing the psalm tunes in a misguided effort to improve them. His real motives were quite different. As in *The Dancing Master*, he was concerned to record accurately the current popular version of tunes that might otherwise have been forgotten and to restore those that had almost dropped out of use. His efforts at reform were directed not at the tunes themselves but at their use. He wanted them to be sung with more uniformity and with greater dignity; he wanted them to be matched more appropriately to the words; ultimately he wanted to bring harmony to the parish church. He succeeded in these aims, not by trying to impose any sudden or drastic change, but by working gradually with the existing materials. With an English practicality that informed all his work, he perceived that congregations could not be forcibly dislodged from an immemorial tradition, but might be led gradually into more productive paths.

[1] Lydia M. Middleton's article on Playford in the *Dictionary of National Biography* contains good biographical information, but the most complete account of his life is Margaret Dean-Smith's in the introduction to *Playford's English Dancing Master, 1651: A Facsimile Reprint* (London, 1957). Miss Dean-Smith's article in *MGG*, Vol. X, cols. 1344–52, is also valuable. An account of Playford's music publishing activities is to be found in Frank Kidson, "John Playford and 17th Century Music Publishing," *The Musical Quarterly*, IV (1918), 516–34, but it contains a number of errors and omissions.

[2] This work first appeared in 1654 as *A Breefe Introduction to the Skill of Musick*. In subsequent editions the exact title varied: some editions were numbered, others not. Full details of each edition are given in *Playford's Brief Introduction to the Skill of Musick: An Account, with Bibliographical Notes* (London, 1926). In the present article the work is identified simply as *Introduction*, followed by the date of the edition.

[3] This work first appeared in 1651 as *The English Dancing Master*: the word *English* was dropped in subsequent editions. Full details in Dean-Smith, *Playford's English Dancing Master, 1651*.

332

The real nature of Playford's work has been obscured partly by some false conclusions about the practice of parochial psalmody before and during his time and partly by the neglect of certain facts in his career, more particularly concerning his relationship with the Company of Stationers. These points will be dealt with before we approach the question of what Playford actually did with the metrical psalms and their tunes.

PSALM SINGING BEFORE PLAYFORD'S TIME

In describing the psalmody of the first hundred years after the Reformation, scholars have concentrated their attention almost exclusively on the harmonized settings of the psalm tunes that appeared in collections from time to time. Walter Frere, who wrote the first comprehensive history of the English hymn,[4] formed the impression that harmonized singing of psalms was the rule in the English parish church until it was abolished by the Puritans under Cromwell.

Ravenscroft's Psalter [of 1621] thus represented the last term in a long development, and the most popular, though not in all respects the best application of the English art at its heyday to the psalmody of the Church. . . . Like the Church which it was to serve, it seemed to be at a point of climax, and it was on the edge of disaster. For with the Old Version and the Prayer Book, and the Church itself, it went down before the puritan outbreak of the Commonwealth period, and lay hid for a time waiting for better days and the revulsion of feeling that was bound to come. . . . After the Restoration fresh books were needed to carry on the tradition of Church Hymnody which had been thus interrupted.[5]

Frere was thus inclined to belittle Playford's efforts, which he saw as a debasement of this glorious tradition.

Playford . . . had to catch the popular favour . . . by lowering the standard of his music. . . . His *Whole Book of Psalms*, 1677, represents the descent which he had to make. The best English musical traditions were gone. No longer, as in Elizabeth's day, could every educated man be expected to take his part book and sing his part at sight. . . . It is a small book compared with the former stately folio [of 1671]. . . . The tunes are now set only in three parts. . . .[6]

This romantic picture was not altered by Maurice Frost when he came to revise Frere's work.[7] His own monumental work on the psalm tunes is

[4] *Hymns Ancient and Modern: Historical Edition* (London, 1909). Introduction by Walter H. Frere (later Bishop of Exeter).

[5] Frere, p. lviii.

[6] Frere, pp. lix–lx.

[7] Maurice Frost, ed., *Historical Companion to Hymns Ancient and Modern* (London, 1962). Frost states in his preface that one of his aims is "to retain in his own words as much as possible of what the Bishop wrote." The parts of the introduction quoted above appear at pp. 57–60 exactly as Frere had written them.

a strictly bibliographical study:[8] it describes in detail the contents of certain selected musical psalters, without saying anything about their use; and as far as the English psalter is concerned, it ignores all unharmonized psalm books after 1570. For the 17th century Frost described only the four harmonized psalters: Ravenscroft (1621), Slatyer (1643), Playford (1671), and Playford (1677). Other writers have followed Frere and Frost, but with less caution. One says that Ravenscroft's psalter "became very popular" and that "by the middle of the seventeenth century four-part singing was, where possible, looked upon as normal. . . . This, of course, did not imply that congregations sang in four parts, but that there was an accompaniment and probably some body of singers more skilled than the rest."[9] Another even claims that "after Ravenscroft there is very little publishing [of psalm tunes] until after the Restoration [of King Charles II in 1660]. Ravenscroft's book becomes definitive for England."[10]

The facts are otherwise. One has only to look at the *British Museum Catalogue*[11] to discover that the vast majority of psalm books printed during the period in question contained the tunes unharmonized: this evidence is summarized in Table 1. It is most unlikely that the tunes were ever sung in full harmony by congregations. In the early years of Elizabeth's reign, some city churches retained enough clerks to form a small choir, and it may be that John Day's psalter of 1563 was intended partly to cater for this, though its title page contains no reference to churches and says the four parts "may be song to al Musical instruments, . . . for the encrease of vertue: and aboleshyng of other vayne and triflying ballades." Later harmonized psalters also indicate in one way or another that they are for cultivated domestic use.[12] Choirs and organs had vanished from most churches by 1580. An anonymous writer of the early 17th century used the following arguments in defending cathedral music against Puritan attack:

Now yf it be demanded of them [i.e., of the Puritans] whether yf the singing of psalmes in the Churche at Sermons by the whole multitude, and at other

---

[8] Maurice Frost, *English and Scottish Psalm & Hymn Tunes c. 1543–1677* (London, 1953).
[9] C. Henry Phillips, *The Singing Church* (London, 1946), pp. 126, 130.
[10] Erik Routley, *The Music of Christian Hymnody* (London, 1957), p. 45.
[11] Entries under "Bible. O.T. Psalms. English. Metrical Versions. Sternhold and Hopkins."
[12] Daman (1579) and Daman (1593) state on their title pages that they are for "recreation." Allison (1599) is scored for lute and other instruments that were never used in church. Este (1592) makes no reference to parish church use in title page or preface and moreover has its four parts "so placed that foure may sing ech one a several part in this booke"—a format hardly calculated for church use, either by choir or congregation; similarly with Ravenscroft (1621). Slatyer (1643) is a learned book containing only the first twenty-two psalms, set in Sternhold and Hopkins's English version but also in three other languages. All other harmonized psalters before 1677 use "unauthorized" versions (see fn. 33).

334

TABLE 1

EDITIONS OF *THE WHOLE BOOK OF PSALMS* (STERNHOLD AND HOPKINS)

Decade	No music	Tunes without harmonies	Tunes and harmonies	Total
1562–1570	–	6	1	7
1571–1580	–	12	–	12
1581–1590	–	14	1	15
1591–1600	–	20	4	24
1601–1610	–	28	2	30
1611–1620	1	29	2	31
1621–1630	3	51	1	55
1631–1640	9	57	1	67
1641–1650	18	22	–	40
1651–1660	18	1	–	19
1661–1670	24	2	–	26
1671–1680	24	1	1	26
1681–1690	24	2	–	26
1691–1700	16	–	5	21
1701–1710	26	–	4	30
1711–1720	22	–	5	27
1721–1730	24	–	4	28
1731–1740	21	–	1	22
1741–1750	21	–	–	21
1751–1760	28	–	1	29
1761–1770	30	–	–	30
1771–1780	25	–	–	25
1781–1790	20	–	–	20
1791–1800	13	–	–	13
1801–1810	13	–	–	13
1811–1820	8	–	–	8
1821–1830	4	–	–	4
1831–1840	–	–	–	0
1841–1850	2	–	–	2
1851–1860	1	–	–	1
1861–1870	1	–	–	1

SOURCE: British Museum Catalogue (1971).
NOTE: The above is only a rough guide to trends, since there were some editions printed of which no copy exists in the British Museum.

exercises (namely at the Communion) be meete to be used, I suppose they will acknowledge that it is very meete, adding this[:] that the same be songe, by the whole multitude in a plaine *Geneua* tvne, wch every one can singe, and not in pricksonge, and descant (as they call it): well, this being graunted by them, I demaund further, Nature having disposed all voices both of men and children into fyve kindes . . . whether it is not more for edification of that which is sung to dispose nature by the art of musick to it[s] right ends, vid: by causinge every one to singe his parte allotted to him by nature, rather than to have voyces violated, and drawne out of their naturall compasse, . . . [which] causeth rather yellinge and scrichinge, then singinge, and confusion of voyces rather then edifyinge.[13]

Clearly then, psalm tunes were normally sung in unison. If Este or Ravenscroft hoped that their settings might be used in some parish

[13] London, British Museum, MS 18.B.xix, fol. 8^v. The printed catalogue dates this "early 17th c."; it cannot be before 1603 because of references to the King.

churches, there is nothing to suggest that they were. Samuel Pepys, at home on a Sunday evening in 1664, took part in a sing-through of "Ravenscroft's four-part psalms, most admirable music," with two other men and a boy.[14] He would hardly have used such words if Ravenscroft's settings had been in normal use in church. Had Ravenscroft's book been widely adopted, we should expect to find that the common psalm books would have been revised so that they could be used in conjunction with it. But in fact very few of the twenty-three new tunes introduced by Ravenscroft found their way into the psalm books or attained any popularity during the next fifty years (see Tables 2 and 3). In short, Ravenscroft's psalter had little influence on the music of the parish church in the 17th century. What happened in the 18th century is another matter altogether.

Thus the only printed music in use in parish churches before Playford's time was that in the unharmonized Sternhold and Hopkins psalm book, which had remained substantially the same since it first appeared in complete form in 1562. It provided "proper" tunes for most of the "Divine Hymns"[15] and for about twenty-five to forty-five of the psalms, including almost all those in peculiar meters. For the remaining psalms (all in Common or Short Meter[16]) it gave only a cross-reference, such as "Sing this to the tune of the 3rd psalm." But there is clear evidence that this book was allowed to become out of date as regards the tunes. By the end of the 16th century, the most popular tunes were the single Common-Meter tunes of four lines. In 1594, in the second edition of Este's (harmonized) psalter,[17] we find 103 of the 156 metrical psalms set to a mere four tunes, all of the four-line variety (CAMBRIDGE, OXFORD, and Low DUTCH, C.M.; and LONDON, S.M.). In the table of incipits, Este adds the following significant note (lacking in the 1592 edition): "The Psalmes are song to these 4 tunes in most churches of this Realme." The same four tunes predominate in the harmonized psalters of Allison (1599) and Barley (ca. 1599). Yet editions of the psalm book continued to appear in large quantities without these or any other four-line tunes, reprinting instead the old D.C.M. tunes which in most cases had apparently dropped out of use; the last such edition appeared in 1653.

[14] Samuel Pepys, Diary, 27 November 1664.
[15] The "Divine Hymns," some of which were printed before and some after the psalms, consisted of metrical versions of the canticles, creeds, Lord's Prayer and commandments, the hymn Veni Creator Spiritus, and a number of original hymns. The exact selection varied slightly from edition to edition. See Edna Parks, The Hymns and Hymn Tunes found in the English Metrical Psalters (New York, 1966).
[16] Common Meter (C.M.) is the traditional English ballad meter, consisting of four lines of iambics in the pattern 8.6.8.6. (the numbers show how many syllables each line contains). Double Common Meter (D.C.M.) is an eight-line verse of the same kind. Short Meter (S.M.) is represented by 6.6.8.6, Long Meter (L.M.) by 8.8.8.8.
[17] The Whole Booke of Psalmes . . . composed in foure Parts . . . (London: Thomas Est, the assigne of William Byrd, 1594).

TABLE 2
The Most Popular Common-Meter Tunes in 17th-Century Collections

Tune (Frost)	Name	Earliest printed source	Este 1592	Allison 1599	Barley 1599	Ravens. 1621	Ps. Bk. 1622	Ps. Bk. 1629	Ps. Bk. 1636	Barton 1644	Introd. 1658	Ps. Bk. 1661	Playford 1661	Handmaide 1669	Playford 1671	Playford 1677	St. Mar. 1688	St. Jam. 1697
121	OXFORD	Scottish 1564	27	27	32	3	–	–	x	x	x	x	7	–	1	1	1	–
42	CAMBRIDGE	Daman 1572a	29	31	35	5	–	–	x	x	x	x	2	–	–	8	–	–
129	WINDSOR	Daman 1591	33	1	1	4	–	–	x	–	x	–	26	x	1	8	3	3
19	LOW DUTCH	Este 1592b	1	33	38	4	–	–	–	x	x	x	10	–	1	4	–	3
109	BATH & WELLS	Este 1592	1	1	1	3	–	–	–	–	–	x	–	–	–	3	–	–
103	WINCHESTER	Este 1592	1	1	1	8	–	–	x	–	x	–	2	–	1	4	–	–
111	ROCHESTER	Este 1592	1	1	1	3	–	–	x	–	–	x	–	–	1	5	–	–
172a	CHESTER	Este 1592	–	–	–	4	–	–	x	–	–	x	–	–	–	–	–	–
205	YORK	Scottish 1615	–	–	–	5	–	–	x	x	x	–	20	x	2	7	2	4
209	MARTYRS	Scottish 1615	–	–	–	6	–	–	x	x	x	–	16	–	2	8	4	2
204	DUNDY	Scottish 1615	–	–	–	2	x	x	–	–	–	–	–	–	1	5	4	4
207	ABBAY	Scottish 1615	–	–	–	2	–	x	–	x	x	–	19	–	–	4	2	–
234	ST. DAVID'S	Ravens. 1621	–	–	–	3	x	–	–	–	–	–	–	x	1	3	–	4
239	GLOCESTER	Ravens. 1621	–	–	–	1	–	x	–	–	–	–	–	–	–	4	–	–
246a	MANCHESTER	Ravens. 1621	–	–	–	3	–	–	–	–	–	–	–	–	2	3	–	–
251	WORCESTER	Ravens. 1621	–	–	–	2	–	–	–	–	–	–	–	–	–	–	–	–
233	CHRIST HOSPITAL	Ravens. 1621	–	–	–	–	–	–	–	–	–	–	–	–	–	–	–	–
25	NEW TUNE	Playford 1658	–	–	–	–	–	–	–	–	x	–	6	–	1	9	1	5

NOTE: The table shows, in chronological order by date of first printed source, all C.M. tunes in Ravenscroft that are also found in later sources listed, with the names assigned to them by Ravenscroft; plus the one tune "introduced" by Playford that became popular, with Playford's original name for it. There were a further twenty tunes in Ravenscroft not found in any of the later sources, but there were no C.M. tunes in Playford's 1661 psalm book other than those in the table. Sources are fully cited in the text or in Frost, except the last two, for which see *British Union-Catalogue of Early Music*, p. 828, items 17, 29. "Ps. Bk." means an edition of the psalm book that first appeared at the date stated. In the body of the table, a number shows the number of psalms set to the tune in the source concerned; an x means that the tune appears in the source; a dash means that the tune does not appear.

a Five-line version: later sources omit the last line.
b The first half of a tune found in Daman, 1579 (Frost 54).

TABLE 3
The Most Popular Short-Meter Tunes in 17th-century Collections

Tune (Frost)	Name	Earliest printed source	Este 1592	Allison 1599	Barley 1599	Ravens. 1621	Ps. Bk. 1622	Ps. Bk. 1629	Ps. Bk. 1636	Barton 1644	*Introd.* 1658	Ps. Bk. 1661	Playford 1661	*Handmaide* 1669	Playford 1671	Playford 1677	St. Mar. 1688	St. Jam. 1697
65	SOUTHWEL	Daman 1579	—	—	—	3	—	×	—	×	—	—	—	—	—	—	3	—
45	LONDON	Daman 1591	3	4	4	1	—	—	×	×	×	×	6	×	1	5	3	6

NOTE: The basis of the table is the same as that of Table 2, but the numbers in the body of the table are not comparable with those in Table 2 because there are only six psalms in Short Meter. The tune listed as LONDON (Ravenscroft's name) was renamed SOUTHWEL by Playford.

338

Other editions made half-hearted efforts to bring the book up to date by printing a few four-line tunes:[18] Tables 2 and 3 summarize their efforts. When William Barton printed his own version of metrical psalms in 1644, which he hoped would be approved by Parliament, he included a selection of tunes with the following comment:

> I have collected the most choice and exquisite tunes that are or have been used in all England; I have onely added or altered a little in some, to make them adequate and suitable to several forms of metre, and to bring some choise strains and ditties into more frequent use, leaving multitudes of tunes (in *Ravenscroft*) as unnecessary and burdensome.[19]

Frere's Anglo-Catholic view of the violent disruption of "the tradition of Church Hymnody" during the Commonwealth cannot be supported by evidence. The Puritan assault fell hard upon cathedrals, chapels royal, and collegiate churches, where the music had been provided by organs and choral foundations (both anathema to the Puritans) and had consisted of various types of musical setting of the liturgy set out in the Book of Common Prayer, plus anthems mostly based on the prose psalms. When Parliament abolished choirs, organs, and liturgy in 1644, and soon enforced its will by military power, nothing was left of cathedral music; and in 1660 a great effort was needed to procure new organs and to train choirs. This story has been told often enough.[20]

In parish churches, on the other hand, organs had long been in disuse; choirs were unknown; and the liturgy, though laid down by law exactly as in cathedrals, had long been merely spoken in parish churches.[21] The only music had consisted of metrical psalms sung by the whole congregation, unaccompanied and unharmonized. When Parliament replaced the liturgy with an extemporized form of worship devised by the Westminster Assembly of Divines, the *musical* part of parish worship was unaffected. The singing of metrical psalms had been a Puritan innovation in the first place, never admitted into the liturgy but tolerated by Queen Elizabeth and her successors. Now in the Puritan ascendancy

---

[18] One such revision has its prototype in a 1622 edition (*Short Title Catalogue*, 2576.5) which introduced two short tunes from Ravenscroft: Frost 233 and 246a. Another, of 1629 (STC 2612), introduced four: Frost 65 (S.M.), 207, 233, and 234. A third, of 1636 (STC 2664) introduced ten: Frost 42, 45 (S.M.), 51, 99, 103, 109, 111, 172a, 205, 209; but only two of these ten came from Ravenscroft. (Tune references refer to Frost, *English and Scottish Psalm & Hymn Tunes* [see fn. 8]; STC refers to the *Short Title Catalogue 1475–1640*.)

[19] [William Barton,] *The Book of Psalms in Metre. Close and proper to the Hebrew . . . With Musicall Notes . . .* (London: Printed by Matthew Simmons, for the Companie of Stationers, 1644).

[20] See E. H. Fellowes, *English Cathedral Music*, rev. J. A. Westrup (London, 1969); Christopher Dearnley, *English Church Music 1650–1750* (London, 1970).

[21] As a result of Puritan activity early in Elizabeth's reign, "the estimacion & reputacion of songe in Churches (except *Geneva* psalmes) was in short tyme in no regard (nay in detestacion) with the Comon people." British Museum, MS 18.B.xix, fol. 5ᵛ.

there was no reason to alter it, and the practice continued without much change throughout the Commonwealth and after the Restoration. It is true that the old metrical version was now officially in disfavor—less for any theological reason than for its long association with the Established Church. But the new versions intended to replace it were cast in the same meters and were designed to be used with the familiar tunes.[22] The Long Parliament never agreed on any one version. Rous's version, revised by the Westminster Assembly, did not please the House of Lords; Barton's, favored by the Lords, was rejected by the Commons.[23] There is no evidence that either was ever used in England. Rous's version, still further revised, was adopted in Scotland. In England people went on singing Sternhold and Hopkins, the only version that continued to be published year by year (see Table 1).[24]

The only practice which was possibly an innovation was that of "lining-out." The Westminster Assembly laid down the following rule:

That the whole congregation may join herein, every one that can read is to have a psalm book; and all others, not disabled by age or otherwise, are to be exhorted to learn to read. But for the present, where many in the congregation cannot read, it is convenient that the minister, or some other fit person appointed by him and the other ruling officers, do read the psalm, line by line, before the singing thereof.[25]

The practice continued after the Restoration, soon turning into a kind of chanting by the parish clerk. It survived in country districts until the late 18th century; in Scotland and America well into the 19th. The parish clerk was the sole survivor of more ceremonious days and was supposed to lead the singing, but he was often a poor old man with no musical ability.

To all intents and purposes parish church music remained congregational and unharmonized, before, during, and after the Commonwealth, though there is evidence that a weird kind of heterophony was often practiced, in which the extremely slow notes of a psalm tune were

---

[22] Barton's *Psalms*, as already mentioned, were designed for use with the old tunes and were cast in the same meters (C.M., S.M., L.M., and three others). Rous's version was "fitted to such tunes as have been found by experience to be of most general use"; it has all the psalms in C.M. except four in S.M. and three in L.M.

[23] See Millar Patrick, *Four Centuries of Scottish Psalmody* (London, 1949), p. 95.

[24] On March 30, 1653, Rous informed the Stationers' Company that in order to promote the use of his own Psalms he would "endeavour the procurement of some Act or Ordinance to inhibit the publicke use of those now in use." Two years later Barton proposed that the Company join with him in "suppressing the Old Version and establishing his new (to effect which he insinuates great probabilities)." But all to no avail. (London, Stationers' Hall, Stationers' Company Archives: Court Book C, fol. 277; Court Book D, fol. 5ᵛ. I am grateful to the Worshipful Company of Stationers and Newspaper Makers for allowing me access to their archives.)

[25] From *The Directory for Publick Worship* (1647). Text reprinted in *The Confession of Faith ... The Directory for Publick Worship* (Edinburgh and London, 1903), p. 166.

340

ornamented at private will by the more adventurous members of the congregation.[26] No doubt, in the absence of any strong musical leadership, the singing often degenerated into chaos. Sometimes congregations confused two or more tunes, and sang both at once;[27] at other times the clerk selected a tune which did not fit the meter of the psalm.[28] A gruesome description of country psalm singing has survived from a slightly later period.

> Then out the People yawl an hundred Parts,
> Some roar, some whine, some creak like Wheels of Carts:
> Such Notes the *Gam-ut* yet did never know,
> Nor num'rous Keys of Harps'cals on a Row
> Their Heights or Depths cou'd ever comprehend.
> Now below double *A re* some descend,
> 'Bove *E la* squealing now ten Notes some fly;
> Streight then as if they knew they were too high
> With headlong hast down Stairs they again tumble;
> Discords and Concords, O how thick they jumble,
> Like untam'd Horses, tearing with their Throats
> One wretched Stave into an hundred Notes.[29]

Certainly this is an exaggeration; if we believed it literally we would have to credit 17th-century congregations with a total compass of five octaves! The writer attested this description to have been true "till of late years in most *Churches* and *Chappels*[30] around Lancashire," suggesting that a reform had recently taken place. The great change in parish church music in the closing years of the 17th century was the rise of the voluntary choir. This change, which has gone entirely unnoticed in history books, was to a great extent the result and complement of John Playford's efforts.

It is obvious from the prefaces to his psalm-tune collections that Playford was greatly concerned about the state of psalmody and was eager to improve it. But the task was a formidably difficult one. Part of

---

[26] For example, *A new and easie method to learn to sing by book* (London, 1686), pp. 100–101, sets out the tune SOUTHWEL in the ordinary way and then goes on to say that "The notes of the foregoing Tune are usually broken or divided, and they are better so sung, as is here prick'd": an ornamented version follows.

[27] Barton, Preface: "The want of such an help as this . . . makes the Congregation often to mistake, and fall sometimes into severall tunes at once, which disturbs the spirits and dulleth the devotion."

[28] Pepys *Diary*, January 5, 1662: "The jest was, the Clerk begins the 25th psalm, which hath a proper tune to it, and then the 116th, which cannot be sung with that tune, which seemed very ridiculous." Psalm 25 was S.M., Psalm 116 C.M.

[29] Elias Hall, *The psalm-singers compleat companion* (London, 1706), pp. 1–2. The punctuation has been emended in this quotation, to clarify the meaning.

[30] "Chappels": this refers exclusively to places of Anglican worship which, for one reason or another, did not have the standing of parish churches; there were many such in Lancashire. The word was not at this date used for dissenting meeting-houses.

it was to provide correct and up-to-date musical texts of the tunes in use, to replace the old psalm books which no longer had much connection with actual practice. This Playford did, as we shall see. But few members of a congregation would or could read musical notation. They had to be led: by organs, where this was possible; by parish clerks, if parish clerks could be made efficient; by a musically educated group of singers, if such could be formed. Through all these means a gradual improvement did eventually take place. Playford stimulated it and provided music well designed for the purpose.

PLAYFORD AND THE STATIONERS' COMPANY

In 1603 King James I had granted to the Worshipful Company of Stationers the exclusive privilege of publishing all psalters and psalms, in verse or in prose, with or without music, in any format and in any English version, except as part of the Book of Common Prayer, in which the monopoly was held by the King's Printer.[31] The privilege was of course an extremely lucrative asset. It was confirmed by a second charter in 1615; it was apparently respected during the Commonwealth;[32] it was reasserted at the Restoration; and it is probably in force today, so far as England is concerned, though no metrical psalter for Church of England use appears to have been printed since 1861.

In the 17th century the Stationers' Company used the monopoly chiefly for the benefit of the poorer London printers. As a result, the standard of printing in the psalters was generally low. Only Sternhold and Hopkins's version of the metrical psalms was printed for parish-church use, except during the Commonwealth, because it was believed

---

[31] Cyprian Blagden, *The Stationers' Company: A History, 1403–1959* (London, 1960), p. 92. The complete text of the charter of 1603 can be seen in E. Arber, ed., *A Transcript of the Registers of the Company of Stationers of London, 1554–1640 A.D.* (London, 1875–77), Vol. III, pp. III. 42–III. 44. Although the wording seems to be all-inclusive, it was not in practice used to cover anything except the *complete* psalter. Selections of psalms were seldom published by the Company, but frequently by others without permission or acknowledgment of the Company's monopoly.

[32] The legal position was uncertain, since the privilege rested on a royal grant which might or might not be recognized by Cromwell. When John Field tested the position by publishing an edition of Sternhold and Hopkins on his own account in 1653 (Wing, *Short Title Catalogue 1641–1700* [New York, 1945], B2451), the Company sought counsel but took no action. In 1655, however, hearing that Field and another publisher had been promised a Patent from the Lord Protector for "sole Printing the English Bible and Psalmes," the Company, acting on legal advice, vested its copyright in the Psalms in George Sawbridge, the Treasurer, during the pleasure of the Court (Court Book C, fol. 288ᵛ; D, fols. 1, 2ᵛ, 3). Sawbridge thereupon entered by title all the books in which the Company had held a monopoly, or a great many of them, in the Company's Copyright Register, in the same way that ordinary books were entered for the protection of individual publishers' copyright (see *A Transcript of the Registers of the Worshipful Company of Stationers from 1640–1708 A.D.* [London, 1913–14], entry for 26 April 1655).

342

that it had been designated by authority.[33] Naturally the demand for this psalm book was large and constant. It was often bound up with the Bible or with the Book of Common Prayer. This created a special opportunity in 1662, when the revised Prayer Book was printed and, according to the Act of Uniformity passed in that year, was to be provided in every parish church throughout the land. The Stationers saw to it that the metrical psalms were attached to these Prayer Books, which were printed by the King's Printer.[34] Large numbers of the psalm book were printed in the years that followed, in various formats from folio to 24mo, and in various type faces. When the entire stock of the Company was destroyed in the Great Fire of September, 1666, among the first books printed "for beginning a Stock again" were "5000 Psalmes 12° for Bibles."[35] This remained by far the most popular format (see Table 4). But as Table 1 shows, the vast majority of these psalm books contained no music. Before 1640 it had been usual for metrical psalm books to be provided with tunes, while the number of editions with harmonies was relatively insignificant. After 1660 tunes were rarely provided, but a certain number of harmonized psalters were available until well into the 18th century. The Old Version of Sternhold and Hopkins maintained its popularity throughout the 18th century despite the existence of the New Version of Tate and Brady, issued by authority of William III in 1696. But the custom of printing either version complete with tunes died out altogether. Instead, tunes were printed in separate books for the use of choirs.

From 1660 onwards, twenty-five editions of Sternhold and Hopkins

[33] Early editions were stated on their title pages to be "Newly set fourth and allowed, according to the order appointed in the Quenes Maiesties Iniunctions." From 1567 the wording was commonly as follows: "Newly set forth and allowed to be song in all churches, of all the people together, before & after morning and euenyng prayer: as also before and after the Sermon." This drew attention to the Injunctions of 1559 and was designed to assert the legality of metrical psalm singing in church; but it was interpreted by later generations as an authority for the particular version which therefore excluded the use of any other. This view was challenged by Richard Goodridge in the preface to his version, *The psalter or psalms of David* (Oxford, 1684); but throughout the 18th century many staunch churchmen resisted the influx of new translations and of hymns because they believed that Sternhold and Hopkins, together with Tate and Brady's "New Version" which William III had purported to authorize in 1696, were the only verses that could legally be sung in the Church of England. The matter was settled only in 1820, when the case of *Holy and Ward* v. *The Rev. Thomas Cotterill* was determined by Chancellor G. V. Vernon in the Consistory Court of York. The Chancellor held that even the King in Council could not, by a strict construction of the Statutes of Uniformity, authorize any alterations in the liturgy; but he declined to give any practical effect to this view. This judgment determined that any metrical psalms or hymns were equally unauthorized, but equally to be tolerated in practice. See Jonathan Gray, *An Inquiry into Historical Facts Relative to Parochial Psalmody* (York, 1821). See also John Julian, *A Dictionary of Hymnology*, 2d ed. (London, 1907), pp. 863–64.

[34] Stationers' Company Archives, Court Book D, fol. 75.

[35] *Ibid.*, English Stock Book (1663–1723).

TABLE 4
TWO FORMATS OF METRICAL PSALMS HANDLED BY THE STATIONERS' COMPANY

Period	12mo psalms (a)	Folio psalms (b)	(b) as % of (a)
March 1663–March 1666	40,664 sold	1,669 sold	4.1
Sept. 1666–March 1669	27,480 sold	none sold	0.0
March 1669–March 1676	112,362 sold	1,400 sold	1.3
Jan. 1677–Dec. 1681	69,016 delivered	1,535 delivered	2.2
Jan. 1682–Dec. 1686	45,890 delivered	811 delivered	1.8
Jan. 1687–Dec. 1691	43,070 delivered	225 delivered	0.4
Jan. 1692–Dec. 1696	73,683 delivered	186 delivered	0.2

NOTE: The statistics are derived from the English Stock Books of the Stationers' Company. There are only two folio editions that could be included in the figure for 1663–66: Playford's of 1661 and the other folio of 1661 (see fn. 45). In September, 1666, the entire stock was destroyed in the Great Fire. The next folio edition was the 1669 reprint of Playford's. The last detailed stocktaking is recorded in March, 1676. Thereafter no precise figures of sales are available; the figures show the number of copies delivered to the Treasurer of the English Stock in five-year periods. In 1679 another folio edition had been issued, in roman type without music; this is not distinguished from Playford's in the figures. The last reprint of Playford's psalm book appeared in 1687. There were other formats, all without music, but their numbers were insignificant compared with those for the 12mo books, most of which were sent to the King's Printer for binding with Bibles and prayer books. After 1692, however, the 24mo format began to rival the 12mo in quantity. From 1660 to 1687 the only psalm books with music were in folio.

contained music: and the man who was responsible for twenty-three of them was John Playford. Such a commanding position could only have been gained through the Stationers' Company. Indeed Playford was closely linked with the Company throughout his career. He was born in 1623, son of a Norwich shopkeeper. He is thought to have gained his knowledge of music through membership in Norwich Cathedral Choir; he later moved to London as apprentice to John Benson, Stationer, to whom he was articled for seven years on March 23, 1640.[36] During the Civil War and Commonwealth he carried on an underground press which distributed royalist pamphlets, and at one time he was threatened with arrest;[37] he was always a Church-and-King man, as his subsequent career demonstrates. He was declared a Freeman (i.e., a qualified publisher) on April 5, 1647, but the Company probably feared to promote so controversial a man during Cromwell's regime. After the Restoration of King Charles II, however, his position improved. His promotion to the Livery on April 20, 1661, was no doubt due to behind-the-scenes pressure.[38] His election to the Court of Assistants, the Company's governing body, did not come until June 20, 1681, and then only as the result of a mandate from the King. Soon afterwards Playford was alotted a livery share in the English Stock, the trading organization that managed

[36] All dates New Style.

[37] Dean-Smith, *Playford's English Dancing Master*, p. xiii.

[38] Full details of Playford's relations with the Stationers' Company are given in my article, "John Playford and the Stationers' Company," to be printed shortly in *Music and Letters*.

344

the Company's monopoly in psalms, primers, and almanacs. Earlier, in 1669, he had turned down a much smaller share in the Stock, in a somewhat cantankerous letter that did nothing to endear him to his fellow stationers,[39] and until the royal mandate of 1681 his progress in the Company's hierarchy had been slow. In the successive purges of the Company's Court of Assistants and Livery that took place in 1684 and 1685, he was one of the few who survived unscathed—once again, no doubt, because of royal protection. He died in late 1686 or early 1687. If he was not beloved in the competitive world of printers and publishers, he was highly esteemed by poets and musicians. Nahum Tate, poet laureate and psalmodist, produced a "Pastoral Elergy on the Death of Mr. John Playford" which was movingly set to music by Henry Purcell:

> Gentle shepherds, you that know
> The charms of tuneful breath
> That harmony in grief can show,
> Lament for pious Theron's death!
> Theron, the good, the friendly Theron's gone!
> ... Yet Theron's name in spite of fate's decrees
> An endless fame shall meet.

And, if we are to believe another (anonymous) elegist,

> His wond'rous Skill did wealthy Fabricks raise,
> Fair *Albion's* list'ning Stones obey'd his lays,
> And stand the signs of *Gratitude* and *Praise*.
> All Sons of Art adorn'd their Rev'rend *Sire*,
> And made his Mansion a perpetual Quire.[40]

PLAYFORD'S *INTRODUCTION*—EDITIONS OF
1658 TO 1670

* Playford began to publish psalm tunes in the year 1658[41]—at a time when there seemed little hope of the Restoration of Church and King for which he must have longed. In the edition of his *Introduction* printed in that year he inserted a modest collection of tunes, which he headed thus:

The Tunes of the Psalmes As they are commonly sung in Parish-Churches. With the Bass set under each Tune, By which they may be Play'd and Sung to the Organ, Virginals, Theorbo-Lute, or Bass-Viol.

It is needless to say that under the Commonwealth there could be no question of using any of these instruments in church. Playford continued, however, with a "Preface":

[39] The letter, copied into the Minutes (Court Book D, fol. 160), is printed in full in my article just referred to.

[40] Playford, *Introduction*, 11th ed. (1687), sig. a.

[41] His two editions of William Child's *The first set of psalmes of III voyces*, in 1650 and 1656, were mere reprints of the engraved edition of 1639.

Courteous Reader,

These following Tunes of the Psalms are of much use, not onely for young Practitioners in Song, but for those Parish-Clerks which live in Countrey Towns and Villages, where their Skill is as small as their Wages: But to them of this City of London, which are most of them Skilful and Judicious men (in this matter) it will add little to their Knowledge; yet I hope and wish it may to some of their Congregations, who I am very sensible have great need of instruction herein.

There are many more Tunes than I have here set down, but these I chose rather from the rest, as being all of them such as the Congregation will Joyn in, and are better acquainted with these than the other Tunes.

Vale,
J. P.

Each tune was underlaid with the first stanza of one of Sternhold and Hopkins's psalms. It is not a matter of great surprise to find that the tunes chosen by Playford as most familiar in 1658 were in many cases the same as those chosen by Barton as most familiar in 1644; agreement with the 1636 revision of the psalm book is also notable. Of the grand old D.C.M. and peculiar meter tunes from the early psalm books, Playford included those for Psalms 1, 51i, 81, 100i, 113, 119, 125ii, and 148.[42] Of the newer C.M. and S.M. tunes he selected those shown in Tables 2 and 3. The four tunes singled out by Este in 1594 as the most popular are still there. Among the others are three of Ravenscroft's innovations.

Only one hitherto unpublished tune was included by Playford. He called it NEW TUNE and set it to Psalm 96, but the preface rules out the possibility that he composed it. This bizarre tune has its own story.[43] It appears to have originated as a counterpoint to OXFORD. For although four-part harmony was emphatically not the norm, there are examples of crude attempts at two-part harmonization. They sometimes gave birth to a new tune which then separated from its parent. Another example is COLESHILL, derived from DUNDEE;[44] and in Barton's psalms we find a tune named "Dutch bass tune, used commonly in Cambridge, and of late in Aldermanbury, it agrees in consort with the tune following, so that it is all one whether you take, for they may be sung both together." But Playford said nothing about performing his NEW TUNE with OXFORD, though he printed them on the same page. Perhaps he was afraid the authorities would have disapproved of such a practice.

The same tunes were repeated in the editions of 1660, 1664, 1666,

[42] Six psalms in Sternhold and Hopkins (Ps. 23, 50, 51, 100, 125, 136) appear in two different metrical versions. These are distinguished in this article by means of lower-case roman numerals.

[43] See Nicholas Temperley, "The Adventures of a Hymn Tune—II," *Musical Times*, CXII (1971), 488-89.

[44] Routley, p. 52. See also Nicholas Temperley, "Kindred and Affinity in Hymn Tunes," *Musical Times*, CXIII (1972), 905-9.

346

and 1667, with trivial alterations, and in 1670 with the addition of another old tune—Frost 180, to Psalm 112, with the name GENEVA. This was the tune long associated with Cox's metrical Lord's Prayer and in Germany named *Vater unser*. It never reappeared in the *Introduction*, but it turns up in all three of Playford's psalters. In the 1660 *Introduction* and thereafter, the second paragraph of the preface was deleted and replaced by this:

> There are many other Tunes in our English Psalm Book, but these being the most usual and vulgarly known, are here inserted; And for such whose Skill or Curiosity desire to see or Hear more, I refer them to the most Exact Edition of Mr. Ravenscroft's Psalm Book in 4 parts, Printed in 1621.

He need no longer disguise the merits of harmonized singing, and he could now proudly call Sternhold and Hopkins "our English Psalm Book"; for the King was returning and with him the liturgy and customs of the Church.

Playford printed the tunes in the same keys in which they had appeared in earlier sources, with two exceptions—Low DUTCH and WINCHESTER, both transposed up a tone from F to G. As to rhythm, however, he often gave a version slightly differing from those in earlier sources, and sometimes the actual notes vary—in two cases (Low DUTCH and OXFORD) substantially. It seems certain, in view of Playford's policy as later outlined in his 1677 preface, that he made these changes as a result of observing common practice of his day, not through a desire to "improve" the tunes, which in any case must have proved futile in a predominantly oral tradition. His allocation of tunes to psalms is rather conservative: only CAMBRIDGE and Low DUTCH are set to psalms with which they are not associated in any earlier collection. The basses call for no special comment; they are quite orthodox, instrumentally conceived, and are not consistently derived from any earlier harmonized psalter. Example 1 shows one of the tunes from the 1658 *Introduction*.

PLAYFORD'S 1661 PSALM BOOK

Playford had needed no permission to print psalm tunes. But a complete book of psalms with tunes fell under the Stationers' monopoly. An opportunity of revising the tunes was provided by the Restoration of Charles II: the Company must have decided to take advantage of it, though there is no record of such a decision in the Court Minutes. At first the job was given to someone (not Playford) who, to judge by the result, was scarcely competent to perform it. One copy survives of an edition dated 1661,[45] bound up with a prayer book of the 1603 version. It is an extremely conservative publication in a typographical style that

[45] British Museum, C.82.g.6 (2). Wing, B2475.

Example 1

"St. David's Tune," from the *Introduction* (1658), set to Psalm 8

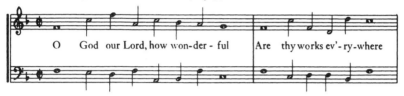

O   God our Lord, how won-der-ful   Are thy works ev'-ry-where

Whose fame sur-mounts in dig-ni-ty   A-bove the hea-vens clear.

had not been seen for some time: black letter,[46] folio, with the words set out in long lines across the page (fourteen syllables to a line for C.M. psalms).[47] The selection and allocation of tunes are eclectic: some go back to old double tunes, some to Este, some to Ravenscroft, others to earlier revisions of the psalm book. There is an entirely new tune for Psalm 14, which, however, is so badly misprinted as to make little sense; in general the music printing is poor. For the first time the cross-references for psalms without their own tunes are thoroughly revised, apparently with some care, though the references are still mostly to tunes of neighboring psalms. It seems that this edition must reflect a deliberate decision to revise the book, perhaps emanating from the Stationers' Company. But it had no successor and must have been regarded as a failure.

Another revised psalm book appeared in 1661.[48] Also somewhat conservative in appearance (folio, black letter), it turns out on inspection to represent a thorough musical reform. "The tunes of the psalmes in this edition is carefully revised and corrected by J. P.," the title page

[46] The last year in which black-letter editions exceeded roman type editions was 1625; the last black-letter edition before 1661 was in 1647. Roman type had been associated with Calvinism on the Continent, and there may have been some such connotation in England. By 1660, black letter was definitely old-fashioned, but it may have been chosen deliberately for this psalter to emphasize continuity with the pre–Civil War tradition and the restoration of established religion.

[47] The prototype for this design was the folio edition of 1565.

[48] *The whole booke of psalmes collected into English meeter by Thomas Stern-hold, John Hopkins, and others: . . . with apt notes to sing them withall . . . The tunes of the psalmes in this edition is carefully revised and corrected by J. P.* (London: printed by S. G. for the Company of Stationers, 1661). This edition is not listed in Wing. Two copies are known to the writer: one at Cambridge University Library (Eff.65(2)), the other at the University of Illinois (uncatalogued).

TABLE 5

TUNES FOR THE PSALMS IN PLAYFORD'S 1661 PSALM BOOK

Psalm	Tune (Frost)	Meter*	TUNE							ALLOCATION				Alt. c/r (Frost)
			Orig.	Este	Rav.	1629	1636	Bar.	Intr.	Orig.	Este	Rav.	Intr.	
1	15	D.C.M.	trad.	x	x	x	x	–	x	trad.	x	x	x	–
3	17	D.C.M.	trad.	x	x	x	x	–	–	trad.	x	x	–	205
4	121	C.M.	1564	x	x	–	x	x	x	Rav.	–	–	–	–
5	209	C.M.	1615	x	x	–	x	x	x	new	–	–	–	–
6	129	C.M.	1591	–	x	x	x	–	x	new	–	–	–	–
8	234	C.M.	Rav.	x	x	–	–	x	x	new	–	–	–	–
12	42	C.M.	1572	x	x	x	x	x	x	new	x	x	–	234
18	36	D.C.M.	trad.	x	–	x	x	–	x	trad.	–	x	–	–
19	25	C.M.	*Intr.*	–	x	–	–	–	–	new	–	–	–	–
23i	19	C.M.	Este	–	x	–	–	x	x	*Intr.*	–	–	x	–
25	45	S.M.	1591	x	x	–	x	x	x	1591	–	x	x	–
27	205	C.M.	1615	–	x	–	x	x	x	Rav.	–	x	x	–
30	51	D.C.M.	trad.	x	x	x	x	–	–	trad.	x	x	–	129
44	63	D.C.M.	trad.	x	x	x	x	–	–	trad.	x	x	–	234
50i	69	XXXXYY	trad.	x	x	x	x	–	–	trad.	x	x	–	–
51i	71	D.L.M.	trad.	x	x	x	x	x	x	trad.	–	x	x	–
59	4	D.C.M.	trad.	x	x	x	–	–	–	Rav.	x	x	–	205
68	85	D.C.M.	trad.	x	x	x	–	x	–	trad.	x	x	–	234
69	86	D.C.M.	trad.	x	x	x	x	–	–	trad.	x	x	–	129
77	93	D.C.M.	trad.	x	x	x	–	–	x	trad.	x	x	–	25
78	95	D.C.M.	trad.	x	x	x	x	–	–	trad.	x	x	–	132
80	205	D.C.M.	1615	x	x	–	–	x	x	new	–	–	–	–
84	103	C.M.	Este	x	x	x	x	–	x	Este	x	x	x	–
100i	114	D.C.M.	trad.	x	x	–	x	x	x	trad.	x	x	x	25
103	117	C.M.	trad.	x	x	x	x	–	–	trad.	x	x	–	–
104	119	L.M.	Rav.	–	x	–	–	–	–	Rav.	x	x	–	–
112	180	D.C.M.	trad.	x	x	x	x	–	–	trad.	x	x	x	–
113	125	55556565	trad.	x	x	x	x	x	x	trad.	x	x	x	–
119	132	888888	trad.	x	x	x	x	x	x	trad.	x	x	–	–
120	135	8888888888888	trad.	x	x	x	x	–	–	trad.	x	x	–	–
121	136	666666	trad.	x	x	x	x	–	–	trad.	x	x	–	–
122	137	866877	trad.	x	x	x	x	–	–	trad.	x	x	–	–
123	138	668668	trad.	x	x	x	x	–	–	trad.	x	x	–	–
124	139	XXXXXX	trad.	x	x	x	x	–	–	trad.	x	x	–	–

Psalm	No.	Metre	Tune							Tune				Alt.
125i	144	888866	trad.	x	x	x	x	—	—	trad.	x	x	—	—
125ii	178	D.L.M.	trad.	x	x	x	x	x	—	Este	x	—	—	—
126	145a	ZZZZXX	trad.	x	x	x	x	—	—	trad.	x	x	—	—
130	149a	76767676	trad.	x	x	x	x	—	—	trad.	x	x	—	132
132	150	D.C.M.	trad.	x	x	x	x	—	x	trad.	x	x	—	209
135	93	D.C.M.	trad.	x	x	x	x	x	x	Rav.	—	—	—	—
136i	114	†L.M.	trad.	x	x	x	x	—	—	new	x	—	x	132
137	157	D.C.M.	trad.	x	x	x	x	—	—	trad.	x	x	x	132
145	169	D.C.M.	trad.	x	x	x	x	—	—	trad.	x	x	—	—
148	174	6664444	trad.	x	x	x	x	x	x	trad.	x	x	x	—

* Numbers indicate syllables in each line; X for 10, Y for 11, Z for 12. For C.M., etc., see fn. 16.

† See text, pp. 352–53.

NOTE: Under TUNE, an x shows which of the principal earlier sources contained the tune; under ALLOCATION, an x shows which sources allocated the tune to the psalm concerned. "Alt. c/r" indicates alternative tunes listed by cross-reference; "trad." means "in English psalm books ca. 1570–1620." Three tunes (Frost 93, 114, 205) were printed twice.

350

tells us. If there were any doubt that the initials stood for John Playford, it would be dispelled by the fact that many variant versions and tune allocations in the book correspond to those in Playford's *Introduction* and in no other source before 1661. We may also recall that in the same year Playford was promoted to the Livery of the Company, possibly as a result of royal command; very likely the same influence played a part in securing the Company's commission to revise the tunes. For it was not a question of Playford's simply publishing the psalms on his own account by leave of the Company. He edited the tunes *for* the Company, and his changes were adopted in all subsequent editions of the psalm book with tunes.[49] In all its history this was the only thorough-going musical reform the psalm book would ever get.

Playford provided tunes for eighteen of the hymns and forty-three of the psalms—about the same number as the traditional psalm book. The remaining psalms he supplied with cross-references. He retained the tunes of the hymns virtually unchanged and also interfered very little with the tunes of psalms in peculiar meter. He also left more than half the old D.C.M. tunes intact, restoring some that had been replaced by single C.M. tunes in earlier revisions. In all, thirty-one psalms were printed with traditional tunes. For some of them he provided alternative cross-references. Those without a cross-reference were either in an unusual meter for which only one tune was available or were so firmly wedded to a traditional tune that it would have been futile to suggest an alternative. In this second category are Psalms 1, 51i, 100i, 119, 125ii, and 148, all of which were also printed with the same tunes in the 1658 *Introduction*. Tables 2 and 3 have already shown that in his choice of short tunes Playford was following much the same path that his predecessors had taken. These were the popular tunes of the time. The only one that had never appeared in an edition of the psalm book was the one called NEW TUNE in the *Introduction*. Table 5 sets out the complete list of tunes that Playford printed in this edition, apart from those for the hymns.

Judging from Table 5 alone one would say that this is a conservative book: and so it is in its selection of tunes, even reaching back to rescue some tunes that were on the verge of oblivion. But the balance is entirely altered if one returns to Table 2 to see how many of the psalms Playford set to the newer four-line tunes. The difference is due to the cross-references, and it was here that Playford made his greatest change.

---

[49] The following post-1661 copies of Sternhold and Hopkins with tunes have been found. All incorporate Playford's revisions of 1661, though they do not have the sentence referring to "J. P." on their title pages.

(1) T. N. for the Company of Stationers, 1669. Wing, B2946. Brit. Mus., 468.b.13(3).

(2) William Godbid and Andrew Clark for the Company of Stationers, 1677. Not in Wing. Trinity College, Cambridge, C.15.43.

(3) J. M. for the Company of Stationers, 1687. Wing, B2561. Brit. Mus., 3434.h.2.

The majority of his cross-references are to a group of five C.M. tunes: WINDSOR, ST. DAVID'S, YORK, MARTYRS, and LOW DUTCH. Thus the general plan of the psalter is seen to be similar to those of Este, Allison, and Barley in the 1590's, where also the majority of the psalms were set to a small group of four-line tunes, and different from that of Ravenscroft, who tried to introduce a large number of new tunes, setting no more than eight psalms to any one of them.

In choosing only a few tunes for most of his cross-references Playford was doubtless merely reflecting their popularity. But in allocating each psalm to one tune among these few, his policy was different. Here he was free to innovate because of the practice of lining-out. Though this had been introduced by the Westminster Assembly ostensibly to help the illiterate, the real reason may have been to facilitate the introduction of a new translation. Thus Rous had written in the preface to his version:

As for any inconvenience which may be supposed to fall out at first, by bringing Psalms into use hitherto not used, and whereof the copies are not yet common, that is prevented by the *Directory* [of *Public Worship* (promulgated by the Westminster Assembly)], where it is recommended that in the Congregation the Psalm be read line by line before it is sung.[50]

Although Playford disapproved of this "late intruding Scotch manner" of lining-out, as he called it, he took full advantage of it in all his psalters by matching each psalm to a tune that suited the words in expression. This idea, so characteristic of 17th-century aesthetics, had been put forward by Ravenscroft.

I have therefore endeavoured for the fitting of every *Heart* to that *Psalme*, which *it* shall most affect, to place special *Tunes*, proper to the nature of each *Psalme*.[51]

But a careful study of Ravenscroft's allocations reveals that in fact he did no such thing. His preface lists seven psalms of tribulation, to be sung with a low voice and in a long measure; twenty of thanksgiving, to be sung with a moderate voice and measure; and seventeen of rejoicing, to be sung with a loud voice in a "swift and jocund" measure. Yet he made no effort to select tunes suited to these moods. Some of the psalms of rejoicing he set to remarkably gloomy tunes in the minor mode (e.g., Ps. 99, to MARTYRS; and Ps. 47, to WORCESTER). If it be objected that a tune that sounds gloomy to us may have sounded joyful to Ravenscroft, the answer is that he was not consistent with his own classification. Two of his "psalms of tribulation" (102, 143) are set to the same tunes as two his "psalms of thanksgiving" (105, 48 respectively).[52]

---

[50] *The Psalms of David in English Meeter* (London: Miles Flesher, for the Company of Stationers, 1646), preface.

[51] Thomas Ravenscroft, *The Whole Book of Psalms* (London, 1621), preface.

[52] Moreover, Ravenscroft's allocation contains numerical patterns that indicate a largely arbitrary procedure. He set Ps. 86, 87, 88, 89, 90, 91, 92, and 93 to the same

352

Playford inserted in the 1661 psalm book the "Treatise made by Athanasius the Great, concerning the Use and Vertue of the Psalmes" —another conservative feature—which included a classification of the psalms according to mood and function. In this treatise, Ravenscroft's seven psalms of tribulation were listed under their better-known title, "the seven penitential psalms of David." Playford set four of them to WINDSOR, a minor-mode tune of doleful monotony (see Ex. 2). The

Example 2

Psalm 6, from the 1661 Psalm Book (set to Frost 234, WINDSOR)

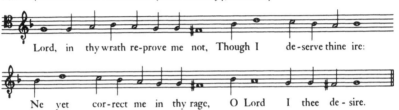

other twenty psalms he set to this tune were without exception psalms of prayer, penitence, or self-pity. By contrast the cheerful ST. DAVID'S (already quoted in Ex. 1) he set almost without exception to psalms of praise, triumph, and thanksgiving, including those classified in the "Treatise" as psalms of praise. The one exception was Psalm 2, which is one of the many prayers for the destruction of enemies. Many of the other psalms of this essentially unchristian type were set to YORK, for which the chief association in Playford's mind appears to have been the strength of the Almighty (e.g., Ps. 14, 27, 83, 109, 129, 144). Low DUTCH he used for psalms of trust and serenity (Ps. 23, 36, 37, 43, etc.) but also for some of jubilation (Ps. 63, 100). MARTYRS served variously for praise (Ps. 34, 96, 105), prayer (Ps. 31, 47, 54), and to express the fear of death (Ps. 39, 90).

This was an important innovation. Playford's 1661 psalm book was the first English hymn book that made a sustained attempt to match words and music appropriately. But the matching was only from the point of view of expressive content. In matters of verbal rhythm Playford showed himself even more insensitive to English stress patterns than the original versifiers. Wishing for some reason to set Psalm 136 (first version) to the tune of Psalm 100 (now known as OLD HUNDREDTH), he was hindered by the fact that the former was in the meter 8.10.8.10, while

tunes as Ps. 32, 33, 34, 35, 36, 37, 38, and 39 *respectively,* and there are many such arithmetical sequences. His tunes for Ps. 1–31 are either new or drawn from English psalters; those for Ps. 32–37 and 39 are from Scottish psalters; those for Ps. 40, 42, 43, and 45 are from Welsh sources. A second such "cycle" begins with Ps. 55 and a third with Ps. 106. The cycles are not entirely regular and are broken by psalms in peculiar meters or double tunes, but they are clearly discernible.

the latter was in ordinary Long Meter (8.8.8.8.). The extra syllables, however, occur in the line that repeats itself in each verse: "For his mercy endureth for ever." Playford solved this little problem by altering this line to "For his mercy dures for ever," thus at one stroke reducing the entire psalm to Long Meter. It does not seem to have worried him that all the stresses in this revised line were precisely wrong. He repeated this outrageous revision in 1677.

Playford had done what he could to improve the tradition of un-accompanied singing in the parish church. In the 1661 psalm book he brought the selection of tunes up to date, matched them appropriately to psalms, and encouraged the revival of some old tunes that were dying out. In the *Introduction* also, he provided correct and up-to-date versions of the most popular tunes, with basses for practice or for domestic use. In both cases he may have been catering principally for parish clerks.[53] The 1661 psalter and its later reprints were all in folio and in black letter; numerically, the vast majority of psalters printed and sold by the Stationers' Company after 1660 were in smaller sizes, in roman type, and without tunes (see Table 4). So the tunes would not have been seen by the ordinary churchgoer. In these circumstances the number sold was considerable.

MUSICKS HAND-MAIDE

Playford next turned to accompaniment. For the rest of his life one of his great ambitions was to restore harmony to the parish church: an un-promising goal in the almost total absence of organs, choirs, or any tradition of part-singing in church. His first effort in this direction was a modest but not insignificant one. He issued a sheet of music headed "The Tunes of Psalms to the Virginal or Organ." Though it is bound in with the 1663 edition of *Musicks Hand-maide* in the British Museum copy, there are sound reasons for thinking it was printed in 1668 or 1669.[54] It consists of only four tunes:

[53] The 1677 reprint of this edition was probably issued in response to a request from the Company of Parish Clerks to the Company of Stationers "to print ye Psalmes wth Musicall Notes," considered by the Court on September 10, 1677 (Court Book D, fol. 284^v). Playford's 1677 three-part psalter cannot have been connected with this request because the Company had already received £10 from Playford for permission to print it (see p. 364 below).

[54] The music type is the same as that used in Tomkins's *Musica deo sacra* (1668), and it seems likely that it was designed for this purpose rather than for an insignificant single leaf of psalm tunes. Thus the psalm tunes would not have been printed before 1668. A publisher's advertisement which seems to be conjugate with the leaf containing the tunes includes Henry Lawes's *Select Ayres and Dialogues* which was reprinted in 1669 under a different title (*The Treasury of Music*); it also includes "*Musicks Recreation* on the *Lyra Violl* containing 150 Choice Lessons . . .": this work contained 150 pieces in the 1669 edition but only 123 in the previous extant edition, that of 1661. So it seems that 1669 is the most likely year for the advertisement and hence for the psalm tune settings. Both the tunes and the advertisement are also

354

Frost No.	Meter	Key	Heading
45	S.M.	a	The Tune of the 25 Psalm
205	C.M.	G	The Tune of the 71 Psalm: called, *Yorke*-Tune
129	C.M.	a	The Tune of the 6 Psalm: called, *Windsor*-Tune
234	C.M.	G	The Tune of the 95 Psalm, or S. *Davids*-Tune.

They are printed on six staves in a very full harmonization including thick left-hand chords (see Ex. 3). Together with other music printed by

Example 3

"The Tune of the 95 Psalm, or S. *Davids*-Tune," from *Musicks Hand-maide* (1663)

Godbid at about the same time they represent the earliest effort by an English printer to set up chords in type[55] and provide a very rare example of the style of organ accompaniment of psalm tunes in the 17th century.[56]

The main reason to connect these settings with Playford is that he was the publisher of *Musicks Hand-maide* and was closely associated with William Godbid, the printer of the tunes. The three common-meter tunes are the ones allocated to the largest number of psalms in the 1661 psalter, and the other is the one allocated to all Short-Meter psalms there (see Tables 2 and 3). The association of WINDSOR with Psalm 6 reflects the

---

bound in with the 1678 edition of *Musicks Hand-maide* in the Newberry Library copy, but not in the British Museum, Dundee Public Library, and Houghton Library copies: the Library of Congress copy has the psalm tunes without the advertisement. I am grateful to the librarians concerned and in particular to Donald Krummel and Oliver Neighbour for help with this intricate problem.

[55] Apart from an isolated instance in Tobias Hume's *Ayres* (1605).

[56] So far, no fully written-out organ accompaniments to psalm tunes have come to light in any 17th-century English MS.

1661 psalter and no earlier source. But Psalms 71 and 95 were not matched to York and St. David's in any other Playford publication. Moreover the keys, precise melodic forms, and harmonizations of the tunes do not agree with other Playford sources. It is not impossible, therefore, that another musical editor was responsible for these settings.

Although these four tunes could serve for the great majority of metrical psalms, it seems likely that the settings were intended mainly as *examples* of how a tune might be accompanied on the organ. The number of parish churches with organs at this date was pitifully small —probably not more than two in the whole of London[57] —but Playford was ever optimistic and hoped, perhaps, to encourage the wealthy to donate organs by showing what might be done with them. Meanwhile the settings were available for domestic use or for cathedrals and collegiate churches in which metrical psalms were sung. They are notable for their almost total lack of ornament. By comparison, settings of the early 18th century have trills, turns, and appoggiaturas, as well as interludes between the lines; but they have no chords, other than octaves, for the left hand.[58]

PSALMS & HYMNS IN SOLEMN MUSICK

Playford now began to explore the possibilities of part-singing. If anyone was qualified to launch a new tradition of harmonized psalm singing in the parish church, he was that man. Well versed in the cathedral tradition,[59] he had demonstrated his mastery over musical theory in the *Introduction*. As clerk to the Temple Church from 1653, he was experienced in the practice of psalmody, and in the 1661 psalter he had shown the possibilities and the limitations of the existing tradition. It is clear from his writings, in particular the prefaces to the 1671 and 1677 books, that he yearned for the solemn sonority of full harmony in the parish church. We do not know when he first conceived the ultimate object of printing a complete psalter with harmonized tunes. He may well have hesitated long before preparing such a work, which could only repay the trouble and expense involved if it was adopted in considerable numbers by churches. The demand for it was not evident. Even in London churches, for which it was chiefly aimed, organs were few and parish clerks of doubtful competence.

The 1671 collection[60] may be seen as a trial run. It was a more hesitant publication than the later work, with less clear aims. Playford

---

[57] See fn. 68.

[58] See, for example, *The Psalms by Dr. Blow Set full for the Organ or Harpsichord as they are Play'd in Churches or Chapels* (London, 1731).

[59] Canon Noel Boston has plausibly suggested that he was a chorister at Norwich Cathedral in boyhood. After the Restoration he sang as a vicar-choral at St. Paul's Cathedral. See Dean-Smith, *Playford's English Dancing Master*, pp. xi, xii.

[60] *Psalms & Hymns in Solemn Musick of Foure Parts On the Common Tunes to the Psalms in Metre: Used in Parish-Churches. Also six hymns for one voice to the*

356

hedged his risk a little by trying to please more than one public. On the one hand he hoped the book would be adopted by churches; and to this end he included a number of metrical psalms complete with the tunes to which they were traditionally sung.

The Common Tunes are all Printed in the *Tenor Part*, and in their proper key, with the *Basse* under each Tune, as convenient to be Sung to an *Organ, Lute,* or *Viol*. And to have this Musick more full and solemn, I have Compos'd to them two other Parts, viz. two *Contratenors*. All Four Parts moving together, being Composed to Mens *Voyces*, and each Part in such a Compass of *Notes* as may be performed with ordinary Voyces: And in such places where there is *Treble Voyces*, those may sing the *Tenor* or *Common Tunes*.[61]

But Playford knew that very few parish churches yet had an organ and none a lute or viol. These suggestions were chiefly for the benefit of accomplished musicians out of church, in the tradition of earlier har-monized psalters such as Este's and Ravenscroft's. So, too, were the alter-native translations of many psalms, which he printed in roman type to distinguish them from the "authorized" Sternhold and Hopkins versions in black letter. He knew that these versions could not be used in church, though he hoped they might be authorized.[62] He went further by in-cluding a number of hymns from a Roman Catholic source[63] and "six hymns for one voice to the organ" in the manner of solo songs. Moreover, in the longer psalms he gave a *selection* of verses, instead of printing them complete divided into sections as was customary in the common psalm book. Here he may have had a double motive: to provide selections of convenient length for home use and to suggest that such curtailment might be properly introduced in church.[64]

As for the tunes, Playford had no desire to innovate, but only to conserve and revive the best.

Those many *Tunes* formerly used to these *Psalms,* which for excellency of Form, Solemn Ayre, and sutableness to the Matter of the *Psalms,* are not In-feriour to any *Tunes* used in *Forreign Churches*: But at this day the *Best,* and

---

organ . . . By John Playford (London, printed by W. Godbid for J. Playford, 1671). It was neither published by, nor registered with, the Stationers' Company, presumably because their monopoly did not in practice extend to selections from the book of psalms. However, on September 13, 1672, fifty-two copies of a book of "Psalms in folio for services" were delivered to the Treasurer's Warehouse: this may well have been Playford's book (Stationers' Company: English Stock Book).

[61] *Psalms & Hymns,* preface.

[62] ". . . and it were to be wished, that one of these Translations, (if Authority thought fit,) might be allowed and used in our Churches: And this may be easily done, It being the custom at this time for the Clerk to read every Line to the People before it is Sung; who may without any disturbance, Inform the Congregation, that according to a more refin'd Translation, they are to sing such a *Psalm*; the *Common Tunes* agreeing exactly to these as they did to the old." *Psalms & Hymns,* preface.

[63] Frost, ed., *Historical Companion,* p. 59.

[64] Even long psalms were evidently sung in their entirety at this period. See, for example, Pepys *Diary,* 6 Jan. 1661 and 5 Jan. 1662.

almost all the *Choice Tunes* are lost, and out of use in our *Churches:* nor must we expect it otherwayes, when in and about this great City, in above One hundred Parishes, there is but few *Parish Clerks* to be found that have either Ear or Understanding to Set one of these *Tunes* Musically as it ought to be: It having been a Custom during the late Wars, and since, to Chuse men into such places, more for their *Poverty* then *Skill* and *Ability;* Whereby this part of Gods Service hath been so ridiculously performed in most places, that it is now brought into Scorn and Derision by many People.

In this passage Playford seems to contradict his earlier opinion of London parish clerks: in the *Introduction* he had said that they were "most of them Skilful and Judicious men (in this matter)." The contradiction cannot well be explained by a sudden deterioration in the abilities of parish clerks, because the comment from the 1658 *Introduction* was repeated in all editions up to 1670. A possibility that seems plausible at first sight is that Playford wished to flatter the clerks in the *Introduction* but in *Psalms & Hymns* was addressing himself to a different public altogether. But there is direct evidence to the contrary, for he presented a number of copies of *Psalms & Hymns* to the Company of Parish Clerks of London for use at their weekly singing practices.[65] It seems that the clue must lie in the parenthetical phrase "in this matter" in the *Introduction.* Playford considered the clerks of London fully competent to lead a psalm in unison (though he withheld even this degree of esteem from their country colleagues); but he doubted their capacity to sing in harmony. Now, therefore, he provided harmonized settings of all the well-known tunes, designed primarily for male voices though adaptable for mixed singing: and he hoped to train the clerks to sing them thus. It seems that the Company of Parish Clerks had the tunes copied out in manuscript part-books, which they continued to use at their practices even after the three-part 1677 psalter had appeared.[66] Playford gave them another copy of the 1671 book in 1685. It is more than likely that he himself supervised the weekly choir practices of the Company. Benjamin Payne in *The Parish Clerk's Guide* said that Playford was "one to whose memory all parish clerks owe perpetual thanks for their furtherance in the knowledge of psalmody."[67]

---

[65] Peter H. Ditchfield, *The Parish Clerk* (London, 1907), pp. 121–22; E. A. Ebblewhite, *The Parish Clerks' Company* (London, 1932), pp. 76–80. Most of the Company's possessions were destroyed in the Second World War, but one copy of *Psalms & Hymns* survives in a damaged state and is preserved in the Guildhall Library, London. It is inscribed by Playford with the date April 1, 1671.

[66] The records themselves are not extant, and Ebblewhite's description of them is not entirely clear. It appears that the Company possessed twenty of these manuscript part-books in 1672, more than twenty at later dates in the 17th century, and that five of them remained in 1932.

[67] John Harley, *Music in Purcell's London* (London, 1968), p. 102, cites this passage from *The Parish Clerk's Guide*, 1685. I have not been able to find a copy; the earliest edition listed in Wing is 1692. It seems unlikely that Payne would have written of the "memory" of a man who (in 1685) was still living.

358

What is not entirely clear is the purpose of training the clerks to sing in harmony, apart from the mere pleasure of the weekly rehearsals. Since early Elizabethan times parish churches had had only one clerk apiece. How could one man, however well trained in part-singing, introduce even two-part harmony in a church in which the congregation depended on him to lead the tunes? Congregational rehearsal and parish choirs, whether professional or voluntary, were equally unknown in the 1670's. The number of London churches with organs was still insignificant.[68] Did the parish clerks form themselves into quartets or small choirs and go from one church to another to lead the psalms in harmony? Or did Playford encourage them to form and train choirs in their churches? There is no record of either proceeding at this early date. Playford was himself clearly aware of the problem, though he offered no solution:

Yet, as it is, it [the psalter] is not wholly perfect; for I have done but one half in Setting the *Musick*, which yet remains as a dead letter: It being your part to Complete it, and to add *life* to its *Harmonious Body*, by your sweet *According Voyces*, singing the same in *perfect Tune* and *Time*, which is the *Soul* of *Musick*.[69]

One senses an uncertainty of purpose in this enterprise of Playford's. From the purely commercial point of view it was not a promising venture. He might hope to sell a few copies to private music-lovers and perhaps to cathedrals, collegiate churches, and Oxford and Cambridge colleges, none of which excluded metrical psalms from their repertories. But parish churches, for whose benefit the book was ostensibly designed, were unlikely to buy it and would have difficulty in using it if they did. It was never reprinted. In 1677 Playford wrote that it

was received with good acceptation among many true Lovers of Divine Musick: . . . the only exception that ever I heard against it, was that the largeness of the Volume, and the not having the *Psalms* in their order, made it not so useful to carry to Church.[70]

That was as near as he would come to admitting a failure. But he had learned his lesson, and in his next venture he would abandon his "domes-

---

*   [68] Only two London parish churches are known to have had an organ at any time between the Restoration of 1660 and the Great Fire of 1666: St. Mary Woolnoth (*ca.* 1663) and St. John, Hackney (1666). The former was destroyed by the fire and not rebuilt until 1681. The following acquired organs between the fire and 1680: St. Giles-in-the-Fields (1671); St. Giles, Cripplegate (1671); St. Dunstan-in-the-East (1672); St. Martin-in-the-Fields (1674?); All Hallows, Barking-by-the-Tower (1675); St. Botolph, Aldgate (1676); St. Sepulchre, Newgate (1676); St. Margaret, Westminster (1676); and St. Dunstan, Stepney (1679–81). In the case of a few churches, records are incomplete, but firm dates have been obtained for the first organ after the Restoration in the great majority of churches: the writer has compiled this information on a card index.

  [69] *Psalms & Hymns*, preface.

  [70] Playford, *Whole Book* (1677), preface.

tic" public and go all out to cater for congregational needs, at the same time seeking to bring harmony within the reach of the parish church.

There are few surprising innovations in the tunes of *Psalms & Hymns.* In the great majority of cases Playford set the psalms to tunes with which they had been associated for many years, as he said in the preface. Many of the old D.C.M. tunes were revived, though not as many as in the 1661 psalm book —which is not surprising, since only a selection of thirty-four of the "authorized" psalms was included. Two old tunes were put to a new use: Frost 10, traditionally set to one of the Divine Hymns ("The Lamentation of a Sinner"), appeared with Psalm 11; Frost 32, the old tune for Psalm 14, was allotted to Psalm 86. Tables 2 and 3 show that most of the popular four-line tunes were included, in many cases allocated to psalms with which they had not been matched before. Playford also brought in a tune not yet known to the English psalm book: Frost 222, found in the Scottish psalter of 1635 as a "common tune" under the name of NEWTOUN. Playford renamed it LONDON NEW, under which name it has remained popular to this day, and joined it to an "unauthorized" version of Psalm 150 by Henry King, Bishop of Chichester. (He was later to allot it to the standard versions of Ps. 47, 93, and 150 in the 1677 psalter.) The NEW TUNE of the *Introduction* and 1661 book, described above, reappeared with Psalm 8 under the name LITCHFIELD.

There are six completely new tunes in the book, so that at first sight it looks as if Playford did want a certain amount of innovation. But on closer inspection it emerges that all the tunes except one are very closely related to earlier tunes, as will be seen from the details below.

EXCETER—Frost 332b (to Ps. 146). The first two lines are identical to a tune found in Prys's Welsh psalter of 1621 (Frost 332) and in Wither's *Hymns and Songs* of 1623 (Frost 332a). The last two lines are entirely different.

WORCESTER—Frost 46 (to Ps. 26). This is strikingly similar to WINDSOR (Frost 129), quoted in Ex. 2. The key and harmonic structure are identical, as are twenty of the twenty-eight notes.

HEREFORD—Frost 152a (to Ps. 133); ST. MARY—Frost 234c (to Ps. 103); CAMBRIDGE SHORT—Frost 154a (to Ps. 134, S.M.). These three are all members of a large family of tunes whose ramifications are set out in some detail elsewhere.[71] All appear to be derived from WINCHESTER (Frost 103): ST. MARY by amalgamation with LINCOLN (FROST 243a), HEREFORD more directly (seventeen notes out of twenty-eight identical apart from minor rhythmic differences), and CAMBRIDGE SHORT from HEREFORD, with perhaps a flashback to an early ancestor, the old tune for Ps. 77 (Frost 93).

The remaining new tune is set to Psalm 116 (Frost 130). It is something of a curiosity, for it is in the old Double Common Meter—perhaps the only *new* tune in this meter from the entire 17th century. This is so unusual that Frost suspected it came from "some earlier edition of the Old

---

[71] See my article cited above, fn. 44.

360

Version."[72] It does indeed bear resemblance to an earlier example, the old tune to Benedictus (Frost 3). The harmonic schemes are similar, and twenty-five notes out of fifty-six are the same. But several lines are strikingly different, so that one hesitates to pronounce the later tune a derivative of the earlier.

None of the six new tunes is in any way striking, and it seems unlikely that Playford printed them in order to "introduce" them. More probably it was a case of setting down a number of tunes which had evolved far enough from their ancestors to deserve recognition in their own right. Although Playford did have his own ideas about good and bad in a tune (as shown in the quotation from the preface on pp. 356–57 above), his overriding concern was that the tunes in use should be properly and "solemnly" sung.

Only two or three tunes appear in significantly changed forms. Some are transposed: five tunes had been inconveniently high and one inconveniently low in earlier sources; this did not matter in the 1661 psalm book, intended like its predecessors for unaccompanied singing, but now transposition was necessary to accommodate four rather low-pitched voices which might be accompanied by an organ.[73]

In harmonizing the tunes, Playford essentially added two counter-tenor parts, one high, the other very low; without them the tenor and bass settings were similar to those in the *Introduction*. The resulting four-part texture is rich and dark, especially when a soprano line is added in octaves with the tenor melody, as Playford suggests in the preface (Ex. 4). Voice-leading is careful: the bass is angular, but the counter-tenor parts move smoothly, generally to the nearest available note. The range of chords is quite conservative: triads in root position or first inversion, with an occasional cadence suspension. There is never the slightest departure from strict homophony.

PLAYFORD'S *INTRODUCTION*, 1672 to 1687

In his next edition of the *Introduction* (1672) Playford decided to make some alterations in the psalm tunes, bringing them into line with the tunes in *Psalms & Hymns*. They were now printed without basses, but with a sol-fa letter under each note for those who could not read music notation. A new preface said:

The Tunes of *Psalms* are of general use, all who are true Lovers of Divine *Musick* will have them in estimation, they may be called Holy *David's* Musick,

---

[72] Frost, *English and Scottish*, p. x.

[73] The interval of transposition was at least a fourth in each case. Up a fourth: Frost 10; down a fourth: Frost 1, 149a, 157, 178; down a fifth, Frost 32. Probably Playford decided that if the best key were only a whole tone away from the traditional key, it was better to leave it unchanged. Transpositions of a third were not possible, since the only keys in use were F major, C major, G major, D minor, and A minor—no doubt because of tuning difficulties.

51

Example 4 *

Psalm 95, from *Psalms & Hymns* (1671), with St. David's Tune

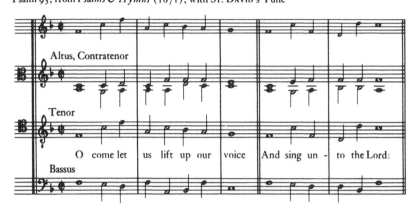

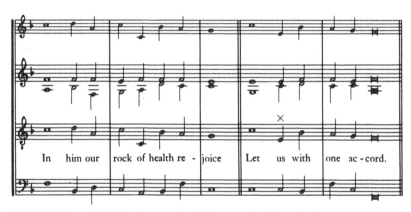

* An ✕ in this and the following examples indicates an altered note in the tune.

they are easie and delightful; those who are principally concern'd are *Parish-Clerks,* as being the Leaders of those Tunes in their Congregations, for whose use and benefit, I have set down these following Directions, as also the Names of Notes under each Tune.

The "Directions" are concerned with pitching the tunes, making it clear that they are designed for unaccompanied singing. Playford goes on to recommend *Psalms & Hymns* "as proper to sing to the Organ, Theorbo, or *Bass-Viol.*" So by leaving out the basses he evidently wanted to induce parish clerks to buy the full four-part version—less for his own financial gain probably than for the encouragement of full harmony.

52

TABLE 6

PLAYFORD'S *INTRODUCTION*, 1670, 1672, AND 1674, COMPARED WITH *PSALMS* & *HYMNS*, 1671

Tune (Frost)	Meter	Name	Introduction			Psalms & Hymns 1671
			1670	1672	1674	
15	D.C.M.	PSALM I	I	–	I	I, I*
71	D.L.M.	PSALM LI	51ii	–	51ii	51ii
99	D.C.M.	PSALM LXXXI	81	–	81	81
132	D.C.M.	PSALM CXIX	119	–	119	119
174	66664444	PSALM CXLVIII	148	148	148	148
125	888888888888	PSALM CXIII	113	113	113	113
114	L.M.	PSALM C	100i	100i	100i	100i, I*, 118*
178	L.M.	TEN COMMANDMENTS	125ii	125ii	125ii	125ii
180	888888	GENEVA	112	–	–	112
85	D.C.M.	PSALM 68	–	–	68	68
121	C.M.	OXFORD	4	4	4	4, 4*
42	C.M.	CAMBRIDGE	12	117	12	117
19	C.M.	{LOW DUTCH	23	–	23	–
		{CANTERBURY	–	23	–	23
205	C.M.	YORK	73	94	27	43, 43*, 128
209	C.M.	MARTYRS	39	145	39	145, 5*
103	C.M.	WINCHESTER	84	84	84	84, 84*
234	C.M.	ST. DAVIDS	95	95	95	95, 95*
25	C.M.	{NEW TUNE	96	–	–	–
		{LITCHFIELD	–	96	96	8, 8*
129	C.M.	WINDSOR	116	116	116	131
111	C.M.	WESTMINSTER	–	141	141	141
222	C.M.	{LONDON	–	149	–	–
		{LONDON NEW	–	–	135	150*
46	C.M.	WORCESTER	–	–	26	26, 26*
333a	C.M.	HACKNEY	–	–	61	–
152a	C.M.	HEREFORD	–	–	133	133
243c	C.M.	{HARTFORDHIRE	–	–	103	–
		{ST. MARY	–	–	–	103
332b	C.M.	EXCETER	–	–	145	146, 146*
45	S.M.	{CAMBRIDGE SHORT	25	–	25	–
		{	50ii		50ii	
		{	67		67	
		{	70		70	
		{	134		134	
		{SOUTHWEL	–	25	–	25
154a	S.M.	{NEW TUNE	–	–	25,134	–
		{CAMBRIDGE SHORT	–	–	–	134

* An "unauthorized" version, not that of Sternhold and Hopkins.
NOTE: Numbers in the body of the table are of psalms to which the tunes were allocated in each source. Tune names are as given in the different sources.

Table 6 shows that in this 1672 edition, compared with that of 1670, the choice, allocation, and naming of the tunes were brought much closer to those of *Psalms & Hymns*, although many of the old long tunes were omitted. Playford now had a pair of complementary books to offer: *Psalms & Hymns* for parish clerks and for those who would try to sing in harmony, at home or in church; the *Introduction* for those who could only manage the tunes, including the less accomplished parish clerks. By bringing the two into conformity he envisaged that they might be used simultaneously—perhaps, even, by choir and congregation. Such an idea was new. No book of tunes had ever been printed to conform exactly with Este, Ravenscroft, or any other harmonized English psalter.

The idea was over-optimistic. The alterations were resisted. In the next edition of the *Introduction* (1674)[74] Playford rescinded most of the changes of 1672. The sol-fa letters were omitted; the basses were restored (but were altered to conform with *Psalms & Hymns*); the old psalm allocations were reinstated; even the old tune names came back in two cases (see Table 6). Four long tunes omitted in 1672 now returned, and a fifth (Ps. 68) joined them. All that was left of the 1672 changes was two new tunes (WESTMINSTER, LONDON NEW) and most of the preface. Now, however, Playford added six new short tunes, not found in earlier editions, some, but not all, from *Psalms & Hymns*.

This reversion seems to lend further support to the conclusion that the 1671 *Psalms & Hymns* had turned out a failure. Customers did not appreciate changes in the *Introduction* designed to conform with a book which they did not want; and they presumably demanded a return to the old plan. After this, the psalm-tune section of the *Introduction* stayed the same, apart from the omission of the preface and correction of a few errors, in both the remaining editions of Playford's lifetime (1679, 1683) and in the one just after his death (1687), which may well have been prepared by him.

THE WHOLE BOOK OF PSALMS
IN THREE PARTS (1677)

Playford was now ready to concentrate all his experience—ecclesiastical, musical, typographical, and commercial—into a new publication which would be a complete edition of the psalter with the tunes harmonized in three parts. A number of considerations must have led him to this decision. *Psalms & Hymns* had been taken up by the London parish clerks but had made little headway in the churches. As he had learned, it was too large for convenience; and it did not present all the psalms in sequence. There were other features that told against its popularity. Its "unauthorized" versions and hymns must have aroused the suspicions of some of the clergy. Its four male parts demanded too great a leap forward from the unison singing that had been usual. The notation was old-fashioned: Playford had not only used the archaic black letter for the Sternhold and Hopkins texts, but in the music he had used C clefs for all parts except the bass. His traditionalism was deeply ingrained, but now he realized that it had stood in the way of his purpose. He defended the old clefs in 1672, in opposition to the radical views of Thomas Salmon; but he continued:

---

[74] The 1674 edition is available in a modern reprint (Ridgewood, N. J., 1966). The 1683 edition, very similar as regards the psalm tunes, is available on microcard.

364

As to my *Psalms* in Four Parts, which are Printed in three *Tenor* Cliffs and a *Bass;* I could have printed them as well in Three *Treble* Cliffs [and a Bass], had I thought all had been so ignorant in the use of our Cliffs as I am assured you are: It being usual and common for Men to Sing the Songs which are prick'd in a *Treble* an Eighth lower, where the Parts are so Composed, that they do not interfere with *Bass*.[75]

It sounds as if he had already realized his mistake. At any rate in 1677 he quietly changed his mind.

The new psalter showed by its title that it belonged in the direct line of the common psalm books. It was called *The Whole Book of Psalms: with the Usual Hymns and Spiritual Songs; together With all the Ancient and Proper Tunes sung in Churches, with some of Later Use. Compos'd in Three Parts, Cantus, Medius, & Bassus: In a more Plain and Useful Method than hath been formerly Published.* It was "printed by W. Godbid for the Company of Stationers, and are sold by John Playford near the Temple-Church." Since this was the complete psalter, Playford must ask the Company's authority for the enterprise. In a quarterly account dated September 1, 1677[76] it is recorded that the English Stock "rec[eive]d of Mr. Playford to print 1000 Psalmes £ 10: 0. 0." The new format was octavo, which made the book "useful to carry to Church" and as easy to manage in the pew as on the clerk's reading desk. Roman type was used throughout.

All the psalms were printed, as well as a revised selection of "Divine Hymns" which included several new texts.[77] Every psalm and hymn had a tune printed with it, underlaid with the first stanza. In a long and informative preface, after the usual ransacking of Bible and early Church Fathers for proofs of the authority and divinity of psalm singing, Playford reviewed the present state of psalmody.

. . . Time and long use hath much abated the wonted reverence and estimation it had for about an hundred years after [the Reformation]. . . : The Reasons whereof, as I conjecture, are chiefly these; 1. The faults some find with the *Translation:* 2. The dislike that others have for the *Tunes:* And 3. The ill custom of *Reading* every Line by itself before they sing it.

He then dealt with each of these objections in turn, withholding censure this time from parish clerks. He admitted that the translation was antiquated and in many places obscure, and pointed out that he had remedied some of the worst passages. As for those that found fault with the tunes,

[75] Letter, Playford to Salmon, dated Aug. 26, 1672. In Matthew Locke, *The Present Practice of Musick Vindicated* (London, 1673), p. 86.
[76] Stationers' Company, English Stock Book.
[77] There were a new Hymn after Communion, Hymn for Sunday, Morning Hymn, and Hymn on the Divine Use of Musick. Bishop Cosin's translation of *Veni Creator Spiritus,* inserted in the 1662 Prayer Book as an alternative to the old translation in the Ordination Service, was likewise included here. The version of the Lord's Prayer set to the tune previously associated with Coxe's version (Frost 180) was reduced to only two six-line stanzas, replacing nine in the original.

"they are only such as want skill to sing them." Four psalms (111, 121, 124, 130) had difficult tunes in irregular meters, so, Playford said, he had provided alternative translations in Common Meter.[78] He had tried out French and German tunes, but stoutly maintained that he found "our *English* Tunes, both for Air and Gravity, well suiting the words, rather to excel than to be any jot inferior to them." Then he stated his policy:

My endeavour in this Edition is, in the plainest method I may, to set down all the Old Tunes that ever were in common use in our Churches; and where any of those Tunes, through long use, have met with some little variation, I have taken care to print them exactly according to present use and practice.

He admitted, though, that Continental Reformed churches sang better, because they taught their children the psalms, and also "they have their *Psalm Books* printed most exactly with the Musical Tunes to each Psalm, so that their Congregations are generally perfect in the Tunes." After the minister has appointed the psalm and given the pitch for the tune, the people sing "without making any stops or stays 'till the *Psalm* is ended." As for lining-out, he attacked the custom, because it "doth much obstruct the Tune by such long pauses, whereby the Ayre and Harmony thereof is lost"; and also because if the clerk should miss a line, much confusion would result. He granted that lining-out might be useful "in some small Villages near the Sea, or in the Borders of *Scotland*"; but in London "you have not three in a hundred but can read." When the custom was abolished "you shall observe more to make use of their Books, and give better attention both to the Matter and the Musick."

Playford went on to suggest that the clergy could well take more interest in the music of the church[79] and should appoint musically competent persons as clerks.[80] He commended the Parish Clerks of London for their diligence in practicing psalm singing in their Hall. Finally he gave a detailed rationale for the collection:

Since [publishing *Psalms & Hymns* in 1671] I was much importuned by some Persons in the West Countrey to set out a new Edition of Mr. *Ravenscroft's Psalms;* but I did not approve thereof, for many Reasons I gave them under

---

[78] These translations were printed in addition to the "authorized" versions. Three of them had appeared in *Psalms & Hymns.*

[79] It might have seemed presumptuous on the part of a mere stationer to criticize the attitudes of the clergy. But Playford's social standing was probably equal to that of many clergymen: his brother was rector of a parish. His complaint was one of the first in a long series, which became increasingly strident towards the end of the 18th century, about clerical apathy towards church music. But the great majority of the clergy continued to scorn psalmody until the Evangelical movement.

[80] The Canons of 1603 had laid down that the minister of each parish was to appoint a clerk who was "known to the said Parson, Vicar or Minister, to be of honest Conversation, and sufficient for his Reading, Writing, and also for his competent skill in Singing (if it may be)." But according to Playford the last-mentioned qualification had seldom been sought since the Civil War (see above, p. 357).

366

my hand; some of which were these: First, The Four Parts being compos'd by divers men, who setting their *Cliffs* in several places, render it confused and difficult to Practitioners. Secondly, The Four Parts were so compos'd with mixture of Trebles, that they could not all be sung by men without admitting Boys. Thirdly, Intruding among our *English* Tunes, many Outlandish, *Welsh* and *Scotch* Tunes, of neither good *form* nor *ayre*. Lastly, The *Tunes* were not there put down as they are sung at this present, likewise several *Tunes* now in use are not to be found therein. To remedy all this, I thought it less pain to set forth a new one, than to take away these inconveniences in the old. . . Wherefore upon *deliberate consideration*, and likewise the *judgment* of some of the best skill'd in this Art, I concluded to compose all the *Musical Tunes* into *Three Parts*, viz. *Cantus, Medius*, and *Bassus*. . . The *Church Tune* is placed in the *Treble Part*, which is the *Cantus*, with the *Bass* under it, as most proper to joyn *Voice* and *Instrument* together, according to holy *David's* prescription *Psalm 144.9*. And since many of our Churches are lately furnished with Organs, it will also be useful for the Organist; Likewise to all such Students in the *Universities* as shall practise Song, to sing to a Lute or Viol. The *Medius Part* is composed as is proper, not to rise above the *Church Tune*, to cloud or obscure the *Ayre* thereof, except in such places as it could not be well avoided. The *Bass* is composed in such a compass of Notes, as will sute an indifferent Voice both below and above. All *Three Parts* may as properly be sung by Men as by Boys or Women. To that end, the two *Upper Parts* are constant in G *sol re ut Cliff*, and the *Bass* in the *F fa ut*, its proper *Cliff*: All *Three Parts* moving together in Solemn way of *Counterpoint*: Also every *Tune* put in such *Keyes* as is most sutable to the *Ayre* thereof: Lastly, you will find every *Psalm* fitted to *Tunes* sutable and proper to the *Matter*: Psalms of *Prayer* and *Confession*, to solemn grave *Flat Tunes*; Psalms of *Thanksgiving* and *Praise*, to lively chearful *Sharp Tunes*. Likewise all such *Hymns* and *Psalms*, whose Tunes are long, and may seem difficult to some, have directions over them to be sung to other short Common Tunes.

Of course, the greatest novelty was the decision to print the psalms in three parts only, with the tune uppermost. It was this, together with the dropping of C clefs, that made the collection so readily accessible to a wide circle and eventually so useful to volunteer choirs. It was adapted for use with an organ (although despite Playford's statement there were still very few organs in London by 1677[81]— and the number in country parish churches was even smaller); or for men's voices alone; or for men with women and children. The harmony is conceived, as before, in terms of two predominant parts, the tenor and the bass; the second tenor is less striking melodically, serving largely to complete the harmonies. In spite of Playford's statement in the preface, it lies above the tune almost as often as below. In Example 5 the harmony has been set out with all three parts doubled an octave above, as Playford recommends when women and children are singing. In some tunes (not that in Ex. 5) this produces consecutive fifths where consecutive fourths appear between the two tenor parts, yet the effect is not unpleasant, particularly if (as would no doubt

[81] See fn. 68.

Example 5

Psalm 95, from *The Whole Book of Psalms in Three Parts* (1677), with St. David's Tune

have been the case) the great majority of persons present are singing the tune in one octave or the other.

Playford transposed tunes far more readily in this collection than in previous ones. With organs beginning to be more common and perhaps bass viols already in use in some country churches, it was important to set a pitch that would not discourage congregations or choirs from singing. No less than thirty-five of the fifty-three tunes found in earlier sources are in a different key—by far the commonest transposition being up one tone. The keys of A major and E minor, not found in earlier psalters, are used freely, and G major and A minor also occur more often than before. A first reading of the passage about keys in the preface (quoted above) might suggest that Playford deliberately chose "sharper" keys for the more cheerful tunes; but in most cases the transposition can be fully explained on grounds of compass. Playford seems to have considered $e-e'$ or $f-f'$ the best octave for a tune, and he altogether avoided notes below d or above g'.[82] Eleven of his transpositions have the effect of avoiding notes outside this maximum range; a further twenty-one improve the general tessitura of the tune, centering on b or c' for preference. Only two remain where the transposition does not seem to improve the compass by Playford's standards. These are ST. DAVID's (up from F major to G major, giving a compass $g-g'$) and the old Te Deum tune (raised from D minor to E minor, giving a compass $e-g'$). ST. DAVID's is one of the most jubilant of tunes and was consistently set by Playford to psalms of praise; the Te Deum tune (also set to Ps. 41) was also associated with joyful words. It may be that in these two cases Playford wanted a higher pitch and a "sharper" key for aesthetic reasons. But WINDSOR, one of the gloomiest tunes in the book and reserved for psalms of abject misery, is also raised a tone, from G minor to A minor: this must surely be for the sake of pitch alone, its new compass being $g\sharp-e'$. A great many of the transpositions involve the old double tunes. In more than a century the level of pitch had dropped appreciably.

Playford included all the tunes found in *Psalms & Hymns* (some greatly altered) with the addition of others, mostly from earlier sources. He seems to have been particularly concerned, as in the 1661 and 1671 psalters, to keep alive the better survivors among the old D.C.M. tunes: he chose no less than fifteen in this unfashionable meter—many more, for example, than in any edition of his *Introduction* and nearly as many as in his 1661 psalm book. True, he provided cross-references to alternative tunes. His alterations of tunes were far more extensive than before, and have been the principal target for criticism of his work.[83] In such tunes as CANTERBURY, MAN-

[82] Pitch would have been fixed only in churches where there were organs. Renatus Harris's organs of the period had a pitch of about $a' = 428$, somewhat lower than today's concert pitch. Thus Playford's tessitura would be about right for modern congregations, or perhaps a little high. Tenor voices were more common in his day than in ours, probably because average body height was less.

[83] "He was an 'improver' who anticipated by two centuries the often nefarious activities of Monk." Routley, p. 45.

CHESTER, NORWICH, and PETERBOROUGH his version differs in several notes from those of Este, Ravenscroft, or *Psalms & Hymns.* As it is difficult to see any positive purpose to alterations such as those in Example 6, one is inclined to accept Playford's word for it that he

Example 6
Alterations in the tune Low DUTCH / CANTERBURY (Frost 19)

a. Este (Ps. 4) and Ravenscroft (Ps. 12, 60, 114, 131)

b. The 1661 Psalm Book (Ps. 41, 95)

c. *Psalms & Hymns* (1671) (Ps. 23)

d. *The Whole Book* (1677) (Ps. 12, 23, 105, 146)

Versions b and d have been transposed to F major to facilitate comparison.

was merely recording changes that had already happened. In the case of ST. DAVID's (Exx. 1, 5) he may have found that the wide compass and large leaps made the tune a difficult one for congregations to manage. Whether in this case his alterations merely recorded what had already occurred or were suggestions for improvement, it is im-

370

possible to say for certain. The fact that only the second version has survived tells in favor of the former explanation.

Playford made even more changes in many of the old proper tunes. A large number of these differ in two or three notes from the previously established versions. Again it is difficult to think of any convincing motive for these alterations other than that of accuracy. Many of these tunes were probably little used, and Playford, if he wanted to revive them, would have been concerned to provide a version that was "correct" in the minds of those few people who did still remember them (see Ex. 7). He also altered both tune and text of Psalm 121

Example 7

a. Frost 144 in Este, Ravenscroft, and psalm books from 1562 to 1661 (Ps. 125)

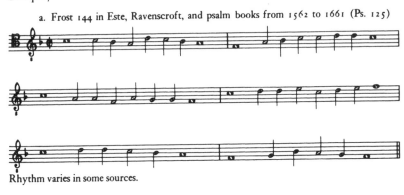

Rhythm varies in some sources.

b. Frost 144 in *The Whole Book* (1677) (Ps. 125)

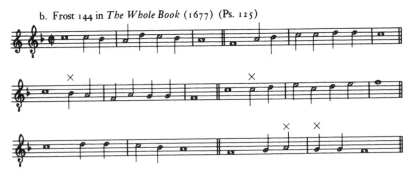

to convert it from 866877 to 866888; and he made a still more drastic alteration to the tune of Psalm 111, changing the tune from 666.666. 667.667 to 666.666 (only the first three lines are as in the original tune) and altering the text correspondingly. These alterations must have been deliberate. Playford probably wanted to restore, in some form, two good tunes that had dropped out of use because of the complexity of their meters. As already stated, he also provided alternative translations of both these psalms.

Playford added three "new" tunes—that is, tunes not found in any earlier printed source. As before, all of them seem to be derivatives of earlier tunes. *

SALISBURY—Frost 143b (set to Ps. 22, 56, 64, and 79) is simply a C.M. adaptation of Frost 143a, which had appeared in Allison's psalter (1599) with Ps. 125ii (L.M.) and in *Psalms & Hymns* with an "unauthorized" version of Ps. 121.

WESTMINSTER—Frost 362c (set to Ps. 40, 76, 97, and 115) is a C.M. adaptation of Orlando Gibbons's Song 34 (Frost 362a, L.M.), used in *Psalms & Hymns* with an "unauthorized" version of Ps. 104.

BRISTOL—Frost 22 (set to Ps. 6, 60, and 83). Its first line is the same as Frost 8 ("The Humble Suit of a Sinner"), but the rest of the tune diverges. A more likely ancestor is Frost 395, one of the tunes printed with Barton's *Psalms* (1644). Though only twelve of the twenty-eight notes are the same, the tunes share the same key, general contour, and harmonic plan; and significantly, the same name.

In the first two cases the transformation of a Long-Meter tune to Common Meter has taken the simplest possible form: the two eight-syllable lines remain unchanged, while the other lines are shortened to six notes with little change in their contour or harmonic plan (see Ex. 8). This is just the kind of change which might have taken place

Example 8

a. Song 34, from Wither's *Hymnes and Songs of the Church* (Frost 362a)

b. WESTMINSTER, from Playford's *The Whole Book* (1677) (Frost 362c)

through confusion of meters by a parish clerk—a phenomenon that is actually recorded by Pepys.[84] The evolution of the third tune was probably more complex.

[84] See fn. 28.

372

In tune allocations Playford of necessity stuck to tradition for the tunes of irregular meter and also for most of the D.C.M. "proper" tunes. He tried to secure the revival of some of these by setting them to additional psalms as well as those to which they had been traditionally wedded.[85] Similarly the OLD HUNDREDTH was now extended to a garbled version of Psalm 136 similar to that already described in connection with the 1661 psalm book, to the alternative version of Psalm 121, and to the new Morning Hymn. In all these cases Playford paid careful attention to the mood of the words. For the short tunes Playford thought out a new set of tune allocations, sometimes adopting Este's, sometimes Ravenscroft's, sometimes his own of 1661 or 1671, sometimes a new combination, but always carrying out the undertaking in his preface: to fit every psalm to a tune "sutable and proper to the Matter." He thus tried to take over the responsibility for choosing tunes from the ignorant or capricious hands of the parish clerk.

In this psalter Playford gave of his best. He hoped, no doubt, to make money; but his primary motive was to raise parish church music from the depths to which it had sunk—not as a result of Puritan attack but from indifference and apathy, particularly from the clergy and gentry. He had done about as much as a man in his position could do. In the end his efforts could succeed only when joined to other forces.

At first the reaction was not particularly encouraging. A second issue, also dated 1677, had an "Advertisement" attached, in which Playford complained of having fallen "under the lash of some censorious Criticks, who want not a convenient stock both of ignorance and impudence, to raise a Reputation to themselves by disparaging others; who maliciously would be quarrelling both at Musick and Metre." He then gave a table of errata for the music and a list of alterations made in the text. He concluded:

Some may suppose other Faults in the Musick where there is none, because in some common Tunes they find a Note or two altered according to present use in our Congregations, wherein I have followed not only my own experience for six and twenty years, but also the judgment of others, especially of that great Master of this Science, and curious Observer of this sort of Musick, Dr. *Chr. Gibbons*, His Majesties late Organist.[86]

No further payments from Playford to the Stationers' Company for the Psalms are recorded during his lifetime, so presumably the first 1,000 printed in 1677 were enough to satisfy public demand.

---

[85] The tune for "The Lamentation of a Sinner" is also set to Ps. 77 and 141; the Magnificat tune to Ps. 33; the "Veni Creator" tune to Ps. 132; the tune for Ps. 81 to Ps. 98 and 135; the tune for Ps. 119 (perhaps the most popular of all the D.C.M. tunes) to Ps. 61, 89, and 145.

[86] Christopher Gibbons, son of Orlando, was private organist to Charles II from 1660 until his death on October 20, 1676.

LATER DEVELOPMENTS

Some seventeen years after the publication of the *Whole Book of Psalms . . . in Three Parts*, Playford's son and successor[87] was caught printing copies of a psalm book without the Company's permission:

Henry Playford A member of this Company Sūmoned to appear at this Court to answer a charge ag' him—for printing part of Davids Psalmes in Meeter with musicall notes (being this Companies Coppy) without leave or license of this Court he acknowledgeing his Error in not first asking leave and agreeing with this company and submitted to y[e] Court to do therein with him as they shall thinke fitt desireing this Court to consider the nature of [the] thing alleadging that as compiled only to teach to sing Psalmes well he hoped it would rather promote the sale of this Companies Psalmes then hinder their Sale and therefore prayed they would be favourable to him therein w[ch]. this Court takeing into their consideration were pleased to fine him but five pounds w[ch]. he promised to pay the Warden on demand.[88]

It would seem then that the original stock of 1,000 copies had become exhausted, and Henry Playford had illicitly printed an unknown number of extra ones. A few months later he obtained leave to print a further 1,000 copies "in the same Volume (i.e., format) he had before printed it,"[89] for a commission of ten pounds. He published the second edition in 1695.[90] It contained some alterations of a minor nature.[91] Soon, however, he was back for more: on November 2, 1696, he asked leave to print a further 1,500 copies and was granted this in exchange for a £15 commission, plus ten shillings as a fine for beginning the printing before leave had been granted. Evidently the demand for the book had increased markedly. Thereafter, printings became more and more frequent, as can be seen from Table 7. The

[87] Henry Playford was born in 1657, bound apprentice to his father in 1674, admitted to the Livery of the Stationers' Company in 1685, and had been made an Assistant by October, 1687.

[88] Stationers' Company Archives, Court Book F, fol. 200[v] (5 March 1694). The only psalm collection known to be published by the Playford firm at this time was the *Whole Book* of 1677. It is odd, however, that the Minute refers to "*part* of Davids Psalmes." It is conceivable that it refers to *A Collection of some Verses out of the Psalms of David composed in two parts. . .* Collected by Daniel Warner, Printed by E. Jones: London, 1694. Henry Playford is not named in this book but may well have been responsible for it.

[89] *Ibid.*, fol. 209 (20 June 1694).

[90] *The Whole Book of Psalms . . . Compos'd in Three Parts . . .* By John Playford. The Second Edition, Corrected and Amended. In the Savoy, Printed by Edw. Jones, for the Company of Stationers. And are to be sold by Henry Playford at his Shop near the Temple Church, and at his House in Arundel-Street in the Strand: 1695.

[91] The preface was greatly shortened. A one-page essay, "Of the virtue and efficacy of the psalms," replaced a single paragraph in the first edition. The table of psalms and hymns was replaced by an index of tunes with incipits. The type was completely reset: all the Divine Hymns were now relegated to the back of the book, instead of the traditional arrangement (maintained in the first edition) of some before, some after. Eight-line stanzas were now divided into two four-line stanzas, and a metrical *Gloria Patri* added at the end of Ps. 68, 80, 85, 86, 94, 101, 102, 107, and 148. The alternative versions of Ps. 111, 121, 126, and 130 were omitted, as was the Prayer after the Ten Commandments. Many key-signatures were modernized.

374

TABLE 7

Editions of Playford's *Whole Book of Psalms. . . Compos'd in Three Parts*

| | Title Page | | No. of copies authorized | Stationers' Co. Records | |
Edition	Publisher	Date		Date	Assignee
[1st]	John Playford	1677	1,000	R 1 Sep. 1677	Mr. Playford
2d	Henry Playford	1695	1,000	A 20 Jun. 1694	Henry Playford
3rd	Samuel Sprint and Henry Playford	1697	1,500	R 8 Jun. 1697	Mr. Playford
4th	Samuel Sprint and Henry Playford	1698	2,000	A 7 Feb. 1698	Mr. Sprint
5th	Samuel Sprint and Henry Playford	1699	2,000 / 3,000	R 15 May 1699 / R 18 Dec. 1699	Mr. Sprint / Mr. Sprint and Mr. Playford
6th	Samuel and John Sprint and Henry Playford	1700	3,000	R 27 May 1700	Mr. Sprint
7th	Henry Playford	1701			Mr. Playford
8th	Henry Playford and John Sprint	1702	2,200	R 21 Nov. 1702	
9th	John Sprint	1707			
10th	John and Benjamin Sprint	1709			
11th	John and Benjamin Sprint	1712			
12th	John and Benjamin Sprint	1713			
13th	John and Benjamin Sprint	1715			
14th	John and Benjamin Sprint	1717			
15th	John and Benjamin Sprint	1719			
16th	John and Benjamin Sprint	1722			
17th	John and Benjamin Sprint	1724			
18th	John and Benjamin Sprint	1729			
19th	Richard Ware	1738			
20th	C. Ware, T. Longman, T. Caslon, B. Davey and P. Law	1757			

NOTE: A = authority to publish granted by Court of Assitants (Court Book).
A = receipt of commission entered (English Stock Book).
The commission was £10 per 1,000 copies, which represented 6 2/3% of the retail price (advertisements show that the book was sold at 3 shillings).

book had become a best-seller. By 1738 the 19th edition had been reached, with no further changes of any substance except for the addition of one new tune in 1700.[92] Playford's selection and harmonization of the psalms became definitive for the first half of the 18th century, and it influenced many other psalmody books of the time.

Meanwhile, Henry Playford had in 1694 reprinted the *Introduction* with a number of changes. The selection of psalm tunes was considerably reduced, and it was revised. Tune names, keys, basses, and (in the case of OXFORD) even the meter of the tune were brought into exact conformity with the *Whole Book* of 1677.[93] In fact the psalm tunes with their basses now looked exactly as they did in the *Whole Book*, where, it will be remembered, the tune and bass were printed together, with the medius and bass parts separately. The next edition of the *Introduction* (1697) had the same arrangement and also advertised (p. 39):

The whole Book of *Psalms* and *Hymns* in 3 Parts, are Printed in a Pocket Volume: With an *Alphabetical Table* for the ready finding any Tune throughout the whole Book, and what *Psalms* are sung to each Tune. To which Book (when you are perfect in these) I refer you.

Thus Henry Playford was making the *Introduction* conform to the 1677 psalter, as his father had made it conform with the 1671 *Psalms & Hymns*. If the object was to promote the psalter, it was a success this time. But there must have been once again protests against the changes in the *Introduction*. In the 1700 and all remaining editions, the tune selection represents a compromise, combining all the principal features of both the 1674–87 editions and those of 1694–97.[94]

[92] The new tune was ST. JAMES, for Ps. 19. It had first appeared in *Select Psalms and Hymns for the use of the Parish-Church and Tabernacle of St. James's Westminster* (London, 1697) and is believed to be the composition of Raphael Courteville, who was organist at that church. Notation was gradually modernized between the 2d and 19th editions: round notes replaced diamond-shaped ones in the 18th. Some editions were printed with a brief introduction giving the gamut, scales, etc.

[93] W. Barclay Squire attributed this revision of the basses of the psalm tunes to Henry Purcell, on the grounds that the title page of the 1694 edition contains the words "Corrected and Amended by Mr. Henry Purcell" (Squire, "Purcell as Theorist," *Internationale Musik-Gesellschaft, Sammelbände*, VI [1904–5], 521–67). But the title page of the very similar 1697 edition makes it clear that Purcell revised only Part III of the book, "The Art of Descant." Part I was "newly Written . . . by an Eminent Master in that *Science*"; it contains no reference to the psalm tunes and ends at p. 32 with the words "and so I bid you heartily *Farewell*." The psalm tunes follow with a fresh title, and comparison with the 1677 psalter leaves no possible room for doubt that the settings are Playford's.

[94] Thus Frost 45 is printed twice: once in G minor, as CAMBRIDGE SHORT, with the rhythm and bass of the *Introduction* of 1674–87; and once in A minor, as SOUTHWEL, with the rhythm and bass of the 1677 *Whole Book* and the *Introduction* of 1694–97. The same thing was done with Frost 19 (Low DUTCH or CANTERBURY, in G or A respectively) and Frost 333a (HACKNEY or ST. MARY'S, in D minor or E minor).

376

It is evident from Table 7 that a remarkable increase in the demand for Playford's *Whole Book* began about 1695, reached its peak about 1700, and remained at a high level for several decades. The 20th and last edition of 1757 was a complete revision undertaken by Joseph Fox, parish clerk of St. Margaret's, Westminster. He omitted five of Playford's tunes and added fifteen new ones, plus three anthems. But the old editions continued in use for many years more and probably lasted as long as the Old Version of Sternhold and Hopkins remained in use—that is, until well into the 19th century in many country churches. Copies have been found among the manuscript music of village choirs of the 1820's and '30's. Playford's book became, in fact, the standard material for the volunteer parish choir and remained so until the nature of that institution was altered as a result of the religious movements of the 19th century.

The origins of the parish choir in England have never been thoroughly investigated. Here it must suffice to say that there is reason to believe that the parish choir emerged during the 1690's under the influence of the Religious Societies which were an important element in the High Church movement of that time. One clergyman gave an informative description of such a choir to Dr. Josiah Woodward, author of *An account of the rise and progress of the religious societies* (published anonymously in 1701).

When I first came to my Parish, I found, to my great Grief, the People very Ignorant and Irreligious; the Place of Divine Worship indecently kept; the Publick Service neither understood, nor attended; the Ministration of the Lord's Supper supported only by the Piety of three or four Communicants, and the Divine Ordinance of Singing Psalms almost laid aside. Now, whilst I consider'd by what Means I might redress this General Neglect of Religion, I was of Opinion, that the setting up of such a Religious Society, as I had known in the City of *London*, would be very proper, but I feared it would be impracticable in the Country; so that at first, I began to teach three or four Youths the Skill of Singing Psalms orderly, and according to Rules, which greatly tended, through the Grace of God, to awaken their Affections towards Religion, and to give 'em a relish of it. The Improvement of These in Psalm-Singing, being soon observ'd by Others, many Young Men desir'd to be admitted to the same Instruction, which being Granted, and the number of them increasing daily; they readily submitted to the Rules of a Religious Society, and have ever since been careful Observers of 'em. By whose Means, a General Reviving of Piety, and a Solemn Observance of the publick Ordinances of God, hath been produc'd amongst Us.[95]

Here was an example of that encouragement by the clergy which Playford had thought would be "much to the Advancement of this Divine

Service of singing Psalms." It seems highly probable, though direct evidence is lacking, that such singing societies found Playford's psalter exactly suited to their needs, particularly where there was no organ to provide harmony. They seem to have flourished particularly in provincial towns and even villages and to have multiplied in the early years of the 18th century. At first their purpose was solely to lead the psalm singing, but in due course they began to want more elaborate music to sing by themselves—first at private meetings or practices and then (not without strong opposition from some portions of the clergy) in church.

The first attempt to cater for this new demand was Henry Playford's *Divine Companion* of 1701, which was "fitted and for the use of those who already understand Mr. John Playford's Psalms in three parts. To be used in Churches or Private Families, for their Greater Advancement in Divine Musick." In dedicating this collection to the Archbishop of York, Playford wrote:

As my Father before me, has made it His Business to excite the publick Praises of God, by the Musick of the Psalms, which bear His name; so I could not but think it my Duty to follow. . . by contributing farther towards the advancement of so noble a design.

The collection included psalms, hymns, and anthems. In the preface Playford made it quite clear that the anthems were not for cathedral use:

We have, 'tis true, had Anthems long since sung, and continued in our Cathedrals and Chapels. . . But our Parochial Churches, which are equally dedicated to Gods Glory, and innumerable, in respect of those before mention'd, have been altogether destitute of such necessary assistances to Praise their Maker by. . . This has made me importunate with my Friends to compile such a set of short and easy Anthems as may be proper for the Places they are designed for, and from such little beginnings in the practice of Musick, endeavour to persuade them into a knowledge of things of a Higher Nature, as Harmonia Sacra, &c.

This book appeared in four later editions (1707, 1709, 1715, 1722) and was followed by other collections of a similar nature;[96] after 1710 there was a growing stream of such books, usually containing a selection of metrical psalms with harmonies as well as some anthems, both parts being strongly influenced by John and Henry Playford's collections, respectively. The North of England was especially prolific in this direction. Many of the books were explicitly designed for "country churches," and the usual scoring of the music was John Playford's: two tenors and bass.

[96] For example, Elias Hall, *The psalm-singer's compleat companion* (London, 1706); John Bishop, *A sett of new psalm tunes . . . With variety of anthems* (London, [ca. 1710]); John and James Greene, *A Book of Psalm-Tunes in Two, Three and Four Parts*, 2d ed. (Sheffield, 1713).

The Playfords also tried to cater for the difficulties faced by choirs in churches that lacked organs. In 1699 Henry Playford published *The Psalmody or the plainest and easiest directions to play the psalm tunes by letters instead of notes.* The directions gave a description of the "Psalterer," an instrument "invented by Mr. John Playford" which was similar to the bass-viol, but had only two strings tuned an octave apart, with chromatic frets labeled with letters. The tunes and basses of the commonest psalm tunes were printed with the directions.[97]

John Playford cannot fully have anticipated the development of parish choirs, which seems to have made little headway until about ten years after his death. But it is tempting to believe that he originated, in practice as well as theory, the three-voice male choir, often accompanied by a bass viol, which became the norm for parish churches later on. In the Temple Church where he was clerk, he may well have tried out his psalm settings, training a group of singers to render them properly, possibly with the help of his "Psalterer."[98] The idea may have spread from there to the Religious Societies of London and thence to parishes in the country. At any rate there is little reason to doubt that Playford's painstaking work with the psalm tunes provided the material for hundreds of parish choirs in the 18th century and served to revive and propel forward the flagging tradition of English psalmody, which had reached its lowest point in his time.[99]

[97] An incomplete copy of this booklet has survived in Cambridge University Library (MR240.c.65.1). No instrument of this description appears to be extant, but it seems to have had a certain currency in the first half of the 18th century. A similar instrument is described in James Leman's *A new method of learning psalm-tunes, with an instrument of musick called the psalterer* (London, 1729), a copy of which is in Aberdeen University Library. See also W. Sherwin, *An help to the singing psalm-tunes... With directions for making an instrument with one string* (London, 1725).

[98] The Temple Church, which was not a parish church, had no organ until Father Smith's was installed after the famous competition with Renatus Harris in 1685.

[99] I wish to express my gratitude to the University of Illinois for the funds which made this study possible.

The Old Way of Singing:
Its Origins and Development

IN PLACES WHERE CONGREGATIONS are left to sing hymns without musical direction for long periods, a characteristic style of singing tends to develop. The tempo becomes extremely slow; the sense of rhythm is weakened; extraneous pitches appear, sometimes coinciding with those of the hymn tune, sometimes inserted between them; the total effect may be dissonant. At certain periods in British and American history this style has been called "the Old Way of Singing," or the "Common" or "Usual" way. Social changes have led to efforts to get rid of it; then it has been strongly denounced and ridiculed, and eventually replaced by "Regular Singing" (in which the leading singers are taught to read music notation or solfa symbols).

Until recent times the Old Way of Singing, if mentioned at all, was treated as an unacceptable, primitive practice that preceded the introduction of anything recognizable as music. The first to treat it sympathetically was George Pullen Jackson, who described the "surge songs" that he heard in black churches of the Southern states, but believed that the "last vestiges" of this practice had "disappeared from the white man's churches" before the mid-nineteenth century.[1] Closer attention was given to the subject in connection with the controversies about singing in New England Congregational churches of the 1720s. Allen Britton, in his pioneering dissertation on American tunebooks, concluded that the Old Way was an indigenous phenomenon (a natural inference from the absence of descriptions of it elsewhere):

> It is important that the reader be aware at least of the almost immediate growth on our shores of a new musical idiom, the further development of which was continually hampered by most of the forces allied with the teaching of note reading.[2]

Scholars were now beginning to feel some interest in the nature of this music, but at first they had to rely largely on the pejorative

---

[1] George Pullen Jackson, *White and Negro Spirituals* (New York, 1943), p. 251.
[2] Allen P. Britton, "Theoretical Introductions in American Tunebooks to 1800" (Ph.D. diss., Univ. of Michigan, 1949), p. 85.

descriptions of Thomas Symmes, Cotton Mather, and the other leaders of the reform movement of the 1720s.

But more recent research has uncovered similar practice in other areas. Gilbert Chase found that it had been described and notated in Scotland by Joseph Mainzer in the 1840s,[3] and a sound recording has been made in a Gaelic-speaking church of the Scottish Highlands.[4] Robert Stevenson pointed out, and my own studies have confirmed, that it was common in English churches in the seventeenth century.[5] Above all, William Tallmadge found that the practice is still extant in many white Baptist churches of the southern Appalachian region.[6] At a conference on rural hymnody organized by Professor Tallmadge at Berea, Kentucky, in April 1979, a group of singers from Mount Olivet Old Regular Baptist Church, Perry County, Kentucky, sang several "lined hymns" in a way that was strikingly close to that of the seventeenth-century English parish church, though the tune reper-tory was quite different.[7] So it now looks as if the New England controversy was a mere incident in a much larger history, extending (at the least) over several centuries of Anglo-Saxon culture. In this article I shall try to discover the extent of the Old Way of Singing in time and place, to explore its nature, and to explain its existence and development.

It is not difficult to account for the long survival of the Old Way of Singing once it has been established. Conservatism is always a strong force in religious music, and indeed in religious customs in general: many elements in Christian liturgies are older than Christianity itself. Religion, after all, deals in eternal truths, and this means in practice that the older members of any community tend to guard the customs they knew in their childhood, which seem eternal. Unfamiliar things thrust in from outside seem to threaten this sacred body of customs. Regardless of theological or rational considerations, any attempt to

---

[3] Joseph Mainzer, *The Gaelic Psalm Tunes of Ross-shire* (Edinburgh, 1844); Gilbert Chase, *America's Music from the Pilgrims to the Present* (New York, 1955), p. 32; see also John Spencer Curwen, *Studies in Worship Music*, [1st series] (London, 1880), p. 72.

[4] "Gaelic Psalm Tunes from Lewis" (Tangent Records; TNGM 120).

[5] Robert M. Stevenson, *Protestant Church Music in America* (New York, 1966), p. 27; Nicholas Temperley, *The Music of the English Parish Church*, 2 vols. (Cambridge, 1979), I, 91–96.

[6] William H. Tallmadge, "Baptist Monophonic and Heterophonic Hymnody in Southern Appalachia," *Yearbook for Inter-American Musical Research*, XI (1975), 106–36.

[7] The papers read at the conference, including an earlier version of the present article, are being prepared for publication by William Tallmadge. For a more detailed description of the singing there, see Nicholas Temperley, "The Old Way of Singing," *The Musical Times*, CXX (1979), 943–47.

interfere with religious traditions will almost always meet with stiff reaction.

So it was with the Old Way of Singing. John Chetham, the Yorkshire schoolmaster who compiled an influential psalmody book published in 1718, wrote of the difficulty of getting country congregations to accept the new style of singing "by rule": "What terrible outcries do they make . . . against any alterations; and if their understanding does not help 'em to any arguments against the thing itself, they immediately cry out Popery."[8] When reforms were introduced in one country parish, an old woman "called the singers very opprobrious names, saying they had put her out of her tune that she had sung forty years."[9] In Scotland the opposition to reform was even stronger, and was supported by many of the clergy on Calvinist principles.[10] In the southern United States, Tallmadge found that disputes tended to arise each time the singing schools and reformers moved in: sometimes, the more conservative group would split off and form a new church to preserve the purity of their singing.[11] Indeed the more democratic organization of churches in America—the freedom to split—may largely account for the longer survival there of the Old Way of Singing.

But while conservatism may explain the survival of the Old Way, it was obviously not responsible for its origin. When, where, and how did it come into being? I will assume that we need not look further back than the Reformation, for it seems clear that in the late medieval Church the people did not sing in worship at all. The music was entirely in the hands of priests and professional musicians. If anything like the Old Way existed then, it can only have been in secular folksongs.

Popular singing as part of worship was an invention of the reformers: first the Bohemian Brethren, then the Lutherans, Zwinglians, and Calvinists, then Anabaptists, Anglicans, and Presbyterians, then Congregationalists and Separatists; much later, Baptists. They used metrical texts because these could be fitted to folk tunes already known to the people as secular songs. Later, new tunes of similar character were added to the repertory. Calvin and his followers, believing that only the songs of scripture should be sung in worship,

---

[8] John Chetham, *A Book of Psalmody*, [1st ed.] (London, 1718), Preface.
[9] Thomas Moore, *The Psalm Singer's Compleat Tutor and Divine Companion*, 2nd ed. (Manchester, 1750), p. iv.
[10] Millar Patrick, *Four Centuries of Scottish Psalmody* (London, 1949), pp. 145, 155.
[11] Tallmadge, private communication.

514

turned the psalms into meter to take advantage of the immense popularity of hymn singing among the followers of Hus and Luther.

Calvinists, unlike Lutherans, were not much concerned with the musical effect of congregational singing. All that mattered was that each person sing the songs of the Bible, with understanding, and from the heart. Thus Heinrich Bullinger, an influential leader in the German Reformed church, said in a sermon published in 1569, and soon translated into English:

> Let no man think, that prayers sung with man's voice are more acceptable to God, than if they were plainly spoken or uttered; for God is neither allured with the sweetness of man's voice, neither is he offended, though prayer be uttered in a hoarse or base sound. Prayer is commended for faith and godliness of mind, and not for any outward show.[12]

The Reformed sects were at first suspicious of all aids to music that would simply "tickle the ear," and tended to ban choirs, organs, instruments, and counterpoint. Zwingli ordered organs destroyed and choirs disbanded at Zurich in 1527. But organs were gradually reintroduced in many Reformed parts of Continental Europe before 1600.[13] In Holland, although the Synod of Dordrecht had banned organs from worship in 1574, they continued to be used for concerts in churches, and from about 1640 onwards, they generally accompanied metrical psalms throughout the State Church.[14] The chief reason advanced for the introduction of organs by their leading advocate, Constantin Huygens, was to improve congregational singing, which, he said, often sounded "more like howling and screaming than like human singing."[15]

So the Reformed musical practice split into two streams. Many Continental Reformed churches, like the Lutherans, integrated the new congregational song into the art-music tradition; the use of organs, choirs, music books, and the leadership of professional musicians automatically "regulated" the hymnody or psalmody and kept it in touch with developments in art music. Several English

[12] Heinrich Bullinger, "Of the Form and Manner How to Pray to God" [1569], *The Decades of Henry Bullinger*, ed. T. Harding, 4 vols., Parker Society Publications, 7–10 (Cambridge, 1849–1852), IV, 196.

[13] Walter Blankenburg, "Church Music in Reformed Europe" (trans. Hans Heinsheimer), in Friedrich Blume, *Protestant Church Music: A History* (New York, 1974), pp. 507–90.

[14] Henry A. Bruinsma, "The Organ Controversy in the Netherlands Reformation to 1640," this JOURNAL, VII (1954), 205–12.

[15] Constantin Huygens, *Gebruyck of Ongebruyck van 't Orgel inde Kercken der Vereenighde Nederlanden* (Leiden, 1640), p. 109; cited Bruinsma, p. 211.

promoters of regular singing held up the Continental Protestant churches as models. Luke Milbourne said in a sermon to the Company of Parish Clerks of London in 1713: "both the *High and Low Dutch*, and *French*, have taken more Care of their *ordinary Psalmody* than we have done."[16] And an advocate of instrumental accompaniment in 1729 wrote: "The French and Dutch Protestants here with us, sing their Psalms much better than we, though their Tunes are more difficult than ours, as well as more in Number; whereas we, for the most part (excepting those Churches where they have Organs) sing our Psalms, as if it were a new or strange Exercise."[17]

It is, indeed, the presence or absence of organs that demarcates the two practices. Organs were banned completely in Scotland and among dissenting groups in England until the nineteenth century. They were almost unknown in parish churches in England between 1570 and 1660, and still lacking in most country churches (because they could not afford them) until the nineteenth century, though present in cathedrals and the larger town churches. There were no organs in English-speaking America, even in Anglican churches, before 1714. But there were also groups on the Continent that continued to ban both organs and choirs. These were the radical Protestant groups, loosely termed Anabaptists, who were disappointed with the moderate reforms of Zwingli and Calvin, and particularly with their collaboration with state governments to form established churches. The Anabaptists continued to practice unaccompanied congregational singing, which was so far removed from art music that it is not mentioned at all in the most authoritative work on the music of Protestant churches, Friedrich Blume's *Protestant Church Music*. A few schismatic groups in the Netherlands have also resisted the introduction of organs until the present day.[18]

In all these areas, the congregational singing was left to take care of itself for several generations; and in all of them, the Old Way of Singing or something similar developed. I will look most closely at what happened in England and in English America. But I will also briefly examine the situation among the American Mennonites (descendants of the Anabaptists), which has striking similarities to the Anglo-American practice.

[16] Luke Milbourne, *Psalmody Recommended, In a Sermon Preach'd to the Company of the Parish Clerks* (London, 1713), p. 24.

[17] James Leman, *A New Method of Learning Psalm-Tunes, With an Instrument . . . Call'd the Psalterer* (London, 1729), pp. iii–v.

[18] Bruinsma, "The Organ Controversy," p. 212.

516

Let us now see what happened to congregational singing in England when it continued for several generations without organ accompaniment or musical direction. When congregational psalm tunes were first introduced in London parish churches in 1559, according to contemporary accounts, they were immediately taken up by thousands, and spread like wildfire through the churches.[19] This suggests that the English, like the Germans and the French before them, began their psalmody by making use of folk tunes already well known to the people. It is said that Thomas Sternhold himself had sung his psalm versions to the tune of "Chevy Chase,"[20] and the metrical psalms were given the nickname "Geneva jigs," possibly by Queen Elizabeth and certainly by others.[21] The jig was a dramatized form of ballad in dialogue, often performed on the stage with dancing. All this indicates that at first the psalms were sung in a lively style similar to that of the folk ballad, and in some cases using the same tunes.

But when we ask what the music of folk ballads was like at the beginning of Elizabeth's reign, the question is surprisingly difficult to answer. There is an almost total lack of musical sources from the period. Hundreds of ballad texts were printed in broadside form, but without music; and the tunes associated with them are known only from sources dating from centuries later, or (in a few cases) from keyboard or lute intabulations of around 1600 that may or may not preserve the rhythms and styles of the ballads as sung by ordinary people.

Precisely *one* broadside surviving from Elizabethan times includes music notation,[22] and this is transcribed in Example 1.[23] As will be seen, it is very different in character from the famous tunes generally associated with early English ballads and folk lyrics—tunes like "Chevy Chase," "Walsingham," "Greensleeves," or "Barbara Allen"—that have come down to us only from eighteenth-century or

[19] Hastings Robinson, ed., *Original Letters of the Reformation*, 2 vols., Parker Society Publications, 53 (Cambridge, 1846–47), II, 40–41; trans. Temperley, *English Parish Church*, I, 43.

[20] G. Gregory Smith, ed., *Elizabethan Critical Essays*, 2 vols. (Oxford, 1904), I, 178, 193.

[21] Temperley, *English Parish Church*, I, 67.

[22] Claude M. Simpson, *The British Broadside Ballad and Its Music* (New Brunswick, 1966), p. 158.

[23] The only known copy is in the British Library, shelfmark Huth 50/27. It is reproduced in facsimile in John Ward, "Music for *A Handefull of Pleasant Delites*," this JOURNAL, X (1957), facing p. 168; and partially in Donald W. Krummel, *English Music Printing 1553–1700* (London, 1975), p. 43.

Example 1

A Newe Ballade . . . To the tune of Damon and Pithias (1568)

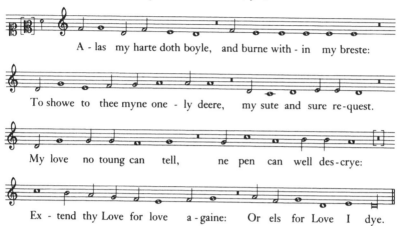

A - las my harte doth boyle, and burne with - in my breste:

To showe to thee myne one - ly deere, my sute and sure re-quest.

My love no toung can tell, ne pen can well des-crye:

Ex - tend thy Love for love a - gaine: Or els for Love I dye.

even later sources or from intabulations, or have been recovered recently from folk singers.[24] "Damon and Pythias" seems to have little in the way of melodic structure or interest; above all, it has no clear rhythm, and cannot easily be fitted into duple, triple, or compound time, though the text is in a regular double short meter. This strange tune has baffled scholars ever since its discovery. To Chappell it was "worthless as music, and, I suspect, very incorrectly printed. It seems a mere claptrap jumble to take in the countryman";[25] to Simpson it was "quite unlike the usual Elizabethan ballad tune" and suggested plainsong;[26] John Ward found it "recitation-like" and thought it might be "a remnant of a popular style hitherto unnoted."[27] Andrew Sabol, however, discovered the same melody in a manuscript source with words that definitely linked it to Richard Edwards's play *Damon and*

---

[24] Ward, "Music," p. 179, has concluded that the *popular* singing of ballads began only in the mid-sixteenth century, and was inspired by courtly singing. Edward Doughtie has persuasively argued that Thomas Sternhold, far from adopting an already popular ballad meter ("common meter," 8.6.8.6) for the majority of his metrical psalms, "*made* the meter popular through his translations of the psalms" (*Lyrics from English Airs*, ed. with an Introduction by Edward Doughtie [Cambridge, Mass., 1970], p. 17).

[25] J. Lilly, *A Collection of Seventy-Nine Black Letter Ballads and Broadsides* (London, 1867), p. 278. The clef is, in fact, misplaced: the correct emendation was first made by Sabol (see n. 28 below).

[26] Simpson, *The British Broadside*, p. 158 and n. 1.

[27] Ward, "Music," pp. 168–69.

76

Pythias, performed in 1564.[28] In this version (Ex. 2) the tune no longer seems amorphous: it fits into a solid triple meter, and the rests between the lines turn out to represent brief instrumental interludes between vocal phrases.

Example 2

"Awake, ye woeful wights" from British Library, Add. MS 15177

The striking thing about the tune for our purposes is its general resemblance to the early psalm tunes printed with Sternhold and Hopkins's *Whole Book of Psalms,* first published in complete form in 1562. Example 3 shows a tune from that book. It is typical of those sixty or seventy psalm tunes of the period that were not taken from French or German sources, but apparently composed anonymously by English musicians between 1550 and 1562. It has all the characteristics, positive and negative, of "Damon and Pythias," and is printed in the same note values. It, too, has rests between the lines that seem to interfere with what little rhythmic drive it possesses; perhaps they, also, represent interludes in an instrumentally accompanied performance. It, too, does not fit into any regular musical meter, and wanders rather aimlessly over a compass of about an octave, largely by stepwise movement. When provided with a lute accompaniment (Ex.

[28] Andrew J. Sabol, "Two Unpublished Stage Songs for the 'Aery of Children'," *Renaissance News,* XIII (1960), 222–32. The source is British Library Additional MS 15177 [*ca.* 1600], fol. 3ʳ. For a complete transcription see Temperley, *English Parish Church,* II, Ex. 11(b).

Example 3

Psalm 59 from Sternhold and Hopkins, 1565 folio edition

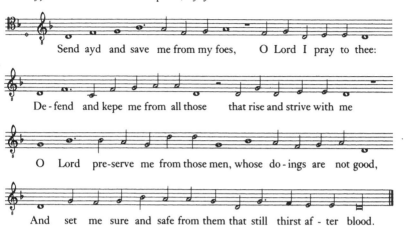

Send ayd and save me from my foes,   O Lord I pray to thee:

De - fend and kepe me from all those   that rise and strive with me

O   Lord   pre-serve me from those men, whose do - ings are   not good,

And   set   me sure and safe from them that still   thirst af - ter   blood.

4) this tune also becomes more rhythmical. So we can suppose (tentatively, because of the paucity of the evidence) that both the psalm tune and the ballad tune represent, as Ward suggested, a "popular style hitherto unnoted" that did not long survive the sixteenth century as far as secular folk music is concerned, and that could be transformed by accompaniment into something approximating art music.

Example 4

Psalm 59 from Allison (1599)

Voice

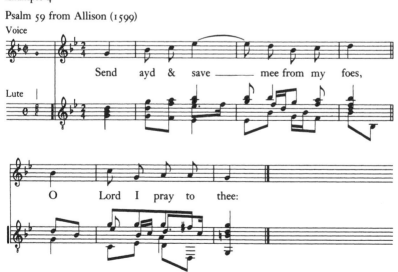

Send   ayd   &   save ____ mee from my   foes,

Lute |

O   Lord   I   pray   to   thee:

520

We know that most of the tunes printed in the Sternhold and Hopkins editions soon dropped out of use, though they continued to be printed in the books as one printer copied from another. The later editions (after 1600) have so many misprints that they could not well have been used for actual performance. The table of contents in the second edition (1594) of Thomas East's *Whole Booke of Psalmes* clearly states that four tunes[29] were the only ones in use "in most churches of this Realme"—and all four are tunes of the short variety (three common-meter, one short-meter), half as long as the ones printed in the common psalm book, much simpler and more memorable in character, and largely confined to a compass of about a fifth.[30] By East's time, ordinary churches had no organs, choirs, or musical leadership. The parish clerk, who was supposed to lead the singing,

Example 5

Oxford tune

(a) From East (1592), Psalm 10, tenor

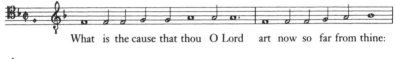

What is the cause that thou O Lord   art now so far from thine:

And keep-est close thy coun - te-nance, from us   this troub-lous time?

(b) From Ravenscroft (1621), Psalm 4, tenor

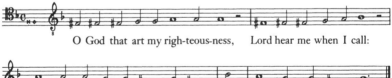

O God that art my righ-teous-ness,   Lord hear me when I call:

Thou hast set me at   li - ber - ty,   when   I   was bound and thrall.

[29] Frost 121, 19, 42, 45. "Frost" refers to Maurice Frost, *English and Scottish Psalm and Hymn Tunes* c. *1543–1677* (London, 1953), where the tunes are transcribed and numbered.

[30] Incidentally, this disposes of the often-repeated theory that the first New England settlers brought with them the knowledge of a large repertory of tunes, which then gradually dwindled to some five or ten by about 1700. It was based, no doubt, on the large number of tunes printed in the psalm collections of Sternhold and Hopkins, Ainsworth, and Ravenscroft. But if East is to be believed, most of these tunes were not part of the popular knowledge. They were known, if at all, only to cultivated musicians such as those who performed Ravenscroft's four-part settings in their homes.

was usually uneducated, poorly paid, and without musical talent or training.[31]

One of the four common tunes, OXFORD, is one of the simplest and most basic of all psalm tunes. It is first found in the Scottish psalter of 1564, and it appears in almost every psalmody collection from England, Scotland, or America between 1590 and 1720. Example 5 shows it in the tenor part of East's and Ravenscroft's settings of 1591 and 1621 respectively. It may be noted as significant that the time signature ₵, used for this tune by East, was altered by Ravenscroft to ₵, although the same basic note values (semibreve and minim) were used. The tune will not fit into either common or alla-breve meter. The significance of the change of time signature is one of tempo. The signature ₵ meant "slow" at this time: Praetorius said it denoted *lento* or *langsam*.

By contrast, Example 6 shows one of the few ballad tunes printed at this period, also in a Ravenscroft publication, and it is notable that here the quarter note is the basic value, though the time-signature is again ₵. At first one might conclude that ballad singing had speeded up in the fifty years since the "Damon and Pythias" broadside (Ex. 1).

Example 6

"There were three ravens" from Ravenscroft, *Melismata* (1611), treble

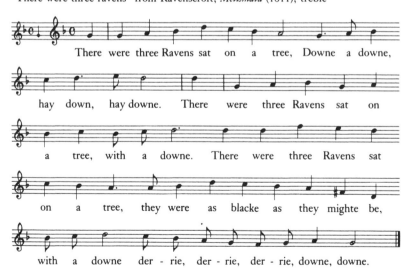

> There were three Ravens sat on a tree, Downe a downe,
> hay down, hay downe. There were three Ravens sat on
> a tree, with a downe. There were three Ravens sat
> on a tree, they were as blacke as they mighte be,
> with a downe der - rie, der - rie, der - rie, downe, downe.

[31] Nicholas Temperley, "John Playford and the Metrical Psalms," this JOURNAL, XXV (1972), 331–78, esp. 338–39; Temperley, *English Parish Church*, I, 43–45.

522

But this was probably not the case. There has been a continuous devaluation of note values almost throughout the history of music notation, and it is more likely that the speed of singing secular folksongs had remained much the same, while the notation appropriate to represent that speed had changed. By contrast the psalm tunes were still shown in the same notation, but the notes now indicated a slower speed than they had fifty years before.

Examples 7 and 8 offer a similar comparison from two publications by John Playford later in the seventeenth century. At first, in the 1658 edition of his *Introduction to Music*, Playford tried to make OXFORD a triple-time tune, but in later editions he reverted to the ¢ time-signature (as shown in Ex. 7). He also used this signature for secular tunes (Ex. 8); a further devaluation had evidently taken place since Ravenscroft's time. But while the secular tune is in quarter and eighth notes, the psalm tune is still in minims and semibreves.

So it looks as if psalm tunes and folksongs, originally the same in style and character, had diverged in the course of fifty or a hundred years to a point where they no longer resembled each other. The psalm tunes by 1650 may have been as much as four times slower than

Example 7

OXFORD tune from Playford, *An Introduction to the Skill of Musick*, 7th ed. (1674), set to Psalm 4 (bass omitted)

O God that art my righ-teous-ness,   Lord hear me when I call:

Thou hast set me at li-ber-ty,   when I   was bound and thrall.

Example 8

"All in a Garden Green" from Playford, *The Dancing Master* (1651)

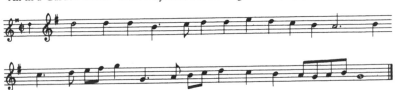

the folk tunes. There is plenty of other evidence that psalm tunes were sung extremely slowly in the seventeenth and eighteenth centuries, perhaps as slowly as two or three seconds to the minim (metronome 20). A Scottish precentor in 1787 defined a semibreve as being "as long as one can conveniently sing without breathing."[32] The Pilgrims and the Puritans would already have known very slow singing of a few short tunes before they left English shores—there is no room for doubt about this.

Why did psalm tunes and folksongs diverge in this way? Folksongs were often accompanied by dancing, or by fiddles or lutes, or at least perhaps by clapping, stamping, or other bodily movements. None of these things was possible in church. The arrangements of psalm tunes with lute accompaniment (like Richard Allison's) and those for four voices (like East's and Ravenscroft's) were for cultivated domestic use; there is no evidence that they were ever used in church. No English organ settings of psalm tunes have survived between the two in the Mulliner Book of *ca.* 1550[33] and those used by Thomas Tomkins at Worcester Cathedral, printed in 1668.[34] People had to sing the tunes without assistance; the less confident singers no doubt waited for the leaders to move on to the next note, and then followed them after a time lag; and so a natural "drag" developed that imperceptibly slowed the normal speed of singing as the years went by. As we shall see, this same process also accounts for other features of the Old Way of Singing.

Naturally, as they slowed down, the tunes lost the distinctive rhythms of the early days, and by the time of Playford they have all been ironed out into standardized rhythmic patterns, basically in duple time, as in Example 7. The first and last note of each phrase is usually a semibreve, the others are minims: sometimes there is a slight variation by syncopation, as in the last phrase of OxFORD. (Compare the lively rhythmic variety of "All in a garden green," Ex. 8). At a somewhat later date, Thomas Mathew, compiler of a psalmody collection, tried to restore the correct rhythms of the tunes by explaining the different note values in his preface: "but," he added,

---

[32] William Taas, *The Elements of Music* (Aberdeen, 1787), p. 34. For additional evidence see Temperley, *English Parish Church*, I, 91–92.
[33] *The Mulliner Book*, ed. Denis Stevens, Musica Britannica, I (London, 1951), Nos. 82, 109.
[34] Thomas Tomkins, *Musica Deo sacra* (London, 1668), p. 308. For further discussion see Nicholas Temperley, "Organ Settings of English Psalm Tunes," *The Musical Times*, CXXII (1981), 123–28.

524

the Clerks are seldom so exact as to keep these distinct *Times* in the Churches: They do generally observe but one *Time* [i.e., but one note-value], as indeed is most easie, and therefore most agreeable to the capacities of the greater number in Congregations and Families, and that is (usually) about a *Minim* and a half, or three pulses, or three quarters of a *Semibrief*.[35]

Later descriptions show an even more complete loss of rhythm:

But the greatest Difficulty is to sound every Note according to its due Measure of Time; and here it is that the Singers in most Country Churches go quite out of Rule, by drawing out the Sound of some Notes twice or thrice longer than they ought to do, thereby spoiling the Musick, and this so affectedly too, that they seem to think it makes the very finest Harmony: So have I observ'd them in some Places to strain themselves in forcing out some, and especially the last Note in a Line, that they have hardly had Strength to begin again: And whereas they should have sounded the longest of their Notes no longer than a *Semibreve*, and the rest proportionably, they have made no Difference [between semibreves and minims] in singing five or seven Notes together, but have sounded each of them so long, that I could distinctly count five or six; but whilst they were sounding the last Note, I could count nine or ten, which is most irregular, tedious, and intolerable, and takes up as much Time in singing what they call two Staves, as would serve very well for five or six.[36]

The natural tendency to drag, spread over many generations, clearly accounts for the slowness and lack of rhythm that was a feature of the Old Way of Singing. And of course, if there was no underlying rhythmic beat, there was nothing to keep the congregation together. Different individuals would pass from one tone to the next at different times, and this explains the dissonance that was frequently matter for complaint. An anonymous New England reformer in 1725 said that "while some affect a quicker motion, others affect a slower and drawl out their notes beyond all reason."[37] In Scotland in 1756 Thomas Bremner described how "one corner of the church, or the people in

---

[35] T[homas] M[athew], *The Whole Booke of Psalmes, As They Are Now Sung in the Churches* (London, 1688), preface.

[36] James Green, *A Collection of Psalm Tunes*, 4th ed. (London, 1718), p. x. Both Mathew and Green, it may be noted, still treat the semibreve in common time as an absolute unit of duration, and many eighteenth-century tunebooks give its value as four seconds. Hence when Green speaks of "counting five or six," etc., he is counting approximately in seconds.

[37] *A Brief Discourse Concerning Regular Singing* (Boston, 1725), cited in Britton, "Theoretical Introductions," p. 25.

one seat, had sung out the line before another had half done."[38] If such descriptions are accurate they reflect a state of affairs in which all semblance of orderly communal singing had broken down. But in less extreme cases the same tendency towards individual variation may have led to a mode of singing that had its own conventions and disciplines.

A persistent characteristic of the Old Way is the addition of extra notes, which for the time being we may call ornaments, in such profusion as to make the tune scarcely recognizable: "some affect a quavering flourish on one note, and others upon another which (because they are ignorant of the true musick or melody) they account a grace to the tune."[39] As a result, Thomas Walter complained, "there are no two churches that sing alike. Yea, I have myself heard . . . OXFORD tune sung in *three* churches (which I purposely forbear to mention) with as much difference as there can possibly be between YORK and OXFORD, or any two other different tunes."[40] Nevertheless, each of the three churches, it would seem, had its own relatively unvarying way of singing the tune. The New England reformers were inclined to explain these local variations by the idea that in the absence of notes or rules, "every leading singer would take the liberty of raising any note of the tune, or lowering of it, as best pleased his ear; and add such turns and flourishes as were grateful to him."[41] Similarly Thomas Walter complained that "our tunes are . . . left to the mercy of every unskilful throat to chop and alter, twist and change, according to their infinitely divers and no less odd humours and fancies."[42] It is of course possible that individual "fancies" would result in the tunes being changed in this way, and such a process is a part of oral transmission in many tune repertories. But the peculiar type of changes in the Old Way of Singing suggests a rather different explanation.

Example 9 shows the earliest known attempt to represent the Old Way of Singing in musical notation. It comes from an English psalmody book of 1686,[43] and the anonymous author, although advocating singing "by book," seems to approve the Old Way, for he

---

[38] Robert Bremner, *The Rudiments of Music*, 3rd ed. (London, 1763), p. xv; cited in Patrick, *Four Centuries of Scottish Psalmody*, p. 139.

[39] *Brief Discourse*, cited in Britton, "Theoretical Introductions," p. 85.

[40] Thomas Walter, *The Grounds and Rules of Musick Explained* (Boston, 1721), p. 3.

[41] Thomas Symmes, *The Reasonableness of Regular Singing, or Singing by Note* (Boston, 1720), p. 8; cited in Chase, *America's Music*, p. 28.

[42] Walter, *The Grounds and Rules*, p. 3; cited in Chase, *America's Music*, p. 26.

[43] *A New and Easie Method to Learn to Sing by Book* (London, 1686), pp. 100–101.

84

Example 9

Two versions of SOUTHWELL tune from *A New and Easie Method* (1686), set to Psalm 25

(a) Plain version (bass omitted)

says "The Notes of the foregoing *Tune* are usually broken or divided, and they are better so sung, as is here prick'd." He prints the tune SOUTHWELL (Frost 45, one of the four common tunes singled out by East) first in simple form, and then "broken or divided" in a way that surely represents the Old Way of Singing.[44] A later attempt (Ex. 10),

---

[44] This example has also been transcribed and discussed by Sir John Stainer, "On the Musical Introductions Found in Certain Metrical Psalters," *Proceedings of the Royal Musical Association*, XXVII (1900–1901), 30; and by Stevenson, *Protestant Church Music*, p. 27.

85

THE OLD WAY OF SINGING   527

Example 10

Setting of Psalm 4 from Chetham (1718) (bass omitted)   *

Those Psalms which the Clark gives out Line by Line, are generally sung in these Tunes, which is call'd the Old way of Singing.

dating from 1718, is explicitly so designated.[45] It is also plausible that certain organ settings of the common tunes dating from the same period are attempts to imitate the Old Way. One of these [46] is shown in Example 11. They are quite distinct in style from Continental organ chorales of the period.

These representations should not be taken too literally. Music notation has its limits, as many transcribers of folksong and non-Western music have discovered; in art music also, such vocal ornaments as the portamento can only be approximated in notation. In Example 11 the limits of the notation are also the limits of a keyboard instrument, which can provide only discrete pitches. The descriptions of the Old Way suggest that it would defy exact representation in a single melodic line. The transcribers, whether consciously or not, were no doubt altering the music in the direction of art music. Each of the three examples uses a different rhythmic scheme to show the multiple groups of notes, from which we may infer that the actual rhythm was vague and unstandardized. They all have certain features in common, however. They show movement largely by step, probably representing portamento; and the extra notes occur in the later portion of each beat, between one note of the tune and the next. The

---

[45] Chetham, *A Book of Psalmody*, p. 70.
[46] Daniel Purcell, *The Psalms Set Full for the Organ or Harpsichord* (London, 1718).

528

Example 11

"Windsor tune given out" from Daniel Purcell (1718)

note on the beat is invariably the main note of the tune, not an "ornamental" or added note; and here lies a sharp difference from the late-Baroque style of ornamenting art music, where trills, appoggiaturas, turns, and even slides generally had the effect of delaying the main note.

One way to explain these added notes is by the same process that accounts for the loss of tempo and rhythm. The leading singers of any group move to the next note of the tune; the stragglers, who are more timid, whose sense of pitch is unreliable, or (less probably) who do not know the tune, gradually follow them, sliding slowly up or down toward the next note, occasionally overshooting it, and then reaching it by a pitch-matching process: everyone assembles on the new note for a brief interval, drawing a new breath, before the long and arduous journey to the next tune note begins. When this proceeding has been heard, Sunday after Sunday, year after year, people will continue to imitate it, even if there is no longer any need for them to follow after the leading singer, for it will have become a ritual. I believe that Examples 9, 10, and possibly 11 are efforts to represent this effect in simplified form, using conventional music notation. One phrase from an unflattering verse description of English country psalmody gives some support for my theory:

> Now below double *A re* some descend,
> 'Bove *E la* squealing now ten notes some fly;
> Straight then, as if they knew they were too high,
> With headlong haste downstairs they again tumble.[47]

---

[47] Elias Hall, *The Psalm-Singer's Compleat Companion* (London, 1706), p. 2.

The phrase "as if they knew they were too high" suggests, to me at least, singers trying to match their voice to the pitch held by the leaders. Again, in a description of Scottish psalmody of the early nineteenth century, a witness spoke of "a wandering search after the air by many who never caught it."[48]

But there was another process at work in English psalmody that may also have contributed to the character of the Old Way of Singing. It could be called popular harmonization. Tallmadge has written of a harmonic element detected in lining hymnody of today, often with voices moving in parallel fourths or fifths in the manner of organum.[49] The harmonic element I have found in English folk psalmody is less archaic than that, and is more probably related to faburden. In the fourteenth and fifteenth centuries this often consisted of parallel six-three chords added to the chant, and in England especially, the faburden part (i.e., the part a sixth below the chant) often took off on its own and was itself treated as a *cantus firmus*.[50] In the sixteenth century, faburden developed into a form of improvised harmonization in four parts: any professional choir could, at sight, improvise a correct set of four-part harmonies for any piece of plainsong, largely in note-for-note common chords with suspensions at the cadence. Because the procedure required no notes, its use cannot be substantiated by examples in musical notation from before the Reformation. But immediately after the Reformation, models of faburden were printed to show how the practice could be adapted to the singing of metrical psalms in English. Robert Crowley provided a four-part setting of Psalm 1 as a supplement to his metrical psalter of 1549: the tenor part is the 7th psalm tone, and the setting clearly represents established faburden practice.[51]

It seems likely that skilled singers, deprived of the positions they had held before the Reformation in cathedrals, monastic foundations, and as chantry priests or conducts in ordinary parish churches, continued to use their facility to enrich the singing of metrical psalms.

[48] Patrick, *Four Centuries of Scottish Psalmody*, p. 141.
[49] Tallmadge, "Baptist Monophonic and Heterophonic Hymnody," pp. 113–14.
[50] See, for instance, Brian Trowell, "Faburden and Fauxbourdon," *Musica disciplina*, XIII (1959), 43–78.
[51] Robert Crowley, *The Psalter of David Newely Translated into Englysh Metre* (London, 1549), folded insert. The music is reproduced in *Grove's Dictionary of Music and Musicians*, 3rd ed. (London, 1928), IV, 268. For another example see F[rancis] S[eager], *Certayne Psalmes* (London, 1553), tune for Psalm 146. Frost, who transcribed this "tune" as No. 294, did not realize that it is simply a faburden setting of the 6th psalm tone. The tune OXFORD may have derived from Gregorian chanting, though it does not closely resemble any one of the psalm tones.

The example from Edward VI's reign shows how metrical psalms were at first chanted. But the same kind of harmonization could be applied with even greater ease to the later syllabic psalm tunes. No doubt it was, by the choirs of lay-clerks that survived in some churches in the early years of Elizabeth I; and the simple settings in John Day's *Whole Psalmes in Foure Partes* of 1563 may well represent this practice. But the choirs succumbed to Puritan attack and lack of funds, and the practice of harmony in parish churches survived in a more fragmented form.

At any rate there is no doubt that several psalm tunes "generated" other tunes as faburdens or descants, which then took on a separate life of their own. One of the most striking such pairs of tunes is shown in Example 12. We have already met with OXFORD: here it is shown in the form in which it appeared in Playford's *Introduction* (compare Ex. 7). On the very same page Playford printed an even stranger tune called LITCHFIELD (Frost 25) with an independent bass.[52] He did not mention any connection between the tunes, but they fit perfectly together. The basic movement is in parallel sixths.

Example 12
Upper voice: OXFORD tune as printed in Playford (1674)
Lower voice: LITCHFIELD tune as printed in Playford (1674)

In other cases two tunes are partially identical, diverging only occasionally into two-part harmony. Indeed the earlier and later versions of OXFORD (Exx. 5 and 7) are related in this way, as are other pairs which Frost interprets as different versions of the same tune.[53]

The evidence that this process was indeed taking place does not depend solely on finding tunes that fit. For instance, it was described by Charles Butler, though in a confusing way.[54] And I have discov-

---

[52] The same juxtaposition, copied from Playford, occurs in the music supplement to the 9th edition of the "Bay Psalm Book" (Boston, 1698; facs. repr. in Richard C. Appel, *The Music of the Bay Psalm Book*, I.S.A.M. Monographs, V [Brooklyn, 1975]).

[53] For example, CANTERBURY (Frost 19a) and Low DUTCH (Frost 19); see Temperley, *English Parish Church*, I, 74–75; II, Ex. 15. Further examples of harmonically related pairs of psalm tunes may emerge from a computer project now in progress.

[54] Charles Butler, *The Principles of Musik* (London, 1636; repr. New York, 1970), p. 44.

ered actual examples of paired tunes in musical notation, in an obscure book of which the only known copy is at the University of Illinois. The Latin title can be translated as follows: "Certain Psalms of David Translated into Latin Meter, with the Addition of Ten of the Psalms Set to Their Musical Notes (As in the Anglican Version). For the Use of the Academic Establishment, When University Sermons are Held."[55] This book was bound up with the Latin version of the Book of Common Prayer, which was allowed to be used at Oxford and Cambridge on the grounds that the scholars and students there could understand the language. Several of the tunes are partially harmonized. One of them is shown in Example 13. It combines two tunes that are normally found independently in seventeenth-century sources and are listed separately by Frost. When the upper note of each two-part chord is chosen, the resulting tune is WINDSOR (Frost 129); the lower notes yield COLESHILL (Frost 392a). We must conclude that COLESHILL (the later tune) originated as a descant or sub-descant to WINDSOR. It is significant that this unique notation occurs in a "learned" source, suggesting that this kind of improvised harmonization was kept up, if at all, largely by educated persons, though not necessarily professional musicians.

Example 13

Setting of Psalm 1 from *Psalmi aliquot Davidici* (1681).

Be - a - tus vir non am - bu - lans, cum pec - ca - to - ri - bus

Se pra - vis non as - so - ci - ans, nec san - ni - o - ni - bus.

The particular interest of this pair of tunes lies in its relationship to the example of the Old Way of Singing represented in Example 10. This could equally well be regarded as a version of either of the melodies shown in Example 13, WINDSOR or COLESHILL. To put it another way, the ornate melody seems to wander from one tune to the other, or to cover both of them. Nothing of the sort is true in Example 11, which is clearly a version of WINDSOR, not of COLESHILL. But it could well be that Example 10 had its origin in the harmonized version

[55] *Psalmi aliquot Davidici in metrum latinum traducti. Cum adjectione decem psalmorum ad notas suas musicas (ut in anglicana versione) compositorum. In usum accademiae cum conciones habeantur ad clerum.* Londini: Excudebat M.F. & venales prostant apud Ric. Davis, Oxonii. 1681.

found in Example 13, and that in this case the "pitch-matching" process caused untutored singers to oscillate from one tune to the other.

This "harmonic" aspect of the Old Way of Singing throws new light on an otherwise obscure passage from one of the New England pamphlets, quoted by Alan Buechner:

> Many congregations . . . in their singing have borrowed and taken some half a line, some a whole line, out of one tune and put it into another. . . . Nor are the musical counter parts set to the tunes . . . in the late customary way [i.e., the Old Way], [in such a way as] to make the melody, most harmonious.[56]

Tallmadge's descriptions of lining hymnody in the Kentucky region reveal a rather similar phenomenon—short segments of the tune are harmonized; the harmonic interval is most often a fourth or fifth, but, in some cases, it was found that the women sang a sixth above the men, in a style closer to that of English improvised harmonization of the sixteenth and seventeenth centuries.[57] The harmony based on fourths and fifths, found also in shapenote singing, is something else again, and it may have come in with the tune repertory of Scots-Irish folksong.

All the phenomena so far considered appear to have originated in the Church of England. But a feature added to the Old Way, called "lining out," was introduced in England during the ascendancy of Presbyterianism. The Westminster Assembly of Divines, set up by Parliament in 1644, published *A Directory for the Publique Worship of God Throughout the Three Kingdoms of England, Scotland, and Ireland* (London, 1644), which included a section "Of Singing of Psalms":

> That the whole Congregation may joyne herein, every one that can reade is to have a Psalme book, and all others not disabled by age, or otherwise, are to be exhorted to learn to reade. But for the present, where many in the Congregation cannot read, it is convenient that the Minister, or some other fit person appointed by him and the other Ruling Officers, do reade the Psalme, line by line, before the singing thereof.

---

[56] Peter Thacher *et al.*, *An Essay Preached by Several Ministers . . . Concerning the Singing of Psalms* ([Boston, 1723], repr. in Samuel H. Emery, *The Ministry of Taunton* [Boston, 1853]), I, 274–75; cited in Alan C. Buechner, "Yankee Singing Schools and the Golden Age of Choral Music in New England, 1760–1800" (Ed.D. diss., Harvard Univ., 1960), p. 36.

[57] Tallmadge, "Baptist Monophonic and Heterophonic Hymnody," p. 114.

It is clear that this reform had nothing to do with music (unless indeed it had the subtly anti-musical intention of undermining the artistic integrity of the psalm tunes). Its avowed object was the strictly Calvinistic one of making sure that the people heard, understood, and sang the biblical words. It was later called by Playford a "Scotch custom," but in fact the Scottish commissioners at Westminster had opposed it, and had been overruled. Later on, it was universally adopted in Scotland, and lasted there much longer than in England. An additional purpose was to introduce new versions of the psalms, more literal in their translation of the Hebrew. The Westminster Divines hoped to agree on a new translation suited to the old tunes, and then to impose it on the people by having parish clerks read out the lines. In England they did not succeed in ousting Sternhold and Hopkins,[58] but lining out survived the Restoration of Church and King in 1660. In Scotland a new translation was published in 1650 and soon universally adopted.[59] In New England, where a similar movement had led to a two-stage revision (the "Bay Psalm Book," published in 1640 and again revised in 1651), lining out was quickly introduced: it was defended by John Cotton, one of the editors of the Bay Psalm Book, in 1647.[60] The object of promoting the new translation was achieved, for we hear no more of the Old Version of Sternhold and Hopkins in the colonies of New England.

In the Church of England it is evident that lining out became associated with the Old Way of Singing, and lasted only until the Old Way was superseded by organs (in town churches) or by voluntary choirs (in country churches). Compilers of psalmody collections between 1690 and 1730 frequently recommend that lining out be laid aside. For instance Francis Timbrell, in the preface to *The Divine Musick Scholar's Guide* (*ca.* 1725), states that "those who make use of these books, may Sing without ye Scots way of reading ye words, & do it in a Standing posture." (A similar association is evident in the heading of Example 10 above.) By 1741 a writer in *The Gentleman's Magazine* regretted that, with the coming of the "singers," lining out had been given up "in most Parishes."[61] In remote country churches where the Old Way survived, lining out generally survived with it.

Nonconformist or "dissenting" bodies in England had to conduct their worship secretly after 1660, until the passing of the Toleration

---

[58] Temperley, *English Parish Church*, I, 81.
[59] Patrick, *Four Centuries of Scottish Psalmody*, pp. 100, 114–16.
[60] John Cotton, *Singing of Psalms a Gospel-Ordinance* (London, 1647), pp. 62–64.
[61] "On the Abuse of Psalmody in Churches and Proposals for Remedying it," signed "Rusticus," *The Gentleman's Magazine*, XI (1741), 82.

534

Act (1690). Thereafter, the Independents (Congregationalists) and Presbyterians sang in the Old Way, with lining out, until singing by note was introduced. Meanwhile the Baptists engaged in a long controversy as to the propriety of any singing in worship. Isaac Watts, in the preface to his *Psalms*, recommended that "all Congregations . . . would sing as they do in foreign Protestant Countries without reading Line by Line."[62] Nevertheless, many dissenting congregations clung tenaciously to lining out, even when the Old Way had been replaced by choral singing.[63] At least two writers in the early nineteenth century, addressing themselves to English dissenters, found it necessary to argue against lining out at some length.[64] The Methodists seem never to have adopted either the Old Way or lining out, at any rate in England.

Before the end of the seventeenth century lining out had turned into a kind of monotoned chant. An Oxfordshire singing teacher spoke of "the ill custom of reading the words in a continued tone or unison in most churches."[65] A guidebook for parish clerks gives a vivid idea of what it was like in the early eighteenth century:

> Let us that are *Clerks* so read the *Psalm*, that as much as in us lies we may preserve *Harmony* and *Decency* in this Part of *God's Worship*, and prevent, if possible, the *Scorn* and *Contempt* that may be cast upon it by *Atheistical* and *Factious* People: For which purpose, in Reading the *Psalm*, read it Tunably, *i.e.* in a *Singing Tone*, and after the manner of *Chanting*, say,
> Psal. 23 *The Lord-is-on* ↳ *ly-my-sup-port*,
> *and-he that-doth* ↳ *me-feed*, &c.
> Psal. 25 *I-lift-my-Heart* ↳ *to thee*,
> *my-God-and-Guide* ↳ *most-just*, &c.
> allowing the Time of a *Crochet* or *Pulse beating* to each *Syllable* in Reading, and that the Break betwixt the falling from one Line to the taking up of

[62] Isaac Watts, *The Psalms of David Imitated in the Language of the New Testament* (London, 1719), p. xxxi.

[63] For instance, Isaac Smith, in the preface to *A Collection of Psalm Tunes* (London, [*ca.* 1780]), warned that "the clerk should always have a pitch pipe with him in the desk. When the Psalm is read, let him immediately name the tune to which he intends to sing it; then having given out the first line, let the key note be sounded aloud" (p. 2). This collection consists of music in three parts for the use of congregations led by choirs, and the fact that most of its texts are from Watts's psalms and hymns clearly indicates that it was intended primarily for the use of Congregational, Presbyterian, or possibly Baptist churches. Smith himself was clerk of Alie Street Congregational Meeting House, London.

[64] William Cole, *A View of Modern Psalmody* (Colchester, 1819), pp. 58–62 and 62n.; [David Everard Ford], *Observations on Psalmody: By a Composer* (London, 1827), p. 109: "In many dissenting chapels the effect of the Psalmody is destroyed by the giving out of the lines."

[65] Daniel Warner, *A Collection of Some Verses Out of the Psalms of David* (London, 1694), preface.

the next, may be so quick, as that due *Harmony* may be kept in some measure, notwithstanding the Reading; or at least not so much marred as it happens when the Reader is blundering or unskilful therein.

I have put a *Crotchet-Rest* after the Four first *Syllables*, to denote a little Pause; which, if carefully observ'd in Reading, the same will appear *Musical*, much after the manner of *Plain-Song* us'd in *Cathedrals*, or the *Chanting* of the *Psalms*. This way of Reading the *Psalm* was constantly practis'd and commendably perform'd by the ingenious Mr. *John Playford, Clerk* to the Honourable Society of the *Temple*, to whose Memory all the *Parish-Clerks* owe perpetual Thanks, for the great Pains he took for their furtherance in the Knowledge of *Psalmody*.[66]

In later times precentors would improvise a melody for the lining out: this is found both in nineteenth-century Scotland[67] and in present-day Kentucky.[68] But, as Tallmadge was the first to point out,[69] this melody does not (as might be expected) take the form of an anticipation of the musical phrase about to be sung by the congregation.

The evangelical "singing sermon" can lead straight into the lining-out of a hymn. The origin of this style of preaching is usually attributed to the leaders of the Great Awakening of 1730–50: Tallmadge quotes Goen as stating that George Whitefield is considered "the father of 'persuasive intonation'."[70] So it is worth mentioning here that "singing preachers" were not unknown at a much earlier date. An English Independent [i.e., Congregationalist] writer of the Commonwealth period declared that

> if there be any such thing as preaching, and prayer, and exhortation, it must be different from singing, even to the most ignorant; for no man will say, when a man meerly speaks or preaches, he sings, without his tone do make them call him a singing preacher or talker, as too many out of either affectation or custome, have given just cause to suspect.[71]

In the Church of England, where spoken responses to the minister were part of the liturgical order, it seems that some kind of monotone was used for them rather than a plain speaking voice. A high-church writer expressed the wish that "people had the art to speak in some

---

[66] B[enjamin] P[ayne], *The Parish-Clerk's Guide* (London, 1709), pp. 70–71.

[67] Mainzer, *The Gaelic Psalm Tunes*.

[68] "Old Hymns Lined and Led by Elder Walter Evans" (Sovereign Grace Recordings 6057 and 6444).

[69] Tallmadge, "Baptist Monophonic and Heterophonic Hymnody," pp. 110–11.

[70] *Ibid.*, p. 110.

[71] Cuthbert Sydenham, *A Christian, Sober and Plain Exercitation on the Two Grand Practicall Controversies of These Times: Infant-Baptism, and Singing of Psalms*, 2 vols. (London, 1653), II, 168.

536

kind of Concord with the Minister, either that their Voices might be Unisons with his, or a Fifth or an Eighth from it: For there is a *Speaking* as well as a *Singing* together, that is very harsh, by reason of a discordancy in the Voices of those that perform it."[72] So it would appear that the change from reading to singing that took place in the practice of lining out was part of a more general trend of the seventeenth century.

In the course of the seventeenth century we begin to hear complaints about psalm singing, not on the old Calvinistic grounds that the people did not understand it, but on the new ground that the effect of the music was unsatisfactory. The high-church Archbishop Laud, whose efforts to enforce Anglican ceremonies in the 1630s spurred on the Puritan emigrations to America, clearly expressed the basis for this point of view:

> It is true, the inward worship of the heart is the true service of God, and no service acceptable without it; but the external worship of God in His Church is the great witness to the world that our heart stands right in that service of God. . . . These thoughts are they, and no other, which have made me labour so much as I have done for decency and an orderly settlement of the external worship of God in the Church.[73]

After the interruption of the Commonwealth, this high-church or Arminian view prevailed more and more strongly in the Church of England. There was greater emphasis on the corporate nature of worship, less on the individual worshipper. Increasing material prosperity made the "hoarse or base sound" of the Old Way seem unacceptable to middle-class people who were familiar with art music; they began to feel that God, too, would not accept it, and that only the best possible music should be used in His service.

So we find determined efforts to get rid of the Old Way of Singing. The simplest way to abolish it was to install an organ, and organs were put up in many London and other large-town parish churches towards 1700. In the poorer parishes that could not afford organs, other ways of "improving" psalmody were attempted: John Playford was one of the pioneer reformers. Many parishes witnessed the establishment of societies of young men, called "religious socie-

---

[72] [Thomas Seymour], *Advice to the Readers of the Common-Prayer, and to the People Attending the Same* (London, 1682), p. 20.

[73] William H. Hutton, *The English Church from the Accession of Charles I to the Death of Anne* (London, 1903), p. 53.

ties," which met under the supervision of the clergyman to pray, discuss religious matters, and sing psalms. The first of these was formed in 1678. Among other activities these societies learned to sing by note, often with the help of a singing master, so that the members could spread themselves around the church and "improve" the singing. Such groups soon formed themselves into a parish choir that sang increasingly elaborate music, departing from their original object of leading the congregation. *A New Version of the Psalms* (Tate & Brady, 1696) was offered not because it was closer to the Hebrew but because its poetry was better; and the new tunes that went with it, by such as Jeremiah Clarke and William Croft, were similarly more artistic than the old. Lining out was no longer necessary. Bass viols were introduced to keep the singers on pitch, and by the later eighteenth century small bands had been formed to assist the choirs in the performance of anthems, fuging tunes, and the rest.[74] Choirs in English country churches are found as early as 1685; they were common by 1710, and normal by 1730. After that the Old Way survived only in small, remote churches where choirs could not be formed. But even in these places the congregation gradually dropped out of the singing, leaving the parish clerk to carry on almost, or entirely, alone. A speaker at the Church Congress of 1864 recalled that this had been the case in a small church near Ely in his youth:

> All the singing was done by the clerk. There was not even a school child to help him. He used to stand up and give out two lines of an hymn and then sing it, after which he read out two lines more, and so on. The good old man was a blacksmith, and used to practise his psalmody whilst blowing the bellows at his forge. Among other embellishments with which he used to adorn his performance, was an extraordinary shake, which he was accustomed to execute at the end, or wherever else it was required to give effect.[75]

As one might expect, the development of singing by note, linked as it was with a retreat from Calvinistic theology, took longer to develop in the nonconformist churches in England, and in the churches of Scotland and New England. It was not until about 1710 that a group of dissenting ministers, mostly Presbyterian, formed a

---

[74] I have treated this subject in fuller detail elsewhere (*English Parish Church*, I, Chap. 6), and am now only outlining it to show how the Old Way of Singing met its end.

[75] *Report of the Proceedings of the Church Congress Held at Bristol, October . . . 1864* (Bristol, 1865), p. 310.

538

society in Eastcheap, London, to give instruction in psalmody.[76] The tune supplements to Isaac Watts's *Psalms and Hymns*, which was the chief singing book of the Congregationalists, were strictly monophonic until the late eighteenth century. The Baptists were still further behind in the process, and continued to dispute the propriety of singing in worship until at least 1780. In Scotland the movement for regular singing began in the middle of the eighteenth century, but it met with hard and long resistance. Before it prevailed there was an era in which "precenting" had become a fine art, reducing the congregation almost to silence, as in the English church where the blacksmith held forth alone.[77]

The movement for regular singing reached America first in the Anglican colonies to the south. Evidence recently assembled by Mason Martens has shown that in Maryland, particularly, an effort was made at the close of the seventeenth century to introduce Anglican religious societies. Dr. Thomas Bray, who had been a leading promoter of religious societies and regular singing in England, visited Maryland in 1700 as the commissary of the Bishop of London and provided books and teachers to start regular singing in the parishes there.[78] Similar movements began at this time in Philadelphia and New York. In Virginia, William Byrd recorded the introduction of the new way in 1710.[79]

In Boston, where the Church of England was an embattled minority, an Anglican religious society was founded in 1704;[80] Tate & Brady's metrical psalms, first imported in London editions, were reprinted in New York in 1710, and a Boston edition with tunes was printed for the use of King's Chapel in 1713. The following year the Brattle organ, the first church organ in English-speaking America, was installed at King's Chapel,[81] and from then on Bostonians had ample opportunity to hear what "regular" psalm singing was like.

[76] Louis F. Benson, *The English Hymn: Its Development and Use in Worship* (New York, 1915), pp. 89–90.

[77] Patrick, *Four Centuries of Scottish Psalmody*, pp. 194–97.

[78] Mason Martens, "Tate and Brady's *New Version* of the Metrical Psalms and Its Introduction into the American Colonies" (paper delivered at the national meeting of the American Musicological Society, Washington, D.C., 1976).

[79] Byrd and his wife were given two books by the singing teacher, and on 24 December 1710, went to church, where "we began to give in to the new way of singing psalms." *The Secret Diary of William Byrd of Westover 1709–1712*, ed. Louis B. Wright and Marion Tinling (Richmond, Va., 1941), pp. 272, 276; cited in Stevenson, *Protestant Church Music*, pp. 53–54.

[80] William S. Perry, ed., *Historical Collections Relating to the American Colonial Church*, 5 vols. (Hartford, 1870–78, repr. New York, 1969), III, 76–79.

[81] Henry W. Foote, *Annals of King's Chapel*, I (Boston, 1882), p. 211.

Cotton Mather, though violently opposed to the organization of the Church of England in Massachusetts, admitted in his diary in 1718: "The psalmody is but poorly carried on in my flock, and in a variety and regularity inferior to some others. I would see about it."[82] It seems clear that the Anglican developments provided both a challenge and a model to the Congregationalists of New England, and sparked the singing-school movement of the 1720s. Judge Sewall wrote in his diary for March 16, 1721: "At night Mr. Mather preaches in the schoolhouse to the young musicians. . . . House was full and the singing extraordinarily excellent, such as has hardly been heard before in Boston. Sung four times out of Tate and Brady."[83] In the Congregational tradition, a meeting with a sermon was the nearest equivalent of the devotional conference of the Anglican societies: in both cases the meeting ended with singing. There was still to be a long and hard-fought battle before regular singing was widely accepted, and indeed some groups never accepted it; but even in New England the retreat from Calvinism had made headway, and there was growing appreciation of "decency and order" in public worship (to quote a catchphrase of the day).

After the second Great Awakening of around 1800, revival hymnody of various kinds swept through the Middle Atlantic, Southern, and Western states, and with the aid of shapenote hymn-books there was a vast extension of the ability to sing from notes. Entirely new tune repertories replaced the old metrical psalm tunes, and even penetrated the conservative rural churches that resisted all attempts at reform of singing practice. In a few hundred churches of the mountain areas of Kentucky, Virginia, and North Carolina, Regular and Primitive Baptists still sing in the Old Way with lining out. From among them Tallmadge has collected 322 examples of lining hymnody. "Among these are 47 selections from the 'long-boy' and camp meeting hymnody; 101 items from late 19th and 20th century gospel type hymnody . . . and 172 examples of lining hymns which, in text and style, and probably tune, relate directly to the Baptist singing during the eighteenth century."[84] The detailed history of this late survival awaits further exploration.

In conclusion, I should like to look briefly at the singing of the Mennonites, a small, self-contained, and invariably rural sect that has

---

[82] Buechner, "Yankee Singing Schools," p. 63.
[83] *Ibid.*, p. 79.
[84] Tallmadge, "Baptist Monophonic and Heterophonic Hymnody," p. 114.

540

preserved traditions inherited from the Anabaptists of the sixteenth century.[85] There were several immigrations of Mennonites from Holland and Germany to North America, chiefly in the eighteenth and nineteenth centuries. A subdivision of the Mennonites is the Old Order Amish. Just as they have continued to oppose technological innovations such as electricity and automobiles, so they have tended to resist organs and the encroachments of newer styles of music. George Pullen Jackson was aware of the resemblance of their music to the Old Way of Singing.[86] One of the first systematic studies of Mennonite music was made by Bruno Nettl. Further work in this area has been done more recently by Sandra Moore of the University of Illinois.

Example 14 shows one of the earliest attempts to transcribe Amish hymnody, made by Joseph W. Yoder in Pennsylvania early this century. Yoder gave the following explanation of his transcription method:

> All the notes between two consecutive bars are sung to one syllable. This necessitates slurring throughout the entire piece, and as slurring is one of the characteristics of these tunes, the marks indicating slurs are omitted, but understood. The whole notes represent a sustaining of the voice almost as long as a whole note in 2-2 time; the half note somewhat shorter and the quarter note a quick swing of the voice, a mere touch of the voice to that note; and the double notes represent a rather long sustaining of the voice. A slight stress of the voice on the first part of each syllable is probably as near to the accent as we can come, as there is little if any accent.[87]

Yoder was unable to identify the tune being sung. Nettl, however, confirmed Jackson's hypothesis that in this singing the first note sung to each syllable was generally the proper note of the melody, and the remainder a kind of ornamental melisma.[88] Guided by this we may extract the original melody from which this song is likely to have been derived. This has been done in the white notes of Example 15 (disregarding black "passing" notes in Example 14).

One of the earliest American songbooks of the Mennonites, the *Unpartheyisches Gesangbuch* (Lancaster, Pa., 1820), lists the hymn of

[85] C. Henry Smith, *The Mennonites of America* (Scottdale, Pa., 1909).

[86] George Pullen Jackson, "The Strange Music of the Old Order Amish," *The Musical Quarterly*, XXXI (1945), 275–88.

[87] C. Henry Smith, *The Mennonites of America*, pp. 437–38. I have added numbers and double bars in Ex. 14 to clarify the phrase structure.

[88] Bruno Nettl, "The Hymns of the Amish: An Example of Marginal Survival," *Journal of American Folklore*, LXX (1957), 323–28.

Example 14

Transcription of Amish singing made in Pennsylvania by Joseph W. Yoder, *ca.* 1905

Weil nun die Zeit

vor - han - den ist, Dasz wir hie

müs - - sen schei - - - den;

So woll uns Gott zu

die - ser Frist Ge - - nä - dig -

lich ge - lei - - ten; Dasz

wir be - - trach - - - ten fort

und fort Sein jetzt ge - - -

hör - tes hei - - lig

Wort Und uns

mö - - gen be - - - rei - - - ten.

542

Example 14 ("Weil nun die Zeit vorhanden ist") as No. 348, with the designation "Mel. Wann wein stündlein." Consultation of Zahn[89] gives several sixteenth-century tunes to a hymn of this name, two of which (Exx. 16, 17) bear similarities to the one shown in Example 15.

Example 15

Melody extracted from the first principal note in each syllable of Ex. 14

Most of the time the Mennonite tune seems to follow the tune of Example 16, and the correspondence is close enough to place the relationship beyond reasonable doubt. The brackets above the notes in Example 15 show correspondences to the tune of Example 16; where the bracket is a broken line, the correspondence depends on black notes in the tune below, representing passing or non-initial

Example 16

Tune printed in 1596 for "Wenn mein Stündlein vorhanden ist" (Zahn 4482b)

[89] Johannes Zahn, *Die Melodien der deutschen evangelischen Kirchenlieder* (Gütersloh, 1889–93), tunes 4482b, 4483.

101

notes from the transcribed Amish tune of Example 14. This leaves, however, several prominent notes in the Amish tune that do not correspond to Example 16. Many of these, most strikingly in the openings of phrases 1 and 3, are related to the other early chorale tune, Example 17. These correspondences are shown by brackets below the notes in Example 15. The two sets of correspondences between them cover all except two notes of the Amish melody.[90]

Example 17

Tune printed in 1569 for "Wenn mein Stündlein vorhanden ist" (Zahn 4483)

In view of the apparent influence of popular harmonization on the Old Way of Singing, one may next ask whether the two early chorales are themselves harmonically related. Certainly they have the same general form (*ABABA'CD*), which they share with Example 15, and the first and last notes of each phrase harmonize perfectly. Both are largely monosyllabic with a three-note melisma in the last phrase. The tune in Example 17 begins and ends on the mediant, a feature more common in an inner part of a harmonized setting than in a monophonic melody, and its sixth phrase certainly sounds like an inner part. But an attempt to fit the tunes together exactly, such as that in Example 18, requires some rhythmic manipulation to make it work.[91] This "quodlibet" is much less neat than that of the paired English tunes. Comparing it with Example 14, one finds that in some parts of the

[90] One of the two notes not accounted for, the *e* in phrase 4, is an unexplained variant of the *d* in phrase 2. It should be borne in mind that Ex. 14 is presumably an honest attempt to write down what was actually sung, analogous to Exx. 9 and 10; whereas Exx. 7, 8, 16, and 17 are more in the nature of ideal or theoretical models of the tunes they represent. This alone may account for many differences.

[91] The presence of unprepared fourths and consecutive fifths in this reconstruction is no bar to its validity. If the English analogy is accepted, the two tunes may have derived from two voices of a four-part harmonization, and either one may have been the higher in pitch. Furthermore, either tune could itself have been a composite of two parts of an earlier harmonization.

544

Example 18

Suggested harmonic relationship between Ex. 16 and Ex. 17

tune (phrase 2, for instance) one can easily imagine that the Amish congregation was originally responding to a two-part performance such as that in Example 18. Elsewhere there is no clear relationship. I would certainly not insist on the influence of popular harmonization on Mennonite singing without a much larger sample of tunes.

On the other hand, there can be little doubt that Example 14 represents a very slow version of an old chorale tune related closely to that of Example 16, with added notes; and many similar examples have been found by Moore from her own field recordings. What is more, the transformation has followed much the same process as in the Old Way of Singing: generally (though not always) the first note on each syllable corresponds with the main note of the tune; movement is largely by step, and can be interpreted as a wayward path from one note to the next.

In short, the singing of the Mennonites can be regarded as a variant of the Old Way of Singing. Its existence, independent of the Anglo-Saxon tradition, suggests that this style of singing is to some extent a "natural" development, within the general framework of Protestant worship, rather than the product of specifically Anglo-Saxon cultural determinants. I believe it offers clear support of the "pitch-matching" hypothesis as the main explanation for the development, and, in addition, further tentative links with the "popular harmonization" that undoubtedly took place in English churches.

V

The Anglican Communion Hymn

Part 1. Hymn Singing in the Church of England: Tradition and the Law

The Church of England, with its descendants and offshoots in the Episcopal and Methodist traditions, combines Catholic and Reformed elements in its liturgical heritage, but has taken very little from Lutheran practice. Its congregational singing in earlier times was. on the Calvinist model, emphasizing metrical psalms rather than hymns because of their direct scriptural authority. Calvin himself, though he had not absolutely excluded hymns of human composition, had in effect decided the issue for his own Church when he wrote in the preface to the French psalm book: "Look where we may, we will never find songs better, nor more suited to the purpose, than the Psalms of David: which the Holy Ghost himself composed."[1] These sentiments were echoed by John Knox and William Whittingham in the preface to their Genevan service book of 1556,[2] which provided only metrical psalms and the Ten Commandments for congregational singing. The Nunc Dimittis (also scriptural) was added in 1558. Anglicans and Presbyterians, both of whom derived their congregational songs from this book, continued to use metrical psalms, more or less exclusively, until the Evangelical revivals of the 18th and 19th centuries.[3]

But in the case of the Church of England the ban on hymns was never complete. Thomas Cranmer had at one time wanted to include translations of the medieval breviary hymns in the Book of Common Prayer of 1549,[4] but only one survived—the *Veni Creator Spiritus*—and that only in the Ordination Office, which is not a congregational service. Among the Protestant exiles of Mary Tudor's reign (1553-8) there were at least two parties: the Puritans, led by Knox and Whittingham, whose practice is represented by the Geneva book; and the "Anglican" party who based their practice on the Prayer Book.[5] Evidence has recently come to light that in at least one of the English colonies on the Continent at this period hymns as well as metrical psalms were used in worship: this will be discussed in a later installment of this four-part series.

The Elizabethan settlement, as is well known, was a compromise imposed by royal authority, an effort to accommodate the views of all but the most extreme factions, all the way from those who shared Roman Catholic beliefs in all matters except papal authority to those who wanted to complete the Reformation of the English Church on strictly Presbyterian lines. In cathedrals a style of worship was maintained that was essentially the Sarum Use of pre-Reformation times, purged of invocations to the Virgin and Saints, prayers for the dead, and other unacceptable elements, and translated into English, to which the old plainsong, faburden, and polyphony were adapted and sung by choirs with organ accompaniment. In parish churches, on the other hand, although the identical service book was used, the words were spoken by priest and people, and the only music was the unaccompanied congregational singing of metrical psalms or hymns. (By 1570 few parish churches still retained choirs or organs.[6])

These metrical texts were not in the Book of Common Prayer, nor were they authorized by the Act of Uniformity (1559), which required the use of that book and none other in all churches of the realm. The omission was no doubt deliberate, but the strength of the Puritan party in the early years of Elizabeth's reign was such that it was found politically expedient to allow the singing of metrical texts in the parish churches and even in the cathedrals.[7] (Of course, the reason why *metrical* texts were associated with Puritanism and disapproved by high-church conservatives was that they could be sung by congregations, with all that that implied theologically and politically. By contrast, only trained choirs could chant the prose liturgy.) The oft-quoted clause of Elizabeth's *Injunctions* of 1559 allowed this practice in the following words:

And yet nevertheless, for the comforting of such that delight in music,

it may be permitted that in the beginning, or in the end of common prayers, either at morning or evening, there may be sung an hymn, or such like song, to the praise of Almighty God, in the best sort of melody and music that may be conveniently devised, having respect that the sentence of the hymn may be understood and perceived.[8]

One cannot fail to be struck by the fact that this passage allows the singing of a "hymn," although it was frequently used to justify the performance of anthems (in cathedrals) and of metrical psalms (in parish churches). Does it mean that, after all, hymns were sung in Anglican churches under Elizabeth and her successors?

Edna S. Parks has addressed herself to this very question. She has drawn attention[9] to the presence of a number of original hymns in Sternhold and Hopkins's *Whole Book of Psalms* (completed in 1562 with the Geneva psalm book of 1556 as its nucleus), which was the only collection of metrical psalms used in the Church for more than a hundred years after its appearance. She has further published an index of no less than 1,157 English hymns which antedate the publications of Isaac Watts, the so-called "Father of English Hymnody."[10] Yet these facts cannot in themselves establish that hymns were used in public worship. Many of those in Ms. Parks's index, as she herself remarks,[11] were mere religious poems, to be read silently, and were only taken into hymn books at a much later date. Others were for the private (often clandestine) devotions of Anglicans, Protestant dissenters, or even Catholics.

The Church of England has always been governed by law, and until the Toleration Act (1689) the law compelled all English citizens to worship according to its dictates, except between 1644 and 1660 when Parliament banned the Book of Common Prayer and laid down other forms of worship. It is to the law and its enforcement that we must turn in the first instance to determine the practice of congregational singing in public worship. As already noted, the Act of Uniformity laid down the use of the Book of Common Prayer, and the Injunctions of 1559 permitted a "hymn, or such like song" before or after services. But *The Whole Book of Psalms*, though *printed* by royal privilege, was never legally authorized for *use* in public worship. The title page from 1560 onwards claimed that the book was "allowed according to the order appointed in the Queen's Majesty's Injunctions"; but also that it was "very meet to be used of all sorts of people privately for their godly solace and comfort: laying apart all ungodly songs and ballads, which tend only to the nourishing of vice, and corrupting of youth." This private purpose had, indeed, always been one of the main objects of metrical psalms and hymns in the eyes of reformers, including Luther and Calvin. It was not until 1566 that John Day, the printer of the book, made bold to add a new phrase to the title: "allowed to be sung in all churches, of all people together, before and after morning and evening prayer, as also before and after sermons." Here Day, presumably with at least the connivance of authority, was not only claiming that the texts and music in his book were covered by the authorizing words of the Injunctions, but was sneaking in an additional time for singing them: "before and after sermons." Since sermons could not legally be delivered in church except in their due place as part of the communion or ante-communion service until the passing of the Act of Uniformity Amendment Act (1872), this addition implied a definite interpolation of metrical psalms or hymns *within* the liturgy,

hence considerably raising their status. And we know from Holinshed (1577) that metrical psalms were indeed frequently sung before and after the sermon,[12] as they have been ever since that time. What is more, although the Queen had only permitted "an hymn" before or after service in her Injunctions, she went much further in several special or occasional services which she issued, under the general authority conferred on her by the Act of Uniformity. The first Accession Service, for example, printed in 1576, and *required* to be celebrated in every parish church, included "the xxi. psalm in metre before the sermon, unto the end of the vii. verse. and the c. psalm after the sermon."[13] A revised version of this service, printed in 1578, had instead of the psalms three metrical hymns, none of them included in Parks or Julian, fitted to the tunes of metrical psalms in the common psalm book.[14]

With such authority it is no wonder that people thought they were allowed to sing metrical psalms or hymns, before and after the sermon as well as before and after the service, even though there was still no strict legal authority for the former practice. The words on the title page of the 1566 psalm book, repeated in hundreds of later editions, came at last to acquire almost the force of law. This impression was strengthened by the issue of Tate and Brady's *New Version of the Psalms* in 1696, which carried a purported authorization by the King in Council stating that they were "permitted to be used in all churches, &c., as shall think fit to receive them." Although this order was later found to have no legal effect (since only Parliament could change the liturgy, while any hymns outside the liturgy were already authorized by the 1559 Injunctions), it was almost universally believed in the 18th century that only the Old and New Versions could be used

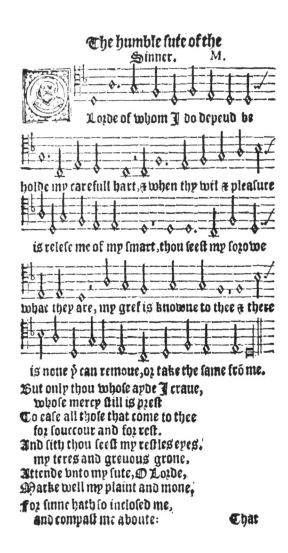

The humble sute of the Sinner. M.

Lorde of whom I do depend be

holde my carefull hart, & when thy will & pleasure

is relese me of my smart, thou seest my sorowe

what they are, my gref is knowne to thee & there

is none ῾ can remoue, or take the same frō me.
But only thou whose ayde I craue,
　whose mercy still is prest
To ease all those that come to thee
　for souccour and for rest.
And sith thou seest my restles eyes,
　my teres and greuous grone,
Attende vnto my sute, O Lorde,
　Marke well my plaint and mone,
For sinne hath so inclosed me,
　and compass me aboute:　　　　　That

The Humble Suit of a Sinner as first printed in
The Whole Booke of Psalms, 1562.
By permission of the Houghton Library, Harvard University.

in church. Even the Evangelical leader William Romaine disapproved of hymns for this reason,[15] and the belief was publicly claimed as late as 1814.[16] It was being more and more blatantly ignored by Evangelical clergy, however, and at last in 1820 it was tested in court when a group of parishioners of St. Paul's church, Sheffield brought an action against their Evangelical vicar, Thomas Cotterill, for introducing his *Selection of Psalms and Hymns* in the church. A thorough legal investigation was undertaken by G.V. Vernon, chancellor of the Consistory Court of the Diocese of York. In his judgment on 6 July 1820 he concluded that the status of hymns was exactly like that of metrical psalms: neither was part of the liturgy, but both could be used before and after services.[17] This important decision opened the way for the free use of hymns in the Church of England, and made possible the flood of Victorian hymn books, representing all shades of churchmanship, and incorporating the hymns of Watts and Wesley, translated Lutheran hymns, and Roman Catholic hymns of both medieval and post-Tridentine origin. In practice the order confining the singing to before and after service was not widely observed.

We can see, therefore, that in earlier times the only hymns likely to have been sung congregationally, apart from any occasional ones included in special services promulgated by authority, were those in Sternhold and Hopkins's *Whole Book of Psalms*. Most editions of this book contained 24 metrical texts in addition to those of the 150 psalms in numerical order. These texts, sometimes referred to as the "Divine Hymns," were not all hymns in the strict sense. They represented among them the views of various groups among the Marian Protestant exiles. Some were metrical versions of various portions of the Prayer Book liturgy: the Veni Creator from the Ordination Service; the Canticles, including the Venite (which is merely Psalm 95), from Morning and Evening Prayer; the Apostles' and Athanasian Creeds, Ten Commandments (in versions by Whittingham and Norton), and Lord's Prayer (in versions by Cox and Norton). Two further metrical psalms (117, 134) by Thomas Becon appeared after the main psalm sequence as "An Exhortation Before Morning Prayer" and "An Exhortation Before Evening Prayer," titles presumably reflecting the words of the Injunctions. Two are translations of German hymns, "Give peace in these our days, O Lord" after W. Capito and "Preserve us, Lord, by thy dear Word" after Luther, probably brought back from Strasbourg by the exiles who had settled there.

There remain, however, seven original hymns, which can rightly be called the foundation of English hymnody. The earliest of these in date of first publication (1556) is *A Thanksgiving after the Lord's Supper* ("The Lord be thanked for his gifts") which will be the subject of the third article in this series, as it represents the beginning of a continuous Anglican tradition of communion hymns. "The spirit of grace grant us, O Lord" is a four-verse addition to Whittingham's Ten Commandments. Another, "Come Holy Sprite, the God of might," is designated for singing "before sermon." The remainder have no liturgical function, and may well have been originally designed for private devotions: (see list).

John Markant was also the translator of four of the psalm versions and was a country clergyman in the early

Title	First Line	Author	First Printed
A Lamentation	O Lord, in thee is all my trust	anon.	1560
The Lamentation of a Sinner	O Lord, turn not away thy face	Markant	1561
The Complaint of a Sinner	Where righteousness doth say	anon.	1561[18]
The Humble Suit of a Sinner	O Lord, of whom I do depend	Markant	1562

years of Elizabeth's reign. Nothing is known of his activity during the Marian period.

Of all the 24 additional texts, these last four are the most clearly "hymns"—in an almost Evangelical sense, for they express deep personal preoccupation with sin, and faith in the atonement as the only source of salvation.[19] All four were printed with tunes to themselves, rather than cross-references to psalm tunes (which was all that was provided for some). The tunes, all in the penitential D minor mode (Dorian or transposed Aeolian), are among the finest in the book. The one for A Lamentation (see example, page 14) may well be by Tallis, for it had appeared first in a four-part setting ascribed to "M. Talis" in Day's Certaine Notes (1560). It is a superbly shaped and constructed melody, even if it invokes a more profound gloom than we are inclined to accept today; perhaps it is based on the plainsong.

These hymns were certainly popular, and their tunes were many times harmonized,[20] and sometimes parodied with secular texts.[21] They are found in collections of parish-church music well into the 18th century,[22] and the 6th edition of the Supplement to the New Version of Psalms (1708) contained a new tune to The Lamentation of a Sinner. Only one piece of direct evidence has come to light on the use of hymns in parochial worship in Elizabeth's time: Melchior Smyth, vicar of Hessle

and Hull (Yorkshire), stated in legal proceedings in 1564/5 that "to avoid tediousness he appointed the hymn to be sung called Come Holy Spirit, at the beginning of every sermon, wherein the Queen, and her Council, the nobility, the states both of the spirituality and temporality were prayed for."[23] This precisely describes the hymn "Come Holy Sprite," which, as already pointed out, was designated "to be sung before the sermon."

The four non-liturgical hymns were probably also used in worship. Three of the texts (the ones beginning "O Lord") were set many times over as polyphonic choral pieces, sometimes based on their proper tunes and sometimes not. They were far more often treated in this way, indeed, than any of the metrical versions of psalms or canticles. A Lamentation, for instance, is found in settings by Fidow, Gibbons, Giles, Hall, J. Holmes, Hooper, W. Lawes, Peerson and Ravenscroft as well as Tallis.[24] Moreover several of the manuscript sources of these settings are definitely associated with cathedral or collegiate choirs. Gibbons's setting is also in Clifford's wordbook of 1663.[25] If these texts could be sung after service in cathedrals, as this evidence suggests, it seems more than likely that they were also sung congregationally in parish churches, where the people had the texts and tunes in the psalm books bound at the back of their Bibles and prayer books.

Footnotes

[1]Jean Calvin, "La Forme des pieces et chants ecclésiastiques," in *Pseaumes octantetrois de David mis en rime françoise par Clement Marot et Theodore de Beze* (Geneva, 1551; facs. edn. 1973), fol. A7ʳ.

[2]*The Forme of Prayers and Ministration of the Sacraments* (Geneva, 1556) (*Short Title Catalogue* [hereafter *STC*] no. 16561), p. 19.

[3]See Nicholas Temperley, *The Music of the English Parish Church* (Cambridge, 1979); Millar Patrick, *Four Centuries of Scottish Psalmody* (London, 1949); Louis F. Benson, *The English Hymn* (Richmond, 1915, repr. 1962).

[4]Francis Procter, *A History of the Book of Common Prayer* (London, 1864), p. 174.

[5]Edward Arber, ed. *A Brief Discourse of the Troubles at Frankfort 1554-1558 A.D.* (London, 1907); Christina H. Garrett, *The Marian Exiles* (Cambridge, 1938).

[6]Temperley, pp. 43-4.

[7]M. M. Knappen, *Tudor Puritanism* (Chicago, 1939), p. 182.

[8]Walter H. Frere & W. M. Kennedy, eds., *Visitation Articles and Injunctions of the Period of the Reformation*, Alcuin Club Collections, nos. 14-16 (London, 1910), vol. III, p. 8. [All spellings are modernized except in titles.]

[9]Edna D. Parks, *The Hymns and Hymn Tunes Found in the English Metrical Psalters* (New York, 1966), p. vii.

[10]Edna D. Parks, *Early English Hymns: An Index* (Metuchen, 1972).

[11]Parks (1972), p. iv.

[12]Richard Holinshed, *Holinshed's Chronicles* (London, 1807; facs. edn. 1965), vol. I, p. 232.

[13]*STC* 16479; W. K. Clay, *Liturgies in the Reign of Queen Elizabeth*, Parker Society Publications, no. 30 (Cambridge, 1847), p. 548.

[14]*STC* 16480; Clay, pp. 558-61.

[15]William Romaine, *An Essay on Psalmody* (London, 1775).

[16]*The Gentleman's Magazine*, LXXXIV (1814), p. 532.

[17]Jonathan Gray, *An Inquiry into the Historical Facts Relative to Parochial Psalmody* (York, 1821), pp. 46-53.

[18]Parks (1966), p. 15, states that this was first published in 1562, but it had appeared in the 1561 edition of the Geneva psalm book (*STC* 16562; copy: Paris, Bibliothèque nationale.)

[19]For the texts, see Parks (1966).

[20]Parks (1966), pp. 29-83.

[21]See Claude M. Simpson, *The British Broadside Ballad and its Music* (New Brunswick, 1966), pp. 70, 260.

[22]See, for instance, Elias Hall, *The Psalm-Singers Compleat Companion* (London, 1706); John & James Green, *A Collection of Choice Psalm-Tunes*, 3rd edn. (Nottingham, 1715).

[23]John S. Purvis, ed., *Tudor Parish Documents of the Diocese of York* (Cambridge, 1948), p. 212, cited Parks (1966), p. 14.

[24]Ralph T. Daniel & Peter le Huray, *The Sources of English Church Music 1549-1660*, Early English Church Music Supp. Vols. I-II (London, 1972), vol. I, p. 57.

[25]James Clifford, *A Collection of Divine Services and Anthems Usually Sung in His Majesty's Chappell and in All Collegiate Choirs of England and Ireland* (London, 1663).

A PRAYER (later called THE LAMENTATION)

Tune harmonized, and perhaps composed, by Thomas Tallis

1. O Lord, in thee is all my trust: Give ear un-to my woe-ful cries.

Re-fuse me not that am un-just, But, bow-ing down thy heav'n-ly eyes,

I do still la-ment

Be-hold how I do still la-ment My sins where-in I thee of-fend.

for them shall I be

O Lord, for them shall I be shent, Sith thee to please I do in-tend?

shent = ruined; sith = since

2. No no, not so, thy will is bent
    To deal with sinners in thine ire;
But when in heart they shall repent,
    Thou grant'st with speed their just desire.
To thee, therefore, still shall I cry
    To wash away my sinful crime:
Thy blood, O Lord, is not yet dry,
    But that it may help me in time.

3. Haste now, O Lord, haste now, I say,
    To pour on me the gifts of grace,
That when this life must flit away
    In heav'n with thee we may have place,
Where thou dost reign eternally
    With God, which once down did thee send;
Where angels sing continually,
    "To thee be praise, world without end."

Text and music are taken from the earliest known source, John Day's *Certaine Notes*, partly printed in 1560 but not issued until 1565 (*STC* 6418-9). The second and third verses are set out in full with slight differences in the music, and the whole is completed with a simple plagal Amen.

Certain changes were made when the tune was reprinted in monophonic form in *The Whole Booke of Psalmes*, 1562 (*STC* 2430) and harmonized in *The Whole Psalmes in Foure Partes*, 1563 (*STC* 2431). The last note of each 8-note phrase becomes a breve, to indicate a pause, and the rhythm is simplified at measures 27-8: the altered form of the tune may be seen in Maurice Frost, *English & Scottish Psalm & Hymn Tunes c. 1543-1677* (London, 1953), no. 186. The words were also slightly altered: 'cries' to 'cry', 'eyes' to 'eye', 'thee offend' to 'do offend.' A number of changes were made in the alto and tenor parts in the 1563 book, chiefly in rhythm and in the additon of passing notes. In all these early sources the piece was called simply *A Prayer:* the name *The Lamentation* appears only in later editions.

All barlines are editorial. Spelling and punctuation are modern.

The Anglican Communion Hymn

Part 2. The Communion Hymn:
A Continuous Tradition

The Anglican Order of Communion, "commonly called the Mass" as it was subtitled in the 1549 Book of Common Prayer, was of course closely derived from the Roman Mass, translated, simplified, and, in points of theological importance, revised. It tended, however, to divide into two parts. The Ante-Communion, which followed immediately after Morning Prayer whenever that service was conducted, included a sermon or homily and the collection of alms. The Eucharist itself, with the prayers for the consecration and administration of the bread and wine, was said only on days when there was an actual celebration of the sacrament, and was normally attended only by those who intended to communicate. This bipartite structure is still clear in modern editions of the Prayer Book.

Not long after the Reformation, the importance of communion began to be downplayed: celebrations became less frequent, and tended to be treated as little more than an occasional appendage to Morning Prayer; attendance dropped steadily. By contrast, Ante-Communion continued to be said every Sunday, and, within it, the sermon gained greater and greater importance, until at last it became the centrepiece of the whole service. A similar process was taking place in virtually every Protestant sect at this time. In England many churches had only four "sacrament Sundays" a year by the 18th century. A low point was reached in the year 1800, when, according to an eye witness, only six people took the sacrament at St. Paul's cathedral, London, on Easter Sunday, the one day in the year when all Anglicans were theoretically required to communicate.[1]

Neither portion of the Order of Communion provided for congregational singing. As I have already shown, there was a strong tradition of singing metrical psalms or hymns before and after the sermon, when the full congregation was present. In cathedrals the choir and organist generally left their posts at the end of Ante-Communion,[2] and most choral settings of the communion service from the 16th to the 19th century include only texts drawn from Ante-Communion; thus they lack settings of the Gloria in Excelsis.[3] It might be supposed, then, that in parish churches also, the reduced congregation of communicants would have remained silent during the latter, sacramental part of the communion service.

But a careful search reveals substantial evidence that the custom of singing during the people's communion was retained in some churches, and was still in being (though hardly vigorous or widespread) when the liturgical revival took place under the influence of the Oxford Movement in the 19th century. The custom had its origin, no doubt, in the *communio* and *post-communio*, psalm verses or antiphons which had been chanted at this point in the Sarum Mass,[4] and which had varied from season to season. In Cranmer's 1549 Prayer Book they were replaced by a single text, the translated Agnus Dei (transferred to this point from another part of the Mass), with the rubric: "In the Communion time the clerks shall sing, O Lamb of God . . . and when the Communion is ended, then shall the clerks sing the Post-Communion." Clerks were professional musicians in minor orders who made up the choir. Marbeck's *Book of Common Praier Noted* (1550) set the Agnus Dei to an adapted version of the Sarum chant for the same text, and a few other Edwardian settings survive.[5] In the 1552 revision of the Prayer Book, however, the Agnus Dei with its rubric was omitted, and from then on no mention was made in the Prayer Book of any singing before, during, or after the administration of the sacrament, except for the Gloria in Excelsis, to be "said or sung."

The reason for the omission of the Agnus Dei has never been explained. It can hardly have been on theological grounds, for an almost identical text was retained both in the Litany and in the Gloria in Excelsis, which now followed the sacrament. Possibly the Agnus Dei was omitted because, in practice, congregational singing of metrical texts had already replaced it. There was some authority for such practice, for the Act of Uniformity (1549) had allowed that "it shall be lawful for all men as well in churches, chapels, oratories, or other places to use openly any psalm or prayer taken out of the bible, at any due time, not letting [i.e.,

hindering] or omitting thereby the service or any part thereof." And there was a model at hand in the practice of the French and Dutch protestant refugees at the church of Austin Friars, London (established in 1550). They, following Calvin's practice, sang a metrical psalm after communion.[6]

If there is no positive evidence that congregational singing took place during communion in England during Edward VI's reign, there is no doubt that it did among the English Protestant exiles on the Continent during the reign of Mary Tudor (1553-8). In the Genevan service book of 1556, Knox and Whittingham enjoined the singing of Psalm 103, "My soul, give laud unto the Lord," from the Sternhold and Hopkins collection, after the sacrament.[7] Another group, probably at Wesel, sang a hymn specially written for the purpose, "The Lord be thanked for his gifts." Because of the historical importance of this, the first communion hymn in the English language, it will be discussed separately in the third article of this series. I shall now trace the practice of singing at communion from the time of Elizabeth I's accession (1558), when this hymn soon found its way into the appendix of John Day's *Whole Book of Psalms*. The title of the hymn is *A Thanksgiving after the Receiving of the Lord's Supper*. It is not entirely clear whether it was sung by those persons who had received the sacrament, as they waited in their seats while others received, or at the end of the whole service after the blessing (the time at which the metrical psalm was sung according to the Genevan service book). Its length, 124 lines, is a slight indication of the former use. In William Daman's *The Psalmes of David in Englishe Meter* (1579) the title of the same hymn was changed to *A Thanksgiving to be Sung at the Ministering of the Lord's Supper*, indicating a use more intimately associated with the

Fig.1. The Puritan Concept of Communion
Source: [Richard Day], *A Booke of Christian Prayers*, [2nd ed.] (London, 1578).

sacrament itself. Bishop Lewis Bayly's *The Practise of Pietie* (c. 1610), long popular among Puritans, prescribed among the duties to be observed after receiving Communion "first, public thanksgiving both by prayers and singing of psalms," and recommended Psalm 22, 23, 103, 111, or 113 for the purpose.[8] Another Puritan, the poet George Wither, provided a new hymn of even greater length (200 lines), to meet, as he said, "the custom among us that during the time of administering the blessed sacrament of the Lord's Supper there is some psalm or hymn sung, the better to keep the thoughts of, the communicants from wandering."[9]

The most detailed description from the 17th century comes from the Anglican clergyman and later Irish bishop, Edward Wetenhall, in an appendix (first printed in 1669) to his famous "Method of private devotion" entitled *Enter into thy Closet*. He advised the following conduct for the devout churchman after receiving the bread:

When I have now eaten . . . it may possibly so come to pass, that the generality of the assembly is singing: if therefore the psalm be pertinent and sense (as it is to be lamented many which are sung in the Church are scarcely so) it is meet I join with them: if it be not, I see not how I can join with them any further, than by praising God in my mind, by meditating in such pertinent sense as

possibly the translators of the psalms have corrupted . . . : and thus meditating, wait till it comes to my turn to drink of that holy cup. . . . Having thus received, in case of such psalm sung, as before allowable, I join therein; otherwise, I employ my devotion as I did after my partaking of the bread till all having received, the church prayers afterwards begin.[10]

Quite clearly, then, singing during the administration of the sacrament was a normal practice, even in Puritan circles, though it may have been a metrical psalm more often than a hymn. John Playford, in his three-part psalm book of 1677, provided a metrical paraphrase of the Gloria in Excelsis ("All glory be to God on high"), with a new tune, to be sung "after the Holy Communion":[11] this was reprinted in several collections. Daniel Warner, another eager psalmodist, in 1694 printed Psalm 103 in Sternhold's version with the WESTMINSTER and the heading "At the Communion."

The high-church movement of Queen Anne's reign (1702-14) was partly promoted by parochial religious societies, which encouraged both congregational singing and more frequent attendance at communion.[12] Tate and Brady's *Supplement to the New Version of Psalms* (1700), which was authorized by the Queen in Council in 1703, contained three "additional

Matth XVIII 1.20 I Cor. XI.23 24. 25. 26..

Fig.2. A High-Church Ideal of Communion in Queen Anne's Time
Source: C. Wheatly, *The Church of England Man's Companion*, 2nd ed. (Oxford, 1714).

hymns for the Holy Sacrament," all paraphrases of scripture. One of these, "To God be glory, peace on earth," was sung "instead of the first psalm, every first Sunday of the month" at meetings of a religious society in a London parish, no doubt by way of rehearsal for the sacrament, which was traditionally celebrated on the first Sunday of each month.[13] A scheme of this kind is found in several sources in the first half of the 18th century. Edmund Gibson, bishop of London, included a "Method or course of singing in church" in the Charge to the clergy of his diocese delivered in 1724, which gave a selection of metrical psalms to cover the services in a parish church for six months.[14] In addition to the psalms for each Sunday, there were "psalms proper, to be sung on particular days and occasions" that included five "for the Holy Sacrament." All the texts were taken from the Old Version of Sternhold and Hopkins, and all were psalms. But a Nottingham publication of 1734, after giving Gibson's scheme and providing music to go with all the psalms selected, added "Five hymns for the Holy Sacrament"—the three from Tate and Brady ("To God be glory, peace on earth" was now entitled *The Thanksgiving in the Church Communion Time*) and two others.[15] Similarly a selection of metrical psalms for use at Gosport parish church (near Portsmouth), published about 1745, had a supplement of "Hymns for the Festivals and other solemn Occasions," which included the three communion hymns from Tate and Brady. A calendar for a "course of two months" at the end of the book shows that one of these was sung as a "Communion Hymn" on the monthly "Sacrament Sundays" with the tune YORK.[16]

The custom of singing a communion hymn may have persisted in such provincial places, but in general it was probably on the wane during the long religious decline of the Georgian Church. A correspondent wrote to *The Gentleman's Magazine* in 1749: "Would it not be very laudable to revive the primitive custom of singing a suitable psalm, or hymn, at our communions?"[17] There is little trace of this "primitive custom" in ordinary London parish churches in the later 18th century. But in country churches, where the voluntary choir and band was a well established institution, the communion hymn was still sung. Examples are to be found in such widely used and imitated country psalmody collections as William Tans'ur's *A Compleat Melody* (five editions, 1734-43) and William Knapp's *A Sett of New Psalm Tunes and Anthems* (eight editions, 1738-70). Some collections even had anthems designed to be sung by country choirs during the sacrament.[18] In America this Anglican tradition was officially recognized in the Prayer Book of the Protestant Episcopal Church, where a rubric "Here may be sung a Hymn" was inserted before the administration.

The other area in which the sacramental hymn was preserved was in the Methodist revival, which began as a strict high-church movement within the Church of England—indeed it was, in some sense, directly descended from the religious societies of Queen Anne's time.[19] The new fervour brought by the Wesleys to the observance of communion is nowhere better seen than in their *Hymns for the Lord's Supper* (1745). In the preface to this collection, based on Daniel Brevint's *The Christian Sacrament and Sacrifice* (1673), Wesley avowed the doctrine of Real Presence in the sacrament, which had been explicitly abrogated at the Reformation; and, as we shall see, he expressed this doctrine in several of the hymns. There were no less than 166

Fig.3. Church of St. Peter and St. Paul, Fressingfield, Suffolk: The Chancel
      Photo: Ray and Gillian Harris

communion hymns in the book. Some of them found their way into general Methodist collections and thence into Anglican books: four are in *Hymns Ancient and Modern Revised* (1950).[20]

As the Methodists gradually drifted away from the church, the custom of singing communion hymns was kept up within the Church of England by the Evangelical clergy. Martin Madan's popular "Lock Collection"[21] contained 170 hymns, including a special section of "Sacramental Hymns" which were widely used in Evangelical circles.[22] Basil Woodd, an Evangelical leader of the next generation, brought out in 1794 *The Psalms of David, and Other Portions of the Sacred Scriptures, Arranged according to the Order of the Church of England, for Every Sunday in the Year; also for Saints' Days, Holy Communion, and Other Services.*[23] Its title was perhaps designed to reassure conservatives, but in fact it included many original hymns as well as metrical psalms. William Richardson (1745-1821), the conservative Evangelical rector of St. Michael-le-Belfry, York, compiled a selection of metrical psalms for the use of York churches in 1788 that included only one hymn: one of the communion hymns from Tate and Brady.[24] Indeed at about this time many editions of Tate and Brady's *New Version*, which was frequently bound up with the Prayer Book, were provided with a modest supplement of hymns. Some of these even included the now well-known communion hymn by the Congregationalist Philip Doddridge (first published in 1755), "My God, and is thy table spread?"[25] John Bacchus Dykes, the Victorian hymn-tune composer, who was brought up in a strictly Evangelical tradition, told the Church Congress in 1871 that "when [he] was a lad, [he] was accustomed to hear Doddridge's hymn . . . sung during Communion."[26]

This would have been in the 1830s at St. John's church, Hull, where Dykes's grandfather, a prominent Evangelical, was incumbent from 1791 until his death in 1847.[27]

We have seen how in the early 19th century even conservative churchmen began to accept the use of hymns in general, especially after a legal decision of 1820.[28] A great impetus to hymn singing was given by the leaders of the Oxford Movement in the 1830s, when they discovered the medieval hymns of the Latin Breviary and realized that hymns were Catholic as well as Evangelical. They were also concerned to restore many details of Catholic worship that had been lost at the Reformation, among them the hymns of the Communion Service. J.M. Neale in his *Mediaeval Hymns* (1851) and *Hymnal Noted* (1854) provided translations of pre-Reformation hymns for communion or for the Feast of Corpus Christi, such as *Pange lingua* and *Verbum supernum prodiens*,[29] fitted to their original plainsong melodies. Others were taken from post-Tridentine Catholic sources. Thomas Helmore, the leading musician of the Oxford Movement, in 1867 advocated "prefixes, affixes, and additional music introduced into the body of the Communion Service," including "Eucharistic hymns while the people are communicating . . . The interspersing other hymns than those already provided in the body of the service, if a license, as I suppose we must allow, is yet so justifiable on grounds of convenience, edification, spiritual comfort, and above all, of Catholic usage, that we may claim allowance for the practice."[30]

Helmore represented the avant-garde, but the middle-of-the-roaders were not far behind. Hymn books tended increasingly to be organized according to the Church year, with a special section for Communion. *The*

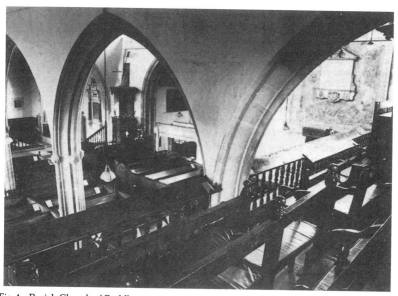

Fig.4. Parish Church of Puddletown, Dorset, Looking Down from the West Gallery
Photo: Ray and Gillian Harris

Church Psalter and Hymn Book of William Mercer of Sheffield, published in 1854 and the most successful hymn book of its decade,[31] had a section of five communion hymns, among them Doddridge's "My God, and is thy table spread?" and two of Wesley's, while the originally high-church but ultimately all-conquering *Hymns Ancient and Modern* (1861) took them from many sources, including the works of modern writers, in a section that grew to 41 communion hymns in the revised edition of 1950. An Anglo-Catholic manual for choirmasters published in 1901 advocated singing during the sacrament chiefly because it was a revival of the medieval *communio:* "A short 'Communion,' i.e., a sentence or hymn after the *Agnus Dei* to continue the devotion of those not communicating, and *while the administration of the Communion is going on,* is very useful, if wished." The author suggested sev-

eral short anthems and several hymns which might be used for this purpose.[32] The practice of singing the Agnus Dei or other hymns at this point in the service had been legally vindicated by an important judgment in 1890, in which the Archbishop of Canterbury, Edward Benson, surveyed the history of the custom from the Reformation onwards.[33]

Thus the wheel had come full circle, with the restoring of Catholic practice more than three centuries after its abolition. Yet, as I have shown, there had never been a time in the Church of England when the old custom had been entirely extinct; it could serve evangelical as well as liturgical purpose, and could be adapted to any theological framework. In the next two articles I shall consider the communion hymns that were used in the 16th, 17th, and 18th centuries, and the tunes to which they were sung.

A word should perhaps be added about the physical setting of communion, which changed radically in course of time, reflecting theological change. The Puritan notion of communion was of an actual supper, distributed by the minister and consumed by the congregation gathered around a plain wooden table in the body of the church, as shown in Fig. 1. (page 95) It prevailed for the first hundred years after the Reformation. Any singing would have been done unaccompanied, by the communicants themselves, standing or even seated round the table. The high-church conception, introduced briefly by Archbishop Laud in the 1630s and more lastingly after the Restoration of Charles II in 1660, is illustrated in Fig. 2. (page 96) The communicants kneel before a stone altar in the chancel, at the east end of the church, and receive the elements individually from the priest. This is hardly a convenient arrangement for singing, but, increasingly after 1700, parish churches had choirs to sing on the congregation's behalf, and organs became more common.

Fig. 3 (page 98) shows the chancel of a medieval church in Suffolk, looking east. The 15th-century choir stalls survived the Reformation, but they would not again

house a choir until the mid-19th century: at that date, also, a cross would once more adorn the altar. In front of the altar is seen the modest communion rail at which the congregation knelt to receive the sacrament. Fig. 4 (page 100) shows the church of Puddletown, Dorset (Thomas Hardy's church), also a medieval building, but with 17th-century furnishings, erected under pressure from Laud. The altar is hidden at the left of the picture, but the communion rail, surrounding it on three sides, can be seen; so can the pulpit and box pews. In the foreground is the west gallery that housed the 18th-century choir and band, and later the organ (out of sight at the right of the picture). On "Sacrament Sundays" the vicar, after descending from the pulpit, would go to the vestry to change his gown for a surplice, and take his place at the altar to consecrate the bread and wine. Communicants would come, a few at a time in order of social precedence, to kneel at the altar rail; then they returned to their pews, to sing, meditate, or listen to an anthem from the gallery, until all had partaken of the sacrament. Then the vicar would read the closing words of the service from his place beside the altar, and dismiss the people with his blessing.

Footnotes

[1]Horton Davies, *Worship and Theology in England,* III (Princeton, 1961), p. 58.

[2]See, for instance, John A. Latrobe, *The Music of the Church* (London, 1831), p. 283; John A. Baxter, *Harmonia Sacra* (London, 1840), p. xi.

[3]Edmund H. Fellowes, *English Cathedral Music,* 4th ed. (London, 1948), pp. 30-3.

[4]Francis Procter, *A History of the Book of Common Prayer,* 6th ed. (London and Cambridge, 1864), pp. 314, 325.

[5]Ralph T. Daniel and Peter le Huray, comp., *The Sources of English Church Music 1549-1660* (London, 1972), p. 67.

[6]Nicholas Temperley, *The Music of the English Parish Church* (Cambridge, 1979), I, pp. 17-18.

[7]*The Forme of Prayers and Ministration of the Sacraments . . . Used in the Englishe Congregation at Geneva* (Geneva, 1556), p. 79.

[8]Lewis Bayly, *The Practise of Pietie,* 3rd ed. (London, 1613), pp. 468, 785. This is the earliest surviving edition (STC 1602): the date of publication of the first edition is not known.

[9]George Wither, *The Hymnes and Songs of the Church* (London, 1623). This and other English communion hymns will be described in my fourth article.

[10][Edward Wetenhall], *Perswasives with Directions to the Frequent and Holy Use of the Lords Supper. By way of Appendix to the Method of Private Devotion* (London, 1669), pp. 403-6.

[11]John Playford, *The Whole Book of Psalms . . . in Three Parts* (London, 1677): 19 later editions, 1694-1757. The tune is printed in Maurice Frost, *English and Scottish Psalm and Hymn Tunes c. 1543-1677* (London, 1953), no. 199.

[12]J. Wickham Legg, "London Church Services In and About the Reign of Queen Anne," Transactions of the St. Paul's Ecclesiological Society, VI (1906-10), 1-34.

[13]*A Form of Publick Devotions, to be Used by a Religious Society, Within the Bills of Mortality* (London, 1713, reprinted Boston, 1728).

[14]Edmund Gibson, *The Excellent Use of Psalmody* (London, [1725]).

[15]R[ichard] W[illis], *The Excellent Use of Psalmody* (Nottingham, 1734).

[16]Temperley, I, p. 125, fig. 4.

[17]*The Gentleman's Magazine,* XIX (1749), p. 438.

[18]For example, William Knapp, *A Sett of New Psalm Tunes and Anthems* (London, 1738); Abraham Adams, *The Psalmist's New Companion,* 10th ed. (London, [c.1775]); Joseph Key, *Eleven Anthems, Book II* (Nuneaton, [c.1790]).

(Continued on page 105)

The Anglican Communion Hymn
(Continued from page 101)

[19]Frederick W. Wilson, *The Importance of the Reign of Queen Anne in English Church History* (Oxford, 1911), pp. 42-3.

[20]Nos. 394, 395, 420, 421.

[21]*A Collection of Psalms and Hymns . . . published by the Reverend Mr. Madan.* London: Printed by Henry Cook: and Sold at the Lock Hospital, near Hyde Park. 1760. The first edition with music appeared in 1769.

[22]Louis F. Benson, *The English Hymn: Its Development and Use in Worship* (Richmond, 1915; reprinted 1962), p. 330.

[23]Benson, p. 351.

[24][William Richardson], *A Collection of Psalms* (York, 1788); 20 later eds. See Nicholas Temperley, *Jonathan Gray and Church Music in York*, St. Anthony's Hall Publications, No. 51 (York, 1977).

[25]Benson, p. 347.

[26]*Report of the Proceedings of the Church Congress Held in Nottingham, . . . 1871* (London, [1871]), p. 378.

[27]J.T. Fowler, ed., *The Life and Letters of John Bacchus Dykes* (London, 1897), pp. 1, 6.

[28]See the first article in this series, *The Hymn* 30, 1 (January 1979), p. 11.

[29]*Hymns Ancient and Modern Revised*, nos. 383, 384.

[30]Thomas Helmore, *On Church Music* [a paper read to the Church Congress at Wolverhampton in 1867] (London, 1868), pp. 18-19.

[31]Benson, p. 508.

[32]James Baden Powell, *Choralia: A Handy Book for Parochial Precentors and Choirmasters* (London, New York & Bombay, 1901), p. 130.

[33]*Read & Others v. The Bishop of Lincoln: Law Times*, LXIV n.s. (1891), pp. 149-80. The archbishop's judgment was largely upheld on appeal to the Privy Council.

The Anglican Communion Hymn

Part 3. The First Communion Hymn

The first communion hymn in the English language, entitled "A Thanksgiving After the Receiving of the Lord's Supper," won a permanent place in *The Whole Book of Psalms* (also known as "Sternhold and Hopkins") which, for more then a century after its publication in 1562, was almost the only book used for congregational singing in England. In addition to metrical versions of all 150 psalms and nine alternate versions, this book in its complete form (1569) contained 21 additional texts, some scriptural, some liturgical, and some original. Of the nine original hymns, the Communion Hymn was the one which the great hymnologist John Julian regarded as "historically of the most importance."[1]

This hymn, as I showed in my last article, was frequently sung during or after the administration of the sacrament in English parish churches. It is a remarkable poem of 124 lines. It is not a paraphrase of the Gloria in Excelsis or any other known text, but evokes unusual symbolism and imagery which I will discuss later in this article. The first task is to establish its origin and authorship.

The development of *The Whole Book of Psalms* took place in three main stages:

(A) *Edwardian editions.* Thomas Sternhold's psalm versions were published in a collected edition after his death with the addition of seven versions by John Hopkins.[2] This was several times reprinted, the last time in 1554.

(B) *Geneva editions.* During the reign of Mary Tudor (1553–8) some of the Protestant exiles formed a Calvinist church at Geneva which published a service book in 1556. Attached to this was a metrical psalm collection,[3] using the Edwardian edition as a nucleus, but the versions were revised—probably by William Whittingham, who added some more psalm versions of his own. This was the first edition to contain tunes. It was further enlarged in 1558, and, after the accession of Elizabeth I, in later Geneva editions produced by those who had remained abroad: these led eventually to the Scottish psalm book of 1564.

(C) *Elizabethan editions.* Beginning in 1559 a series of editions appeared in London, mostly printed by John Day, culminating in *The Whole Book of Psalms*,[4] which built on the Geneva editions and added new versions by Hopkins, Thomas Norton, and others, including a number of hymns. It was reprinted hundreds of times over a period of three centuries, and from about 1650 was known as the Old Version.

The complex relationships among these various editions have been studied by a number of scholars,[5] though a definitive work on the subject has yet to be written.

The Communion Hymn makes no appearance in the Edwardian and Geneva editions, which exclude all but scriptural texts. Like the other hymns of liturgical origin or of new composition, it has hitherto been found only in the Elizabethan editions, where it can be traced back no further than 1561. (The 1560 edition, which probably did contain it, survives only in a copy with the relevant pages missing; the 1559 edition, known to have been printed by Day but suppressed by authority, has not survived at all.[6]) In all Elizabethan editions that contain it, the hymn is printed anonymously.

But an edition has recently surfaced at the Houghton Library, Harvard University, which does not belong in any of the three categories listed above. It is a very small book, incomplete and without imprint or date, printed in a continental Gothic typeface associated with the Puritan printer Thomas Singleton (see Fig. 1). It has been concluded on bibliographical grounds that this book was probably printed at Wesel, a small German city near the Dutch border, in 1556.[7] A colony of about a hundred English exiles was established at Wesel in 1555, but was dispersed in 1557 when the magistrates of the town asked the colonists to leave; they moved, under their pastor Thomas Lever, to Aarau in Switzerland.[8] The contents of the book are consistent with its use by this colony, and possibly by other moderate Protestant groups that wished to continue their worship in the form laid down by the Edwardian Book of Common Prayer. These, who would later form the

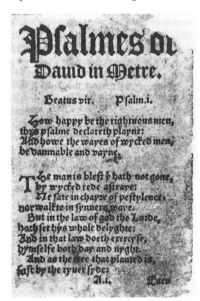
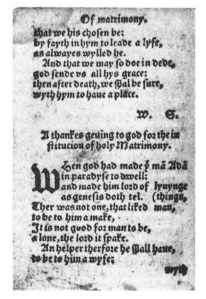

Figs. 1 and 2
Psalmes of David (Wesel?, 1556?, *STC* 2426.8), actual size
Fol. A1ʳ: the title page, with the beginning of Psalm 1
Fol. L5ᵛ, showing the end of the Communion Hymn with the signature W.S.
(By permission of the Houghton Library, Harvard University)

nucleus of the Anglican church, had split off from the "Puritan" party in a well-recorded series of disputes at Frankfurt;[9] the Puritan group, led by Whittingham and John Knox, made its headquarters at Geneva, where the service book and the Geneva Bible were produced.

The Wesel psalm book is the earliest source for several of the hymns that later appeared in Elizabethan editions, among them the Communion Hymn, which appears over the signature "W.S." (Fig. 2 shows the end of the hymn with the signature). The same letters are appended to two metrical versions of the Ten Commandments and three other original hymns. Among the latter is *A Prayer to God for his Afflicted Church in England* which gives us a vivid picture of the plight of sincere Protestants in those times of cruel persecution:

O God, that are the ready help
Of those that call on thee,
Save and defend thy little flock
That now in danger be. . . .

Those, who thou hast in prison laid
For breaking of thy law,
Deliver them, and give them grace
To live in better awe.

O God, do not take them away:
Their likes to us are scant:
We have such need of learned men,
Their lives we may not want.

And if thou wilt that they shall die,
To plague us for our sin,
Yet let them not deny thy truth,
But still abide therein. . . .

And those that fly, O Lord above,
Thine arm be their defence:
And make their journeys prosper well,
That for thee are gone hence.

Let not the sea molest their gait,
Nor wind their voyage stay:
And send them friends in foreign lands
To further them alway.

And those that be at liberty,
And still do here remain,

Give them thy grace stedfast to be
And feel no earthly pain. . . .

The word "here" in the last-quoted stanza suggests that the poem was written by someone still in England, but it has been found in no book printed in England. Oddly enough the first stanza turns up as a metrical conclusion to be added to the psalms in the Scottish psalm book of 1595.[10]

The obvious question, then, is: Who was the mysterious W.S.? Christina Garrett, in her book *The Marian Exiles,* mentions a certain William Samuel (d. 1569), who had served the Duke of Somerset (Protector, i.e., effective ruler, of England during the latter part of Edward VI's reign) and who became a resident of Geneva on 7 January 1557, and joined Knox's congregation there on 8 May.[11] In 1558, we learn, he described himself as a minister of Christ's Church. Evidently he was a leader of the Puritan party. What happened to him after that is not known. But a reference to the *Dictionary of National Biography* reveals that he was a considerable poet or versifier. Indeed he planned no less a project than a metrical version of the entire Bible, and did actually complete the Old Testament, explaining in the preface to the Pentateuch:

My mind is that I would have my country people able in a small sum to sing the whole contents of the bible, and whereas in times past the musicians or minstrels, were wont to sing feigned miracles, saints' lives, and Robin Hood, instead thereof to sing undoubted truths, canonical scriptures, and God's doings.[12]

One of Samuel's works listed in the *DNB* is called "Preces pro afflicta ecclesia Anglicana," which sounds very much like the verse quoted above. And, indeed, a publication of 1566 by Robert Crowley (1518–88), another Puritan poet and exile, actually quotes from the poem and attributes it to Samuel: "by the titling, you see it was printed beyond the seas, in Queen Mary's time, for that it is entitled *A prayer to God for his afflicted Church in England*, and as it there appeareth manifest, it is the work of W. Samuel, which is a man unto me of very small acquaintance: but a preacher he is."[13] Crowley is trying to defend Samuel from a charge of belief in the Calvinist doctrine of predestination; but in so doing he has established the identity of W.S. and hence shown us positively that William Samuel was the author of our Communion Hymn.

William Samuel's Communion Hymn (printed in full on pp. 182-5 below) owes its great length, no doubt, to its function, that of concentrating the minds of communicants on the meaning of the sacrament while it is being administered to a possibly large congregation. It owes its meter and *abcb* rhyme scheme, both derived from Sternhold, to the fact that metrical psalms and hymns in these early days were probably sung to a common body of tunes, at first ballad tunes like "Chevy Chase," later other tunes on the same model. As poetry it aims no higher than the Sternhold and Hopkins psalms, which have been called "doggerel': its purpose is not high art, but the driving home of theological beliefs in language that ordinary people could understand. At times it is barely grammatical. Nevertheless it contains some unusual imaginative touches.

Like the other English hymns of the period, it emphasizes the Reformed doctrine of justification by faith alone, and the vanity of trusting in anything other than Christ for salvation (lines 11-12, 57-60). It stresses the nature of communion as a mere sign and memorial (65-8), not as a re-enacted miracle, and it focuses on the Crucifixion rather than the Last Supper as the event to be recalled in the communion

service. We find none of the expression of joy at the receiving of the sacrament that one would find in a Wesleyan communion hymn: the only strong emotion conveyed is that of man's unworthiness and sense of sin. In this way the hymn brought home the great change in the meaning of the sacrament that the reformers desired. It was no longer the performance of a mystical ceremony which in itself carried the means of grace: it was a reminder of man's total dependence on the atonement for his hopes of salvation.

The self-abasement of the first 20 lines is developed in the next passage (21-48) in which the rest of creation is passed in review, and compared favorably with man: even the ox and mule serve Christ better than we do. Human worthlessness is finally summed up in lines 49-56. At this point, close to despair, Samuel shows how Christ provided the only way out (57-64). This eight-line stanza, centrally placed, gives the essence of the hymn's message. What follows is a careful explanation of the Calvinist view of how the sacrament of communion is related to Christ's sacrifice (65-72). But this dry theology is brought to life in the next 40 lines, which give a series of colorful images and similes derived from the making of bread (73-92) and of wine (93-104). These passages are gruesome, and are in accord with the morbid emphasis on physical suffering found in much North European art at this time. A final pair of similes links the making of bread and wine out of corn and grapes to the unity of Christ's Church (105-16). The hymn ends with a clear reference to the doctrine of predestination, and the customary exhortation to be virtuous—not for the purpose of attaining salvation but to demonstrate that we are predestined to achieve it. Samuel's ideas may or may not be original, but they are certainly far bolder than anything else in the

English hymns of the period.

Samuel's Communion Hymn was not provided with a tune of its own in the Elizabethan psalm book, but was marked to be sung to the tune of Psalm 137. This is, as it happens, one of the grandest of the early English psalm tunes: it is so impressive that Robert Bridges, who had a very low opinion of these tunes in general, was inclined to suppose that it must have been composed by Louis Bourgeois at Whittingham's request![14] The tune has been revived in various modern hymn books as OLD 137TH, but in both *Hymns Ancient and Modern* and *The English Hymnal*, from one or other of which most later collections derived the tune, it was given in forms that detract from the individual character of the original. The original version of the tune has some rhythmic surprises, but when the difficulties have been mastered it will be found both moving and memorable. It can well be sung, as the first reformers must have sung it, in an unaccompanied unison. Of several 16th-century harmonizations, I have provided one that has the tune in the top voice; this setting by William Parsons (page 186 below) is plain, somewhat austere, yet serviceable. It retains the sense of triple time in the fifth and seventh phrases that is one of the most attractive features of the tune.

William Daman in 1579 provided a new tune for this hymn, but it is of little distinction.[15] Thomas East[16] set it to the four-line tune OXFORD, one of the most popular at the time, while Ravenscroft[17] allotted it to MARTYRS. That the hymn was still in use at least in the earlier 17th century is strongly suggested by Wither's remarks, quoted before,[18] but there is no knowing whether it was still sung to the tune of Psalm 137. Playford in 1677 replaced it with another hymn, to be described later; and thereafter it is found only in retrospective collections such as those directly based on Ravenscroft.[19]

A Thanksgiving After the Lord's Supper, in Meter

By WILLIAM SAMUEL

The Lord be thankèd for his gifts
　And mercy evermore
That he doth show unto his saints:
　To him be laud therefore.
Our tongues cannot so praise the Lord　　　　5
　As he doth right deserve;
Our hearts cannot of him so think
　As he doth us preserve.

His benefits they be so great
　To us that be but sin,　　　　　　　　　10
That at our hands for recompense
　There is no hope to win.
O sinful flesh, that thou shouldst have
　Such mercies of the Lord:
Thou dost deserve more worthily　　　　　15
　Of him to be abhorred.

Nought else but sin and wretchedness
   Doth rest within our hearts,
And stubbornly against the Lord
   We daily play our parts.   20
The sun above in firmament
   That is to us a light
Doth show itself more clean and pure
   Than we be in his sight.

The heavens above, and all therein,   25
   More holy are than we:
They serve the Lord in their estate,
   Each one in his degree.
They do not strive for mastership,
   Nor slack their office set,   30
But fear the Lord and do his will;
   Hate is to them no let.

Also the earth and all therein
   Of God it is in awe:
It doth observe the former's will   35
   By skillful nature's law.
The sea, and all that therein is,
   Doth bend, when God doth beck:
The spirits beneath do tremble all
   And fear his wrathful check.   40

But we, alas, for whom all these
   Were made, them for to rule,
Do not so know or love the Lord
   As doth the ox or mule.
A law he gave for us to know   45
   What was his holy will:
He would us good, but we will not
   Avoid the thing is ill.

Not one of us, that seeketh out
   The Lord of Life to please,   50
Nor do the thing, that might us join
   Our Christ and quiet ease.
Thus we are all his enemies,
   We can it not deny:
And he again, of his goodwill,   55
   Would not that we should die.

Therefore when remedy was none,
   To bring us unto life,
The Son of God, our flesh he took,
   To end our mortal strife.   60
And all the law of God our Lord
   He did it full obey,
And for our sins upon the cross
   His blood our debts did pay.

And that we should not yet forget   65
   What good he to us wrought,
A sign he left, our eyes to tell
   That he our bodies bought.

In bread and wine, here visible
Unto thine eyes and taste,   70
His mercies great thou mayst record,
If that his spirit thou hast.

As once the corn did live and grow
And was cut down with scythe,
And threshèd out with many stripes,   75
Out from his husk to drive;
And as the mill with violence
Did tear it out so small,
And made it like to earthly dust,
Not sparing it at all: 80

And as the oven, with fire hot,
Did close it up in heat,
And all this done that I have said,
That it should be our meat:
So was the Lord, in his rich age,   85
Cut down by cruel death:
His soul he gave in torments great,
And yielded up his breath.

Because that he to us might be
An everlasting bread,   90
With much reproach and trouble great
On earth his life he led.
And as the grapes in pleasant time
Are pressèd every sore,
And pluckèd down when they be ripe,   95
Nor let to grow no more,

Because the juice that in them is
As comfortable drink
We might receive, and joyful be,
When sorrows make us shrink: 100
So Christès blood out-pressed was,
With nails and eke with spear,
The juice whereof doth save all those
That rightly do him fear.

And as the corns by unity   105
Into one loaf is knit,
So is the Lord and his whole Church,
Though he in heaven sit.
As many grapes make but one wine,
So should we be but one,   110
In faith and love, in Christ above,
And unto Christ alone,

Leading a life without all strife,
In quiet, rest and peace,
From envy and from malice both,   115
Our hearts and tongues to cease.
Which if we do, then shall we show
That we his chosen be,
By faith in him to lead a life
As always willed he: 120

And that we may so do indeed,
God send us all his grace;
Then after death, we shall be sure
With him to have a place.

Glossary of archaic words and meanings

6 *right:* duly

35 *former:* creator

38 *beck:* signal

75 *stripes:* blows

76 *his:* its

101 *eke:* also

The text above follows the earliest source, *Psalmes of David* [Wesel?, 1556?], *STC*

2426.8, with modernized spelling and punctuation. Two other early sources were compared: *Psalmes of David* (London: John Day, 1560/1), *STC* 2429, and *The Whole Booke of Psalmes* (London: John Day, 1562), *STC* 2430. The following variant readings were found:

60 *end*] *mend* (2430)

85 *rich*] *ripe* (2430)

Footnotes

[1] John Julian, *A Dictionary of Hymnology*, 2nd edn. (London, 1907; facs. repr. 1957), p. 1541.

[2] *Al such psalmes of David as Thomas Sternolde . . . did in his lyfe tyme drawe into English metre* (London, 1549): *STC* 2420. ("STC "numbers refer to the revised *Short Title Catalogue* now in progress.)

[3] *The Forme of Prayers and Ministration of the Sacraments, &c. Used in the Englishe Congregation at Geneva* (Geneva, 1556): *STC* 16561. [Part 2:] *One and Fiftie Psalmes of David in Englishe Metre, whereof .37. were made by Thomas Sterneholde.* See Maurice Frost, *English & Scottish Psalm & Hymn Tunes c. 1543-1677* (London, 1953), p. 3.

[4] *The Whole Booke of Psalmes, Collected into Englysh Metre by T. Starnhold I. Hopkins & Others* (London, 1562): *STC* 2430. See Frost, pp. 13-15.

[5] Neil Livingston, *The Scottish Psalter of 1635* (Glasgow, 1864); Julian, pp. 857-66, 1538-41; Frost, pp. 3-18; [Walter H. Frere &] Maurice Frost, eds. *Historical Companion to Hymns Ancient & Modern* (London, 1962), pp. 31-45.

[6] Edward Arber, ed., *A Transcript of the Registers of the Company of Stationers of London: 1554-1640 A.D.* (5 vol. Birmingham, 1894), I, p. 124.

[7] I am indebted to Miss Katharine F. Pantzer for drawing attention to the existence of this book, which she is numbering 2426.8 in her revision of the *Short Title Catalogue;* and for telling me her conclusions about its provenance and date.

[8] Christina H. Garrett, *The Marian Exiles: A Study in the Origins of Elizabethan Puritanism* (Cambridge, 1938; repr. 1966), pp. 47, 50-3.

[9] Edward Arber, ed., *A Brief Discourse of the Troubles at Frankfort 1554-1558 A.D. Attributed to William Whittingham, Dean of Durham.* London, 1907.

[10] Livingston, Appendix, p. vi.

[11] Garrett, pp. 281-2.

[12] William Samuel, *The Abridgemente of Goddes Statutes in Myter* (London, 1551): *STC* 21690, fol. A2r.

[13] Robert Crowley, *An Apologie, or Defence, of Those Englishe Writers & Preachers which Cerberus the Three Headed Dog of Hell, Chargeth with False Doctrine, Under the Name of Predestination.* London, 1566: *STC* 6077. (In the quoted passage Crowley was himself quoting the anonymous "Cerberus.")

[14] Robert Bridges, "A Practical Discosure on Some Principles of Hymn-Singing," *Journal of Theological Studies,* I (1899-1900), pp. 40-63 (p. 56).

[15] Frost, tune no. 191.

[16] *The Whole Booke of Psalmes: With their Wonted Tunes . . . Composed into Foure Partes* (London: Thomas Est, 1592): *STC* 2482.

[17] Thomas Ravenscroft, ed., *The Whole Booke of Psalmes . . . Composed into 4. Partes* (London, 1621): *STC* 2575.

[18] *The Hymn,* vol. XXX, no. 2 (April 1979), p. 95.

[19] For example, T[homas] M[athew], *The Whole Booke of Psalms, As They are Now Sung in the Churches* (London, 1688); Ravenscroft, rev. William Turner, *The Whole Book of Psalm-Tunes* (London, 1728).

Version by William Parsons, 1563

MEDIUS CONTRA TENOR

The Lord be than - ked for his gifts And mer - cy ev - er - more

TENOR BASSUS

That he doth show un - to his saints: To him be laud there - fore.

Our tongues can - not so praise the Lord As he doth right de - serve;

Our hearts can - not of him so think As he doth us pre - serve.

The music of this version is a setting by William Parsons in *The Whole Psalmes in Foure Partes* (London: John Day, 1563: *STC* 2431). Note values have been halved and the music transposed up a tone. Time signatures, barlines, and accidentals are editorial. In the original, all phrases except the last end with a half note and half rest, and the rhythm of m. 20 is a half and two quarters. (These changes have been made on the basis of other early sources of the tune.)

The Anglican Communion Hymn

Part 4. From Wither to Wesley

During the first 200 years after the English Reformation, it was customary in many Anglican churches, as I have shown, to sing a hymn or metrical psalm during or after the administration of the sacrament. A number of hymns were written or used for this purpose. In this concluding article I shall consider the more imporant Anglican communion hymns of this period, one at a time, in chronological order. After the first line of each hymn I give its author, date, meter, and length; then follow page references to Julian (*J*) and Parks (*P*).[1] Next comes a discussion of the hymn's content, use, and the tune or tunes to which it was sung.

1. *The Lord be thanked for his gifts.* (William Samuel, c.1556, DCM, 124 lines. *J*, 1541; *P*, 114.)

This, the first Anglican communion hymn, was discussed and printed in full in the third article of this series.[2]

[1a. *With glory and with honor now. P,* 139.]

According to Maurice Frost,[3] a new hymn beginning in this way was printed by William Damon in *The Psalmes of David in English Meter* (London, 1579), with the title "A

Thanksgiving to be Sung at the Ministering of the Lord's Supper," and was set to Damon's tune for Psalm 149. The words, however, have no apparent connection with communion, and in fact they turn out to be the second half of Psalm 149 in the metrical version of Sternhold and Hopkins. On closer inspection of the source it turns out that this "hymn" is merely a continuation of Psalm 149, which begins on the previous page.[4] The heading which deceived Frost (and also Parks, who listed this as an original hymn) is merely a running head, referring to the beginning of No. 1 ("The Lord be thanked for his gifts") further down the same page.

2. *That favor, Lord, which of thy grace.* (George Wither, 1623, DCM, 200 lines. Not in *J* or *P*.)

An important original contribution to the repertory was made by George Wither (1588-1667), as part of his determined effort to broaden and elevate the poetry of Anglican worship. In addition to versions of the psalms and other scriptural lyrics, he provided in *The Hymnes and Songs of the Church* (London, 1623) a comprehensive selection of original hymns for festivals, seasons and occasions. In this case there is no doubt that the hymns were meant to be used in church, and Wither obtained a patent from King James ordering the Stationers' Company to bind up the book with every copy of Sternhold and Hopkins's *Psalms.*[5] The Company managed to evade the order, and Wither's hymns had to wait until the 19th century before they passed into common use.

Wither's hymn "For the Communion," also headed "Song LXXXIII," is given a clear purpose by the author's prefatory remarks: "We have a custom amongst us, that, during the time of administering the blessed sacrament of the Lord's Supper, there is some psalm or hymn sung, the better to keep the thoughts of the communicants from wandering after vain objects: This song therefore (expressing a true thankfulness, together with what ought to be our faith concerning that mystery, in such manner as the vulgar capacity may be capable thereof) is offered up to their devotion, who shall please to receive it." The text begins with a milder assertion of Calvinistic theology than we found in No. 1. It clearly states the doctrine of justification by faith alone, but equivocates concerning the real presence of Christ in the elements: "We do no gross realities/ Of flesh in this conceive,/ Or, that their proper qualities/ The bread and wine do leave;/ Yet, . . . though the outward elements/ For signs acknowledged be,/ We cannot say thy sacraments/ Things only signal be./ . . . Thy Real Presence we avow,/ And know it so divine/ That carnal reason knows not how/ That presence to define." Wither thus leaves precise doctrine unstated ("This mystery, we must confess,/ Our reach doth far exceed"), and similarly avoids explicit reference to election and predestination. In the

later stanzas of the hymn it becomes clear that his purpose is ecumenical, and that he sees the sacrament as a mystical union in which sectarian differences, so strident in his time, could be submerged in the common love of Christ: "Oh, let us not hereafter so/ About mere words contend,/ The while our crafty common foe/ Procures on us his end:/ But if in essence we agree,/ Let all with love assay/ A help unto the weak to be,/ And for each other pray./ Love is that blessed cément, Lord,/ Which must us reunite;/ In bitter speeches, fire and sword,/ It never took delight:/ The weapons those of malice are,/ And they themselves beguile/ Who dream that such ordainèd were/ Thy Church to reconcile." The last two stanzas express this feeling in calmer and milder terms, and would be well suited for use at communion today, especially where an ecumenical emphasis is desired. They have been transcribed on the next page.

The tunes of Wither's hymns were provided by no less a composer than Orlando Gibbons (1583-1625). They were written in a variety of meters to suit the verse, and only one of them, "Song 3" (Frost 351), was in the popular common meter. Perhaps it is significant that Wither's Communion Hymn was in this meter, and hence could easily take the place of Samuel's hymn. It was directed to be sung to Song 3, which was printed earlier in the book to go with the Song of Deborah and Barak. This is a fine, strong tune, and deserves revival. Like the rest of Gibbons's melodies, it was provided with a bass only: I have supplied inner vocal parts to complete the implied harmonies.

3. *Behold we come, dear Lord, to thee.* (John Austin, 1668, 888888, 42 lines. J, 131; P, 21.)

For the Communion

George Wither (1588-1667)

Orlando Gibbbons (1583-1625)

Lord, let that flesh and blood of thine Which fed us hath to - day
And with each o - ther, for thy sake, So tru - ly let us bear,

Our hearts to thy true love in - cline, And drive ill thoughts a - way.
Our pa - tience may us dear - er make, When re - con - ciled we are.

Let us re - mem - ber what thou hast For our mere love en - dured,
So, when our cours - es fi - nished be, We shall as - cend a - bove

Ev'n when of us des - pised thou wast, And we thy death pro - cured.
Sun, moon and stars, to live with thee, That art the God of love.

Source: George Wither, **The Hymnes and Songs of the Church** (London, 1623), Song LXXXIII, stanzas 24, 25, with proper tune (Song III). Spelling and punctuation modernized. The last soprano note in measure 8 is F in the source. The alto and tenor parts are editorial. The false relation in measure 14, produced by the tenor B-flat, is characteristic of Gibbons's style, and seems to arise naturally from the progression of the parts here. But if it is found too colorful, the following tenor part may be substituted for this phrase

This hymn, written by the Roman Catholic John Austin (1613-69) and published as the first hymn in *Devotions in the Ancient Way of Offices* (Paris, 1668), has no direct reference to communion, but was designed for Sunday Matins. It was reprinted by John Playford in 1671, set to the tune of "Vater unser" (Frost 180). For his 1677 collection Playford reduced the verses to common meter and set them to a dull four-line tune (Frost 200). From there, Daniel Warner took the hymn into his *Collection of Some Verses Out of the Psalm* (London, 1694), fitted them to the old tune for Psalm 18 (Frost 36), and called them * "An Hymn. Before the Communion."

* 4. *All glory be to God on high.* (Anonymous, 1677, CM, 36 lines. J, 425; not in P.)

A paraphrase of the Gloria in excelsis, first appearing in John Playford's *The Whole Book of Psalms . . . Compos'd in Three Parts* (London, 1677). This important collection was at first not widely used, but in 18 subsequent editions printed between 1695 and 1738 became the chief standby of parish-church choirs, and was both a source and a model for countless later collections. Before 1700 this communion hymn had already appeared in two other books, Daniel Warner's (see No. 3 above) and the third edition of Abraham Barber's *Psalm Tunes in Four Parts* (York, 1698). Playford and Barber set it to the tune MARTYRS (Frost 199), Warner to BRISTOL (Frost 22). It is a crude piece of verse, full of faulty verbal accents.

5. *All ye that serve the Lord his name.* (John Patrick, 1679, DCM, 32 lines. Not in J or P.)

John Patrick (1632-95) was an Anglican clergyman and, from 1671, Preacher to the Charterhouse in London. His *Psalms* (1679) was one of many efforts to improve on the Old Version, and in 1694 it was rumored that "there would be very speedily an Act of Parliament for the annexing it to the Bibles." But this privilege was accorded instead to Tate & Brady's *New Version of the Psalms* (1696), and Patrick's psalms won their widest acceptance among Congregationalists: indeed Isaac Watts acknowledged his debt to them in his own *Psalms of David* (1719). Patrick inserted several hymns, chiefly paraphrased from scripture, at the end of his *Psalms*; and this hymn was taken "out of several passages of the Revelations," and was not designed for use at communion. It is a general hymn of praise, but a reference to the Atonement in its last stanza makes it fit for communion use. Richard Willis, in *The Excellent Use of Psalmody* (Nottingham, 1734), used it as one of five "Hymns for the Holy Sacrament," and set it to the fine tune ST. MATTHEW'S (*AMR* no. 478).[6]

6. *But, Lord, thy mercy my sure hope.* (Tate & Brady, 1696, LM, 20 lines. Not in J or P.)

This appears in William Knapp's *A Sett of New Psalm-Tunes and Anthems* (London, 1738), a country psalmody collection emanating from Poole, Dorset, where Knapp was parish clerk. It is designated "For ye Holy Sacrament." This is not an original hymn, but is Psalm 36, verses 5-10, from Nahum Tate and Nicholas Brady's *A New Version of the Psalms* (London, 1696). It is a highly suitable passage for the purpose, and it happens to be the text for which Knapp wrote the tune WAREHAM, one of the greatest of Georgian hymn tunes. As the original harmonies are a striking example of 18th-century country psalmody, they are given here with the hymn. The tune, of course, is placed in the tenor. In this style there is no restriction on the use of parallel fifths. (See page 248.)

7. *Thou, God, all glory, honour, pow'r.* (Tate & Brady, 1700, CM, 16 lines. *J,* 801; not in *P.*)

The first of "Three Hymns for the Holy Communion" published in *A Supplement to the New Version of Psalms by Dr. Brady and Mr. Tate* (London, 1700), which was authorized for use in churches by the Queen in Council in 1703 (though, as we have seen, this action was without legal effect)[7] and which reached its tenth edition in 1740. It is a paraphrase of parts of Revelation, chapters 4 and 5, and is strongly influenced (to put it mildly) by lines 17-32 of Patrick's hymn, No. 5 above.

All three hymns were marked "To be sung to any tune of 8 and 6 syllables," and many such tunes, old and new, were provided in the *Supplement.* In Richard Willis's collection (see No. 6 above) this hymn was allocated to a tune called ST. MICHAEL'S, which is closely related to WINDSOR (Frost 129).

8. *All ye, who faithful servants are.* (Tate & Brady, 1700, CM, 16 lines. *J,* 801; not in *P.*)

The second of the three hymns in the *Supplement to the New Version* (see No. 7 above). A smooth paraphrase of Revelation 19:5, 7-8. Willis suggested two alternative tunes, ST. DAVID'S (*AMR* no. 470) or NAMURE, a tune first published in Samuel Shenton's *The Devout Singer's Guide* (London, * 1711).

9. *To God be glory, peace on earth.* (Tate & Brady, 1700, CM, 24 lines. *J,* 425; not in *P.*)

The last of the three hymns in the *Supplement to the New Version* (see No. 7 above). This one is a paraphrase of the Gloria in excelsis, and has its own heading, "The Thanksgiving in the Church Communion Service." It was taken into several 18th century collections; Willis allocated it to the tune NAMURE (see No. 8 above).

10. *Sing Hallelujah to the Lord.* (After Joseph Stennett, 1734, CM, 16 lines. Not in *J* or *P.*)

William Tans'ur (c.1700-1783), an itinerant country psalmody teacher who aspired to be a poet as well as a composer and music theorist, was probably responsible for both text and tune of this hymn, which appeared anonymously in his collection of 1734, *A Compleat Melody,* headed "An Hymn on the Holy Communion. Composed in Three Parts." The first two stanzas, however, were taken almost word for word from a hymn with a similar first line (Parks, p. 107) by Joseph Stennett (1663-1713). Stennett was pastor of a Baptist Meeting House in London, for the use of which he published in 1697 a book of 37 *Hymns in Commemoration of the Sufferings of Our Blessed Saviour Jesus Christ, Compos'd for the Celebration of His Holy Supper*—probably the first collection entirely devoted to communion hymns in English. The hymn has a simplicity, almost a naivety, lacking in the others we have considered. Verse 2 reads: "He gave his body to be broke,/ And unto death to bleed:/ That we his sacred blood might drink,/ And on his flesh might feed." The tune, in G minor, matches the simplicity of the verse, and merits

For the Holy Sacrament

Nahum Tate (1652-1715) and
Nicholas Brady (1659-1726), after Psalm 36: 5-10.

William Knapp (1698-1768)

1. But, Lord, thy mer - cy, my sure hope,

A - bove the heav'n - ly orb as - cends;

Thy sac - red truth's un - mea - sured scope

Be - yond the sprea - ding sky ex - tends.

2. Thy justice like the hills remains;
   Unfathomed depths thy judgments are;
Thy providence the world sustains;
   The whole creation is thy care.

3. Since of thy goodness all partake,
   With what assurance should the just
Thy sheltering wings their refuge make,
   And saints to thy protection trust!

4. Such guests shall to thy courts be led
   To banquet on thy love's repast,
And drink, as from a fountain's head,
   Of joys that shall for ever last.

5. With thee the springs of life remain;
   Thy presence is eternal day.
O let thy saints thy favor gain
   To upright hearts thy truth display.

Source: William Knapp, **A Sett of New Psalm-Tunes and Anthems** (London, 1738), pp. 18-19. Spelling and punctuation modernized.
   The first line might well be emended to "O Lord, thy mercy, my sure hope."

revival better than some of Tans'ur's more pretentious efforts.

11.-18.

The theological trend of communion hymns after 1660 was, not surprisingly, away from Calvinism, but it took the form chiefly of a retreat to suitable metrical psalms and other scriptural paraphrases, and to the Gloria in excelsis, Catholic in origin but unimpeachable because of its presence in the Book of Common Prayer. With the communion hymns of John and Charles Wesley, however, we reach an entirely new phase. Their *Hymns on the Lord's Supper*, published at London in 1745, treat the sacrament from an aggressively Arminian, high-church point of view: there are a number of explicit references to the doctrine of Real Presence.[8] The 166 hymns are arranged under six aspects of the Lord's Supper:

I. As it is a Memorial of the Sufferings and Death of Christ (27 hymns)
II. As it is a Sign and Means of Grace (65 hymns)
III. The Sacrament as a Pledge of heaven (23 hymns)
IV. The Holy Eucharist as it implies a Sacrifice (12 hymns)
V. Concerning the Sacrifice of our Persons (30 hymns)
VI. After the Sacrament (9 hymns)

The Wesleys' communion hymns are notable for their variety of meter, after a long line of common-meter hymns, and for the new tone of individual feeling that they bring to sacramental devotion. In some, the language is too graphic, too strong for ordinary use, for instance in hymn 9: "Come hither all, whose groveling taste/ Ensnares your souls, and lays them waste,/ Save your expense, and mend your cheer;/ Here God him-

self's prepared and dressed,/ Himself vouchsafes to be your feast,/ In whom alone all dainties are." Others express longing for release that only the sacrament can bring: "O thou paschal Lamb of God,/ Feed us with thy flesh and blood,/ Life and strength thy death supplies,/ Feast us on thy sacrifice./ Quicken our dead souls again,/ Then our living souls sustain,/ Then in us thy life keep up,/ Then confirm our faith and hope./ Still, O Lord, our strength repair,/ Till renewed in love we are,/ Till thy utmost grace we prove,/ All thy life of perfect love." (Hymn 35, complete.) In reading this poem one feels driven on from verse to verse as by an irresistible force.

These extraordinary hymns "testify to the deep reverence for the sacramental side of religion that characterized both brothers,'[9] particularly in this early phase of the Methodist movement. They are Anglican in the sense that both Wesleys regarded themselves from first to last as members, and later priests, of the Church of England; that they consistently urged their followers to take the sacrament at their parish churches, and timed their meetings to avoid conflict with the parochial services; and that their view of the sacrament was firmly rooted in the Catholic tradition that continued into the Anglican Church at the Reformation. *Hymns on the Lord's Supper* was many times reprinted—it reached the tenth edition by 1974—and several of its hymns were admitted to the general Methodist collections.

Nevertheless, it is unlikely that these hymns were sung in Anglican churches during the 18th century, except in a few isolated cases where a vicar or rector was receptive to Wesleyan ideas. The movement for hymn singing within the Church was spurred by the Evangelical party, which was predominantly Calvinist rather than Arminian and played down the sacramental side of worship.[10] The few hymns of the Wesleys that found their way into Anglican collections before 1800 generally appeared anonymously.[11] They gradually won their way in the 19th century, as prejudice receded and Anglican hymnbooks began to draw on a wider range of sources. The first edition of *Hymns Ancient and Modern* (1861) admitted several Wesleyan hymns, though none of them communion hymns. But no less than eight of the Wesleys' *Hymns on the Lord's Supper* have appeared in the various later editions, and we may take these as the chief representatives of the Wesleys' work in the repertory of the Anglican communion hymn. They are listed below (the dates are of editions of *Hymns Ancient and Modern* in which they appear):

11. *Author of life divine* (666688): 1875-1950

12. *O thou eternal victim slain* (888888): 1889-1950

13. *Victim divine, thy grace we claim* (888888): 1889-1904

*14. *Father, Son and Holy Ghost* (777777): 1889-1904

15. *How glorious is the life above* (LM): 1904-1950

16. *Hosanna in the highest* (77447.D): 1904-1950

*17. *Saviour, and can it be* (667777): 1916

18. *With solemn faith we offer up* (888888): 1916

The ardor of some of these hymns has been consistently toned down over the years. "O thou, eternal victim slain" became "O thou, before the world began," and several other lines were altered:[12] Julian traced this modification to the *Salisbury Hymn Book* (1857).[13] The intensity of its last line, "My God, who dies for me, for me," was subtly diluted by the change to "My Lord, my God, who dies for me."

But the hymn which might be called *the* Anglican communion hymn of modern times, "Author of life divine,"[14] survives exactly as the Wesleys printed it in 1745, in two stanzas of six lines each. John Stainer's tune AUTHOR OF LIFE was specially written for it in 1875, and is still there as a "second tune" in *Hymns Ancient and Modern Revised* (1950). But a preferable tune, written appropriately enough by Charles Wesley's grandson (but not for this hymn), is GWEEDORE, the "first tune" given for the hymn in *AMR*. This match seems to have been initiated in *The Eton College Hymn Book* (Oxford, 1937).

*19. *My God, and is thy table spread.* (Philip Doddridge, 1755, CM, 24 lines. *J*, 779.)

This classic communion hymn is by Philip Doddridge (1702-51), minister of Castle Hill Congregational Meeting, Northampton, and was written for use at that chapel. It was first published in a posthumous collection of Doddridge's hymns. Anglican churches probably began to use it after it was included in a brief appendix of hymns added to many editions of Tate & Brady's *New Version* in the late 18th century, beginning with a Cambridge edition of 1782.[15] Its use in Anglican communion services in the early 19th century is attested by J. B. Dykes.[16] It won a place in *Hymns Ancient and Modern* from the start (1861), though shorn of its last two stanzas. The usual tune for it was ROCKINGHAM.

We have seen how the custom of singing a hymn during communion survived through all the turmoil that beset the Church of England from the Reformation to the Methodist

Revival. During those two centuries it generated a score of hymns that might be called Anglican communion hymns, either by origin or by later usage. They cover a wide range of provenance, style, theology, literary merit, and emotional intensity, but they add up to a body of verse that is both historically significant and a potential fund of hymns for use today.

Footnotes

[1] John Julian, *A Dictionary of Hymnology*, 2nd ed. (London, 1907, repr. 1957); Edna D. Parks, *Early English Hymns: An Index* (Metuchen, 1972).

[2] *The Hymn*, XXX/3 (July 1979), pp. 178-86.

[3] Maurice Frost, *English & Scottish Psalm & Hymn Tunes c. 1543-1677* (London, 1953), pp. 22, 207.

[4] There is no room for doubt that this is a mere continuation. It lacks the large initial letter used at the beginning of all other hymns in the book; moreover the catchword at the foot of the previous page (p. 74 in the Treble partbook) is "With," the first word of the *text* on p. 75, showing that the headline is a running head rather than an integral part of the page. (I am grateful to the National Library of Scotland, Edinburgh, for supplying xeroxes of the relevant pages.)

[5] [Walter Frere &] Maurice Frost, *Historical Compa-*nion to *Hymns Ancient & Modern* (London, 1962), p. 65.

[6] *AMR = Hymns Ancient and Modern Revised* (London, 1950).

[7] *The Hymn*, XXX/1 (January 1979), p. 9.

[8] Julian, p. 727.

[9] Louis F. Benson, *The English Hymn* (Richmond, 1915, repr. 1962), p. 234.

[10] Benson, pp. 328-49.

[11] Benson, p. 259.

[12] Frere & Frost, p. 349.

[13] Julian, p. 850.

[14] *AMR*, no. 394.

[15] Benson, p. 347.

[16] *The Hymn*, XXX/2 (April 1979), p. 99.

VI

THE ORIGINS OF THE FUGING TUNE

THE FUGING PSALM OR HYMN TUNE is a form whose existence one would hardly suspect from any history of English music.[1] Yet is was a product of the Church of England, and there are more than six hundred and fifty specimens in English eighteenth-century printed sources alone.[2] Its neglect is readily explained by the fact that it lies on the borderline of art music: the musicians who developed it were obscure country singers without professional training; but at the same time it does not fall within the definition of 'folk music' that we have inherited from the Cecil Sharp era, for it is written music designed for rehearsed performance. We may or may not wish to hear or sing these tunes today. But our understanding of eighteenth-century English musical life must be incomplete if it does not take into account a form that was so distinctive and so widely appreciated at the time.

It was American scholars who first paid serious attention to the fuging tune (see Lindstrom 1939; Macdougall 1940, 95–8; Lowens 1953; Barbour 1960, 67–79). Naturally, country church music of the eighteenth century occupies a much more important place in American musical history than in European; America boasts little in the way of opera, art song, or instrumental music, and almost no professional church music, from that period. Many who have studied this music during the last fifty years have been attracted by the freshness of fuging tunes, and by their boldness. Some, grown accustomed to their strange idiom, have come to like them. Early investigators thought they had found a native American product. But Irving Lowens, who was the first to make a methodical study of early New England psalmody and to offer a definition of the fuging tune, established that the form was of English origin (1953, 44). A comprehensive study of American church music in this period is now being undertaken by Richard Crawford, who has already discussed the subject in some detail (1974; 1980; McKaẏ and Crawford 1980). While American scholars have already identified as British most of the tunes that were reprinted in American collections, an independent study of English fuging tunes has yet to appear.

A fuging tune can be defined as a tune designed for strophic repetition with a sacred metrical text, in at least one phrase of which voices enter successively giving rise to overlap of text. A definition as broad as this, however, covers tunes which would not be regarded as typical: for example, ones in which a single voice comes in late in one phrase. The typical fuging tune has fully-fledged imitation, including all voice parts, in at least one phrase, most often the third or the last.

*　　*

---

[1] I have used the spelling of the word 'fuging' adopted by Lowens (1953) on the basis of early sources.

[2] A census of fuging tunes in all British and American printed sources up to 1800 is included in Temperley & Manns 1983.

There is no historical thread connecting the eighteenth-century fuging tune with the *arrangements* of homophonic tunes 'in reports' that had been popular in both England and Scotland in the sixteenth century. A full century separates the last examples of these (in the Scottish psalter of 1635) from the rapid rise of fuging tunes in English country parishes in the 1740s. Nor is there any likelihood of continental influence. Indeed, the rise of the fuging tune is a phenomenon with few parallels in musical history. The country musicians who developed it seem to have taught themselves counterpoint by trial and error, and by pooled experience, rather than by working directly from models in the works of professional composers.

Fuging tunes were written for the use of country parish choirs of a kind that had begun to appear in the 1680s. First, societies were formed, with the primary object of disciplining the young men of a parish by means of religious meetings conducted by the clergyman. Among other activities, the members were taught to sing from notes, to rehearse the traditional psalm tunes, and to lead an improvement in congregational singing (Temperley 1979a, vol. 1, 103–5, 141–62). Once the choir had been formed, however, it frequently began to attempt more ambitious music, encouraged by itinerant singing masters who printed and sold their own collections of church music. Anthems for country choirs were first provided by Henry Playford in 1701 (*ibid.*, 163–4) and soon afterwards by country singing masters. In some northern churches, choirs even began to chant the psalms and liturgy (*ibid.*, 167–70). The psalm tunes themselves gradually became more elaborate and less congregational. Edmund Gibson, Bishop of London, charged his clergy thus:

> I do by no means recommend to you . . . the inviting or encouraging those idle instructors, who of late years have gone about the several counties to teach tunes uncommon and out of the way (which very often are as ridiculous as they are new; and the consequence of which is, that the greatest part of the congregation being unaccustomed to them, are silenced, and do not join in this exercise at all.)

(Gibson 1724). The 'out of the way' elements that were successively brought into psalm tunes at this time were inequality of note lengths, melismas, repeated lines of text, solos and duets, cumulative entries of voices, and – finally – imitative entries with text overlap. The singers learned the music in temporary singing schools organized by the teachers, and sang them from their special pew or gallery in the parish church, unaccompanied.

The first tune with text overlap was by Robert King, organist of St Martin in the Fields, and it was contributed to Playford's *Divine Companion* (1701) as a duet with continuo accompaniment. It was no doubt intended for home use, for its text was a new, anonymous paraphrase of Psalm 101 ('Mercy I will and judgment sing') rather than one of the versions of metrical psalms authorized for use in church. The only reason for mentioning it here is that it was later taken into the fuging-tune repertory, with a third part added, even reaching an American publication of 1764. Another archetypal tune, by an anonymous but evidently well-trained composer, appeared in the second edition of John Chetham's *Book of Psalmody* (1722).[3] Though it has only one minimal text overlap in its

---

[3]   This tune is transcribed in Temperley 1979a, vol.2, no. 39.

original form, it was later 'fugalized', and was the model for several later specimens. Until about 1745, the slow growth of the fuging tune was dominated by these two archetypes and their derivatives (see Table 1). Of the twelve different tunes printed by that date, five were by named composers. Besides King, two more organists, John Broderip and Dr John Alcock, each provided one example.

Table 1   Printed fuging tunes up to *c*1745

Source	Date	New Tunes			Old Tunes
		No.	Fuging section	Origin	No.
51	1701	*670*	2 duet lines	Robert King	
51.2	1707				
51.3	1709				*670*
51.4	1722				*670*
71.2	1722	*106*	1 duet line	Anonymous	*670*
86	1724				
89	-1725				*106*
80.B	*c*1725				*670*
80.C	*c*1725				*670*
86.4	1731				*670*
104	1731-	*597*	2 lines of 4-part imitation	Arthur Bedford	*106*
D1	1733	*653*	1 line of 4-part imitation	Arthur Bedford	
88.3	1733	*857*	1 duet line	Derived from *106*	
		860	1 line with 'late entry'	Influenced by *106*	
107	*c*1733				*106, 860*
111a	1736				*106*
117	1740	*858*	1 line with 'late entry'	Derived from *857*	
118	1740				*857*
111a.7	1741				*106*
118.2	1741				*857*
120	1741	*911*	1 line with 'late entry'	Anonymous	*857, 860*
123	1744	*828*	1 duet line	Influenced by *106*	*106**
124	1745	*383*	1 line of 3-part imitation	Anonymous	
125	1745	*993*	4 duet lines	John Broderip	
126	*c*1745	*567*	1 duet line	John Alcock	

Numbered sources in col.1 refer to the list in Temperley 1979a, 366-90, or to that in Temperley & Manns 1983. Italic numbers refer to the fuging-tune census in Temperley & Manns 1983. In col.2, -1725 means 1725 or before; 1731- means 1731 or after.

* In a 'fugalized' version, with 3 duet lines containing imitative entries.

Most of these early specimens have only two-part imitation, either in lines in which only two voices sing, or where one voice has a 'late entry' and then catches up with the others (ex. 1). Only two tunes known to have been printed before 1745 attempt four-part imitation and clearly prefigure the typical fuging tune. Interestingly enough, these are both the work of Arthur Bedford (1668–1745), the high-church clergyman who had played a prominent part in the formation of religious societies in Queen Anne's time (Temperley 1979a, vol.1, 143). He is known to historians for his love of music and hatred of playhouses (and especially of *The Beggar's Opera*), but it is not so well known that he

144

4

Ex. 1   The end of fuging tune *860*

Text: Psalm 148, Old Version
Source: Israel Holdroyd, *The Spiritual Man's Companion*, 3rd edn. (1733)

was a positive promoter of parish choirs (Bedford 1711, 229–34) until he found that they were beginning to usurp the congregation's right to sing. In 1733 he published *The Excellency of Divine Music*, which he dedicated to 'the Religious Societies in the Cities and Suburbs of London and Westminster, and the Borough of Southwark; as an Acknowledgement of the Zeal, which some of their Members have expressed for the promoting the Glory of God by Divine Musick'. In the course of this sermon he objects to the separation of the choir from the rest of the congregation, so that they alone sing the psalms, proposing instead that they should spread themselves around the church to teach the congregation how to sing. Also, he says, 'such a Society of Singers' might sing 'a short Anthem on every Sunday both Morning and Afternoon before the beginning of Divine Service', and after the service sing 'whatever Psalms, Hymns, or Anthems they pleased . . . because every one might take his own Choice either to tarry or withdraw' (1733, v–vi).

By way of an appendix to this publication Bedford provided 'A Specimen of Hymns for Divine Musick', presumably intended for choirs to sing in this way, after service. The ten pieces are for three or four voices, and include carols such as 'A virgin unspotted' and 'O remember Adam's fall', hymns such as Campion's 'Never weather beaten sail', and 'An Hymn for Easter-Day, The Words out of Playford's Divine Companion, the Musick by A. Bedford'. This last is the one that is unequivocally a fuging tune. It has eight verses in common metre, the first underlaid, the others printed after. The fuging section occurs in the third phrase, and seems designed to illustrate the words occurring at that point in the first verse, 'We then may imitate their mirth'.

Bedford's other fuging tune appears in *The Second Book of the Divine Companion*, William Pearson's undated successor to Henry Playford's book of 1701. This time the text is from Psalm 27 in Sternhold's version, beginning at verse 4 ('One thing of God I do require'), which might suggest that it was meant to be sung in church. The tune has one verse underlaid, with two fuging sections (ex. 2), and a final fuging alleluia.

It is evident that Bedford, though he was careful to avoid consecutives and to observe the rules of dissonance treatment as he understood them (with a lapse at bar 16), had very modest powers as a composer. The music moves stiffly; the harmonic changes are too frequent and lack direction; the characteristics that might make a tune popular are lacking. He keeps text overlap to a minimum, and does not attempt to fit the music to other verses of the psalm.

Reluctance to associate the fully fuging tune with psalm texts was due to clerical opposition (including that of Bedford himself), which in turn was founded on Calvinist theology. The psalms, being divinely inspired, were the only texts that Calvin had thought proper in worship, and the Church of England on the whole maintained this principle to the end of the eighteenth century.[5] The words, following biblical injunctions, were to be sung by all, and they were to be understood.[6] A fuging psalm tune was open to the double objection that it was too difficult for the common people to sing, and that its text overlap obscured the words of the psalm so that the people could not even understand them. Bedford and other high churchmen, who believed in the spiritual value of elaborate music, overcame the difficulty by advocating fuging tunes for use in meetings of religious societies, or before and after service, while proscribing their use in the service itself.

But in the late 1740s there was a decisive breach of this principle, and, within a short space of time, many printed collections from different parts of the country included a number of fuging tunes with metrical psalm texts from the Old or New Version, intended

---

[4] *The Second Book of the Divine Companion: or, David's Harp New Tun'd.* Printed by, and for William Pearson: London, [n.d.]. The date of c1725 given in *The British Union-Catalogue of Early Music* is too early: publishers' advertisements suggest a date no earlier than 1731, and the likely date, judging by the contents, is about 1736–8. The book was reissued by J. Robinson in about 1745 as *The Divine Companion: or, David's Harp New-Tun'd.*

[5] There were exceptions, however: nine original hymns were printed, for instance, in Sternhold and Hopkins's *The Whole book of Psalms* (London 1562). In many churches there was a tradition of singing a hymn during the celebration of communion (Temperley 1979b). It was widely held that only the Old Version (Sternhold and Hopkins) or Tate and Brady's *New Version* of 1696 could legally be sung in church.

[6] For instance, the Reverend George Lavington, in a sermon preached at Worcester Cathedral on the occasion of the Three Choirs Festival, 8 September 1725, said: 'Our *present Church music* has it's share and due *proportion* of *influence* and *use*. Especially *1st*. When it is *plain* and *intelligible* . . . whereas in *compounded music*, consisting of several *parts*, where *different* words are sung at *one* and the *same* time, a common auditor is distracted, and the *sense* overwhelm'd and stifled in the *sound:* no *particular passion* is mov'd; nor consequently *devotion* rais'd . . . I presume men *sing*, especially in the *Church*, with the same design that they *speak*, i.e. so as to be understood . . . Unless, according to St. *Paul, I sing with the understanding,* i.e. so as to be understood . . . there can be no such thing as *edification:* if any kind of *devotion* is raised, 'tis that which hath *ignorance* for its *mother;* and a sort of *Popery* is brought even into *music*' (Lavington 1725, 13–15). Lavington's text was Ephesians 5.18–20; others frequently adduced in this connection were I Corinthians 14.19, Colossians 3.16, and – as showing that *all* are to sing psalms – Psalm 148.112–13, Psalm 150.6, and James 5.13.

6

to replace the traditional psalm tunes and to be used in worship. There is little doubt that by 1750 fuging tunes were being used in this way in many country parish churches.

The growth of this development can be traced primarily in a group of books published between 1746 and 1753, two of which consist entirely or almost entirely of fuging tunes, the others containing a substantial number (four or more) intermingled with plain tunes in a way that suggests their use in public worship. These books will be discussed in some detail. In the same period, there were also a number of books which merely continued the tradition established before by including one, two or three fuging tunes, mostly reprinted from earlier collections: these are listed in Table 2.

Table 2   Books containing 1, 2 or 3 fuging tunes published between 1746 and 1753

Source	Date	Book	Fuging tune content
88.4	1746	Holdroyd, *The Spiritual Man's Companion*, 4th edn	2 FT reprinted from 88.3
134	c1748	East, *The Voice of Melody*, [vol.1]	1 new FT (see below, p.22)
136	-1750	Broderip, *A Second Book of New Anthems and Psalm Tunes*	1 new FT
117.2	1750	Arnold, *The Compleat Psalmodist,* 2nd edn	3 FT, none new
143	-1751	Hinton, *A Collection of Church Musick*	1 FT, not new
123.11	1751	Green, *A Book of Psalmody*, 11th edn	2 FT reprinted from 123.10
111a.8	1752	Chetham, *A Book of Psalmody*, 8th edn	1 FT reprinted from 111a.7
142	c1750-60	Tans'ur, [untitled collection]	3 FT, 1 of them new

For conventions see Table 1; for further details, Temperley & Manns 1983.

Ex. 2   Fuging sections of tune *597*

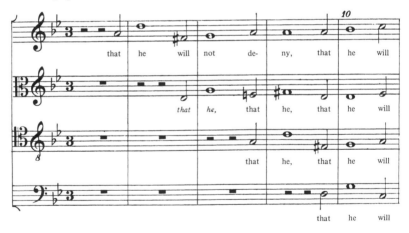

Text: Psalm 27:3, Old Version

Source: *The Second Book of the Divine Companion* [c1731]

The books with which we are primarily concerned are described below. Not all of them carry an imprint date, and it is not a simple task to determine the priority. They are listed here in the order that I have concluded is probably chronological; the reasons are discussed subsequently. Another problem is that most of the tunes were published anonymously, and although many tunes are common to several books, the compilers rarely acknowledge their source. It cannot be assumed, in the absence of any source attribution, that a tune was composed by the compiler of the volume. For these reasons I have felt it necessary to give full bibliographical details for all these books.

8

At the head of each description is a number referring to my list of printed collections of parish church music (Temperley 1979a, vol. 1, 366–90; see also Temperley & Manns 1983),followed by the compiler's surname. In the transcript of the title, original spelling and capitalization have been retained, except that words printed wholly in capitals in the source are here printed with capital initials for principal words only. Under 'format' the descriptions such as '8's' refer to gatherings, not size; dimensions are in centimetres, with the vertical dimension given first. Under 'FT' all fuging tunes are listed in order of their appearance, with page or folio number first; text designations are standardized (OV = Old Version, NV = New Version, IW = Isaac Watts); if no verse of a psalm is specified, the selection begins with verse 1. The italicized tune number refers to Temperley & Manns 1983; 'new' means this is the only or earliest printing of the tune, 'new?' means it is the earliest if the proposed chronology is accepted, 'as in . . .' means 'printed from the same plates as in . . . .'.

129a (formerly 177) BEESLY
Title: A / Collection of / 20 / New Psalm Tunes / Compos'd with veriety of Fuges after a / different manner to any yet Extant / [A later addition to the plate:] Sold by E^d Doe at Oxford, Jos Wimpey at Newbury / Collected Engrav'd and Printed by Mich Beesly [n.p.,n.d.]
Format: 8's; 8.0 x 17.3; [50] pp.; engraved
Date: c1746 (see discussion below)
Locality: Oxon, Berks
Copy: British Library, A.1231.o.(2) (catalogue date [c1760])
Contents: 20 psalm tunes underlaid, with additional verses below
FT: [page nos. are those added in MS at bottom left corners of British Library copy]

p. 136 Psalm 1 [NV]	226	new	p. 158 Psalm 98 [NV]	1161	new?
138 Psalm 5 [NV]	1042	new?	160 Psalm 107, v.23 NV	1112	new?
140 Psalm 9 NV	818	new?	164 Psalm 108 [NV]	381	new?
142 Psalm 11 NV	1033	new?	166 Psalm 128 [OV]	473	new?
144 Psalm 25 [NV]	675	new?	168 Psalm 133 [OV]	948	new?
146 Psalm 27, v.4 [OV]	597	from 104 (c1713)	170 Psalm 136 NV	860	from 105 (1732)
150 Psalm 40 [OV]	531	new	172 Psalm 145 [OV]	326	new?
152 Psalm 57 OV	970	new?	174 Psalm 146 [OV]	1175	new?
154 Psalm 57 NV	88	new?	176 Psalm 148 NV	212	new?
156 Psalm 92 [OV]	115	new?	180 Psalm 150 NV	141	new?

130 EVISON
Title: A / Compleat Book / of / Psalmody. / Containing Variety of / Psalm-Tunes, Hymns, / and / Anthems, / To be Sung / In Two, Three, and Four Parts, / within Compass, as will most naturally suit the Voices / in Cathedral and Country Churches. / . . . / Set forth, and Corrected by James Evison. / London: / Printed by Robert Brown, . . . / For the Author; and sold by Mr. John Bird . . . / . . . and Mr. Thompson . . . / . . . MDCCXLVII
Format: A–Z4, Aa–Ff4; 18.0 x 10.5; 232 pp.; typeset
Date: 1747
Locality: E. Surrey, W. Kent (see discussion below)
Copy: Frost Collection, Royal College of Music, B.II.18a (with owner's inscription "Tx Piercy Feb. 18: 1757" and MS addns. at end)
Contents: pp. [3]–4, Preface; [5–6], List of subscribers; 7–28, Introduction; 29–42, 42 psalm tunes with additional verses below; 93–101, Magnificat (chant-like setting); 102–9, 5 hymns; 110–230, 16 anthems; [231–2], index
FT:

p. 40	BRIDGWATER TUNE	Psalm 47 NV	402	based on 88 in 129a
66	SEAL TUNE	Psalm 145 OV	326	from 129a
86	CRANLEY TUNE	Psalm 27 OV	948	from 129a
88	DARKING TUNE	Psalm 9 OV	345	new

135 WATTS

Title: A Choice / Collection of Church Musick; / . . . / With a / Select Number of Psalm Tunes, / Some with Variety of Fuges / . . . / The Whole Collected and Enlarged / by Joseph Watts, of Fennycompton, / in the County *Warwick* / . . . / [n.p.] Sold by *Joseph Watts*, of *Fennycompton*; and by Mr. *Calcut*, / in *Banbury, Oxon,* 1749 . . .

Format: Separate sheets; 13.5 x 17.5; [94] ff., printed on one side only; ff. [1–2] typeset, the rest engraved

Date: 1749

Locality: Warks, N. Oxon

Copy: British Library, A.1213

Contents: f.[2], letter and poem; [3–8], Rudiments; [9–10], 'A Chanting Tune'; [11–36], 32 psalm tunes with additional verses below; [37–94], 16 anthems, and [72] 'A Chant to Magnifiecate'

FT:

f. [13] Psalm 8 [OV]	*192*	new?	f. [31] Psalm 96 NV	*670*	from 51 (1701) etc.
[14] Psalm 15 [OV]	*219*	new?	[32] Psalm 132 [OV]	*288*	new?
[17] Psalm 40, v.3 [OV]	*66*	new, by 'J.W'	[34] Psalm 145 [OV]	*326*	from 129a or 130
[19] Psalm 57, v.9 [OV]	*690*	new?	[35] Psalm 146 [OV]	*1175*	from 129a
[21] Psalm 77 [OV]	*1060*	new?	[36] Psalm 149 [OV]	*125*	new?
[25] Psalm 100 [OV]	*88*	from 129a			

134.2 EAST

Title: The Second Edition of / the First Book of the / Voice of Melody. / With Great Additions, / The Anthems Entirely new, and great part of the Psalm-Tunes never / before in Print, with some Choice Hymns for several Occasions. / . . . / Collected, Printed, and Sold by William East of Waltham, Leicestershire, / likewise, by M.ʳ Whiteman Stationer in Grantham. / [A later addition to the plate:] for the Use of my Schools. / Of whom may be had the Second Book of the Voice of Melody. / . . . / 1750 / [Engraved by] William Costall

Format: Separate sheets; 14.5 x 17.9; [i], 47 ff., printed on one side only; engraved

Date: 1750

Locality: Leics, S. Lincs, S. Notts

Copy: British Library, A.914.(1)

Contents: ff. 1–2, Rudiments; 3–20, 24 psalm tunes (some claimed as by 'Wm. East' or 'W.E.') with additional verses below; 21, 23, 2 hymns; 22, 2 hymn texts; 23–47, 6 anthems

FT:

f. 4 Psalm 15 OV	*219*	from 135
5 Psalm 47 NV	*378*	new, "by M.ʳ J. Broderip"
9 Psalm 91 OV	*267*	new
15 Psalm 111 NV	*465*	new
16 Psalm 113 OV	*670*	from 51 (1701), etc.
19 Psalm 148 NV	*860*	from 105 (1732), etc.
23 An Hymn for Christmas Day ('Hark, hark, what news')	*419*	new, "by W.ᵐ Knapp"

137 EAST

Title: The Second Book of the / Voice of Melody, / Being a Collection of the / Most Curious Psalm-Tunes / Extant, in Four Parts; / with Variety of Hymns and Anthems; Likewise, M.ʳ Halls Te Deum, / and D.ʳ Tudways Magnificat; all in Score; Compos'd by the most / Eminent Masters for Four, and Five Voices, as Sung in Cathedrals, neatly / Engrav'd and Printed on good paper. / Collected, Printed, and Sold by William East, of Waltham, Leicestershire; like– / –wise, by M.ʳ Whiteman Stationer in Grantham. [Probably a later addition to the plate:] for the Use of my Schools. / . . . / of whom may be had the Second Edition of ᵞ First / Book of the Voice of Melody . . . / . . . 1750. [Engraved by] William Costall.

Format: Separate sheets; 14.5 x 19.7; [i], 99 ff., printed on one side only; engraved

Date: 1750

Locality: Leics, S. Lincs, S. Notts

Copy British Library, A.914.(2), with MS additions

Contents: f.[1], List of subscribers; 2–25, 20 psalm tunes; 26, hymn; 27, 'A Song in the Oratorio of Saul', 28–38, Te Deum; 39–44, Magnificat; 45–99, 9 anthems

FT:

f.	2 Psalm 8 NV	*192*	from 135	f.	16 Psalm 95 NV	*451*	new?	
	3 Psalm 22, v.25 NV	*648*	new		17 Psalm 98 NV	*60*	new, 'by W. Costall'	
	5 Psalm 23 NV	*1073*	new		18 Psalm 108 NV	*690*	from 135	
	7 Psalm 33 OV	*143*	new, based on		19 Psalm 125 OV	*426*	new?	
			948 in 130		20 Psalm 128 OV	*444*	new	
	8 Psalm 34 NV	*125*	from 135		21 Psalm 133 OV	*1092*	new	
	9 Psalm 47 OV	*470*	new		23 Psalm 145 OV	*326*	from 130 or 135	
	10 Psalm 57 NV	*178*	new, based on		24 Psalm 146 OV	*142*	new	
			402 in 130 (or		25 Psalm 148 NV	*370*	from 134	
			88 in 135)		26 Hymn for Christ-	*463*	new	
	11 Psalm 66 OV	*56*	new		mas Day ('Arise			
	12 Psalm 77 OV	*1060*	from 135		and hail')			
	13 Psalm 88 NV	*739*	new					
	15 Psalm 89 NV	*993*	from 125 (1745)					

130.2 EVISON
> Title: A / Compleat Book / of / Psalmody. / Containing Variety of / Psalm-Tunes, / Hymns, / and / Anthems, To be Sung / In Two, Three and Four Parts, within Compass, as will most naturally suit the Voices / in Cathedral and Country Churches. / ... / The Second Edition, with Additions, / Set forth, and Corrected by James Evison. / London: / Printed by Robert Brown, ... / And Sold by John Bird ... / ... and Mr. Thompson ... / ... MDCCLI ...
> Format: A–Z4, Aa–Hh4, Ii2; 17.0 x 10.5; 252 pp.; typeset
> Date: 1751
> Locality: E. Surrey, W. Kent
> Copies: British Library, C.15.v; Royal College of Music, XIII.B.31; and elsewhere
> Contents: pp. 3–4, Preface; 5, poem 'On Vocal Music'; 7–28, Introduction (rudiments); 29–101, 47 psalm tunes with additional verses below; 102–10, Magnificat; 111–8, 5 hymns; 119–249, 17 anthems; 250, doxology texts; [251–2], table of contents

FT:

p. 38	BRIDGWATER TUNE	Psalm 47 NV	*402*	as in 130
64	SEAL TUNE	Psalm 145 OV	*326*	as in 130
84	CRANLEY TUNE	Psalm 27 OV	*948*	as in 130
86	DARKING TUNE	Psalm 9 OV	*345*	as in 130
91	OXFORD TUNE	Psalm 66 NV	*125*	from 135
93	YAR[M]OUTH TUNE	Psalm 108 NV	*690*	from 135
95	CANTERBURY TUNE	Psalm 8 NV	*192*	from 135
96	STROUD TUNE	Psalm 77 OV	*1060*	from 135
100	MEPHAM TUNE	Psalm 150 NV	*141*	from 129a

145a (formerly 176.A) BEESLY
> Title: A / Book of *Psalmody*; / Containing Instructions for Young Beginners ... / ... / To which is added a Collection of *Psalm-Tunes* with select Portions / adapted to each Tune, together with *Anthems, Hymns* and *Canons*; / the Whole Composed for three and four Voices. / ... / [n.p., n.d.] Collected, Engrav'd and Printed, by *Michael Beesly*, and Sold by *Edward Doe*, Bookseller in *Oxford*, by *Thomas Price*, Bookseller in *Gloucester*, by *John Edmund* at *Winchester.*
> Format: 8's; 8.0 x 17.3; [168] pp.; typeset title-page, introduction, and texts; engraved music
> Date: *c*1752 (see discussion below)
> Locality: Oxon, Glos, Hants
> Copies: Mitchell Library, Glasgow (with owner's inscription "J. Buttress 1777", catalogue date [*c*1741])[7]

---

[7] A book with an almost identically worded, but engraved, title page, and with 57 sheets engraved throughout, exists in the British Library, A.1023, with an owner's inscription 'Richd Knibbs, Deddington, Oxon.' It contains 66 psalm tunes, 29 anthems, and other material, but no fuging tunes. I have numbered it 145b.

Contents: p. [3], poem; [4], engraved gamut; [5–17], Introduction (rudiments); [19], 2 chanting tunes;
[20–57], 18 plain psalm tunes (music and additional verses hand-engraved on recto pages, alternate
texts typeset on versos opposite); [58–65], 7 plain psalm tunes and 1 hymn, with additional texts below; [66–71, 74–9], 6 long tunes; [72–3], 1 anthem; [80–111], 16 fuging tunes (2 pp. each);[8]
[112–23], 4 fuging tunes (3 pp. each); [124–70], 7 anthems, with 1 plain tune inserted at p. [153]

FT:

p. [80]	Psalm 8 NV	*192*	from 135 or 137	p. [100]	Psalm 128 [OV]	*473*	as in 129a
[82]	Psalm 9 NV	*818*	as in 129a	[102]	Psalm 132 [OV]	*288*	from 135 or 137
[84]	Psalm 15 [OV]	*219*	from 135	[104]	Psalm 133 [OV]	*948*	as in 129a
[86]	Psalm 57 NV	*88*	as in 129a	[106]	Psalm 136 NV	*860*	as in 129a
[88]	Psalm 66 [OV]	*382*	new?	[108]	Psalm 145 [OV]	*326*	as in 129a
[90]	Psalm 77, v.11 [OV]	*1060*	from 135, 137 or 130.2	[110]	Psalm 146 [OV]	*1175*	as in 129a
[92]	Psalm 92 [OV]	*115*	as in 129a	[112]	Psalm 27, v.4 [OV]	*597*	as in 129a
[94]	Psalm 95 NV	*451*	from 137	[115]	Psalm 66 NV	*125*	from 135 or 137
[98]	Psalm 108 NV	*690*	from 135, 137 or 130.2	[118]	Psalm 125 [OV]	*426*	from 137
				[121]	Psalm 148 NV	*212*	as in 129a

148 KNAPP
Title: New / Church Melody; / Being a Set of / Anthems, Psalms, Hymns, &c. / In Four Parts, / On Various
Occasions. / With a great Variety of other Anthems, Psalms, Hymns, / &c. composed after a Method
entirely new, and ne- / ver printed before. / By William Knapp, / . . . / London: / Printed for R. Baldwin,
in Paternoster-Row; the Author at / Poole; and B. Collins, Bookseller, in Salisbury; and sold by / most
Booksellers in Great-Britain and Ireland . . . . [n.d.]
Format: Unsigned 4, A–Y4, Z8; 14.5 x 9.5; viii, 196 pp.; i-viii typeset, the rest engraved.
Date: 1753 (see discussion below)
Locality: Dorset, Wilts
Copies: British Library, B.647.g. (catalogue date [1751]; owner's inscription "William Costall"); Newberry
Library, Chicago, –VM2082. K67n. 1751 (catalogue date [1751]); and elsewhere
Contents: p.iii–vi, introduction; vii, Advertisement; viii, poem; [1]–2, hymn; 3–104, 12 anthems; 105-6, hymn;
107–58, 23 psalm tunes with additional verses below; 159–72, 4 Christmas hymns and a letter; 172–81,
anthem; 182–7, hymn of King Charles I; 187–93, anthem; 194, doxology texts; [195–6], alphabetical table

FT:

p. 105	A Funeral Hymn		*372*	new
107	PARKSTON TUNE	Psalm 1 NV	*236*	new
109	HAM-PRESTON TUNE	Psalm 7 NV	*1042*	from 129a
112	LONG-HAM TUNE	Psalm 9 NV	*816*	new
114	CREEKMOOR TUNE	Psalm 11 NV	*1033*	from 129a
116	LONG-FLEET TUNE	Psalm 20 NV	*734*	new
119	SANDWICH NEW TUNE	Psalm 21 NV	*320*	new
121	STUDLAND TUNE	Psalm 25 NV	*675*	from 129a
127	KNOWL TUNE	Psalm 50 NV	*350*	new
130	UPTON TUNE	Psalm 57 NV	*970*	from 129a
132	CORFE CASTLE TUNE	Psalm 66 NV	*348*	new
136	WINBORNE TUNE	Psalm 96 OV	*466*	new
138	HAM WORTHY TUNE	Psalm 98 NV	*1161*	from 129a
141	KEYNSON TUNE	Psalm 101 NV	*876*	new
144	POOLE NEW TUNE	Psalm 107 NV	*1112*	from 129a
146	KNIGHTON TUNE	Psalm 108 NV	*381*	from 129a
151	CORFE-MULLEN TUNE	Psalm 135 NV	*1136*	new
153	CANFORD TUNE	Psalm 136 NV	*169*	new
162	A Carol		*381*	from 129a (as Ps. 108 above)
164	The Counsels of Grace A Carol 1750		*350*	new (as Ps. 50 above)

---

[8] The tune for Psalm 100, though its position in the book on pp. [96–7] implies that Beesly classified it as fuging, is
not so under the definition adopted here. It has cumulative voice entries, but no text overlap.

12

The undated items in the list are 129a, 145a and 148. To begin with the last: the catalogue datings of 1751 are probably based on the item 'Carol for Christmas Day 1751' in the book, but the matter is settled beyond reasonable doubt by a publisher's advertisement stating that the work 'will be published' on 24th September 1753.[9] The second edition of the same book has an imprint date of 1754.

The greatest difficulty is in the dating of the Beesly works. There is little bibliographical evidence to help, nor have I found any publishers' advertisement in the *Reading Mercury* or other local newspaper. I have been obliged to rely on claims made in the books themselves, and on their contents in comparison with that of other, dated, books. If 129a was published in about 1746, as I suggest, the strong claim made on its title page would be substantially justified. In 1746 there would have been almost no psalm tunes in print of the kind now published by Beesly, with fully fuging sections in four-part counterpoint. Only the two by Bedford, from the early 1730s, could be considered exceptions. Beesly now printed twenty fuging tunes, of which nineteen could be called 'fully fuging' in this sense (the other one is of the 'late entry' type, and had already been printed several times, first in 1732: see Table 1 above). Among these nineteen is one of Bedford's tunes, the one partly represented in ex. 1. The remaining eighteen are entirely new (on this supposition), and they do indeed exemplify 'a different manner to any yet extant'. Thus a date of 1746 would make the claim essentially, if not literally, true (only eighteen of the twenty being actually 'new').

If on the other hand the *British Union-Catalogue* date of c1760 is right for this book, the claim on the title page is entirely mendacious; moreover it would not have fooled Beesly's fellow-psalmodists for a moment. Not only was the 'manner' extremely familiar by 1760, having been used in at least two hundred tunes in print, but the majority of the actual tunes in the book had already been printed several times. Only two of Beesly's tunes, in fact, are unique to this collection. Two are shared with Evison's first edition (130), one more with his second (130.2), one with Arnold, three with Watts, one with East, seven with Knapp, and many with later collections. Nine of the tunes also appear, printed from the same plates, in Beesly's *A Book of Psalmody* (145a), whose title, be it noted, carries no claim of novelty or originality.

As a matter of fact one piece of external evidence pushes the date back at least as far as 1751. One tune in Beesly's *Collection* is also found in Abraham Milner's *Psalm Singer's Companion* (dated 1751) with the name BEESLY, which strongly suggests that Milner was acknowledging his source for the tune, though of course one cannot rule out the possibility that Milner took it from a manuscript.[10] If Beesly is no later than 1751, he must probably be given credit at least for the tunes shared with Knapp. So the next stage is to examine Knapp's claims of authorship. His title page is (perhaps deliberately) ambiguous: though

---

9   *Salisbury Journal*, no. 810, 3 September 1753. I am grateful to Betty Matthews for this reference.

10 There is little doubt, though, that printed books were the chief means of dissemination for country psalmody: see Temperley 1979a, vol.1, 182–4. (Milner's book is discussed below.)

some of the music is claimed to be 'composed after a Method entirely new, and never printed before', this phrase may refer only to the 'other Anthems, Psalms, Hymns &c.' of the main title. In his preface Knapp is again equivocal:

> Some of the Anthems and Psalm-Tunes are not entirely my own Composition *viz.* the 16th and 19th [Psalms set as] Anthems; but I was desired by some Friends to compose Counters to them, and publish them with my own Works.

He never tells us which or even how many of the psalm tunes were 'not entirely of [his] own composition' or not newly printed. If Beesly's book had appeared after Knapp's, *all* Knapp's psalm tunes would have been newly printed and there would have been no need for the qualifications and ambiguities. It looks very much as though Knapp took them from Beesly without acknowledgement, a procedure that was not at all unusual among country psalmodists.[11]

When we compare tunes that are shared by Beesly, Watts, Evison and East, a new kind of evidence appears in the form of variants. For instance tune *88*, allotted by Beesly to Psalm 57, New Version, appears also, with variation, in Evison, Watts and East. One passage, the third phrase of the tune, suggests that Beesly was not in full control of his technique (ex. 3a): an ugly dissonance suddenly appears in the second bar, while much of the rest of the harmony is quite bare, with many open fifths. In addition to internal parallel fifths, which were widely tolerated in this style, there are parallel movements of whole chords such as the one in the first bar. The other three versions seem to be attempts by other compilers to repair the worst blemishes in the passage. Watts (ex. 3c) changes only the second bar, eliminating the clash; Evison (b) alters this in another way (introducing some bizarre consecutive fifths) and also mitigates the parallelism of bars 1 and 3; East (d) rewrites the passage more thoroughly, and he alone places the barlines correctly for an iambic text. It is difficult to imagine that any of these revisions could have been made *by* Beesly *from* the other versions; what is more, if Beesly were later than all of them, he would have had to take his text from East but his music from Watts, which seems implausible.

Ex. 4 compares two versions of a fuging section of a tune found in Beesly and Evison: no earlier version is known. The Beesly version has some casual dissonance between the tenor and bass parts, which seem to get in each other's way in bars 4 and 6. The Evison version is free of these clashes , and also of the grating consecutive octaves between the soprano and alto in bar 3. It is still far from elegant: but, again, it is surely an improvement.

---

[11] What little information we have about Knapp's character is less than flattering: H. Price, a fellow-citizen of Poole in Dorset (where Knapp was parish clerk, and George Savage was sexton) prayed that he might be delivered 'From doctor's bills and lawyer's fees, / From ague, gout and trap; / And what is ten times worse than these, / George Savage and Will Knapp' (Frere 1962, 697). There remains the bare possibility that although Knapp was the composer of the eight fuging tunes concerned, Beesly printed them before Knapp did; but then one might have expected some mention of the fact in one or both books. In any case this would not affect the dating of Beesly's book, which is the object of all this argumentation.

14

Ex. 3   The third phrase of related fuging tunes *88, 402, 178*

(a)   Tune to Psalm 57, New Version, from Beesly's *Collection* (undated)
(b)   Bridgwater Tune, to Psalm 47, New Version, from Evison (1747)
(c)   Tune to Psalm 100, from Watts (1749)
(d)   Tune to Psalm 57, New Version, from East's *Voice of Melody,* Book II (1750)
The differing tune numbers correspond to differing tenor incipits.

Ex. 4   The first fuging section of tune *326*

(a)   Tune to Psalm 145 in Beesly's *Collection* (undated)
(b)   Seal Tune, to Psalm 145 in Evison (1747)

16

If these inferences are correct, Beesly's book must be earlier than 1747. Recalling his statement on the title page, we note that neither Watts, East, Evison, nor any of the others makes any such claim of innovation, while Knapp's claim turns out to be disingenuous or at least ambiguous. On these grounds, therefore, I feel justified in dating Beesly's *Collection of 20 New Psalm Tunes* at about 1746, choosing a 'conservative' date (*i.e.,* in this instance, one as late as the evidence allows). Had the book appeared much earlier, the chances are that some of its contents would have been reprinted in other books of the early 1740s, whereas actually Evison in 1747 appears to have been the first to make use of them.

This means that Beesly was the prime mover in the development of the fuging tune. Two of the tunes he printed in *A Collection* were quite popular in England and America during the next fifty years[12], and most of the others were reprinted several times. More significantly, his *method* was copied by many compilers, and fuging tunes in the Beesly manner were soon to be sung in country churches all over England and the American colonies. But Beesly makes no claim to have done anything more than 'collect' the tunes. Their composer or composers are likely to remain unidentified.

*   Beesly's *Book of Psalmody* is, by contrast, a derivative publication. This time, there is no claim of innovation; the tunes shared with Evison are printed without emendation, suggesting that Beesly took them from Evison, and they include three from Evison's second edition of 1751; there are also a number of anthems, including several from Knapp's *A Sett of New Psalm-Tunes and Anthems* of 1738 and 1741, but none from the same compiler's *New Church Melody* of 1753. I have therefore assigned a date of [c1752] to this book.[13]

*   *

---

12   His tune for Psalm 133 (*948*) became well known as CRANLEY, and the one for Psalm 107, v.23 (*1112*) was named POOLE NEW by Knapp, to whom it was attributed in many later collections.

13   Another collection published by Beesly is entitled *An Introduction to Psalmody*. It is 'Engrav'd Printed & Sold' but not (according to the imprint) 'Collected' by Beesly, and hence is listed in the *British Union-Catalogue* only by its title (at p.546). However, its physical resemblance to the other two books suggests that Beesly had much to do with its compilation. Many of the same plates were used. This book contains two anthems from Knapp's *New Church Melody*, where they are clearly claimed as Knapp's own compositions; this and other considerations have led me to date the book [c1755] and to renumber it 155a.

D.W. Krummel was kind enough to examine photocopies of three of the four books in the Beesly series, and pointed out an additional reason to support the proposed chronological sequence (*Collection-Book-Introduction*) in preference to the *BUC* datings which place the *Book* and *Introduction* at about 1750 and the *Collection* after them at about 176 John Doe's name, Krummel observes, was a late addition to the plate of the title page of the *Collection*, and is preser on the other two title pages. Thus we have this sequence:

Collection, 1st state	[c1746]	without Doe
Collection, 2nd state		with Doe
Book (145a)	[c1752]	with Doe
Introduction	[c1755]	with Doe

which makes more sense than:

Book and *Introduction*	[c1750]	with Doe
Collection, 1st state	[c1760]	without Doe
Collection, 2nd state		with Doe.

Unless more can be discovered about Michael Beesly, we must assume that he was a typical country singing-teacher of the time, making his rounds perhaps in Berkshire and Oxfordshire, with limited education, modest skill in music (and, incidentally, in engraving), and relatively little success.[14] What distinguishes him from the rest is ambition. He was probably the first to gather in print a number of tunes of the new kind, perhaps composed by one or two creative musicians in his area. His *Collection* is not a general psalmody collection, but a special, pioneering effort. In the next few years other psalmodists caught on, taking some fuging tunes from Beesly's book and adding some more on the same lines. Three geographical routes can be discerned from the lists above (see Map 1): first eastward to Evison, who took two of Beesly's tunes in 1747; then north to Watts in the Banbury area, who took three in 1749, added some, and passed them on in turn to East in the northeast Midlands; and thirdly, southwest to Knapp at Poole. Evison in 1751 took a fresh supply from Watts, and one more from Beesly. After that, fuging tunes soon became common property, and it is more difficult to establish clear lines of dissemination. But in the early stages it is not unlikely that the fuging tune idea travelled quite slowly through adjoining regions. Country psalmody was locally organized; but psalmodists *did* move from parish to parish — it was an economic necessity for them — and several moved from region to region. Neighbouring psalmodists, though they might be rivals, could also be collaborators (Temperley 1979a, vol.1, 176–84).

I have already pointed out that Beesly was not able to write four voice parts in a meaningful way. To say this is not to judge him unfairly by the standards of art music. Regardless of conventions of style, it seems inconceivable that he wanted his music to sound as it does in exx. 3a and 4a. Their oscillation between extreme but meaningless dissonance and equally meaningless blandness indicate that Beesly (or his anonymous protégé) was not in control of his harmony, and did not know how his music would sound.

James Evison's books reveal more than Beesly's about their compiler. They are much more professionally produced, set up in type by a London printer (Robert Brown). Evison allotted names to all his tunes (in all known instances, the names are his own even if the tunes are not), and the majority of them can be identified with an area of east Surrey, west Kent and north Sussex which we can assume to have been his 'bailiwick' as a psalmody teacher. (Map 2 plots the local tune names from the second edition of Evison's book, 130.2; the names off the map are mostly of larger, more distant places.) There is some independent confirmation that he did work in this region.[15] His book is adorned by a dedicatory poem written by Starling Goodwin, schoolmaster and organist of Maidstone, who later published

---

[14] None of his publications is known to have reached a second edition, and the sum total of surviving copies known to me is eight. By contrast, Knapp's two psalmody collections enjoyed eight and five editions respectively, and survive in at least forty copies.

[15] Canon Macdermott found copies of Evison's book at Bosham and Warnham, both in Sussex; the Bosham book had an inscription by a previous owner in Harting, also in Sussex. See Macdermott 1922, 80. Macdermott prints (pp. 86–7) a facsimile of two pages of the book, but he misdates it 1750 (actually they come from the third edition of 1754). The material reappears in Macdermott 1948, 61–2, 46–7, respectively.

18

MAP ①
CENTRAL AND
SOUTH ENGLAND
showing places
mentioned in the
text
NT

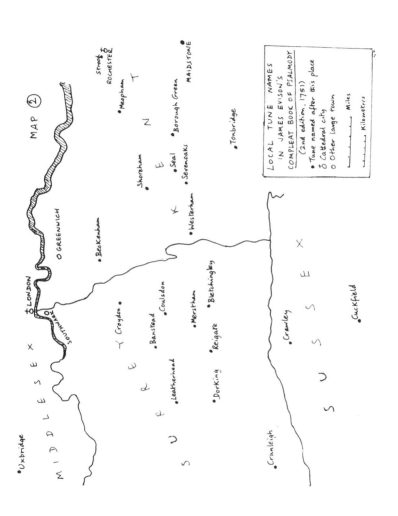

20

The Complete Organist's Pocket Companion (London [c1775]). This suggests some slight link with the world of trained composers.

Unlike Beesly's *Collection,* Evison's book belongs in the tradition of what might have been called the Country Psalmodist's Vademecum: it was complete with rudiments, hymns, anthems and a Magnificat setting, and its psalm tunes were various in style, from simple homophony to florid counterpoint. That the fuging tune was an increasingly popular ingredient is shown by the number he included in successive editions: four in the first, nine in the second and twelve in the third (1754). Few of his tunes were new, and indeed he nowhere makes any claim of novelty. In taking over some of Beesly's he was able to smooth the roughest places, and his versions were often the ones most frequently copied in later books (an example will be given below). But one could not claim for him any notable advance in contrapuntal skill.

Joseph Watts also makes no general claim of novelty for the contents of his comprehensive psalmody book. He seems to have copied the phrase 'Variety of Fuges' from Beesly's title, tidying up the spelling in the process, and he did the same with the three fuging tunes he took from Beesly's *Collection.* Seven others appear to be new, but only one bears his initials, 'J.W.'; the other six cannot be certainly credited to him, since they also occur in Beesly's undated *Book of Psalmody.* The main argument for Watts's priority is that whereas Watts 'tidied up' the three tunes taken from Beesly's *Collection,* he did not do so with the six shared with Beesly's *Book,* so it is more likely that these were copied by Beesly from Watts. Moreover these six tunes begin to show a command of the new medium that had eluded Beesly's composers. They might also be called the hard core of the future development of the fuging tune, both in England and America. All six of them were popular, and two of them, later named NEWBURY (*1060*) and STROUD or OTFORD (*192*), would be more frequently reprinted in eighteenth-century English books than any other fuging tunes (Temperley & Manns 1983). The credit for this success may be assigned with confidence to Watts – to Watts the compiler, not Watts the composer (the one fuging tune he *composed* was never reprinted). As with Beesly, he may have been simply lucky in having among his colleagues a gifted composer whose name has not come down to us.

William East's title pages explicitly indicate that he was a singing teacher as well as a printer, bookseller and compiler, based at Waltham in Leicestershire. Map 3 is based on more direct evidence than that of tune names: it plots the localities of the subscribers to one of his books. We can see that his influence extended over a region with Waltham at its centre, and with a radius of some thirty miles or more. Typically, copies were bought in a number of villages surrounding a larger town (such as Market Harborough), but not in the town itself, where a very different kind of musical practice would have existed in the parish church, with organ and charity children. Where a number of books were subscribed from the same village they probably belonged to the members of the choir. In other parishes a single copy may have been used as the source for hand-copied partbooks.

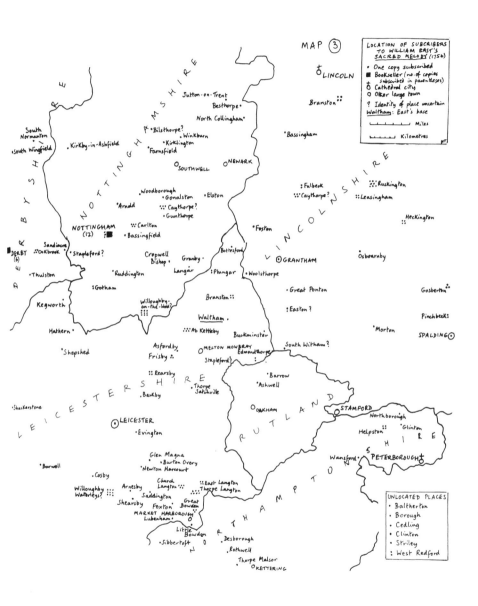

22

East's first book, *The Voice of Melody*,[16] appeared in an undated edition whose title page carries many interesting details not repeated in later editions:

> The Voice of Melody. Or; A Choice Collection of Psalm-Tunes In Four Parts Extracted From the best Authors, both ancient and modern; with Several new Tunes, never yet before in Score; The words Engrav'd at length; and the most Select words taken out of Each Psalm, in the Old Version; regard being principally had to the Plan of the right Reverend Father in God Edmund Lord Bishop of London. To which is added, the Te Deum and Magnificat, with Variety of Anthems, on Several Occasions; The whole being free from Harsh airs, and musical disallowances. . . . Printed by and for William East, in Waltham, near Melton, Leicestershire, for the Use of his Schools; and sold by Mr. Cooke at Uppingham, Oakham and Stamford; M! Rogers of Stamford; Mr. Whiteman of Grantham; and by the Men that carry the Cambridge and Stamford Papers, &c. Engrav'd by William Scott, of Ashley, near Market-Harborough Leicestershire, who will attend any Gentlemen at their Houses (if desired), and Engrave upon Reasonable terms.

It had only one fuging tune in it. But in the second edition, dated 1750 and engraved by William Costall of Caythorpe, East not only expanded the number to seven, but added a 'Second Book' containing no less than twenty-seven fuging tunes. One has the impression that he wished to surpass all previous compilers by gathering in one volume the best fuging tunes from all sources.

In taking over earlier tunes East subjected them to revision, usually in the direction of art music — reducing parallelisms, softening harsh dissonances, and so on. He also printed many new tunes on similar lines to the old, tending towards a standard voice order (bass — tenor — alto — soprano) in the fugal entries. (One advantage of this order which should not be overlooked is that it did not leave intervals of silence when the upper voices were lacking.) East attributed one tune to his engraver Costall, one to John Broderip, and a third to William Knapp.[17] *The Voice of Melody* did not exhaust East's initiative: in 1754 he brought out *Sacred Melody,* which, like Beesly's *Collection,* is a specialized anthology devoted to fuging tunes alone. Its title page contains the earliest known use of the word *fuging* in reference to psalm or hymn tunes: 'The Sacred Melody . . . Containing a Curious and Select Number of Psalm-Tunes, in the Fugeing, Syncopating and Binding Taste . . . '. In his *Collection of Church Musick* (c1755) further fuging tunes appear, bringing East's total to more than fifty.

East clearly possessed greater knowledge and skill than the other psalmodists in this group: ex.3 serves to demonstrate this. It seems that he alone had sufficient control of his resources to make effective choices between alternatives, based on understanding of how

---

16 The only known copy (Frost Collection, Royal College of Music, B.I.10) bears owners' inscriptions dated '1748 Billingborough' and '1750 Wigtoft'; Bishop Gibson died in 1748, and the tunes traced by Maurice Frost include two from the 2nd edition of John Barrow's *The Psalm-Singer's Choice Companion,* which Frost dated c1747. On these grounds Frost dated the East book c1748, and the date seems plausible. For the 'Plan' of Bishop Gibson, see Willis 1734.

17 The attributions to Broderip and Knapp must be viewed with caution. Neither musician printed the tune concerned in his own collections of church music. Note, however, that a William Costall later acquired a copy of Knapp's *New Churc Melody* (see above, p.11).

the music would sound. But his books remained chiefly of local importance. They influenced others printed in the same area, such as those of John Harrott. But neither the fuging tunes East introduced, nor the changes he made in others, were generally adopted.

Lastly, William Knapp, already the compiler of *A Sett of New Psalm Tunes and Anthems* (1738), which would reach eight editions, followed the fashion by bringing out a new comprehensive psalmody book in which seventeen of the twenty-three psalm tunes were fuging. As parish clerk of Poole, Knapp had official charge over the psalm singing in one of the larger parish churches in Dorset, which had not yet acquired an organ. He may well have taught in surrounding parishes, and nine 'singing masters' were among the subscribers to his first book of 1738. This list of subscribers does not give place names, however. Map 4 is based on the tune names of both books,[18] and it seems to show a more close-knit 'bailiwick' than those of Evison and East, in an area about 10 miles by 15 miles. The widening circle of his influence can be charted from the locations of booksellers mentioned on the title pages of successive editions of his books (see Temperley 1979a, vol.1, 180–81).

As I have already suggested, Knapp made heavy use of Beesly's work, without acknowledgment. His emendations improved, and his business methods disseminated, seven of Beesly's tunes. Indeed the most successful of the fuging tunes he printed was one of Beesly's which Knapp named POOLE NEW [19] after his home town (tune *1112*). It was reprinted eight times in England and twenty-six times in America, up to 1800. The only one of his original tunes that spread much beyond his own books was KNOWL (*372*).

*   *

Let us now look at one of the most successful tunes of this germinal period, discuss its character and trace its later history. The tune probably first printed by Joseph Watts for Psalm 8 (*192*), and later known by various names including STROUD and OTFORD, is shown in its original form in ex.5. It is one that is largely free of gross harmonic blunders, which may partly account for its great popularity. It is, indeed, one of the best of the early fuging tunes, more skilful than any of Beesly's. It is also quite typical of the fuging tune as it was later developed, and may well have been a pattern for compilers such as

---

18   The following tune names occur in Knapp's *Sett of New Psalm Tunes* (1738): Sandwich, Durweston, Dorchester, Bere, Litchet, Poole, Gorden, Sturminster, Wareham, Winterbourne and Spetisbury. Those in the 1753 collection are listed above (p.11). Gorden and Clapper have not been identified; Dorchester is outside the area of Map 4 (but see Map 1). All the remainder can be identified, at least tentatively, with places marked on Map 4. For some names, two places are possible (they are shown with question marks on the map). Winterborne is a river, with a whole string of villages named after it (Winterborne Whitchurch etc). I am most grateful to Margaret Holmes, of the Dorset County Record Office, and to Muriel Arber, for their assistance in locating these places. Miss Holmes pointed out, among other things, that Swanage was often called Sandwich in this period, and thus saved me from having to explain why one of Knapp's tunes was named after a town in Kent.

In the second edition of *A Sett of New Psalm Tunes*, published in 1741, Knapp added six tunes named after somewhat larger and more distant places: Bridport, Weymouth, Froom, Yeovil, Taunton, Sherborne (see Map 1).

19   The word 'NEW' distinguished it from an earlier tune which Knapp had named POOLE, but it was soon dropped when the tune was taken over by other compilers.

24

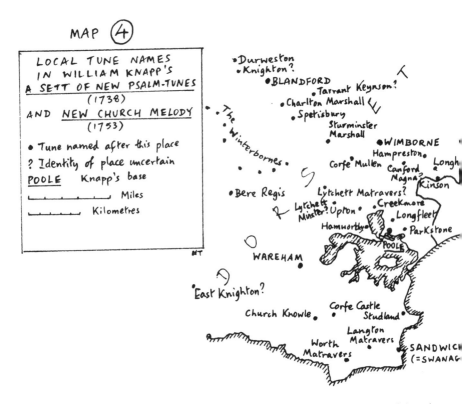

Aaron Williams and Joseph Stephenson who, in turn, influenced later English and American psalmodists.

The tune is in two clearly demarcated sections. The first half is like one of the early Georgian triple-time tunes, many of which are still to be found in our hymn books. Its half-close on the dominant sets off the beginning of the fuging section in a new and faster tempo;[20] the four voices enter at one-bar intervals, coming together for another half-close; and the last phrase rounds off the tune with a strong perfect cadence. There is no doubt, in the first half, that the tenor is the leading voice, carrying the melody, and throughout the tune it is sufficiently prominent and memorable to provide a clear 'lead' to the other

---

20 Watts's introduction indicates that a minim in 3/2 was equivalent to a crotchet in ₵, both occupied the time of one pendulum stroke of a grandfather clock – that is, 60 per minute; while ₵ is "faster" than ₵. Other contemporary introductions, including Beesly's in *A Book of Psalmody*, state that ₵ is twice as fast as ₵, which would mean that the crotchet would be constant at 120 per minute throughout this tune – a dignified pace.

voices. The harmony of the first half is smooth enough, and would not have disgraced a professional; only the movement of the bass in bar 6 seems a trifle clumsy. Departures from conventional grammar occur in the fuging section, with the movement of the outer parts essentially in parallel fifths throughout bars 11–13, the total parallelism between bar 12 and 13, and the unorthodox resolution of the dominant seventh chord at the end of bar 11. In the last phrase only the untreated seventh chord at the end of bar 15 might have caused powdered eyebrows to rise. There are also elements that break no rule of harmony, yet stand out as foreign to contemporary art music: the beautifully archaic '6-5' movement of the alto in bar 13; the open-fifth chords in bars 15 and 17. To end on an open fifth is, indeed, a trademark of country psalmody of the time.

Ex. 5   Tune for Psalm 8 (192) from Watts's Choice Collection (1749)

26

In this particular tune, either by skill or luck or a combination of the two, the section of imitative counterpoint does not produce any great departure from the general harmonic idiom. The most one can say against it is that it has a less clear sense of harmonic direction than the other phrases of the tune: the movement from I to VI in bars 9–10 is repeated in bars 11–12, giving a somewhat static effect. This, also, was to prove typical of fuging sections in general. Some repeat the same chords in every bar until all the voices have entered, and only then continue the harmonic movement. The entry of each voice on the last beat, followed by three repeated crotchets, was also to be a fuging-tune trademark. It probably tended to steady the voices, and made it easy for the choirs to accomplish the imitation without mishap. In this tune no great violence is done to verbal rhythms — another point in its favour, in a practical as well as an aesthetic sense. The fuging section, with its repeat of the verbal phrase by tenor and bass, works equally well with the third lines of the second and third verses printed below the tune ('For in those babes thy might is seen'; 'The sun, the moon, and all the stars'), but not with that of the last verse ('Or what the son of man, whom thou'). It is difficult to say whether compilers paid much attention to such matters. It looks as if Watts did not.

The next to print the tune was East, in *The Second Book of the Voice of Melody*, and he made two alterations which seem clearly deliberate, designed to mitigate the aspect of the tune which was most clearly against the rules: the extended consecutive fifths between soprano and bass in bars 11–13. He changed the soprano in bar 11 to D–D–E–D and the bass in bar 12 to E–B. With these changes, all illicit consecutives in the passage are eliminated except the inconspicuous parallel fifths between soprano and alto. East made another change, however, which actually introduced new parallel fifths: he substituted a minim E for the two crotchets in the bass part of bar 6. He retained the association of the tune with Psalm 8, but substituted the New Version for the Old.

Evison printed the tune in 1751, and it seems that he had both Watts's and East's versions at his disposal. He restored Watts's soprano line in bar 11, but kept East's bass emendation in bar 12. In bar 6 he compromised, substituting two crotchets, G–E, which produced probably the most 'professional' of the three readings. He followed East's text, and for the first time he gave the tune a name, CANTERBURY.

All subsequent printings of this tune can be clearly traced to either East's or Evison's version, and the great majority of them derive from Evison's. East's emendation of the bass, being followed by Evison, is found in all later versions, and thus gives no clue to their descent. The only later printing that follows East in the soprano in bars 6 and 11 is John Harrott's *The Rutland-Harmony or Sacred-Concert* (Stamford 1769). Harrott worked in a region near to East's (see Map 3), and his books are closely related to East's in a number of ways.

Evison's version was taken up by a group of psalmodists in the south (see Map 1). Beesly followed it precisely in his book of *c*1751, and so did Abraham Adams, of Shoreham in Kent, in *The Psalmodist's New Companion*.[21] Adams made a change of notation, by writing the first half of the tune in 3/4 instead of 3/2 and eliminating the double bar

---

[21] The earliest surviving edition of this work is the sixth, dating from about 1760. The second edition was advertised in December 1752 and the fifth in 1756, according to MS notes by Maurice Frost in the Royal College of Music. A work called *A Choice Collection of Psalm Tunes and Anthems*, by Adams, is advertised in *The Organist's Pocket Companion* (*c*1751), and this may have been the first edition of the same work. Adams had a habit of transposing tunes taken from other books into a different key, which helps in establishing a stemma. Several psalm tunes in William Crisp's *Divine Harmony* (1755) are headed 'From A. Adams'. It is impossible to say, of course, whether the earlier editions contained this tune, but those from the sixth (*c*1760) to the twelfth (*c*1795) certainly did. Many of the tunes in these editions are taken from Evison's book, which came from the same region.

28

in bar 5. He also renamed the tune OTFORD. Two later printings probably based on Adams were in Matthew Wilkins's *Book of Psalmody,* hard to date but most probably around 1760, and John Crompton's *Psalm Singers Assistant,* of 1778. They copied the 3/4 but retained the double bar. Crompton called the tune AYLSHAM and set it to a Christmas hymn by the Independent minister Philip Doddridge, though his book was for Anglican use. Wilkins was active in the Chilterns, and Crompton at Southwold in Suffolk.

A more important derivative of Evison's was the version of Abraham Milner, in his *Psalm Singer's Companion* of 1751. The great majority of texts in this book are from the psalm versions of Dr Isaac Watts, which shows that it was intended for the use of Independents (Congregationalists) and possibly some Baptists and Presbyterians (Benson 1915, 122–47). These texts could not be used in worship in the Church of England at this time (see n.5 above), and are hardly likely to have appealed to Anglicans for use at home or in singing schools. Most dissenters' tunebooks until after about 1770 were quite conservative, providing only plain tunes in two or three parts and avoiding the elaboration of Anglican country psalmody. Milner's is the first that included fuging tunes – there are five, none of them new, and three of them are set to texts by Isaac Watts. He sold his book from 'Somerset-Street, near White-Chapel-Bars,' London, according to the title page. (In the absence of organs and charity children, there was no distinction between town and country in the psalmody of dissenters.) Milner must have taken tune *192* from Evison, for his version is musically identical. He set it once again to Psalm 8, but now in the version of Dr Watts, and he renamed it NETTLETON.

The tune's later popularity was largely due to dissenters. Stephen Addington, an Independent minister, included the tune in his *Collection of Psalm Tunes for Public Worship.* It may have been in the first edition of 1779;[22] it was certainly in the earliest surviving edition, the third, of 1780, where it was one of only three fuging tunes; and it was retained in a steadily growing corpus of fuging tunes through subsequent editions down to the fifteenth of 1807. Addington, though he was based right in East's territory at Market Harborough, used Adams as his main source for this and other tunes, as can be seen from the variants and from his use of the name OTFORD. But he omitted the soprano part, and attributed the tune for some unknown reason to 'Dr Hayes'.[23] Isaac Smith, clerk to a Congregational meeting house in London, took the tune and name directly from Addington into the 'new edition with supplement' [c1782] of his *Collection of Psalm Tunes.*

Another dissenting clergyman, Ralph Harrison, minister of Cross Street Unitarian Chapel, Manchester, also used the tune in his influential *Sacred Harmony,* volume 1 (1784),

---

[22] This was advertised in the *Leicester and Nottingham Gazette* in 1779; I am indebted to Karl Kroeger for this information

[23] Apart from the inherent improbability that such a tune was composed by Dr William Hayes (1706–77), professor of music at Oxford since 1741, it would be hard to explain either his relationship with Joseph Watts or the latter's failure to claim so eminent a composer for the tune. The following chain of circumstances is barely possible: an unknown psalmodist adapted the tune from some larger work by Hayes; the tune came to Hayes's notice, perhaps in the first or second edition (now lost) of Addington's book; and Hayes requested Addington to give him credit for it. But this is an uncomfortable speculation. (The other Dr Hayes, William's son Philip, was only eleven years old when Watts published the tune.)

set to Watts's Psalm 24. Harrison was a well-trained musician, and a reformer who wanted to make the music of his services more artistic. This tune, like many in his book, was revised in the direction of more conventional harmony. He left the melody and the fuging section unchanged, but he altered the soprano and alto parts to fill out the chords, including the bare fifth at the end, and to eliminate the non-functional dissonance at bar 15 (ex.6). He also added figures to the bass. Curiously enough he restored East's bass at bar 6, although this reintroduced consecutive fifths, but as this is the only resemblance to East's version I would hesitate to say that it is more than a coincidence. Harrison's main source was evidently Addington, for he included the attribution to Dr Hayes. But he invented yet another name, WORCESTER.

With its inclusion in John Rippon's *Selection of Psalm and Hymn Tunes* (c1792) the tune entered the Baptist repertory, for this quickly became the authoritative Baptist tunebook. Its musical compiler, probably Thomas Walker, also took the tune from Addington, including its name and attribution, but he made another, independent, revision, apparently adding a fresh soprano part to Addington's ATB without even seeing one of the earlier four-part versions (ex.7). As in many late eighteenth-century editions, the intended octave registers of the 'air' and of the uppermost part are by no means clear (see Temperley 1979a, vol.1, 184–90; Temperley & Manns 1983, n.29). Rippon assigned a new text, Watts's Psalm 98, part 2. The tune in this form recurs in both English and American editions of Rippon well into the nineteenth century.

Another type of psalmody book that became more and more common in the later eighteenth century was of a kind that I have called 'ecumenical' (Temperley & Manns 1983), though its *raison d'être* was simply the commercial one of appealing to as broad a market as possible. John Beatson's *Complete Collection of All the Tunes Sung by the Different Congregations in Hull* (c1780) is of this type. Beatson seems to have used Evison as his direct source, taking the name CANTERBURY, but he printed only the tenor and bass. William Dixon, of Guildford, prepared his *Psalmodia Christiana* (1789) primarily for Anglican use, but adapted many of the tunes to the words of Dr Watts as well. He printed this tune without underlay and with an even more unlikely attribution to 'Dr Croft'. His heading 'Psalm 8' did not distinguish the version intended. His name NETTLETON, and his variants, show that he took the tune from Milner. But, like Harrison, he sought to make it more elegant by revising the soprano and alto parts, and by adding figures, grace notes and trills (ex.8). He allowed the non-functional seventh chord and the bare-fifth conclusion to stand, but he eliminated the alto 6–5 in bar 13, the doubled third in bar 7, and the bare fifth in bar 15.

Ultimately the tune found its way to Scotland and to America. Laurence Ding's *The Beauties of Psalmody* (Edinburgh 1792) and Henry Boyd's *Select Collection of Psalm and Hymn Tunes* (Edinburgh and Glasgow 1793) provided tunes for Scottish Episcopal use, and ventured to include a few fuging tunes, *192* among them: Ding may have taken his text from Addington, renaming the tune EASSIE and going back to the Old Version Psalm 8; Boyd perhaps returned to Adams, using the name OTFORD but omitting the *alto* part. The one American compiler who used the tune was Simon Jocelin, in the *Supplement to the Chorister's Companion* (New Haven 1792). He copied Harrison's revised version note for note, omitting only the bass figures, and came up with his own name, DOMINION.

30

Ex. 6   End of tune *192* as altered by Harrison (1784)

Ex. 7   Beginning of tune *192* as altered by Rippon (*c*1792)

Ex. 8   Beginning of tune *192* as altered by Dixon (1789)

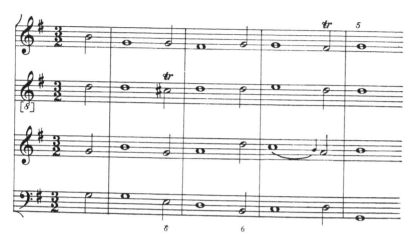

The story of this particular tune is, in many ways, the story of the fuging-tune genre as a whole. Parochial musicians continued to develop the fuging tune in the 1750s and early 1760s, but after that the initiative passed to dissenters and to America (for the later history see Temperley & Manns 1983). In English parish churches, musical reform set in, gathering strength particularly in the 1790s, and more 'correct' forms were provided by professional composers like Samuel Arnold and John Callcott, whose *Psalms of David* (1791) contained a large number, many of them adapted from the works of Handel. These 'respectable' fuging tunes, even the three by Joseph Haydn which were commissioned by William Tattersall for his *Improved Psalmody* (1794), ultimately followed their more uncouth ancestors into oblivion.

But in the more remote country churches fuging tunes would remain in use until the bands of instrumentalists which had grown up around the singers were replaced by a barrel organ or harmonium. Fuging tunes could be heard in some places well after the middle of the nineteenth century (Dickson 1857). In America, they passed from New England to the Southern states in the early nineteenth century and entered the shape-note repertory, where they still flourish today. But that is another story.

*   *

32

BIBLIOGRAPHY

Barbour, J. Murray, 1960. *The Church Music of William Billings.* East Lansing: Michigan State University Press

Bedford, Arthur, 1711. *The Great Abuse of Musick.* London: John Wyatt

Bedford, Arthur, 1733. *The Excellency of Divine Music.* London: C. Rivington

Benson, Louis F., 1915. *The English Hymn.* London: Hodder & Stoughton

Crawford, Richard (ed.), 1974. James Lyon's *Urania.* New York: Da Capo Press

Crawford, Richard, 1980. 'Psalmody: II. North America', *The New Grove Dictionary of Music and Musicians,* ed. Stanley Sadie, 15, 345–7, London: Macmillan

Dickson, William E., 1857. *A Letter to the Lord Bishop of Salisbury, on Congregational Singing.* Oxford: John Henry and James Parker

[Frere, Walter,] rev. Maurice Frost, 1962. *Historical Companion to Hymns Ancient and Modern.* London: Proprietors of Hymns Ancient and Modern

[Gibson, Edmund,] [1724.] *Directions Given by Edmund Lord Bishop of London to the Clergy of His Diocese, in 1724.* London: [n.p.]

Lavington, George, 1725. *The Influence of Church Music.* London: J. & L. Knapton

Lindstrom, Carl E., 1939. 'William Billings and His Times,' *The Musical Quarterly* 15 (1939), 479–97

Lowens, Irving, 1953. 'The Origins of the American Fuging Tune,' *Journal of the American Musicological Society* 6 (1953), 43–52, repr. Lowens, *Music and Musicians in Early America* (New York: Norton, 1964), 237–63

Macdermott, K.H., 1922. *Sussex Church Music in the Past.* Chichester: Moore & Wingham

Macdermott, K.H., 1948. *The Old Church Gallery Minstrels.* London: S.P.C.K.

MacDougall, Hamilton C., 1940. *Early New England Psalmody.* Brattleboro: Stephen Daye Press

McKay, David P. and Richard Crawford, 1975. *William Billings of Boston: 18th-Century Composer.* [Princeton:] Princeton University Press

Temperley, Nicholas, 1979a. *The Music of the English Parish Church.* 2 vols. Cambridge: Cambridge University Press

Temperley, Nicholas, 1979b. 'The Anglican Communion Hymn', *The Hymn* 30 (1979), 7–15, 93–101, 178–85, 243–51

Temperley, Nicholas, and Charles G. Manns, 1983. *Fuging Tunes in the Eighteenth Century.* Detroit: Information Coordinators

W[illis], R[ichard], 1734. *The Excellent Use of Psalmody.* Nottingham: George Ayscough and Richard Willis

* * * *

Originally published in *RMA Research Chronicle* 17 (1981), 1–32

Table converting tune numbers in No. VI to *HTI* numbers

Temperley/ Manns no.	*HTI* no.	Temperley/ Manns no.	*HTI* no.
56	1975	465	1969
60	1978	466	2101
66	1944	470	1973
88	1844	473	1850
106	963a	531	1843
115	1846	567	1749
125	1950	597	1143
141	1855	648	1970
142	1981	653	1371
143	1972	670	604
169	2087	675	1842
178	1974	690	1945
192	1942	734	2096
212	1854	739	1976
219	1943	816	2097
226	1838	818	1840
236	2098	828	1140
267	1967	857	963e
288	1949	858	963c
320	2099	860	1166
326	1852	876	1683
345	1877	911	2332
348	2089	948	1851
350	2091	970	1845
370	1982	993	1788
372	2092	1033	1841
381	1849	1042	1839
382	1960	1060	1946
383	1760	1073	1971
402	1874	1092	1980
419	1682	1112	1848
426	1963	1136	2090
451	1977	1161	1847
463	1887	1175	1853

VII

ORGANS IN ENGLISH PARISH
CHURCHES 1660-1830

Organs in most English parish churches were allowed to decay after about 1570, and the few that remained by 1640 were destroyed or dismantled during the Civil War. After the Restoration only the wealthiest parishes could afford to buy organs. They were acquired by many churches in London and in market towns during the 18th century, but country churches often had to wait until the early Victorian period.

These facts have been known in a general way for some time, and Peter Williams has conducted a methodical study of organs and organ music in the Georgian period (Williams)*. In this paper, I have made an effort to compile accurate statistics; the original purpose was to provide a basis for factual statements on the subject in my forthcoming book, *The music of the English parish church*. It was hardly practicable to try and get information about over 8,000 churches. Accordingly I chose four regions whose economic and social histories seemed to be roughly representative of all parts of the country during the period. London, including Westminster and the adjoining suburbs, could not well be omitted, and the region contained a contrast between the City of London, with nearly a hundred small parishes, and the affluent town of Westminster in which the parishes were too large for the growing population. York, like London, was one of those ancient cities which retained its medieval structure of many poor and underpopulated parishes. The West Riding of Yorkshire was the scene of early industrialisation and rapid population growth, and contained several of those rapidly growing towns which (by contrast with York and London) had far too large a population for the size of the parish church, until they were subdivided in the nineteenth century. Dorset, on the other hand, was a county which changed very little throughout the period under review, remaining almost entirely agricultural, sparsely inhabited, and sleepy. It was the scene of one of the last church bands, heard and described by Canon Galpin in the 1890s (Galpin, 1906).

For each region I made an effort to gain information about the introduction of the first organ after 1660 from reliable secondary sources, and, where these did not exist, to examine vestry minutes, churchwardens' accounts and other archives. It cannot be claimed that the results are likely to be complete. One can rarely be absolutely certain that an organ purchased at a certain time was the first in the church, though various indications will often make this likely. There may be churches that acquired organs by gift without mention in the records, and there may be others whose records have not survived or have eluded my search: this is more likely in the case of country parishes than in London or York, but, on the other

---

*For full citation of sources see the bibliography at the end.

hand, few country parishes had organs before 1830. I should be most grateful to hear of any additions or corrections to the list. Meanwhile, I am sufficiently confident of its accuracy to feel that it does not greatly falsify the picture. The summary tables at the end probably present a fair approximation of the actual state of affairs, and they show how the delay in the acquisition of organs was related to more general differences among the regions.

A London

The list covers parish churches within the area known as the 'Bills of Mortality' at any time between 1670 and 1830, though the fortunes of these churches are followed into the 20th century. It thus *excludes* (a) cathedrals, royal chapels, proprietary chapels, and chapels-of-ease; (b) parish churches destroyed in the Fire of 1666 and not rebuilt; (c) the church of St. Mary Bothaw, demolished in 1669. Parishes that lost their churches generally shared the use of another parish church, as indicated in parentheses after the name of the parish.

The churches are divided into areas, as was customary: (i) The City of London within the walls; (ii) London out-parishes and 'parts adjoining'; (iii) Westminster. Within each area the order is alphabetical, but ignoring the word 'St.'. The information given in each column is explained and amplified below:

Parish

Some names occur in other forms, such as All Saints (for All Hallows), St. Anthony (for St. Antholin), St. Benedict (for St. Bennet), St. Bridget (for St. Bride). In the case of two or more parishes sharing a church, the name given first is the original name of the surviving church; other parishes follow in parentheses.

Houses 1732

The number of houses in the parish in 1732, as recorded in *New Remarks of London.*

Vestry 1732

S – select vestry, G – general vestry, as recorded in *New Remarks of London.* Where there are two or more letters, the church was used by two or more parishes with separate vestries, designated in the same order as the parishes in the *Parish* column.

School 1732

The number of children given a free education by the parish in 1732, as recorded in *New Remarks of London.*

Pop. 1801

The population in thousands of the parish in 1801, to the nearest hundred. Census figures are taken from Parliamentary Papers, Session 1831: XVIII, supplemented where necessary by George: Appendix III. A figure could not be obtained for St. John, Clerkenwell; its population is included in that of St. James, Clerkenwell.

Dates of church

The dates are those between which the church was functioning *as a parish church* between 1660 and the second World War. A terminal date (as -1666) shows when the church was destroyed, demolished, closed, or converted to non-parochial use; an initial date (as 1685-) shows when it was built, rebuilt, or opened as a parish church. The absence of an initial date means 'before 1660 -'; the absence of a terminal date means '- after 1939'. Thus a complete blank means there was a parish church throughout the period. When a second line is used in this column for one parish it means that a new church was built or opened at the initial date shown.

(These facts are well established, therefore detailed sources for them have not been given.)

Date of organ

For each church building allotted a line in the previous column, a date is given that is believed to be the first year in which an organ was in use in that building after 1660. Two dots mean that no organ is known to have been in use in that building after 1660. A terminal date (as -1867) means 'not later than' that year.

Source of organ information

In each case, what is believed to be the most reliable source is cited, and has been followed, though many other sources were also consulted. At All Hallows, Bread St., Freeman stated that an organ was acquired about 1684 (*The Organ* 7, 1922: 178), but the church records do not mention an organ or payments connected with one, and Paterson (1714) does not list an organ at this church. William Babell (1690-1723) was organist there, according to Brown & Stratton. At St. George-in-the-East, Mackeson (1866-95) (an unreliable source in this matter) gives a date of 1728, but there is no mention of one in the vestry minutes of that year, or in *New Remarks of London* (1732). However, there is a gap in the minutes from 1729 to 1766, and the churchwardens' accounts are also missing. According to Brown & Stratton, John James was organist from 1738 to 1745.

Summary statistics will be found below, pp96-97. The list does not exhaust the organs available to London parishioners. Many chapels-of-ease, subordinate to parish churches, also had them. For instance King St. Chapel, built as a 'tabernacle' in 1688, was endowed and licensed as a chapel-of-ease to St. James, Westminster, in 1700, and rebuilt in 1702: it was later known as Archbishop Tenison's Chapel. The building still stands, as St. Thomas, Regent Street, but it did not become a parish church until 1869 and hence falls outside the scope of this list. It had an 'excellent and extraordinary organ' in 1714, according to Paterson.

Parish	Houses 1732	Vestry 1732	School 1732	Pop. 1801 ('000)	Dates of church	Date of organ	Source of organ information
(I) CITY OF LONDON							
St. Alban, Wood St.	259	GG	75	1.8	-1666	..	
(with St. Olave, Silver St.).					1685-	1729	Pearce, 1909: 144
All Hallows by the Tower, Barking	319	S	20	2.1		1675	*The Organ* 30, 1928: 88
All Hallows, Bread St.	108	GG	0	0.6	-1666	..	
(with St. John Evangelist)					1684-1876	*c*1720?	See notes above
All Hallows the Great	206	SG	50	0.8	-1666	..	
(with All Hallows the Less)					1683-1893	1749	*The Organ* 26, 1927: 66
All Hallows, Lombard St.	120	G	40	0.7	-1666	..	
					1694-	1701	MS 57, 1701
All Hallows, London Wall	300	S	80	1.6	-1765	..	
					1767-	1784	M. Fowler: 74; MS
All Hallows, Staining	100	S	6	0.7	-1671	..	
					1675-1870	..	MS 51, 1866-70

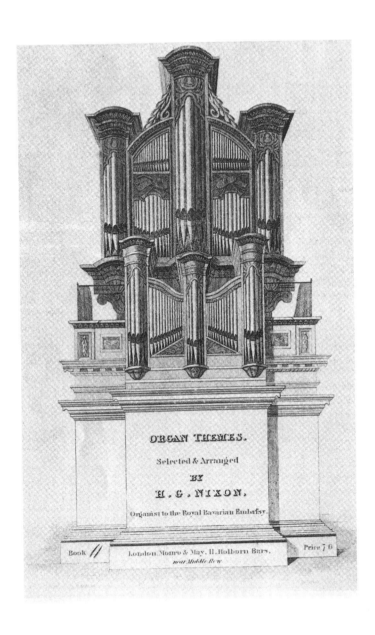

Titlepage from H.G. Nixon's Organ Themes
*(London, c1825), showing a typical or
conglomerate Renatus Harris organ-case*

Parish	Houses 1732	Vestry 1732	School 1732	Pop. 1801 ('000)	Dates of church	Date of organ	Source of organ information
St. Alphege, London Wall	75	G	75	1.0	-1774	..	
					1777-	1843	Carter: 61
St. Andrew-by-the-Wardrobe (with St. Ann, Blackfriars)	577	SG	70	4.0	-1666	..	
					1692-	1774	Pearce, 1909: 164
St. Andrew Undershaft	210	G	80	1.3		1696	Towerson: title page
St. Anne and St. Agnes, Aldersgate (with St. John Zachary)	232	G	50	1.5	-1666	..	
					1681-	1781	McMurray, 1925: 297- 300
St. Antholin, Watling St. (with St. John Baptist, Dowgate)	164	G	0	0.8	-1666	..	
		G			1682-1874	1733	The Organ 28, 1927:217
St. Augustine, Old Change (with St. Faith)	184	SG	0	1.3	-1666	..	Pearce, 1909: 170
					1683-	1766	
St. Bartholomew-by-the-Exchange	118	G	0	0.6	-1666	..	
					1679-1840	1740	The Organ 28, 1927: 218
					1841-1904	1841	The Organ 28, 1927: 218
St. Bennet Fink, Threadneedle St.	?	G	0	0.5	-1666	..	
					1673-1842	1714	The Organ 28, 1927: 220
St. Bennet Gracechurch (with St. Leonard Eastcheap)	106	SS	0	0.7	-1666	..	
					1685-1867	1837	MS 50, 1836-8
St. Bennet, Paul's Wharf (with St. Peter near Paul's Wharf)	200	G	20	1.0	-1666	..	
					1683-1879	1833	Pearce, 1909: 176
Christ Church, Newgate St. (with St. Leonard Foster)	515	G	90	3.7	-1666	..	
					1687-	1690	Pearce, 1909: 27-9
St. Christopher-le-Stocks	92	G	0	0.1	-1666	..	
					1671-1781	..	Pearce, 1909: 179
St. Clement, Eastcheap (with St. Martin Orgars)	132	G	0	0.5	-1666	..	
					1686-	1696	Pearce, 1909: 74
St. Dionis Backchurch	120	G	0	0.9	-1666	..	
					1674-1878	1724	Pearce, 1909: 123
St. Dunstan-in-the-East	322	S	0	1.6	-1666	..	
					1671-	1672	Wren Society XIX, 1942: 18
St. Edmund, Lombard St. (with St. Nicholas Acons)	154	G	0	0.8	-1666	..	
					1690-	1702	Wren Society XIX, 1942: 19
St. Ethelburga, Bishopsgate	120	G	0	0.6		1812	MS 58, 1812
St. George, Botolph Lane (with St. Botolph, Billingsgate)	104	G	40	0.3	-1666	..	
					1674-1899	-1708	Hatton, 1708

Parish	Houses 1732	Vestry 1732	School 1732	Pop. 1801 ('000)	Dates of church	Date of organ	Source of organ information
St. Helen, Bishopsgate	138	G	0	0.7		1683	Survey of London IX, 1924: 21
St. James, Aldgate	150	G	0	0.9	-1874	1815	The Organ 30, 1928: 115
St. James, Garlickhithe	40	G	50	0.6	-1666 1682-	.. 1719	Wren Society XIX, 1942: 21
St. Katherine Coleman	180	S	0	0.7	-1734 1736-1925	.. 1743	The Organ 1, 1921: 33
St. Katherine Cree	300	S	40	1.7		1686	Pearce, 1909: 198
St. Lawrence, Jewry	237	G	10?	0.8	-1666 1677-	1686	Wren Society XIX, 1942: 25
St. Magnus by London Bridge (with St. Margaret, New Fish St.)	192	SG	100	0.7	-1666 1676-	.. 1712	The Organ 17, 1925: 2
St. Margaret, Lothbury	150	G	0	0.6	-1666 1686-	.. 1801	Pearce, 1909: 61
St. Margaret Pattens (with St. Gabriel Fenchurch)	124	G	0	0.7	-1666 1687-	.. c1750	Pearce, 1909: 115-6
St. Martin, Ludgate St.	176	G	110	1.2	-1666 1684-	.. 1684	The Organ 33, 1929: 37
St. Martin Outwich	40	G	0	0.3	-1765 1798-1874	.. 1805	The Organ 38, 1930: 117
St. Mary Abchurch (with St. Lawrence Poultry)	179	G	10?	0.9	-1666 1686-	.. 1822	Pearce, 1909: 130
St. Mary Aldermanbury	135	G	0	0.8	-1666 1677-	.. 1825	MS 55, 1825-6
St. Mary Aldermary (with St. Thomas Apostle)	208	G	0	1.1	-1666 1682-	.. 1781	The Organ 80, 1940: 145
St. Mary-at-Hill (with St. Andrew Hubbard)	127	S	0	1.1	-1666 1672-	.. 1693	Wren Society XIX, 1942: 32
St. Mary-le-Bow (with St. Pancras, Soper Lane and All Hallows, Honey Lane)	156	GGG	0	0.9	-1666 1680-	.. 1802	Pearce, 1909: 43
St. Mary Somerset (with St. Mary Mounthaw)	158	SG	44	0.8	-1666 1695-1872	.. -1838	MS 62, 1838

Parish	Houses 1732	Vestry 1732	School 1732	Pop. 1801 ('000)	Dates of church	Date of organ	Source of organ information
St. Mary Woolnoth (with St. Mary Wool-church Haw)	153	G	0	0.8	-1716	c1663	*The Organ* 21, 1926: 4
					1727-	1727	*The Organ* 21, 1926: 4-9
St. Mary Magdalen, Old Fish St. (with St. Gregory by St. Paul)	403	G	50	2.2	-1666	..	
					1685-1886	1786	*The Organ* 33, 1929: 41
St. Matthew, Friday St. (with St. Peter, Cheap)	137	G	0	0.5	-1666	..	
					1685-1881	1735	Dawe
St. Michael Bassishaw	146	G	0	0.7	-1666	..	
					1679-1893	1762	*The Organ* 39, 1930: 179
St. Michael, Cornhill	130	G	0	0.7	-1666	..	
					1672-	1684	Wren Society XIX, 1942: 47
St. Michael, Crooked Lane	118	G	0	0.6	-1666	..	
					1688-1831	1748	Dawe
							Organ removed, 1794. (*History*, 1833)
St. Michael, Paternoster Royal (with St. Martin Vintry)	200	G	0	0.8	-1666		
					1694-	1780	Pearce, 1909: 219
St. Michael, Queenhithe (with Trinity)	118	S	0	1.4	-1666	..	
					1677-1876	1799	*The Organ* 80, 1940:144
St. Michael, Wood St. (with St. Mary, Staining Lane)	140	G	0	0.8	-1666	..	
					1675-1894	1818	*The Organ* 41, 1931: 56
St. Mildred, Bread St. (with St. Margaret Moses)	100	G	0	0.5	-1666	..	
					1683-	1744	Pearce, 1909: 220
St. Mildred, Poultry (with St. Mary Colechurch)	230	SG	0	0.8	-1666	..	
					1676-1871	1778	*The Organ* 80, 1940: 144
St. Nicholas Cole-Abbey (with St. Nicholas Olave)	106	G	0	0.6	-1666	..	
					1677-	1824	Pearce, 1909: 223
St. Olave, Hart St.	205	S	0	1.2		1781	MS 49
St. Olave, Old Jewry (with St. Martin, Iron-monger Lane)	100	G	25	0.5	-1666	..	
					1676-1888	1814	MS 59, 1814
St. Peter, Cornhill	171	S	0	1.0	-1666	..	
					1681-	1681	Wren Society XIX, 1942: 49
St. Peter-le-Poer	·140	G	0	0.9	-1788	1718	*Weekly Journal*, 22 Nov 1718
					1792-1896	1792	*The Organ* 44, 1941: 242

Parish	Houses 1732	Vestry 1732	School 1732	Pop. 1801 ('000)	Dates of church	Date of organ	Source of organ information
St. Stephen, Coleman St.	461	G	0	3.2	-1666	..	
					1676-	1775	*The Organ* 53, 1934: 54
St. Stephen, Walbrook (with St. Bennet Sherehog)	108	GS	10?	0.5	-1666	..	
					1679-	1765	*The Organ* 80, 1940: 143
St. Swithin, London Stone (with St. Mary Bothaw)	138	G	0	0.7	-1666	..	
					1678-	1809	Mackeson, 1866-95
St. Vedast, Foster Lane (with St. Michael Quern)	76	G	0	0.8	-1666	..	
					1697-	1774	Pearce, 1909: 112

(II) OUT-PARISHES AND 'PARTS ADJOINING', including Southwark

Parish	Houses 1732	Vestry 1732	School 1732	Pop. 1801 ('000)	Dates of church	Date of organ	Source of organ information
St. Andrew, Shoe Lane, Holborn	?	S	160	21.4		1699	Pearce, 1909: 7
St. Ann, Limehouse	1000?	S	0	4.7	1730-1850	1741	Pearce, 1911: 102
					1857-	1857	Mackeson, 1873
St. Bartholomew the Great	324	S	50	2.6		1731	Pearce, 1909: 18
St. Bartholomew the Less	143	G	0	1.0		1794	Pearce, 1909: 174
St. Botolph, Aldersgate	700	S	100	4.1		1773	MS 56, 1772-3
St. Botolph, Aldgate	2500	S	160	8.7		1676	Pearce, 1909: 138
St. Botolph, Bishopsgate	1800	S	50	10.3		1764	MS 60, 1764
St. Bride, Fleet St.	1500	G	100	7.1	-1666	..	
					1687-	1690	Wren Society XIX, 1942: 14
Christ Church, Southwark	?	G	40	9.9	1671-1738	..	
					1741-	1789	Survey of London XXII, 1950: 102-3
Christ Church, Spitalfields	2190?	S	60	15.1	1729-	1735	Pearce, 1911: 4
St. Dunstan-in-the-West	858	S	90	3.0		1674	MS 52, 1674
St. Dunstan, Stepney	5500?	S	93	25.2		1680	MS 71, 1679-80
St. George, Bloomsbury	900	S	202	7.7	1730-	1788	Pearce, 1911: 92
St. George-in-the-East	2000	G	100	21.2	1728-	1738?	See notes above
St. George, Southwark	740	S	50	22.3	-1732	1682	MS 66, 1682
					1736-	1736	Survey of London XXV, 1955: 31
St. George the Martyr, Queen Square	666	S	90	6.3	1723-	1773	Pearce, 1911: 92
St. Giles, Cripplegate	4810	S	200	11.4		1672	Pearce, 1909: 33
St. Giles-in-the-Fields	2000	S	?	28.7		1671	Survey of London V, 1914: 132
Holy Trinity in the Minories	123	G	0	0.6	1730-1899	-1867	Mackeson, 1866-95

Parish	Houses 1732	Vestry 1732	School 1732	Pop. 1801 ('000)	Dates of church	Date of organ	Source of organ information
St. James, Clerkenwell	1900	G	100	23.4	-1788	1734	MS 45, 1733-5
					1792-	1792	*The Organ* 82, 1941: 43
St. John, Clerkenwell	?	?	?	?	1723-	1723	MS 46: fol. 65v-67
St. John, Hackney	600	S	62	12.7		1666	MS 47, 1665-7
St. John, Horsleydown, Southwark	?	?	?	8.9	1732-	1770	Pearce, 1911: 100
St. John, Wapping	1600?	S	66	5.9	1694-	-1793	Pearce, 1911: 116
St. Katherine-by-the-Tower	867?	S	50	2.7	-1824	-1710	*The Organ* 30, 1928: 118
St. Leonard, Shoreditch	2500?	S	100	34.8		1757	Survey of London VIII, 1922: 104
St. Luke, Old St.	..	..	..	26.9	1733-	1733	*The Organ* 124, 1941: 180
St. Mary, Islington	937	G	44	10.2	-1751	..	
					1754-	1772	MS 63, 1770-2
St. Mary, Lambeth	?	G	44	27.9		1701	MS 65, 1701-2
St. Mary, Newington Butts	700	G	30?	14.8		..	
					1793-1877	1794	Mackeson, 1866-95
St. Mary, Rotherhithe	1500	G	8	10.3		1764	Pearce, 1911: 104
St. Mary Matfelon, Whitechapel	3500?	G	100	23.7	-1666	..	
					1673-1875	1715	Pearce, 1911: 121
					1877-1880		
					1882-		
St. Mary Magdalen, Bermondsey	1900?	G	120	17.2		-1700	MS 67, 1705
St. Matthew, Bethnal Green	..	..	..	22.3	1746-1859	1772	Pearce, 1911: 144
					1861-	1861	Mackeson, 1866-95
St. Olave, Southwark	3000	G	100	7.8	-1735?	1700	MS 68, 1700
					1737-1843	1737	Pearce, 1911: 111
					1844-1926	1844	Mackeson, 1866-95
St. Paul, Shadwell	1800	S	100	8.8	1666-	-1800	Pearce, 1911: 110
St. Saviour, Southwark	?	S	160	15.6	-1905	1705	MS 48, 1705
St. Sepulchre, Newgate (Holborn)	?	S	150	11.9	-1666	..	
					1670-	1676	MS 53, 1676; MS 54, 1676
St. Thomas, Southwark	130?	S	30	2.1	1702-1901	..	Mackeson, 1866-95

(III) WESTMINSTER

| St. Anne, Soho | 1500? | S | 80 | 11.6 | 1686- | 1708 | Survey of London XXIII, 1966: 266 |

Parish	Houses 1732	Vestry 1732	School 1732	Pop. 1801 ('000)	Dates of church	Date of organ	Source of organ information
St. Clement Danes	1750	S	140	8.7	-1680	..	
					1682-	1685	MS 75, 1685
St. George, Hanover Square	1432	S	80	38.4	1724-	1725	*The Organ* 54, 1934: 100
St. James, Piccadilly	4300	S	120	34.5	1685-	1691	MS 76, 1691
St. John Evangelist, Smith Square	1600?	S	0	8.4	1728-	1750	*The Organ* 53, 1934: 38
St. Margaret, Westminster	2350?	S	80	17.5		1676	Pearce, 1911: 120
St. Martin-in-the-Fields	5000?	S	?	25.7	-1722	1667	McMaster,
					1724-	1724	1916: 154
St. Mary-le-Strand	266	S	40	1.7	1724-	1790	Pearce, 1911: 108
St. Paul, Covent Garden	600?	S	50	5.0	-1795	1726	Survey of London XXXVI, 1970: 107
					1798-	1798	Pearce, 1911: 95

B York

The list includes all parishes existing between 1660 and 1830 within the city of York. The 1801 population is taken from Parliamentary Papers, Session 1831: XVIII, but no figure could be obtained for St. Olave. The date of the first organ (O), harmonium (H), or barrel organ (B) is given where a reliable source of information could be found: this source is listed in the last column. A terminal date (as -1831) means 'not later than' the year given. It is extremely unlikely that any of the churches left blank in this column had organs in 1801. No chapels-of-ease are known to have existed, so that in this case the list probably presents a complete picture of organs in Anglican places of worship (apart from the cathedral). Summary figures are given below.

Parish	Pop. 1801 ('000)	Date of first organ	Source
All Saints, North St.	0.5	H 1851	MS 102
		O 1856	*Yorks. Gazette*, 19 Jan. 1856
All Saints, Pavement	0.5	O 1791	MS 106: 18
St. Andrew	0.1		
Christ Church (otherwise Holy Trinity), King's Court	0.7	O 1833	MS 106: 33
St. Crux	0.7	O 1836	*Yorks. Gazette,* 5 Mar. 1836
St. Cuthbert	0.6	H 1865	MS 106: 42
St. Dennis	0.7	O 1857	*Yorks. Gazette,* 18, 25 Apr. 1857
St. Helen, Stonegate	0.7	O -1831	MS 106: 56
Holy Trinity, Goodramgate	0.4	H -1867	MS 106: 61
Holy Trinity, Micklegate	0.9	O 1851	MS 106: 65
St. John, Delpike	0.3		
St. John, Ousegate	0.8	B *c*1840	MS 106: 76
		H *c*1845	
		O 1855	
St. Lawrence	0.3	O 1846	MS 106: 83
St. Margaret, Walmgate	0.6	O 1855	*Yorks. Gazette*, 23 June 1855
St. Martin, Coney St.	0.6	O 1837	MS 103
St. Martin-cum-Gregory	0.5	O 1840	MS 106: 94
St. Mary Bishophill Junior	0.4	O 1851	*Yorks. Gazette*, 30 Aug. 1851
St. Mary Bishophill Senior	0.4	O -1849	MS 102a
St. Mary, Castlegate	0.8	O *c*1850	MS 106: 88
St. Maurice	0.6	H 1850	MS 106: 100-1
		O 1881	
St. Michael-le-Belfrey	1.2	O 1687	MS 107
St. Michael, Spurriergate	0.7		
St. Olave		O 1856	*Yorks. Gazette*, 6 Dec. 1856
St. Peter the Little	0.5		
St. Peter-le-Willows	0.2		
St. Sampson	0.9	O 1839	*Yorks. Gazette*, 10 Aug. 1839
St. Saviour	0.6	O 1811	MS 106
St. Wilfred	0.4		

C Yorkshire, West Riding

The list is chronological, and includes only churches that are known to have acquired organs between 1660 and 1830. In this list it has not always been possible to distinguish between parish churches and district chapels or chapels-of-ease. The region included some parishes very large in area, and in many cases the district chapels were parish churches in practice long before they became so in name. Wherever possible the population of the township or other subdivision in which a chapel or parish church stood has been given. In the case of the parish church of a subdivided parish, both the population of the parish and that of the subdivision are stated. Where no population is given, the church was probably built as a chapel-of-ease and was not assigned its own specific district. Other indications as for section B.

Parish, etc.		Pop. 1801 ('000)	Date of first organ	Source
Ripon (collegiate church)	Parish:	10.2	-1663	MS 91, 30 May 1663
	Ripon township:	3.2		
Barnsley (township in Silkstone parish)		3.6	1682	*The Organ* 34, 1929: 113
Leeds		53.2	1713	Hargrave: 320
Wakefield		16.6	1720	*The Organ* 83, 1941: 90
Doncaster	Parish:	6.1	1739	MS 93
	Doncaster borough:	5.1		
Birstall		14.7	1754	Lawton
Sheffield: St. Paul		...	1755	Odom: 68
Halifax	Parish:	63.6	1766	Houseman: 84
	Halifax township:	8.9		
Pontefract	Parish:	6.2	1774	*The Organ* 154, 1959: 73
	Pontefract borough:	3.1		
Rotherham	Parish:	8.5	1777	*The Organ* 25, 1927: 19
	Rotherham township:	3.1		
Thornhill	Parish:	4.3	1785	Lawton
	Thornhill township:	1.5		
Bradford	Parish:	29.8	1786	Cudworth: 112
	Bradford township:	6.4		
Sheffield: St. James		...	1794	Odom: 89
Wakefield: St. John		...	1795	MS 98
Tadcaster	Parish:	2.4	-1800	MS 101
	Tadcaster township:	2.1		
Leeds: St. Paul, Park Square		...	1800	Hargrave: 347
Elland cum Stainley and Fixby (chapel, parish of Halifax)		5.5	1805	Lawton
Sheffield: parish church	Parish:	45.8	1805	Odom: 42
	Sheffield township:	31.3		
Keighley		5.7	1811	*The Organ* 106, 1947: 7
Huddersfield	Parish:	14.8	1812	Ahier: 201
	Huddersfield township:	7.3		

Great Horton: Bell Chapel (parish of Bradford)	3.5	c1812	Cudworth: 120
Bradford: Christ Church	...	1815	Cudworth: 120
Wyke (chapel, parish of Birstall)	1.0	-1819	PC 344a: list of subscribers
Badsworth	0.5	1820	Lawton
Leeds: Holy Trinity, Boar Lane	...	-1825	PC 354: list of subscribers
Wortley (chapel, parish of Leeds)	2.0	-1825	PC 354: list of subscribers
Otley Parish:	6.8	-1825	PC 354: list of subscribers
Otley township:	2.3		
Selby Abbey	3.0	1825	*The Organ* 54, 1934: 75
Sheffield: St. George	...	c1825	Odom: 94
Leeds: Christ Church, Meadow Lane	...	c1826	Taylor: 503
Sheffield: Christ Church, Attercliffe	...	1827	Odom: 100
Holmfirth (chapel, parish of Kirkburton)	...	1828	Lawton
Ripon: Holy Trinity	...	1828	Lawton
Leeds: St. Stephen, Kirkstall	...	1829	*Yorkshire Evening Post*, 26 June 1971
Batley Parish:	6.4	1830	Lawton
Batley township:	2.6		

D Dorset

The list is chronological, and includes only churches that are known to have acquired organs between 1660 and 1830. For further explanation see section **B.**

Parish	Pop. 1801 ('000)	Date of first organ	Source
Wimborne (collegiate church)	3.0	1665	MS 16
Sherborne Abbey	3.2	1700	Mayo
Shaftesbury: Holy Trinity	0.9	1764	Adams: 137
Dorchester: St. Peter	0.8	1787	MS 12
Blandford Forum	2.3	1794	P. Smith: 80; MS 11
Poole	4.8	1799	MS 17
Wyke Regis	0.5	-1809	MS 9
Bridport	3.1	1815	Collins
Dorchester: Holy Trinity	1.0	1824	MS 14
Lyme Regis	1.5	1828	Leather
Wareham: Lady St. Mary	0.8	1829	MS 10

Summary Table 1

Number of London parish churches having organs at the end of each decade, 1660-1830; and the same expressed as a percentage of the number of functioning parish churches.

Year	City		Out-parishes		Westminster		Total	
	No.	%	No.	%	No.	%	No.	%
1660	0	0.0	0	0.0	0	0.0	0	0.0
1670	1	7.1	1	4.2	1	25.0	3	7.1
1680	3	8.6	7	26.9	2	66.7	12	18.8
1690	9	15.8	9	33.3	3	50.0	21	23.3
1700	12	19.4	12	42.8	5	83.3	29	30.2
1710	15	24.2	15	51.7	5	83.3	35	36.1
1720	20	32.8	16	55.2	·5	83.3	41	42.7
1730	23	37.1	17	57.2	7	77.8	47	43.9
1740	26	41.9	22	59.5	7	77.8	55	50.9
1750	30	48.4	23	59.0	8	88.9	61	55.5
1760	31	50.0	24	61.5	8	88.9	62	57.3
1770	34	55.7	27	69.2	8	88.9	69	63.3
1780	39	65.0	31	79.5	8	88.9	78	72.2
1790	44	74.6	33	84.6	9	100.0	86	80.4
1800	44	72.1	37	94.9	9	100.0	90	82.6
1810	48	78.7	37	94.9	9	100.0	94	86.2
1820	52	85.2	37	94.9	9	100.0	98	89.9
1830	55	90.2	36	94.7	9	100.0	100	91.7

Summary Table 2

Percentage of London parish churches having organs and charity schools in 1732, in relation to certain other variables.

For parishes with ...	General vestry	Select vestry	Charity school	No charity school	1-200 houses	201-1000 houses	1001 or more houses	All parishes
...% of churches having organs was ...	39.2	67.6	61.1	27.0	26.0	43.3	62.5	47.9
...% of churches having a charity school was ...	42.8	77.5	100.0	0.0	28.0	80.0	95.8	57.9
1-40 children in charity school ...	12.5	15.0	22.6	..	16.0	13.3	4.2	13.1
41-70 children in charity school ...	8.9	17.5	27.5	..	4.0	36.6	12.5	15.9
71-100 children in charity school ...	17.9	25.0	33.9	..	6.0	23.3	45.8	19.6
101 or more children in charity school ...	3.5	20.0	16.1	..	2.0	7.7	25.0	9.3

Note: For the purpose of computing each percentage figure in the body of this table, only parishes for which all relevant variable quantities were precisely known are included.

‑ ‑

Summary Table 3
Comparative statistics for the selected areas in 1801:

Area	Total population ('000)	Number of parishes	Average pop. per parish ('000)	No. of parishes with organs	Percentage of parishes with organs	Persons per parish organ ('000)
A London: Bills of Mortality	694.8	110	6.3	91	*82.7*	7.6
(I) City of London	63.4	62	1.0	45	*72.6*	1.4
(II) Outparishes and parts adjoining	479.8	39	12.3	37	*94.9*	13.0
(III) Westminster	151.6	9	16.8	9	*100.0*	16.8
B York (City)	16.1	29	0.6	2	*6.9*	8.1
C West Riding of Yorkshire	565.3	190	3.0	16	*8.4*	35.3
D Dorset	115.3	273	0.4	6	*2.2*	19.2

Note: It should be remembered that the statistics for organs are not complete for areas C and D. Other parishes in these areas may have had organs of which no record has been found. This is much less probable in areas A and B.

‑ ‑

Bibliography

Adams
[Adams, T.], *A history of the ancient town of Shaftesbury* (Shaftesbury, [1808])

Ahier
Ahier, P., *The story of the three parish churches of St. Peter the Apostle, Huddersfield* (Huddersfield, 1948)

Brown & Stratton
Brown, J.D. & Stratton, S.S., *British musical biography* (Birmingham, 1897)

Carter
Carter, P. C., *The history of the church and parish of St. Mary the Virgin, Aldermanbury* (London, 1913)

Collins
Collins, J. A., *St. Mary's Church, Bridport* (Bridport, 1906)

Cudworth
Cudworth, W., *Musical reminiscences of Bradford* (Bradford, [1885])

Dawe
Private information from Donovan Dawe, Esq., formerly librarian, Guildhall Library, London

M. Fowler
Fowler, M., *History of All Hallows Church, London Wall* (London, 1909)

Galpin, 1906
Galpin, F. W., 'Notes on the old church bands and village choirs of the past century', *The Antiquary* XLII (1906), 101-6

George
George, M. D., *London life in the XVIIIth century* (London, 1925)

Hargrave
Hargrave, E., 'Musical Leeds in the 18th century', *Thoresby Society Publications* XXVIII (1928), 320-355

Hatton
[Hatton, E.], *A new view of London* (London, 1708)

History
The history and antiquities of the parish church of St. Michael Crooked Lane, London (London, 1833)

Houseman
Houseman, J. W., 'History of the Halifax parish church organs', *Halifax Antiquarian Society: Papers, Reports, &c* (1928), 77-112

Lawton
Lawton, G., *Collectio rerum ecclesiasticarum de diocesi eboracensi*, 2 vols (London, 1840)

Leather
[Leather, F. S.], *Some account of Lyme Regis* (London, 1882)

Mackeson
Mackeson, C., *A guide to the churches of London and its suburbs*, 20 nos. (London, 1866-95)

McMaster
McMaster, J., *A short history of the royal parish of St. Martin-in-the-Fields* (London, 1916)

McMurray
McMurray, W., *The records of two city parishes* [St. Anne and St. Agnes, Aldersgate] (London, 1925)

Mayo
Mayo, C. H., *The official guide to Sherborne Abbey church* (Sherborne, 1925)

MS 9
Dorchester (Dorset), Dorset Record Office: P5/CW3

MS 10
Dorchester (Dorset), Dorset Record Office: P63/VE2

MS 11
Dorchester (Dorset), Dorset Record Office: P70/CW22

MS 12
Dorchester (Dorset), Dorset Record Office: P87/CW2

MS 14
Dorchester (Dorset), Dorset Record Office: P173/CW4

MS 16
Dorchester (Dorset), Dorset Record Office: P204/CW42.

MS 17
Dorchester (Dorset), Dorset Record Office: P227/CW3

MS 45	London, Finsbury Library: St. James, Clerkenwell, vestry minutes.
MS 46	London, Greater London Record Office: P76/JNB/24
MS 47	London, Greater London Record Office: P79/JN1/138-44
MS 48	London, Greater London Record Office: P92/S/452
MS 49	London, Guildhall Library: 858 (1)
MS 50	London, Guildhall Library: 1568A
MS 51	London, Guildhall Library: 1704
MS 52	London, Guildhall Library: 3016 (2)
MS 53	London, Guildhall Library: 3146 (2)
MS 55	London, Guildhall Library: 3570 (4)
MS 56	London, Guildhall Library: 3863 (1)
MS 57	London, Guildhall Library: 4049 (2)
MS 58	London, Guildhall Library: 4241 (5)
MS 60	London, Guildhall Library: 4526 (4)
MS 62	London, Guildhall Library: 5714 (4)
MS 63	London, Islington Central Library: St. Mary, Islington, vestry minutes
MS 65	London, Minet Library, Lambeth: P3/2
MS 66	London, Newington District Library: St. George, Southwark, churchwardens' accounts
MS 67	London, Newington District Library: St. Mary Magdalen, Bermondsey, vestry minutes
MS 68	London, Newington District Library: St. Olave, Southwark, vestry minutes
MS 71	London, St. Dunstan's church, Stepney: St. Dunstan, Stepney, vestry minutes
MS 75	London, Westminster Public Library: B14/CA
MS 76	London, Westminster Public Library: D1756
MS 91	Ripon (North Yorks), Minster Library: Registrum A-E
MS 93	Sheffield (South Yorks), City Library: PR 19/3-4, 19/38-40
MS 98	Wakefield (West Yorks), City Library: St. John, Wakefield, parish records
MS 101	York (North Yorks), Borthwick Institute: PR/TAD
MS 102	York (North Yorks), Borthwick Institute: PR/Y/ASN/12
MS 102a	York (North Yorks), Borthwick Institute: PR/Y/M.Bp.S/
MS 103	York (North Yorks), Borthwick Institute: PR/Y/MCS/18
MS 105	York (North Yorks), Borthwick Institute: PR/Y/SAV/15
MS 106	York (North Yorks), City Library: Y942/7411
MS 107	York (North Yorks), Minster Library. St. Michael-le-Belfrey, vestry minutes and churchwardens' accounts
New remarks of London	*New remarks of London: or, a survey of the cities of London and Westminster, of Southwark, and part of Middlesex and Surry* (London, 1732)
Odom	Odom, W., *Memorials of Sheffield: its cathedral and parish churches* (Sheffield, 1922)
The Organ	*The Organ*, 1921-
Paterson	Paterson, J., *Pietas Londiniensis* (London, 1714)
PC 344a	Jacob, Benjamin, *National psalmody* (London, [1817?])

PC 354	Greenwood, John, *A selection of ancient and modern psalm tunes, chants, and responses* (Leeds, [1825])
Pearce, 1909	Pearce, C.W., *Old London city churches, their organs, organists and musical associations* (London, 1909)
Pearce, 1911	Pearce, C. W., *Notes on English organs of the period 1800-1810.....taken chiefly from the MS of Henry Leffler* (London, 1911)
P. Smith	Smith, P., *Blandford* (Blandford, 1968)
Survey of London	London County Council, *Survey of London*, 38 vols London, 1900-75
Taylor	Taylor, R. V., *The ecclesiae Leodienses* (London, 1875)
Towerson	Towerson, C., *A sermon concerning vocal and instrumental musick in the church, as it was delivered in the parish church of St.Andrew, Undershaft, May 31st, 1696..... the day wherein the organ there erected was first made use of* (London, 1696)
Weekly journal	*The weekly journal*
Williams	Williams, Peter, *English organ music & the English organ under the first four Georges*. (Unpublished dissertation, Cambridge, 1962)
Yorks. gazette	*The Yorkshire gazette*
Yorks. evening post	*The Yorkshire evening post*

Note

The abbreviations and MS nos. are chosen to conform with those used in *The music of the English parish church*, by Nicholas Temperley, where the manuscript sources are more fully described.

_ _

Among the many librarians and curators who have assisted me in the research for this article, I should like to mention particularly Miss M.E. Holmes, of the Dorset Record Office, and Mr. Donovan Dawe, formerly of the Guildhall Library, London. Dr. Harry Diack Johnstone kindly supplied me with the reference to the introduction of an organ at St. Peter-le-Poer, London.

VIII

ORGAN MUSIC IN PARISH CHURCHES, 1660-1730

Writers on English music never tire of blaming the Puritans for everything that isn't as good as they would like it to be. In this tradition, a writer has recently labelled the Civil War and Commonwealth as one in which "the Church lost its music."[1] He forgets that for most people the Church's music was that of the *parish* church, which continued during the Commonwealth with very little disturbance. As far as organs were concerned, there were few opportunities for change, because with rare exceptions there had been no functioning organs in parish churches during the early part of the 17th century.[2] Nor were there any choirs to disband. The music remained in essence what it had always been: unaccompanied congregational singing of metrical psalms. It was not affected by the banishing of the Book of Common Prayer, for it fitted in equally well with a Presbyterian or Independent form of worship.[3]

For the same reasons, the Restoration of 1660 was no landmark in the history of parish church music. But it marks a convenient zero point for the subsequent development of organs. Little time was lost in reinstating organs in the Chapel Royal, cathedrals, and a small number of collegiate parish churches,[4] where they were indispensable for the restoring of choral service. It was quite another matter with ordinary parish churches, where there was no choral service to restore and no endowment for music. Even if money could be found to pay for the instrument itself, few parishes could hope to attract and retain a competent organist, as Thomas Mace pointed out.[5] Consequently, parish churches were slow to acquire organs. Even in London only thirty percent of the churches possessed them by 1700; in 1730 the proportion was still less than half. Elsewhere, a parochial organ was a great rarity.[6] Sometimes the principal church in a cathedral city would acquire one, as for instance St Michael-le-Belfry, York (1687), which shared its organist with the cathedral; similarly at St Peter Mancroft, Norwich (1707). But the churches of the larger market towns did not usually have one until well into the eighteenth century.

If some parishes did nevertheless acquire organs before 1700, the motive was not to introduce choral services: Henry Playford stated in 1701 that "our Parochial Churches ... have been altogether destitute" of anthems,[7] and it was not until 1716 that Dr Thomas Bisse made the revolutionary suggestion that "parish-churches should as much as possible, conform to the customs of the cathedral churches, which are as the mother-churches within the diocese, and should give the rule to them."[8] Before such an idea had taken root, the function of an organ in a parish church was to regulate and adorn the psalm singing. For instance the vestry of All-Hallows-by-the-Tower decided in 1675 to install an organ "for the improvement of the psalmody of this church."[9]

Without an organ, the psalmody was directed by the parish clerk, who would begin by announcing a psalm (generally of his own choosing) from Sternhold and Hopkins's version. He would then "line out" the text, by reading one or two lines in a style that by 1700 had become a kind of monotoned chant, and proceed to sing the same lines with whatever congregational support was forthcoming. The tune, also selected by the clerk, was seldom announced, so there was little hope of a good firm start by the whole congregation; they would come in gradually, and sing extremely slowly (two or three seconds to a note was quite normal), in a sort of heterophony that was painful to cultivated ears.[10] Under these conditions it was hardly possible to introduce new tunes, and indeed virtually no new psalm tune had been added to the English repertory since Ravenscroft's OLD 104TH of 1621. Pepys wrote in 1663: "I was amused at the tune set to the psalm by the clerk of the parish [St Olave, Hart Street], and thought at first he was out, but I find him to be a good songster, and the parish could sing it very well, and was a good tune. But I wonder that there should be a tune in the psalms that I never heard of."[11] Judging from publications of the period, this fixed repertory was no more than fifteen tunes or so. Pepys was lucky to have a "good songster" for a parish clerk: most were poor old men without musical knowledge or talent, "it having been a custom during the late [civil] wars, and since, to choose men into such places, more for their poverty than skill and ability."[12]

Organs were acquired early in the wealthier parishes of London: not, typically, in the City, but in the new districts of Westminster and the outlying suburbs, where the more aristocratic and prosperous inhabitants were now assembled. It was in such parishes that there were sufficient resources to acquire an organ and pay an organist; and it was there, too, that the congregations liked cultivated music. As a second step, children from the newly founded charity schools would be brought in to lead the singing. For instance at St Margaret, Westminster, where an organ had been erected as early as 1676, a charity school was founded in 1688: it was the first of its kind, and was rapidly imitated by others, so that before long there were similar schools in dozens of London parishes, and many outside London as well.[13] The school was often supported by a religious society of young men, who learned to read music, and practised psalms at their meetings. Thus in some churches a polarized choir of trebles and baritones was formed to lead the congregation.(Full SATB settings of psalm tunes, with the tune in the treble, are very rare: one of the few such collections is *The Metre Psalm-Tunes, In Four Parts, Compos'd for the Use of the Parish-Church of St. Michael's of Belfrey's in York* (1702), by Thomas Wanless, who was organist at that church.)

The parish clerk was not superseded by these innovations. At St James, Westminster, the new parish church came into use in 1685; an organ was acquired in 1691; the rector, Thomas Tenison (later Archbishop of Canterbury), refounded the local school as a charity school, and, as we shall see, the psalms were certainly sung by a choir of trebles and basses. Nevertheless, the vestry continued to appoint a "psalm clerk" whose duties specifically included "the setting up of the early and later prayers with the singing of a psalm at each of those services."[14] At St Martin-in-the-Fields, where conditions were similar, it was ordered in 1692 "that the Clerk of the Church, do every morning and afternoon on Sermon Dayes (Fast dayes excepted) give notice in writing to the Organist, before the Service begins, of the psalmes and number of verses he intends to sing and also what tune."[15] Other church records show that an organist was expected to attend twice on Sundays and Christmas Day, and once on a few special days of thanksgiving.

Church records contain little information, however, on the precise duties of the organist, and we have to turn to other sources to discover what these were. Of course the most essential duty was the accompaniment of the metrical psalms. But very few organ settings of psalm tunes have come down to us from

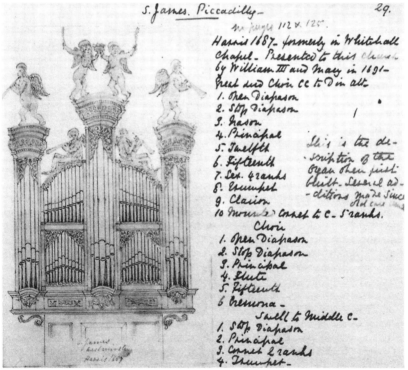

THE ROYAL COLLEGE OF ORGANISTS

St. James, Westminster (now usually called St. James, Piccadilly). Drawing of the organ and specification from the Sperling Notebooks.

the Restoration period. There is nothing in any way comparable to the rich repertory of tune-based organ music found in the Netherlands and North Germany at this time. One voluntary based on the "Old Hundredth," variously attributed to Blow or Purcell, survives. Two printed sets of tunes date from the late 1660s, one by Thomas Tomkins and the other anonymous: they are thickly, rather crudely scored, and probably represent the style of a much earlier period.[16] There are a few manuscript settings of the same description. Then there is a gap until the early 18th century, when we find several much more elaborate sets of organ psalm tunes, both manuscript and printed, often divided into "givings-out" and plain harmonizations with interludes. In the interval before the first set of these was printed in 1703, we must presume that this style of playing the psalm tunes was being gradually evolved.

London organs built in the seventeenth century, particularly in the City, often had only one manual: for example, those at St Dunstan-in-the-East (c.1670),[17] St Botolph, Aldgate (1676),[18] St Martin, Ludgate Street (1684),[19] and All Saints, Lombard Street.[20] A hundred years later, "W.L.," writing in *The Gentleman's Magazine*, stated that organs "with one row of keys are sufficient when the service of the church consists in plain *psalm-singing* only. In that case the psalm tune is given out on some of the softer stops, but the congregation is accompanied in singing the psalm by the full organ throughout. Here, then, no variety is required."[21] At St Peter, Cornhill, the high-church rector, William Beveridge, was one of those few clergymen who took psalm-singing seriously. The Smith one-manual organ there was installed at a cost of £210, no doubt at Beveridge's instigation, in 1681 (soon after he became rector), and was maintained by a gift of his friend Benjamin Thorowgood.[22] Beveridge excited admiration for his unusual support of psalmody: it was thought worthy of remark that he "constantly stood with reverence while he sung the praises of God; ... and when he went into the pulpit, he neither altered his posture, nor forbore to join with the congregation till the psalm was finished."[23]

The giving-out of the psalm tune on a one-manual organ may have been little more than a plain harmonization in two or three parts. John Playford, in his three-part psalm book of 1677, set out the tune in the G clef with the bass below, "as most proper to joyn *Voice* and *Instrument* together, according to holy *David's* prescription *Psalm 144.9*. And since many of our Churches are lately furnished with Organs, it will also be useful for the Organist."[24] One of these settings is illustrated in Example 1: the small notes indicate the medius part, which, however, Playford printed separately.

The organ at the affluent new church of St James, Westminster (now usually called St James, Piccadilly) was transferred from Whitehall Chapel, where it was no longer needed after the departure of the last Catholic queen dowager, Catherine of Braganza. It was presented to the church by Queen Mary II, and its removal, enlargement and installation in 1691 were carried out by Bernard Smith, whose fee of £150 was paid by voluntary subscription.[25] I have been unable to discover how many manuals this organ possessed. The psalms were no doubt performed from the little book entitled *The Psalms and*

Example 1.
WINDSOR tune, from John Playford, *The Whole Book of Psalms* (1677), Ps.17.

Hymns, Usually Sung in the Churches and Tabernacles of St. Martins in the Fields, and St. James's Westminster, published in 1688.[26] The tunes are set out in three parts, two trebles and bass, in a conservative style. In five later editions of this book, however, dating from 1697 to 1704, only St James's church is mentioned in the title, and the tunes are reduced to *two* parts. As no more elaborate organ versions have survived from this period, we must assume that the organist, Ralph Courteville, played from these settings, though of course he would have been free to fill them out either harmonically or melodically. (His own tune ST JAMES, one of the earliest of the new school of psalm tunes and still very popular today, first appeared in the 1697 edition of this booklet.)

Other simple organ settings are found in *Melodies Proper to be Sung to Any of the Versions of the Psalms of David, Figur'd for the Organ*. This booklet was advertised in *The Post Man*, 17-19 July 1716, and has been attributed to Philip Hart, apparently on the grounds that it contains six tunes by him. Hart was deputy organist, later organist, at St Andrew Undershaft, but the collection, even if it was his, cannot be taken as necessarily representing parish church practice. It has the tunes set out on two staves, in two parts with an occasional third part for the left hand, and with bass figures. On the same page, each tune is also given in a version transposed for the flute. The book may have been intended for practising psalm tunes at home.

The more elaborate type of setting with interludes and givings-out is found only in 18th-century sources. There are four sources from the earlier decades, two printed and two in manuscript. All have titles strikingly similar in their wording. The earliest is *The Psalms by Dr. Blow Set Full for the Organ or Harpsicord As They are Play'd in Churches or Chapels*. It was advertised for sale by John Walsh in 1703. Another set by Daniel Purcell, with an almost identical title, was advertised in 1718.[27] (The surviving copies of both works are later issues.) Blow had no known connection with a parish church, and he may have composed his settings for Westminster Abbey, where metrical psalms were sung after the sermon. Purcell was organist of St Andrew, Holborn from 1713 until his death in 1717.

The two manuscript sets are from the substantial books of keyboard and vocal music written out by John Reading (1677-1764) and presented by him to Dulwich College.[28] Reading was organist at this college from 1700 to 1702, and apparently later as well, judging by the ascriptions of some of the pieces in this manuscript. After an interval at Lincoln Cathedral he was chosen organist of St John, Hackney in preference to five other candidates on 28 January 1708, the appointment to run from the following Lady Day. He appeared before the vestry in 1719 to answer complaints concerning the discharge of his duty, and was dismissed in 1727.[29] In that year he was made organist of St Mary Woolnoth, a post he retained until his death.

In one of the Dulwich books, now numbered 92B, Reading calls himself "Organist of St. Johns Hackney" on the title page, and the harpsichord music contains pieces based on songs from operas that were performed in London between 1720 and 1728: it was probably therefore compiled or at least begun during his last years at Hackney. The other Dulwich set (92A) calls Reading "organist of St. Mary Woolnoth, Lombard Street, London," and the harpsichord pieces are taken from operas performed up to 1731, so it is clearly a later compilation for use at St Mary's, though containing much of the same music, in identical or revised form, as the earlier book. (Another book in the set, containing no organ music, bears the date 29 May 1716 on its title page.)

The four sets are remarkably close in their tune repertory, as the table shows. All confine themselves to the old, traditional psalm tunes; the tunes OXFORD and 125TH PSALM were modal in character and were dropping out of use, so it is not surprising that only Blow included these. The Blow settings have no givings-out, only simple four-part harmonizations with short, one-bar interludes between the phrases of the tune (Ex. 2). These interludes, which are quite standardized and trivial, often end on a longer note that leads into the

Example 2.
WINDSOR tune, from *The Psalms by Dr. Blow.*

next tune note (the example is an exception in this respect). An old-fashioned feature is the adding of a lower octave in the bass after the upper octave has been played.

The Purcell settings have absolutely plain four-part harmonizations, with mostly two-part interludes lacking the long note, running straight into the tune — not a very practical feature for congregational singing.[30] The new factor, however, is the separate "giving-out," which goes through the whole tune with extremely elaborate but rather vapid ornamentation, possibly intended to imitate the Old Way of Singing. The harmony is notably thin, mainly the bass alone with occasionally a third part added in the left hand, and it clearly calls for the use of a cornet or other solo stop. These givings-out could still be played on a one-manual organ with a divided Cornet stop for the treble half of the keyboard only.

In the Reading settings, the tunes are harmonized with the maximum sonority — both hands play almost every note in reach. The interludes are generally as before, in continuous semiquavers, but often involve some motivic development on a small scale; in the longer tunes the interludes are cumulative. The tune YORK in the book for St John, Hackney (92B) has additional interludes in the *middle* of the first and third phrases of the tune. The givings-out are less predictable than Blow's or Purcell's, sometimes almost exuberant (Ex. 3). It is fair to say that whereas Blow and Purcell applied a routine procedure to a number of tunes, Reading begins to make a musical composition, applying different figures and ideas each time. We have here the beginnings of a development of tune-based art music, but it was never followed through.

One Reading setting, that of the 81ST PSALM in the St Mary Woolnoth book, has only a single interlude, at the end of the verse. This pattern was forward-looking: it became the norm in later eighteenth-century organ settings of psalm tunes. The ones in *The Organist's Pocket Companion* (*c*.1750), for instance, have an elaborate giving-out in much the same style as before, a plain harmonization of the tune, and a series of little pieces to play between the verses, but nothing between phrases.[31]

Clearly these settings could be played far more effectively on two or even three manuals than on one. We find, after about 1690, that many London organs were enlarged, and that new organs in London churches typically had two manuals, if not three. Largest of all was the famous Jordan instrument at St Magnus, London Bridge (1712), complete with swellbox.

Our *Gentleman's Magazine* correspondent of 1772 pointed out that "in services and *anthems* one or two persons frequently sing alone, and then the whole choir together ... In these sudden transitions from soft to loud two rows of keys are absolutely necessary." The introduction of anthems in parish churches, first proposed by Henry Playford in 1701, may have been one reason for the greater use of two-manual organs. Again John Reading is a significant figure. The Dulwich MS 92A contains anthems designed for use by a choir of children, or of children and young men, such as existed in the churches where he worked. There are anthems by Blow, Humfrey, Purcell and Croft "made into a solo, for a tenor, or treble, by John Reading," and anthems of his own

Example 3.
(a) WINDSOR Psalm Tune given out, by John Reading (Dulwich 92B).

(b) WINDSOR Psalm Tune with the interludes (*ibid.*)

of the same kind. They consist mainly of "verse" sections for the solo voice and continuo, alternating with symphonies for organ; at the end is a short section for *unison* chorus. Reading also published, about 1710, a book of anthems of just this kind.

Extended compositions called "charity hymns," with organ symphonies, were also written for parish churches at this time. Four by Croft, who was probably organist of St Anne, Soho, from 1700 to 1711, were late printed by his pupil John Barker and used at Coventry parish church.[32] William Richardson published in 1729 *The Pious Recreation*, a set of hymns and anthems for a choir of trebles and basses with organ, no doubt performed at St Nicholas, Deptford, where he had been organist since 1697.[33]

In all this music there is a notable preference for thin texture, especially when the organ is playing alone: the only consistent exception is in the plain harmonizations of psalm tunes. An "airy" sound was evidently admired, with contrast between manuals where this was possible, and with a wide gap between tune and bass. This can be taken as a sign that the Italian baroque idiom of the earlier seventeenth century had at last reached the English parish church.

As parishioners went to a good deal of expense to enlarge organs and pay organists, they would naturally want to see a substantial return for their money. Organ solos or voluntaries would have been encouraged. We know that voluntaries were played in cathedrals, not only before, between, and after the services, but in the middle of morning and evening prayer as well, generally before the first lesson: this is explicitly stated by James Clifford.[34] But, as we have seen, it was not until well into the eighteenth century that parish churches began to model their music consciously on that of cathedrals. I have discovered no reference to the use of voluntaries in parish churches before 1700, and the few voluntaries that survive from this period are by cathedral organists such as Christopher Gibbons, Blow, and Purcell.[35] The practice, if it existed at all, was improvisatory, and we have nothing but our imaginations to tell us what parish organists may have played in the Restoration period.

Once again the main development seems to have taken place after 1700. For our knowledge of the early decades of the 18th century we are once again dependent on the Reading manuscripts at Dulwich, though it is entirely possible that Croft's short and simple voluntaries[36] were written for use at St Anne, Soho. He would hardly have needed these for his own use, but it was notorious that in many churches the organist's duty was often performed by a deputy, perhaps one of his students.

The voluntaries in the Dulwich books not only give a good idea of the repertory used by Reading himself at the two churches at which he was organist — and many of the same voluntaries occur in both books. They also include pieces by several composers whose titles as organists of other parish churches are given: for instance "The blind youth, Mr. Stanley, organist of St. Andrus Holbourn;" "Mr. John Barratt, organist of Christ Church [Newgate Street];" "Mr. James, organist of St Tollys [i.e., St Olave's] Church, Southwark." (These details tend to confirm the dating already proposed for the MSS.) Clearly by this time — around 1730 — there were a number of parochial organists who were in the business of composing voluntaries and sharing them with colleagues. Reading also copied, no doubt from cathedral sources, a handful of voluntaries by Blow, Croft and so on. A third book (MS 92D) adds voluntaries by Handel.

An interesting feature of the collection is that Reading divides his material into "1st" and "2nd" voluntaries, suggesting a different function in the service. The "1st" voluntaries are the more elaborate ones, in several movements, and nearly always exploit contrasts of registration, often with echo effects: many of them are empty show pieces (Ex. 4). This type of voluntary was probably played before the lessons. One writer on parish church music defined the voluntary as "an extempore Air or Prelude played on the Organ immediately after the Reading Psalms."[37] The "2nd" voluntaries invariably are fugues, with or without a short introductory movement. I believe that this "2nd" type of voluntary must have been played at the end of the service: if a voluntary was played at all, it was played then, as is made clear in more than one vestry minute.[38] Most of Croft's voluntaries are of this type.

Publication of sets of voluntaries also began in this period.[39] So long as they had been used only in cathedrals and were chiefly improvised, there was

Example 4.
A (1st) Voluntary, in D sol re, Composed by Mr. John
Baratt, organist of Christ Church (Dulwich 92A).

no profit in them, but now the leading music publisher, John Walsh, took advantage of the growing parochial market. In all organ publications it was usual to mention the harpsichord as an alternative, to maximize the market. The first title in which the word "voluntary" appears was a speculative affair, *Voluntarys and Fugues Made on Purpose for the Organ or Harpsichord by Ziani, Pollaroli, Bassani and Other Famous Authors*, printed about 1710. Walsh lifted the contents directly from an edition by Roger of Amsterdam, where the title was *XVII Sonates da organo o cembalo*. It is so far removed from actual English practice that several of the "voluntarys" have pedal parts, and would have been, for this reason, unplayable on any known English organ of the time. It is a sign, however, of the growing strength of Italian influence. Walsh tried again in 1719 with *A Second Collection* [also pirated] *of Toccates, Vollentarys, and Fugues Made on Purpose for the Organ & Harpsicord Compos'd by Pasquini, Polietti and Others*.

The voluntaries of the Georgian period would be distinctly Italianate in character. The landmark of the new style was the first set of *Voluntarys and Fugues Made on Purpose for the Organ or Harpsichord* (1728) composed by Thomas Roseingrave. Walsh used the same title as for his earlier collections, but this time he hit the nail on the head with compositions by the organist of the new and fashionable church of St George, Hanover Square, and presumably performed at that church. There were dozens more such sets during the rest of the century. A sizable proportion of them were the work of parish church organists.[40]

The change to a secular, more Italianate style was widely noted, and not always appreciated. A writer to *The Spectator* in 1712 complained that the religious feelings induced by the sermon, and by an appropriate metrical psalm, were "all in a moment dissipated by a merry jig from the organ loft."[41] Arthur Bedford, high-church vicar of the Temple Church, Bristol, and an amateur musician, complained in *The Great Abuse of Musick* that the solid English church style was being corrupted by foreign influences: "Our *Artists* boast themselves that they imitate the *Italian Fashion*, and which is worse, take their *Patterns*, not from the *Churches*, but from the *Play-houses*, and such like Diversions."[42] I will close with a longer quotation from Bedford. However jaundiced in tone, it throws much light on the matters I have discussed in this article. He objects to the secular style of "the *Voluntary* before the first *Lesson*, or after *Sermon*, and the *Interludes* between the Lines in *Singing of Psalms*," and goes on:

> When ... the *Clark* names the *Psalm*, the Organist ought so to play the Tune, so that it may be plainly understood; and the *Interludes*, that the *Congregation* may know when to begin, and when to leave off. But now the *Notes* are play'd with such a *Rattle* and *Hurry* instead of *Method*, with such Difference in the Length of equal Notes, to spoil the Time, and displease a *Musician*, and so many *Whimseys* instead of *Graces*, to confound the *Ignorant*, that the Design is lost, and the *Congregation* takes their *Tune*, not from the *Organ*, since they do not understand it, but from the *Parish Clark*, or from one another; which they could better have done, if there was no *Organ* at all.[43]

Notes

1. Henry Raynor, *Music in England* (London 1980), p. 90.
2. Nicholas Temperley, *The Music of the English Parish Church*, 2 vols. (Cambridge 1979), I, pp. 51-2;
3. Temperley, I, p. 79.
4. These are St Katherine-by-the-Tower, London (organ before 1710), Ripon (1663), Southwell (1663), Wimborne (1664), Wolverhampton (date unknown), Manchester (1684), and Middleham, Yorks, which had no organ before the 19th century.
5. Thomas Mace, *Musick's Monument* (London 1676), p. 11.
6. Nicholas Temperley, "Organs in English Parish Churches 1660-1830," *The Organ Yearbook* 10 (1979), pp. 83-100.
7. Henry Playford, *The Divine Companion* (London 1701), preface.
8. Thomas Bisse, *The Beauty of Holiness in the Common Prayer* (London 1716), pp. 89-90, n.
9. *The Organ* 48 (1932), p. 72.
10. The "old way of singing" has been described in detail in *The Musical Times* 120 (1979), pp. 943-7.
11. Samuel Pepys, Diary, 9 Aug. 1663.
12. John Playford, *Psalms & Hymns in Solemn Musick of Foure Parts* (London 1671), preface.
13. James Paterson, *Pietas Londinensis* (London 1714).
14. Vestry Minutes, 6 Apr. 1708 (Westminster Public Library D1758).
15. Vestry Minutes, 3 May 1692 (Westminster Public Library F2005).
16. Nicholas Temperley, "Organ Settings of English Psalm Tunes," *The Musical*

Times 122 (1981), contains an example; for others see Temperley, *Parish Church*, II, p. 53.

17. Built by Bernard Smith and presented by Lady Dionys Williamson: see Charles W. Pearce, *Old London City Churches, Their Organs, Organists and Musical Associations* (London 1909), p. 187; Wren Society [Publications], 20 vols. (Oxford 1924-43), XIX, p. 18.

18. Built by Thomas and Renatus Harris and presented by Thomas Whiting: Pearce, p. 138.

19. Built by Smith: Pearce, p. 204; *The Organ* 9 (1923), p. 37.

20. Built by Renatus Harris in 1695, according to Pearce (p. 121), with only one manual (*The Organ* 21 (1926), p. 10). However, the vestry minutes show that a loan to set up an organ was proposed only in 1700, and £22 to maintain it and pay the organist was appropriated on 9 September 1701 (Guildhall Library 4049/2).

21. *Gentleman's Magazine* 52 (1772), p. 562.

22. Paterson, p. 231; Wren Society, XIX, p. 49; Pearce, p. 70.

23. Edward Burton, ed., *The Works of George Bull, D.D., Lord Bishop of St. David's* (Oxford 1827), p. 62.

24. John Playford, *The Whole Book of Psalms ... Compos'd in Three Parts* (London 1677), fol.A3v.

25. Vestry Minutes, 7 Sept. 1691.

26. There is a copy in the Euing Library, Glasgow University.

27. William C. Smith, *A Bibliography of the Musical Works Published by John Walsh During the Years 1695-1720* (Oxford 1968), nos. 130, 539. The Purcell settings were pirated by Daniel Wright, a rival of Walsh, in a work called *The Harpsicord Master Improved* (London [1718?]).

28. Dulwich College MSS 92A, 92B, 92D. I am most grateful to Professor Bunker Clark for lending me a microfilm of these MSS, which he acquired through the good offices of Dr. Harry Diack Johnstone. I have revised my conclusions about the chronology of these sources since writing

in *The Musical Times* (see note 16 above).

29. Vestry Minutes, 28 Jan. 1707, 12 Dec. 1719, 4 Apr. 1727 (Greater London Record Office P79/JN1/138-40).

30. For an example see Temperley, *Parish Church*, II, p. 54.

31. For an example see Temperley, *Parish Church*, II, p. 55.

32. Nicholas Temperley, "Croft and the Charity Hymn," *The Musical Times* 119 (1978), pp. 539-41. One is printed in the *MT* Supplement for June 1978, and another in Temperley, *Parish Church*, II, p. 60.

33. One of the anthems is printed in Temperley, *Parish Church*, II, p. 65.

34. James Clifford, *The Divine Services and Anthems Usually Sung in His Majesty's Chappell and in All Collegiate Choirs of England and Ireland* (London 1663), p. 1.

35. Gibbons was, it is true, organist of St Martin-in-the-Fields for the last two years of his life (1674-6), but his later voluntaries were no doubt composed for Westminster Abbey.

36. For instance the set of twelve in British Library Add. MS 5336.

37. John Arnold, *The Compleat Psalmodist*, 5th ed. (London 1761), fol. F1v.

38. For instance the vestry of St John, Hackney, decided in 1753 to advertise for an organist, stipulating "that on every Sunday throughout the Year a Voluntary shall be played after both Morning and Evening Service" (Vestry Minutes, 11 Aug. 1753).

39. Matthew Locke's *Melothesia* (1673) contained some of his voluntaries, included in the title-page description as "lessons for the harpsichord and organ of all sorts." The *Fugues for the Organ or Harpsichord* published by Philip Hart in 1704 are similar in character to the "2nd Voluntaries" of Reading, but are not so called.

40. Temperley, *Parish Church*, I, p. 136.

41. *Spectator*, no. 338 (28 Mar. 1712).

42. Arthur Bedford, *The Great Abuse of Musick* (London 1711), p. 214.

43. Bedford, p. 212.

Organ Settings of Psalm Tunes With Interludes, 1700-1740

Tune	Frost	Metre	Date	Blow	Purcell	Reading I	Reading II
OXFORD	121	CM	1564	1	—	—	—
CANTERBURY	19	CM	1588	1	1	1	1
WINDSOR	129	CM	1591	1	1	1	1
MARTYRS	209	CM	1615	1	—	1	1
YORK	205	CM	1615	1	1	1	1
ST MARYS (HACKNEY)	333	CM	1621	1	1	1	1
ST DAVIDS	234	CM	1621	1	1	1	1
LICHFIELD (LONDON)	25	CM	1645	2	1	1	1
SOUTHWELL	65	SM	1579	1	1	1	1
100TH PSALM	114	LM	1561	1	1	1	1
81ST PSALM	99	DCM	1562	—	—	1	1
119TH PSALM	132	DCM	1558	1	1	1	1
125TH PSALM	144	$8^4 6^2$	1561	1	—	—	—
148TH PSALM	174	$6^4 4^4$	1558	2	1	1	1
113TH PSALM	125	8^{12}	1561	1	1	1	1

The Frost numbers refer to Maurice Frost, *English & Scottish Psalm & Hymn Tunes* c. *1543-1677* (London 1953), where the tunes are set out in their original forms. The 'Date' is of the earliest British printed source of the tune. The last four columns show the number of organ settings of each tune in the four early eighteenth-century sources: Blow = *The Psalms by Dr. Blow Set full for the Organ* [London: Walsh, 1703]; Purcell = Daniel Purcell, *The Psalms Set Full for the Organ* (London: Walsh, [1718]); Reading I = Dulwich college MS 92B (c.1720-30?); Reading II = Dulwich College MS 92A (c.1730-35?).

IX

Croft and the Charity Hymn[1]

The end of the 17th century was a turning-point for English parish church music. It was then that choirs began to reappear in the churches, after an interval of over a century in which they had been practically unknown. The impulse came from the high-church party, and its original objective was to improve congregational singing of the metrical psalm tunes, which had evolved after generations of neglect into a strange ritual known as 'the old way of singing'.[2] Among the clergy most active in promoting reform were Josiah Woodward, Thomas Bray, Arthur Bedford, and Thomas Tenison, archbishop of Canterbury from 1694. The *New Version of the Psalms* by Nahum Tate and Nicholas Brady (1696), with its tune supplement (1700), and the musical publications of John and Henry Playford provided materials to open the campaign.

Music was only one element of parochial life that needed reform. Of greater concern to the church leaders were the prevalence of vice and crime, the neglect of Christian principles, and non-attendance or irreverent behaviour at divine services. All these problems were attacked simultaneously by the formation of 'religious societies', made up of the young men of a parish, who met regularly under the direction of the clergyman for private devotions and religious discussion.[3] The first of these societies was founded in London as early as 1678. They were exclusively male, and largely of the working and artisan classes. The society of St Giles, Cripplegate, had 254 members in 1718, of whom only seven were described as 'gentlemen'. Meetings included the singing of psalm tunes, and, in time, singing teachers were employed to teach the young men to sing from notes in two or three parts. The movement was greatly strengthened in 1698 by the foundation of the Society for Promoting Christian Knowledge, which soon took the local societies under its wing, and provided them with books (including music).

---

[1]   Published in recognition of the 300th anniversary of William Croft's birth in the year 1678. A supplement in the same issue of the *Musical Times* was an edition of Croft's charity hymn 'To thee, O Lord of hosts', edited by Nicholas Temperley.

[2]   See Chapter IV in this volume.

[3]   See G.V. Portus: *Caritas Anglicana* (London, 1912).

In addition to their private meetings these societies took upon themselves the duty of supporting and enhancing the services of their parish church; in particular they took the lead in singing the psalms, and tried to guide the congregational singing away from the 'old way' and towards the accepted standards of art music. In country churches, where there were not sufficient funds to pay for organs, they formed the nucleus of west-gallery choirs that were an accepted institution throughout the Georgian period, later supported by wind and string instruments. In the larger towns, especially London and Westminster, organs were frequently donated or purchased by subscription, and charity schools were founded, in part for the purpose of providing treble voices for the choir. Here also the SPCK was active. In many London churches in Queen Anne's reign (1702–14) there was a choir consisting of charity children (generally of both sexes) and young men of limited musical ability and vocal powers, supported by a manual organ in fairly good condition. The accession of George I in 1714 soon led to the long hegemony of the Whigs, who strongly discouraged the religious societies, especially in London, because of their Toryism and suspected Jacobite connections. (So it came about that many London churches, for the rest of the 18th century, had choirs of children only, who tended to monopolize the singing as congregations lost interest.)

A limited body of music remains to attest the existence of these polarized choirs of trebles and baritones. Many collections of parish church music on either side of 1700 have one or two parts in the G clef and one in the F clef, but this was an adaptable format that could serve a number of vocal and instrumental combinations, in the home as well as the church. A collection of psalm tunes was published in 1688 for the churches of St Martin-in-the-Fields and St James, Westminster (now known as St James, Piccadilly). Both parishes had religious societies and charity schools, founded under the guidance of Tenison, who was incumbent of both; and both churches had organs. The book,[4] which was many times revised and was used at St. James's for over 50 years, had music in three parts, two with G clefs and the third with an F clef, and was very probably meant for a choir of children and men.

It was natural that choirs would sometimes want to sing more challenging music than simple psalm tunes, and an occasion for this was the charity sermon, often held annually, at which a prominent clergyman would urge the value of charity and religious education, and the plate would be passed round for contributions to support the school. The children, in their fine uniforms provided by the charity, would do their best to melt the hearts of the

---

[4]   *The Psalms and Hymns, usually sung in the Churches and Tabernacles of St. Martins in the Fields, and St. James's Westminster* (London, 1688).

congregation with their singing. Before long special hymns and anthems were being composed for these occasions with texts chosen or specially written for the purpose in hand. From 1704 an even more effective fund-raising event was staged: the annual meeting of all the charity children of London in one church.

John Reading's *Book of New Anthems* (London, *c*.1710) has anthems for trebles, optional bass voices, and organ, and may well have served this purpose, as some of its texts are suitable for charity occasions. There were several musical John Readings about at the time: one of them (1677–1764) was organist of St John, Hackney, from 1708 to 1727, and then of other London churches. To find publications more explicitly catering for treble-and-bass choirs, however, one has to look outside London. At St Nicholas, Deptford, the organist from 1697 was William Richardson, a former chorister of the Chapel Royal and pupil of John Blow. In 1729 he brought out a book called *The Pious Recreation . . . with six hymns for the use of societies and charity-children, likewise anthems for two and three voices, after the cathedral manner*. The hymns and anthems, some of which are on subjects connected with charity, have solos for treble, bass, and 'tenor bass' (baritone); choruses for two trebles and bass; and independent organ accompaniments. There are no alto or tenor parts. Some of the hymns have antiphonal sections marked 'boys' and 'girls'.

The great majority of 18th-century collections of parish-church music catered either for the 'country' choir, unaccompanied with the tune in the tenor, or for the 'town' choir, which increasingly had only treble voices with organ accompaniment. But the Birmingham area was one place in which the choir combining charity children with young men seems to have persisted longer than elsewhere. Publications by Michael Broome, James Kempson and John Barker between 1730 and 1780 are unusual among parochial collections of this period in being in three or four parts with the tune in the treble voice. Broome (1700–1775) was a country singing teacher who began operations in the Chiltern area in the 1720s, worked for a while in East Anglia, then settled in Birmingham, where in due course he became clerk of St Philip's church and a successful publisher and bookseller. In one of his many church music publications, *A Collection of Twenty-eight Psalm Tunes in four parts for the use of Churches and Chapels in and near Birmingham* (Birmingham, 1753), he divided the contents into pieces with the tune in the treble for churches with organs, and those with the tune in the tenor, 'for the use of societies'.[5] Kempson (1742–1822), parish clerk of St Paul's, was also a prominent local musician and publisher.

---

[5]   The latter would have been for village churches in the region, lacking organs.

Our particular interest in John Barker lies in his connection with William Croft, whose tercentenary falls this year [1978]. Barker was born probably in 1710 or a little earlier, and was a Chapel Royal chorister under Croft, being pensioned off in 1724. From 1731 to 1752 he was organist of Holy Trinity parish church, Coventry. He seems to have been in possession of some of his master's music, either in the form of autographs or in copies that he had made himself. He was the copyist of British Library Additional MS 31647, one of the main sources of Croft's harpsichord music, and of a manuscript recently discovered by H. Diack Johnstone[6] containing six otherwise unknown chamber sonatas. In about 1750 he published a collection of parish church music which
* included four hymns by Croft, also unknown in any other source. At his death in 1781 he left a number of manuscripts to Lichfield Cathedral, and there is other music in his hand at Birmingham (Barber Institute MS 5010).[7] Incidentally, two other publications of Croft's music from the Birmingham region should probably be given consideration as independent sources, since they could well have derived from copies in Barker's possession.[8]

Barker's printed collection, of which the only known copy is at Birmingham Public Library, is entitled *A Select Number of the Best Psalm Tunes, extant, for the treble, counter-tenor, tenor, and bass. To which are added, twelve psalm tunes, never before in score, most of them (if not all) set by the late Dr. Croft. Also, a collection of hymns, for the use of charity-children, set by Dr. Croft.* Birmingham: Printed by Mich. Broome, at Purcell's-Head in Lichfield-Street. An unknown hand has added a publication date of 1756, but an earlier date is likely, since Barker describes himself on the title-page as 'Organist, in the Holy Trinity Church in Coventry', a post which he resigned in 1752, to be succeeded by Capel Bond.

The psalm tunes are set for SATB with the tune in the treble. They include 'St Anne' and 'Hanover' (called 'St George's' here), though unfortunately they do not supply more definite evidence than we already have that these tunes were composed by Croft. They are marked 'Set by D[octor] C[roft]', but so are several tunes definitely not Croft's; 'set' evidently refers to the harmonies. Croft could have written these four-part settings for the Chapel Royal, but it

---

[6]   I am indebted to Dr Johnstone for much of this information about John Barker, without which I would not have realized the high probability that the four Croft hymns in Barker's collection are authentic. The information about the Barker MSS at Lichfield comes from Peter Marr.

[7]   I. Fenlon: *Catalogue of the Printed Music and Music Manuscripts before 1801 in the Music Library of the University of Birmingham* (London, 1976), 120.

[8]   Croft: *Six Anthems* (Birmingham: J. Kempson, 1771); Broome: *Divine Harmony: being a Choice Collection of Six Cathedral Anthems* [1 by Croft] (Birmingham: Michael Broome, c1770).

seems not unlikely that they were for a London parish church.[9] The probability is strengthened when we turn to the four 'hymns', which, together with two similar 'hymns' of Barker's and an anthem by Henry Holmes, make up the remaining contents of the book. Everything about these suggests that they were for use in connection with charity sermons.

The four hymns attributed to Croft are as follows:

Hymn I: *Ascribe to God most solemn praise* (G major, solo treble, SSB, organ)
Hymn III: *To thee, O Lord of hosts, do we* (G minor, solo treble, SB, organ)
Hymn IV: *To thee, O Father of mankind* (G minor, solo treble, S, organ)
Hymn VI: *Eternal Father of mankind* (C major, SSB, organ)

The texts have not so far been identified. All relate quite clearly to charity, some so aggressively that they could not well be used today. One (Hymn IV) is a blunt statement of the current Pelagianism:

Each heart and hand that lent us Aid,
  Thou didst inspire and guide;
Nor shall their love be unrepai'd,
  Who for the poor provide.

The text of Hymn I gives the flavour of the occasion with some humour:

Let us to God in greatful Thanks,
  Our chearful Voices raise;
And where the great Assembly meets,
  Set forth his Noble Praise.
To Psalms and Hymns we may aspire,
  Tho' Anthems are too High;
And strive to imitate the Choir,
  In decent harmony.

All have a similar musical scheme: a solemn, rather pleading opening section for the children in unison, with an organ obbligato on a solo stop; then a more cheerful triple-time section, in square phrases generally arranged with strophic or rondo-form repetitions (not in III), with solo verses (except in VI) and

---

9   As Dr Johnstone has pointed out to me, the oft-repeated statement that Croft was   *
organist of St Anne, Soho, from 1700 to 1711 is based on a mistaken identity: the St Anne organist was named Phillip Crofts (see F.G. E[dwards], 'Dr. William Croft', *MT*, xli (1900), 577–85). The naming of the tune 'St Anne', if indeed it is by William Croft, must be regarded as a coincidence. It appeared first in *A Supplement to the New Version* (8/1708), without attribution; its composer is first given as 'Dr. Crofts' in Philip Hart's *Melodies Proper to be Sung to any of the versions of the Psalms of David* (1715).

chorus basses (except in IV). Hymns IV and VI conclude with a common-time Hallelujah. The general style is that of Croft's earlier, 'Restoration' manner.

This is pleasant, certainly not great music, by one of our best composers, and it represents a forgotten phase of our musical and religious life. Hymn III, the accompanying music supplement, is the only one whose words are sufficiently general in their reference to charity to permit modern use, and it may possibly fill a need in choirs where altos and tenors are in short supply. Musically it is perhaps slightly below Hymn I (to be published in my book),[10] but a little better than the other two: its last section has a more extended form than the others. But opinions would differ on this point. All four are polished and, at moments, touching music.

Reproduced by permission of The Musical Times Publications Ltd.

---

[10]   *The Music of the English Parish Church*, ii, ex. 24.

Hymn: To thee, O Lord of Hosts

William Croft
edited by Nicholas Temperley

Anonymous

To thee, O Lord of

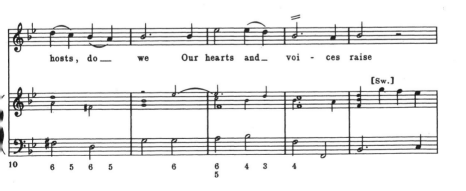

hosts, do we Our hearts and voi - ces raise

In sa - cred hymns of thanks to thee, in sa - cred hymns_ of thanks to thee,_ In set - ting_ forth thy_ praise.

[Sw.]

[Gt.]

To

ease the___ wants of all___ man - kind___ Do's*

streams of boun - ty flow, do's streams of

boun - ty flow;

From thee, O Lord, to love in - clined, from

*Do's = Do his

5

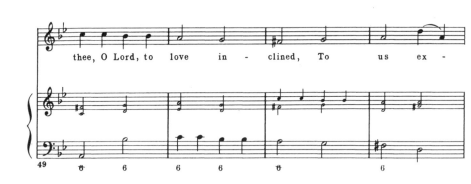

thee, O Lord, to love in - clined, To us ex -

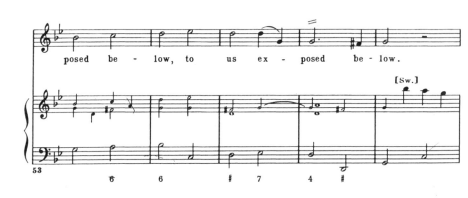

posed be - low, to us ex - posed be - low.

[Sw.]

To

[≡]

[Quicker]
VERSE
[SOPRANO] SOLO

'Tis he in - spires the good_ and just, in - spires the

good and just, His fa - vours to dis - pense:

To take the need - y from the dust, And

stand in their, and stand in their de - fence:

7

CHORUS
[SOPRANOS]

To Fa - ther, Son and Ho - ly Ghost, All glo - ry,_

[BASSES]

To Fa - ther, Son and Ho - ly Ghost, All glo - ry,

[Gt.]

109

hon - our be, Both now and as__ in a - ges past To

hon - our be, Both now and as in a - ges past To

115

all__ e - ter - ni - ty, to all, to all__ e - ter - ni - ty.

all__ e - ter - ni - ty, to all, to all__ e - ter - ni - ty.

121

X

The Hymn Books of the Foundling and Magdalen Hospital Chapels

The association of music with charity is immemorial. Begging players and singers, or "buskers" as they are now called, have importuned in street and home through the ages. Minstrels, mummers, and mystery plays were all associated with raising funds; traditional Christmas carols, such as "Here we come a-wassailing," sometimes directly ask the hearers for food, drink, or money. In eighteenth-century Britain, the use of music for charitable purposes took on new institutional forms.[1]

The urge to found new charities in this period can be explained in part by the new Enlightenment philosophy and its attendant Deistic tendencies. With the declining faith in the probability of divine intervention to relieve suffering came a correspondingly greater emphasis on human endeavor. There was a growing conviction that all the problems of the world could be solved by the application of reason. On the other side of the matter, those who were caught up in the new religious fervor of the Methodist and Evangelical movements were eager to save souls, and an institution offered unequaled opportunities to lead young sinners or victims to Christ.

A particularly acute set of social problems was forcing itself on the attention of the responsible classes. They resulted from the greater sexual promiscuity attendant on early industrialization, urbanization, and the decline of the Puritan ethic. Some charities, like the Foundling Hospital and the Asylum for Female Orphans, dealt directly with the increasing number of births outside marriage among the poor. Others, such as the Magdalen and Lock Hospitals, attempted to tackle the problems of prostitution and venereal disease. In all these cases, sacred music was developed as an attractive feature of chapel worship and, during the reign of George III, was published in specially prepared collections. The importance of these books has long been

---

[1]For a good general treatment of music and charity in this period, see E. D. Mackerness, *A Social History of English Music* (London: Routledge and Kegan Paul, 1964), 109-14. See also Betsy Rodgers, *Cloak of Charity: Studies in Eighteenth-Century Philanthropy* (London: Methuen, 1949). A recent study by Donna T. Andrew, *Philanthropy and Police: London Charity in the Eighteenth Century* (Princeton: Princeton University Press, 1989), suggests an additional motive for charity, the desire to maintain a large and healthy population for commercial and military advantage to the nation.

4

recognized,[2] but the details of their production and the chronology and relationship of the various editions have not been known.[3]

It is the purpose of this paper to establish such facts for the hymn books associated with the two institutions, the Foundling Hospital and the Magdalen Hospital, that were the first in this field among the new London charities.[4] The conclusions will be based principally on three sources of information: first, surviving copies of the books; second, the Hymn Tune Index database;[5] and third, in the case of the Foundling Hospital, the archives housed at the Greater London Record Office.

. . .

The idea of training children of both sexes to lead the singing in worship was well established in England long before the existence of these charities. Grammar school children were taught to sing metrical psalms in the parish church from the early years of the Reformation.[6] Easter Psalms were sung in procession by the orphaned children of Christ's Hospital, in a custom dating back at least to

---

[2]See, for instance, Maurice Frost, comp., *Historical Companion to Hymns Ancient and Modern* (London: Hymns Ancient & Modern, 1962), 100-103; Erik Routley, *The Music of Christian Hymns* (Chicago: G.I.A. Publications, 1981), 75-76.

[3]For instance, for the Foundling Hospital Collection, *The British Union-Catalogue of Early Music*, ed. Edith B. Schnapper, 2 vols. (London: Butterworths, 1957), under "Psalms. English" lists editions dated [c. 1770], 1774, [c. 1790], and 1796; John Julian, *A Dictionary of Hymnology*, 2d ed. (London: John Murray, 1907), 333, lists "Music, 1774, 1779, 1801. Words only, 1797 and 1801"; Frost (*Historical Companion*, 102) also thought the series began in 1774. Cf. Table 1.

[4]Perhaps the most influential of all was the Lock Hospital. This, however, has been discussed elsewhere: see Nicholas Temperley, "The Lock Hospital Chapel and Its Music," *Journal of the Royal Musical Association* 118 (1993): 44-72.

[5]The Hymn Tune Index, in preparation at the University of Illinois, is a computerized index of all hymn tunes associated with English-language texts found in printed sources published from the earliest times until the year 1820. It is to be published in book form by Oxford University Press, probably in 1995.

[6]See Nicholas Temperley, *The Music of the English Parish Church*, 2 vols. (Cambridge: Cambridge University Press, 1979), 1:63.

1610.[7] Charity schools were established in many parishes in London and other cities, beginning with St. Margaret, Westminster, in 1688,[8] and the children in these schools regularly learned the metrical psalms used in worship and led the congregation from a special position in church, generally the organ gallery. As the schools relied on voluntary contributions, it was usual for the children to sing at an annual charity sermon; special hymns and anthems were frequently written for the purpose.[9] From 1704, the charity children of all the London parishes joined together in a mammoth annual meeting at one church; after 1800, it was held at St. Paul's cathedral.

Of all the new London charities, none enjoyed a higher standing than the Foundling Hospital, with its royal charter (granted in 1737) and its parliamentary grants (amounting to over £500,000 between 1756 and 1771, when they ceased).[10] Conceived by the retired sea captain Thomas Coram (1668-1751), who was horrified by the growing practice of abandoning or killing unwanted children, it attracted broad support among the wealthier classes of society and also from leaders of the arts such as William Hogarth, Thomas Gainsborough, Joshua Reynolds, and, above all, George Frideric Handel.

Its official name was The Hospital for the Maintenance and Education of Exposed and Deserted Young Children. At first, all foundlings offered were admitted; when the number became too great, a ballot was instituted. But when Parliament agreed to grant financial support, it made a condition that all children offered should be accepted. The Hospital was then swamped with thousands of entrants every year and had to open country branches and farm out children to private nurses, but the numbers dwindled again after 1771. The children were educated and taught useful handicrafts and were found work when they reached maturity: boys were generally placed with shopkeepers or artisans, or in the armed forces or merchant navy, and girls went into domestic service. From 1758 onwards, blind foundlings were trained to be professional musicians.

---

[7]*A Psalme of Thanksgiving, To Be Sung by the Children of Christs Hospitall, on Munday in the Easter Holy Dayes, at Saint Mary Spittle, for Their Founders and Benefactors. Anno Domini.* 1610, STC 5208.5 (formerly 21521); see Susi Jeans, "The Easter Psalms of Christ's Hospital," *Proceedings of the Royal Musical Association* 88 (1961-62): 45-60.

[8]Temperley, *Parish Church*, 1:101-5.

[9]Temperley, *Parish Church*, 1:127, 134; 2:ex. 24. See also Nicholas Temperley, "Croft and the Charity Hymn," *The Musical Times* 119 (June 1978): 539-41 and music supplement.

[10]R. H. Nichols and F. A. Wray, *The History of the Foundling Hospital* (London: Oxford University Press, 1935), 15, 67. This work is the standard history of the institution and is the source for much of the general information in this and the following paragraph.

6

When the Hospital opened its doors in 1741, the children were at first boarded in houses in Hatton Garden. The permanent buildings, erected in Lamb's Conduit Fields (now Coram's Fields), opened in 1745; they were demolished in 1926 when the Hospital moved to Berkhamsted, Hertfordshire, but the Thomas Coram Foundation for Children still exists nearby at 40 Brunswick Square. The Hospital chapel, in use by 1749 and officially opened in 1753, soon became well known for its music as well as for its elegant architecture and adornments. The performances of *Messiah* under Handel's direction, his "Foundling Anthem" specially written for the Hospital, and his opening of the splendid organ on 1 May 1750 have been thoroughly investigated.[11] The singing of the children at ordinary Sunday services was also a great attraction to fashionable London and became an important source of income to the Hospital through pew rents and voluntary contributions. Music was specially composed and arranged for the Hospital chapel, and the success of the singing led to a demand for this music, which was i   by the publication of a book entitled *Psalms, Hymns and Anthems; for the Use of the Chapel of the Hospital for the Maintenance and Education of Exposed and Deserted Young Children.* It is generally known more informally as the Foundling Hospital Collection.

A firm date of 1774 has been assigned in many catalogues to the relatively common 128- to 158-page edition of this work, presumably on the grounds of an inscription at the base of the title-page engraving: "L. Sanders delin. et incis. in Aqua forti Feb. 1774." The records of the Hospital show that on 11 April 1772 the Subcommittee "taking into consideration the providing new Hymn Books used in the Chapel of this Hospital the Old plates being worn Out and some peices being to be Added are of Opinion that New plates be Engraved for that purpose and refer to the General Committee to give directions Accordingly."[12] On 15 April, the General Committee "Resolved, That new Hymn Books be provided for the use of the Chapel of this Hospital, under the Inspection of Mr. Harrison, And . . . that new plates be engraved for that purpose."[13] It seems almost certain that this order resulted in the earliest edition

---

[11]See, for instance, Otto Erich Deutsch, *Handel: A Documentary Biography* (London: Adam and Charles Black, 1955) and Donald Burrows, "Handel and the Foundling Hospital," *Music & Letters* 58 (1977): 269-84.

[12]London, Greater London Record Office, A/FH/A/3/5/1/10, p. 63. The governing body of the Hospital was the General Court. Responsibility for the administration of the charity was delegated to the General Committee, and day-to-day decisions were taken by the Subcommittee.

[13]A/FH/A/3/2/11, 15 April 1772. William Harrison was an active governor who was frequently called into service on musical matters.

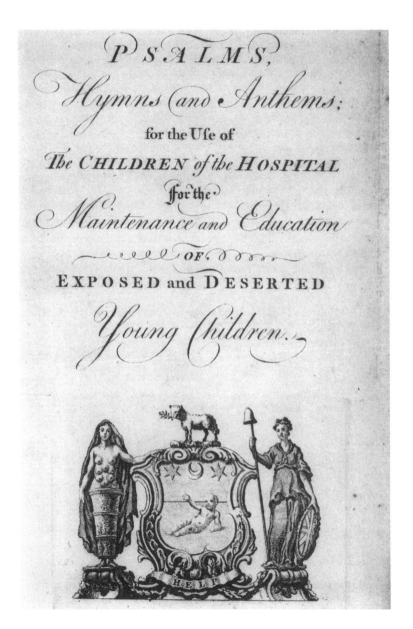

I. Title-page of the Foundling Hospital Collection, edition A/a (1760). University of Illinois at Urbana-Champaign, Rare Book Room, x783.452/P958.

7

with the Sanders engraving, which did indeed have its music printed from new plates, signed "Caulfield sc." (probably John Caulfield the elder)[14] on page 1. This edition is coded B/a in Table 1.

Relative uncertainty attaches to the earlier edition, the one whose plates were said to be worn out in 1772. Four copies of an evidently earlier edition with forty-eight pages and a different title-page, lacking imprint or date, have been located.[15] There is also an apparently incomplete copy, ending at page 12, at the University of Illinois in Urbana-Champaign.[16] The title-page engraving of all these copies is based on a coat of arms designed by Hogarth and granted to the Hospital in 1747. It shows a naked child supported on one side by a lady with eight breasts and on the other by Britannia (reproduced in Plate I).[17]

No order or resolution pertaining to this edition can be found in the minutes of the General Court, General Committee, or Subcommittee, or in the Steward's Accounts. However, a most illuminating document has been preserved among the Steward's records. It is a small cash notebook containing several pages of notes about the printing of "psalm books," with dates in the years 1760 and 1761. The notes were probably made by the Steward of the time, Lancelot Wilkinson, who was responsible for day-to-day receipts and disbursements. They provide information about the cost of printing music which has no parallel for this period of English history.

On the verso of the cover, we read the following:[18]

The Printers Name Nicholas Noyes Dogwell Court White Fryers
The Graver Caulfield Compton Street by Woods Close
Thick super fine Royal perfect costs £2. 2s. 0 p[er] Ream
. . . [Estimates for other types of paper]

---

[14] See Charles Humphries and William C. Smith, *Music Publishing in the British Isles*, 2d ed. (Oxford: Basil Blackwell, 1970), 100.

[15] British Library, C.16.m.; Fitzwilliam Museum, Cambridge, MU.MS. 1272; Newberry Library, Chicago, VM2136.P9759; Washington State University, Pullman, Washington.

[16] Rare Book Room, x783.452/P958.

[17] The sketch and the grant of arms are illustrated in Nichols and Wray, *History*, facing pages 251, 252. The full description of the arms reads: "Parted per fess, Azure and Vert, a Young Child lying naked and exposed, extending it's right hand proper. In Chief a Crescent Argent between two Mullets of six points Or; And for a Crest on a Wreath of the Colours, a Lamb Argent, holding in it's mouth a Sprig of Thyme proper; Supported on the Dexter side by a Terminal Figure of a Woman full of Nipples proper, with a Mantle Vert, the Term Argent being the Emblem of Nature; And on the Sinister side The Emblem of Liberty, Represented by Britannia holding in her right hand, upon a Staff proper, a Cap Argent, and habited in a Vest Azure, girt with a Belt Or, the under Garment Gules." The motto was simply "Help."

[18] One pound (£) = 20 shillings (s.); 1 shilling = 12 pence (d.).

Ch^r Watkins [at the] Crown in Holbourn over against Grays inn Gate
504 sheets is a Ream
Sent Sept 29th to y^e Printer
6. q^r × $^1/_2$ of Super fine Royal. 5 q^r / 6s^{heet} is to Print
200. Copies

The main account begins as follows:

				£	s	d
1760	May	13	Half a ream of paper	0	15	0
			2 Quire of blew Ditto	0	1	6
		16	1 Copper plate	0	9	0
		17	Changed the half ream			
			of Paper for a 11			
			Quire larger	0	7	0
			Changed the blew ditto	1	0	
			Proof paper	0	6	
		18	2 Pewter Plates	0	14	0
		24	4 Ditto	1	8	0
		28	3 Quire & 1 half of Paper	0	7	0
			6 Sheets of Gould &			
			flowered Paper	0	0	7$^1/_2$
			6 Ditto	0	0	7$^1/_2$
		29	Binding & Gilding 12			
			Books	0	2	0
	June 14		Printing 300 Books	1	7	0
				5	13	3

The meaning of this information seems clear. This was evidently
Wilkinson's first experience of publishing. He noted the names and
addresses of the tradesmen he would have to deal with: Noyes the
printer, Caulfield the engraver, and Watkins (no doubt) the supplier
of paper and plates.[19] He even had to make a note of the size of
a ream (504 sheets is 21 quires, rather than the normal 20—the extra
quire probably thrown in as a discount for quantity). On 13 May,
he bought half a ream (240 sheets) of ordinary paper and 2 quires
(48 sheets) of blue paper, perhaps for covers, with the intention of
printing 200 copies of the book. As time passed, the proposal grew.
A larger size of paper was substituted on 17 May, more pages were
decided on between 18 May and 24 May, and by 28 May, the total
number of sheets of white paper had reached 348. In the end, 300
copies were printed, 12 of them bound with ornamental endpapers
and decorated with gilt. The printing required one copper plate and
six of pewter. The copper plate would have been used for the title-page

---

[19]Nicholas Noyes is unknown to Humphries and Smith. This new information also pushes Caulfield's activity back to 1760 and supplies his
address.

9

and the pewter for the rest of the book.[20] This would provide twelve pages of text, if the leaves were folded once after printing, plus a separately engraved title-page.

Attention now focuses on the Illinois copy of the pre-1774 edition, described as "incomplete" in the library catalogue, and having twelve numbered pages. This copy is disbound; the thread that once held it is missing, but three thread holes are present in each folded leaf. There are front and back covers made of a coarse, purplish-brown paper that might once have been "blew." Inside these, the book is made up as follows:

Double leaf 1	pp. [i-ii]: blank
	p. [iii]: title-page, engraved from two small plates;
	p. [iv]: blank
Double leaf 2	engraved music and text: pp. 1, 4 printed from one plate, pp. 2, 3 from another
Double leaf 3	engraved music and text: pp. 5, 8 printed from one plate, pp. 6, 7 from another
Double leaf 4	engraved music and text: pp. 9, 12 printed from one plate, pp. 10, 11 from another
Single leaf	both sides blank

Each copy thus required four and a half double leaves of white paper, so 300 copies would have required 1,350 leaves. The double leaves measure 23 × 31 cm. If each of these was one-quarter of a sheet, 337 sheets would have been needed, each 46 × 62 cm. (or more).[21] This would be nicely covered by the 348 sheets actually bought by the Steward in 1760.

There is little doubt, then, that the Illinois copy[22] is the sole survivor of the first edition of the Foundling Hospital Collection, and that it was published by the Hospital itself in 1760. It is called edition A/a in Table 1. The cashbook yields further information. There is an account of copies sold: the regular price seems to be one shilling, but seven persons were charged 10s. 6d. each (possibly for a dozen copies), while a Miss Cantrell paid 4s. 6d. for three copies— these may have been gilt ones or ordinary copies bound. At a later stage (no date given), there is the note "Books in the Stewards hand plain 51 gilt 3— [total] 54," suggesting that 246 copies had been sold out of the first printing of 300. After that, numbers are not stated clearly; from time to time, profits are passed on to Mr. Harrison.

---

[20]This was the practice of the Walsh firm, for example, in the earlier decades of the century. See David Hunter, "The Printing of Opera and Song Books in England, 1703-1726," *Notes* 46 (December 1989): 336.

[21]The plates, judged by the plate marks in the paper, measured 19 × 26.5 cm.

[22]I have been unable to determine when or from whom the University of Illinois Library acquired this book.

Table 1. Foundling Hospital Tunebooks

Edition	Date	Compiler	Engraver	Pagination	Exemplar
A/a	[1760]	?	J. Caulfield	[2],12	US-U, x788.452/P958
A/b	[1762?]	?	J. Caulfield	[2],48	GB-Lbl, C.16.m.
B/a	1774	?	J. Caulfield	[2],128	GB-Cu, MR250.c.75.1.
B/b	"1774" [1780?]	?	J. Caulfield	[2],141	GB-Lbl, D.596.a.
B/c	"1774" [1790?]	?	J. Caulfield	[2],158	GB-Lbl, E.460.s.
C/a	1796	?	R. Skarrat[t]	[2],170,ii	GB-Lbl, F.1120.x.
C/b	"1796" [1802?]	?	R. Skarrat[t]	[2],138,13, [2],141-274	GB-Lbl, F.1120.y.
C/c	1809	W. Russell	R. Skarrat[t]	See foot-note 44	GB-Lbl, F.1120.z.

Note: Lines grouped together indicate editions with identical musical contents. Library sigla follow RISM.

Table 2. Contents of Foundling Hospital Tunebook, Edition A/a

Page	Title	Text	Text Source	Tune Incipit*	Attribution
1	Foundling's Hymn	Our light, our Saviour is the Lord	Ps.27: 1, 12, …	5123432321	Mr. Smith
2	Psalm 19	The spacious firmament on high	Ps. 19: 1-6 (Addison)	5154329451	Mr. Smith
4	Psalm 23	My shepherd is the living Lord	Ps. 23 (Hopkins)	1548456543	Mr. Scott
5	Psalm 145	The Lord does them support that fall	Ps. 145: 14-16, 19-20 (Tate & Brady), …	1123454327	
6	A Hymn	Father of mercy, hear our pray'rs	unknown	1356123432	Mr. Worgan
8	The Easter Hymn	Jesus Christ is risen today	Lyra Davidica (1708)	1351465345	
9	The Thanksgiving Hymn	To celebrate thy praise, O Lord	Ps. 9: 1-4 (Tate & Brady), …, doxology	1548192313	
10	Anthem	Sing unto the Lord	Ps. 96: 2-4 (BCP)	1333323555	

Note: Ellipsis indicates additional text of unknown origin.

* The first ten notes of the tune, coded according to the method used in the Hymn Tune Index: 1 is the keynote, 2-7 the other notes of the diatonic scale; accidentals, rests, and ornaments are ignored.

In April 1761 comes the entry: "N. B. Matroon [Matron?] has 100 books Steward 300 books." It is clear from this and other entries that more copies were printed from time to time, but there are no dates later than 1761. Evidently then, the book was selling quite well.

In October 1761, Steward Wilkinson absconded with £600,[23] leaving certain moneys unaccounted for. The General Committee investigated and found, among other things, "To so much rece[ive]d from Hymn Books, which he has not accounted for, £5. 13. 0";[24] this would represent the proceeds of over 100 copies.

Who used the books? On 31 December 1759, there were 270 children living at the Hospital in Bloomsbury.[25] Since infants were boarded out up to the age of five and were then educated in the Hospital until they were put out to employment at about fourteen, most of those in residence were of an age that allowed them to sing in the chapel. Others who boarded near the Hospital may have attended Sunday services. An illustration of about 1810[26] shows over 100 children of each sex seated in the organ gallery during a service, while the fashionably dressed congregation occupies the pews below and the side galleries.

It seems unlikely, however, that the printed hymn books were used by the children because the cashbook shows that they were sold for 1s. each. Most probably the children were taught the music by rote, and the books were sold to the congregation, either to use at the chapel or for home use, to help pay the cost of maintaining the chapel and services (which could not properly be defrayed out of donations to the Hospital).[27]

The twelve pages of the 1760 edition contain only eight pieces of music (see Table 2), set out for voice and figured bass with occasional "symphonies" for the organ. They represent current, orthodox Anglican practice in microcosm. Seven have metrical texts; three are called Psalms and four Hymns. Of the Hymns, two are, in fact, metrical versions of psalms; a third is the Easter Hymn that was widely used in parish churches. The eighth piece is an anthem also based on verses from a psalm. There is little concession here to Evangelical views, but the text selection is mildly progressive. The

---

[23]Nichols and Wray, *History*, 270.

[24]A/FH/A/3/2/7, 18 November 1761.

[25]Nichols and Wray, *History*, 55. The total under the governors' care was 6,293, but this included those in branch hospitals and those put out to lodge with nurses.

[26]Rudolph Ackermann, *The Microcosm of London* (London, 1808-10); plate reproduced in *Ackermann's Illustrated London*, ed. Fiona St. Aubyn (Ware: Woodsworth Editions, 1985), 195.

[27]Nichols and Wray, *History*, 201.

11

words were chosen, and in some cases modified, in part to underline the children's dependence on charity. This is true of the first and most important piece, the Foundling's Hymn, which became quite popular—its tune being later adapted to a number of other texts. The text shows beyond doubt that the children themselves were singing:[28]

> Our light, our Saviour is the Lord;
> For nothing need we care:
> The Mighty Lord is our Support;
> What have we then to fear?
>
> When Parents, deaf to Nature's Voice,
> Their helpless Charge forsook,
> Then Nature's God, who heard our Cries,
> Compassion on us took.
>
> Continue still to hear our Voice,
> When unto thee we Cry;
> And still the Infants' Praise receive,
> And still their Wants supply.

The oldest tune in the book is the still popular one for the Easter Hymn, dating from 1708. The anthem, unattributed here, was in fact by Vaughan Richardson (d. 1729), sometime organist of Winchester Cathedral, and had long been popular with country parish choirs. Normally for four voices, it is adapted here for treble and bass. Apart from this, all the music has only a single vocal line. The first three items are by musicians associated with the Hospital: John Christopher Smith (1712-95), Handel's amanuensis, who was the first organist, from 1754 to 1770, and John Scott (d. 1792), the blind organist of St. Michael, Crooked Lane, who was Smith's assistant at the Hospital.[29] John Worgan (1724-90) was a famous London organist.

The next edition (A/b) was produced by adding thirty-six more pages, bringing the total to forty-eight. There is no sign that it appeared in separate numbers of twelve pages each; moreover the words "Caulfield sc." appear on page 13, as on page 1, but nowhere else. The title-page and pages 1-12 were reprinted unchanged. The additional music consists of nine metrical psalms, three hymns (none of them of Evangelical tendency), three anthems, and one set piece.[30]

---

[28]Punctuation regularized.

[29]The two composers are more definitively identified in edition C/c. For Scott's position at the Hospital, see Nichols and Wray, *History*, 233; for his biography, see Donovan Dawe, *Organists of the City of London 1660-1850* (Padstow: Donovan Dawe, 1983), 141.

[30]The term *set piece* is used in the Hymn Tune Index, following occasional eighteenth-century usage, to denote a through-composed setting of a metrical text, as opposed to an *anthem* which has a prose text.

No precise date can be assigned to this edition, since it is not mentioned in the Hospital records. But there are reasons for supposing that it appeared soon after 1760. One is that the plates of pages 1-12 are not noticeably more worn than those of pages 13-48, showing that not more than a few hundred copies of edition A/a can have been sold before the new edition was printed;[31] and we have seen that at least 400 had been printed by 1761. Another is that a new tune in edition A/b, printed with an attribution to "Dr. Heighington" (Musgrave Heighington [1679-1764]), appears in a portion of the Lock Hospital Collection which was probably first printed in 1763,[32] with the note "Altered from Dr. H." On these grounds, it would seem that edition A/b appeared in or near the year 1762.

New composers named in this edition are Heighington, Handel, Mr. Green (unidentified: not Maurice Greene, who was always given his title "Dr."), and Mr. Cook (identified in later editions as Benjamin Cooke [1734/5-93], organist of Westminster Abbey). The most important innovation is the use of two high voices (SS or SA) in many pieces, suggesting that the children's choir was gaining in skill.[33]

The next edition (B/a) has the new title-page engraving already mentioned, dated 1774, suggesting that it was published in that year.[34] The illustration shows a tall, hooded woman apparently suckling a child, surrounded by four other children of various ages, with Hospital buildings in the background. Caulfield again signed as engraver of the music, but it was newly engraved throughout. Some of the pieces in edition A were now dropped, including two of four items by Smith (he had retired as organist in 1770), and there are many new ones to fill the 126 pages of music.[35] The great majority of pieces are now for SS, SA, or SAB. The bass parts may well have

[31]Pewter plates, while generally regarded as softer than copper, could produce two thousand impressions if handled well, according to Hunter, "Printing," 333. But a source from the early nineteenth century suggests that four thousand impressions were obtainable: see *Recollections of R. J. S. Stevens: An Organist in Georgian London,* ed. Mark Argent (London: Macmillan, 1992), 30.

[32]See Temperley, *Lock Hospital Chapel,* 49, 69.

[33]In the 1870s, it was the custom for the girls to sing soprano and the boys alto: see John Spencer Curwen, *Studies in Worship-Music,* 1st ser. (London: J. Curwen & Sons, 1880), 201. It is quite likely that this had been the practice from the beginning.

[34]1774 is at least a *terminus a quo.* Another factor pointing to a date no later than early 1775 is the fact that this edition attributes several tunes to "Mr. Cook," which was corrected to "Dr. Cook" later. Cooke received his Cambridge Mus. D. in 1775 and was the only composer of that name who held a doctorate in music from either Oxford or Cambridge at that time.

[35]Pages 127-28 contain an index of first lines.

been sung by ex-Foundlings, some of whom continued to attend the chapel. There are some new tunes for old texts: Addison's Psalm 19, "The spacious firmament on high," now has the tune most often associated with it today, by John Sheeles (first published about 1740); there is a new tune by James Evance (d. 1811), organist of St. Andrew, Holborn, and All Hallows the Great, and possibly a former inmate of the Hospital. There is now one hymn by Isaac Watts ("Infinite power, eternal Lord"); a new adaptation of Pope's *Universal Prayer* ("Thou great first cause, least understood"); and a gloomy "Hymn for the Children of the Foundling Hospital by Dr. Hawkesworth [1715-73], Set by Mr. Stanley"—John Stanley (1713-86), the famous blind organist of the Temple Church, taught some of the Foundlings to play the organ. The Easter Hymn has now been expanded into a short cantata, and there is a set piece by Thomas Grenville (1746-1827), one of the blind Foundlings who were trained to be musicians; he was organist of the Hospital from 1773 to 1798.[36]

Two later editions (B/b, B/c) have music identical to the 1774 edition, printed from the same plates, but contain added pages of text; the pagination rises to 141 and 158, respectively. These have been dated 1774 by many libraries, because of the date on the title-page engraving; their actual dates will be discussed below.

On 4 June 1777, the General Committee noted that only about £2 was being taken at the chapel doors each Sunday and asked the Subcommittee to suggest ways of increasing the "Income of the Chapel." On the advice of the Subcommittee, it was

Resolved,

> That John Printer be engaged to sing in the Chapel . . . every Sunday Morning and Evening from Michal[s] [Michaelmas] next at a certain Salary.

> That the Children Chant in the Morning Service, We Praise thee O Lord!, or Te Deum, and in the Evening, My soul doth Magnifye the Lord!, or the Magnificat.

> That Mr. Harrison be desired to procure proper Chants for that Purpose.

> That the Evening Service begin at 6 o'Clock from Mich[aelma]s next, as at the Magdalen and Lock Hospitals.

> That the East Gallery be appropriated for well dressed Strangers, without asking Money for Admittance; but the plate to be held at their coming out as at the Magdalen Hosp[ita]l.[37]

---

[36]For his biography, see Nichols and Wray, *History*, 244. He succeeded Stephen Philpot, who was organist from 1770 to 1773 in succession to Smith.

[37]A/FH/A/3/2/14, 4 and 11 June 1777. Printer was another blind Foundling who had been provided with lessons in singing, organ, harpsichord, and violin. For Harrison, see note 13 above.

Clearly, it was felt that the rival charities were outstripping the Foundling Hospital in attracting wealthy patrons by their music, though in fact they too experienced a decline in income from their chapel services at about this time or shortly after. Chanting by children at this date (other than by boys forming part of a full choir in choral foundations) was probably an innovation; it would soon be taken up as an impressive part of the annual performance by the massed charity children of London, witnessed by Haydn in 1791. The measures adopted by the Committee seem to have had little effect on the takings recorded. Large crowds and substantial takings were still to be had, however, at the annual performances of *Messiah* and also at the annual charity sermon.

In 1778, Jonas Hanway (1712-86), the well-known philanthropist, founder of the Magdalen Hospital, and now vice president of the Foundling Hospital, suggested the printing of small wordbooks containing the texts of the hymn book. The General Committee turned down the request because "the Printing the same would prevent the Sale of the Books now used in the Chapel," but they were overruled by the General Court:

> Whereas the Book of Psalms &ca. sung in the Chapel is too expensive for the Purchase of the poorer part of the Congregation in the Chapel,
> Resolved that a small edition of one thousand Copies be printed in twelves without the Music, the pages to correspond with the Pages of the Hymn Book, and that Mr Harrison be desired to see the same executed in the manner he shall most approve, at an expense not exceeding £20. -. -.[38]

That seems to show that the hymn books with music were primarily sold for use in the chapel by the congregation, rather than for outside use, though they were advertised for sale by some music sellers at this period.[39] This in turn suggests that the congregation was encouraged to join in at least some of the hymns.

The wordbooks were printed with the title *Psalms, Hymns and Anthems; Sung in the Chapel of the Hospital for the Maintenance and Education of Exposed and Deserted Young Children. London: Printed in the Year. . . .* The earliest edition so far discovered is dated 1783. Two copies of it exist in a box of some twenty wordbooks of different dates preserved among the Hospital records.[40] In

---

[38]A/FH/A/3/2/13, 25 February 1778; A/FH/A/3/1/3, 1 April 1778.

[39]For instance, by John Welcker in 1776: see his catalogue, British Library, Hirsch IV.1110.(9.), where "Foundling Hymns" are listed at a price of 1s. 6d.

[40]Greater London Record Office, A/FH, Secretary: Chapel, "Psalms etc 1794-1835."

15

accordance with the order of the General Court quoted above, the wordbooks have, in place of true pagination, numbers referring to the pages in the tunebooks. The 1783 wordbook has page references up to 137 corresponding exactly to edition B/b of the tunebook (which has music on pages 1-126, texts on pages 127-37, and an index on pages 138-41). Thus, the latter may be dated circa 1780, and probably no later than 1783.

Wordbooks of 1788, 1794, and 1795 have been examined; they extended the page references to 153, 154, and 155, respectively, but edition B/c has additional texts on pages 143-58 (after the index). It also has a new, unsigned title-page engraving, copied from Saunders' engraving on edition B/a. It cannot be later than 1796, when a new edition of the hymn book appeared (see below); perhaps a date of circa 1790 might be postulated.

Further efforts were made to render the services more attractive. A special Chapel Committee was set up in 1795 (a step that the Lock Hospital had taken in 1781), and for a few years, it was energetic in making improvements. On 26 August 1795, it "Ordered that an Hymn be sung in the Chapel before the Evening Service begins in place of the Voluntary usually performed at present & a Psalm or Hymn be sung after the Prayer beginning Lighten our Darkness[;] that an Anthem be sung before the Sermon & the Evening Hymn after the Sermon." A few months later, the Chapel Committee asked the Secretary to "report upon what has been done with respect to a new publication of the Hymn Book."[41] No report emerged, but in that year, a completely new edition of the hymn book did appear (C/a), with a shortened title *Psalms Hymns and Anthems for the Foundling Chapel,* a new pictorial title-page incorporating a boy and girl with the chapel and other Hospital buildings in the background, a new motto ("But the greatest of these is Charity"), and the imprint "London, 1796." It had 138 pages of music "engraved by Skarrat Britannia St. Battle Bridge." These were followed by a second title-page reading "Additional Anthems and Hymns, The Music of which is not published By the Hospital"; texts, pages 141-70; and a two-page index, the whole "Printed at the Philanthropic Reform, London-Road, St. George's Fields" (this was probably the Philanthropic Society, founded by Hanway in 1788 for the education of criminals' children).

Musically, this edition is no great advance on its predecessors, but there are a few solos, including a second verse of Addison's Psalm 19 with an attribution to "Mr. J. Printer," who no doubt sang this verse as a solo, the first and third verses being sung by the children

---

[41]A/FH/A/3/13/1, 15 January 1796.

to the standard tune. The other added pieces are chiefly traditional texts and tunes, and the only new composer is Thomas Arne, in a tune borrowed from the Magdalen Chapel Collection. Tune names were introduced in this edition.

From this point on, single and double leaves containing additional hymns are found inserted in some copies, and it is difficult to define what constitutes a new edition. A number of copies have seven leaves of music inserted after page 138, paginated 2-13, and these copies seem to amount to a definite edition (C/b), which can be dated circa 1802.

On the resignation of Grenville as organist at Midsummer 1798, the General Court took unusual care in the choice of his successor:

> it being of very considerable Importance to the Charity & to the Revenues thereof, that it should have the full benefit of the present competition of so many able Performers, & that person be elected who is most capable of discharging all the Duties of the appointment, the Governors are earnestly intreated not to solicit or engage any votes until all the candidates have been heard.

Out of eight candidates, three were in the final round, and the voting was as follows:[42]

Mr. [John] Immyns	50
Miss [Emily] Dowding [a Foundling]	41
Mr. [William] Russell	2

However, in March 1800, Immyns resigned, after being rebuked by the Court for neglect of his duties, and this time Russell was elected, and served until his death.

William Russell (1777-1813) was a prominent virtuoso organist as well as a composer of some repute. Soon after his appointment, the chapel organ was altered by his father, an organ builder, "so as to give an opportunity of making more variety in the Voluntaries." A few years later, in March 1805, Russell recommended extensive improvements to the organ, which the General Committee ordered at a cost of £120. However, the Committee told Russell that it "does not approve of any extended introductory preludes to the Anthems and Hymns sung during Divine Service at the Foundling Hospital nor of any Cadences ad Libitum in Church Music and therefore desires that in future they may be omitted."[43] Such strictures may well have diminished the Hospital's revenues in an age when fashionable congregations expected more and more elaborate "performances" as part of the music of worship.

---

[42]A/FH/A/3/14, 28 March and 9 May 1798.
[43]Nichols and Wray, *History*, 223, 225.

17

In 1809, the Hospital published the last of its series of tunebooks, a version of the 1796 edition revised by Russell (edition C/c). The title-page has the same engraved illustration as before, but the date was altered from 1796 to 1809, and the following words added: "Revised Corrected & Completely Figured for the Organ By W. Russell, Mus. Bac. Oxon. Organist of the Chapel." Many of the old plates were used, but with additions, mainly attributions to composers.[44] There are also a number of new compositions by Russell, all dated 1808 or 1809. One is an ambitious through-composed setting of Psalm 46, with an elaborate organ accompaniment invoking "the sublime" in a way possibly suggested by the aria "Rolling in foaming billows" from Haydn's *Creation*. So Russell, debarred from "Cadences ad Libitum," succeeded in introducing some virtuoso material by writing it into the printed accompaniment of a vocal work. The wordbooks kept pace with editions of the hymn book, and from 1801 onwards, they carry the imprint "London: Printed by Luke Hansard."

During the 1790s, John Printer, a solo singer in the chapel since 1777, had been joined by another blind Foundling, Jane Freer (1784-1845), who soon became the star performer.[45] The emphasis on paid professional singing grew, and in about 1811, the governors went outside the ranks of former Foundlings by hiring an opera singer, John Kendrick Pyne (1785-1857), as principal tenor soloist and singing teacher. By 1827, a professional quintet was doing most of the singing, at an annual cost of £206. In 1835, an observer wrote: "A portion of the service is chaunted in the best style, and anthems are delightfully sung by the male and female [adult] singers."[46] In the 1870s, the then-current organist, Christopher Edwin Willing (1830-1904), conducted a choir of 100 children and six professional singers. The psalms were sung antiphonally: one verse by the girls, the next by the professionals with the boys doubling the *alto* part. As J. S. Curwen observed, "the want of 'balance' is the chief defect of the service."[47] This type of singing drew huge crowds throughout the Victorian period, until the professional choir was finally abolished in December

---

[44]The pagination of this edition is irregular. After the title-page leaf and 140 numbered pages of music, there follow 45 pages of text numbered 139-83; then from 45 to 57 pages of music, bearing, instead of consecutive pagination, references to pages in the preceding section; then a two-page index, of which the first page is numbered 184. Clearly, the unpaginated section is an insertion, varying in size and content from one copy to another.

[45]Nichols and Wray, *History*, 240-41.

[46]*The Metropolitan Ecclesiastical Directory* (London: T. Hurst, 1835), 53.

[47]Curwen, *Studies*, 201.

239

1917 and the singing was once again carried solely by the voices of the children.[48]

The fifty years from 1760 to 1810 thus represent a first period of the Foundling Hospital chapel, when the basis of its music was the singing of hymns (and later chanting) by the children themselves. The Hospital governors, by means unknown, succeeded in staving off commercial piracies of their hymn book and designed it entirely for use in their own chapel, though it may well have been used privately as well. An inevitable result was that the music at the Foundling Hospital was less influential than the parallel developments at the Magdalen Chapel, to which we turn below. Three hymns written for the Foundling Collection survive in common use today: the anonymous "Spirit of mercy, truth and love"; "Praise the Lord, ye heavens, adore him," adapted by Russell to Haydn's famous "Emperor" tune in edition C/b; and perhaps James Edmeston's "Lead us, heavenly father, lead us."[49] No tune first printed in the Foundling Collection is in common use today.

. . .

The Magdalen[50] House, later called the Magdalen Hospital, was founded by Jonas Hanway, Charles Dingley, and others in 1758 as a haven for penitent prostitutes. The founding committee of seven laymen first met on 13 April 1758. They maintained close relations with the committee of another charity, the Asylum for Female Orphans, founded in the same year by John Field, and "intended as a preventive measure to supplement the work of the Magdalen Hospital."[51] A merger was even considered, but it was decided to keep the two charities separate in order to protect the moral education of the orphan girls.

The Hospital's first permanent location was at the former London Hospital between Prescott and Chambers Streets, Whitechapel; it moved to Blackfriars Road, Southwark, in 1772. In 1868, it took up its final location, a new set of Gothic buildings in Streatham High Street, where it was developed into an Approved School in 1934. Ten years later, it became a remand home, which finally closed in 1966. The records have been lost: the Magdalen Hospital Trust does not know whether they still exist. But the principal history of the

[48]Nichols and Wray, *History*, 231.
[49]This is headed "Written for the children of the London Orphan Asylum (air Lewis)" in Edmeston's *Sacred Lyrics* (London, 1821). It has not been found, however, in the Foundling Hospital wordbooks, and it is possible that it was written for the Asylum for Female Orphans.
[50]Pronounced "Maudlin."
[51]Rodgers, *Cloak of Charity*, 50.

19

institution was based on them and is presumably reliable,[52] though providing only scanty information about the music of the chapel and none about the hymn books.

A chaplain, Jonathan Reeves, was appointed at once, and there was a "little chapel" by the end of 1759. Horace Walpole described a visit to it in January 1760:

> At the west end were inclosed the sisterhood, above an hundred and thirty, all in greyish brown stuffs, broad handkerchiefs, and flat straw hats with a blue ribband, pulled quite over their faces. As soon as we entered the chapel, the organ played, and the Magdalens sung a hymn in parts; you cannot imagine how well.[53]

On 5 November 1761, a minute recorded that the old organ was to be sold and a new one built.[54]

The inmates of the Magdalen Hospital were able-bodied girls: if they had been affected by venereal disease, they would have been sent to the Lock Hospital.[55] Many were little more than children, the average age being about fourteen. Like the Foundlings, the Magdalens could be asked to sing to help arouse interest and support for their cause. On the other hand, there were risks involved in having them too openly displayed to the public view. In 1761, therefore, following a precedent set by the Ospedali of Venice,[56] the chapel was fitted with galleries where the girls sang from behind a grill.

---

[52]H. F. B. Compston, *The Magdalen Hospital: The Story of a Great Charity* (London: Society for Promoting Christian Knowledge, 1917). Crompston, on p. vi, thanks the Warden for "full access to the archives." His book is the chief source of the information in this and the preceding paragraph.

[53]W. S. Lewis and Ralph S. Brown, Jr., eds., *Horace Walpole's Correspondence with George Montagu, I,* The Yale Edition of Horace Walpole's Correspondence (W. S. Lewis, general editor), Vol. 9 (New Haven: Yale University Press, 1941), 273. According to official reports, the number of Magdalens in the Hospital was 105 in February 1761 and 115 in March 1765: see William Dodd, *An Account of the Rise, Progress and Present State of the Magdalen Charity* ([London]: W. Faden, [1761]), 8; 3d ed. (London: W. Faden, 1766), 6. Walpole's description of the girls' uniforms may be compared with Plate II.

[54]Crompston, *Magdalen Hospital,* 162 n. 2.

[55]See Temperley, "Lock Hospital Chapel," 47.

[56]Samuel Sharp, *Letters from Italy in the Years 1765 and 1766* (London: R. Cave, 1766), wrote the following description of the singing at the Incurabili, a hospital for venereal patients and penitent prostitutes: "However beautiful the girls may be, they trust only to their melody, being intercepted from the sight of the audience, by a black gauze hung over the rails of the gallery in which they perform: It is transparent enough to show the figures of women, but not in the least their features and complexion" (28). Jean-Jacques Rousseau gave a similar description in his *Confessions.* See Denis Arnold, "Orphans and Ladies: The Venetian Conservatories (1680-1790)," *Proceedings of the Royal Musical Association* 89 (1962-63): 31-47.

A MAGDALEN in her UNIFORM.

II. Frontispiece of the Magdalen Hospital Collection,
edition B2/b [1772?] British Library, E.602.y.(1.).

20

A similar arrangement was made when the octagonal chapel was opened at the new site in May 1772: it was fitted with "two galleries for the accommodation of these women, who are, however, concealed from the rest of the congregation by pieces of green canvas, stretched upon frames, and placed at the front of each gallery."[57] Another threat to the girls' virtue was, it seems, the presence of a male organist and singing instructor. From 1769 onwards, the organist was always female and was sometimes styled the "organess."[58] A revised set of bylaws adopted in 1791 stipulated that the office must always be held by a woman, who was also to attend twice a week "to instruct the women who sing in the chapel." It was further laid down that "No person is allowed to go into the Organ-loft, except the Organist and the women in the House."[59]

Large congregations were drawn to the chapel, in part by the colorful preaching of Thomas Dodd (1729-77).[60] The singing of psalms, hymns, and responses by the Magdalens became a great attraction of London society, mentioned in several guidebooks and memoirs. It probably reached its height in the 1770s. As in the Foundling and Lock Hospitals, a decline in choral singing seems to have begun in the 1780s, when a taste for solo singing began to prevail. A Mrs. Bell was in demand as a soloist. In the 1798 competition for the position of organist, candidates were required to play the first chorus from *Messiah* "from the score" and any other piece of their own choosing, and to sing "the Old Hundredth as set by Luther, two verses solo and two in duo with Mrs. Bell."[61] Looking back on the good old days in 1840, a former governor, Sir Edward Cust, wrote to the Committee that music had been "one of the leading causes of the former popularity of our chapel. The mystery of unseen voices, the monastic nature of our institution, the screen behind which a portion of the congregation is placed, who are the subject of our prayers and often appealed to by the preacher—

---

[57]*The London Guide* (London, 1782), 149. The arrangement is visible in an illustration by Ackermann: see *Ackermann's London*, 13.

[58]Compston, *Magdalen Hospital*, 169 n. 2. See Table 3 for the succession of organists in the early decades of the Hospital's existence.

[59]*Bye-Laws and Regulations of the Magdalen Hospital* (London: Printed for the Hospital, 1794), 27-28.

[60]Dodd, an eloquent orator in what Walpole termed the French style (Lewis and Brown, *Walpole's Correspondence with Montagu*, 274), was also a prolific writer. His vivid narratives of the fallen women and their repentance undoubtedly aroused public interest in the charity. But he was never, as many sources state, the permanent chaplain of the Hospital (Compston, *Magdalen Hospital*, 66 n. 1). He was publicly hanged for forgery in 1777.

[61]Compston, *Magdalen Hospital*, 162. This famous tune was often attributed to Luther.

all conspire[d] to make the pomp and ceremony of public worship at the Magdalen a more peculiar attraction."[62] In 1883, after the move to Streatham, the Magdalen Collection of hymns was finally replaced by *Hymns Ancient and Modern*.

Unlike the Foundling and Lock Hospitals, the Magdalen Hospital did not publish its own book of hymns with tunes. Although the term "Magdalen (Chapel) Collection" is often found, it refers loosely to a number of separate commercial publications which this paper will attempt to sort out. The Hospital did publish, beginning in 1759, a booklet entitled *The Rules, Orders and Regulations of the Magdalen House*, which carried the texts of hymns used in the chapel by way of an appendix; and they were also incorporated in several editions of *An Account of the Rise, Progress and Present State of the Magdalen Charity*, which was compiled by Dodd. The 1759 *Rules* had only three hymn texts; in the 1761 edition, the number had increased to twenty-seven (see Table 5). Later, an Anthem and an Ode (described below) were added. In 1769, the selection was revised and divided into twenty-five metrical psalms, mostly from Tate and Brady's *New Version*, and seventeen hymns, which included the Ode; and, from this year also, the texts were available as a separate publication.

The emphasis in these texts is somewhat different from that of the Foundling Collection. As might be expected, prominence is given to the subjects of sin and repentance. There is a preponderance of hymns over metrical psalms, not only popular and orthodox texts by Ken and Addison, but one by Watts and seven by his Independent successor, Philip Doddridge. The latter include two powerful and vivid sacramental hymns, "My God, and is thy table spread?" and "And are we now brought near to God?" These, first printed as recently as 1755 in a collected edition of Doddridge's hymns, were strong meat for Anglicans and would certainly have been new to many of the Anglican hearers at the Magdalen services. There were new translations of Latin hymns, not only *Veni, Creator Spiritus* (in use in the Church of England since the Reformation) but also *Dies irae*. The intention clearly was to remind inmates of the awful fate that awaited them if they did not repent and throw themselves on the mercy of Christ. To accomplish this, the Hospital authorities went outside the orthodox Anglican fare. However, the selection was not as advanced as that of the Lock Hospital Collection, which drew chiefly from Methodist and Dissenting sources.

---

[62]Compston, *Magdalen Hospital*, 165.

The first book of music associated with the Hospital was compiled and published by Thomas Call, probably the first organist to the charity (see Table 3). It was entitled *The Tunes As They Are Used at the Magdalen Chapel, Properly Set for the Organ, Harpsicord and Guittar*, London: Printed for and sold by Mr Thos Call at his lodgings at Mr Bennett's Stay Ware House near Great Turnstile Holbourn, and at the Magdalen House (Table 4, edition A/a). It was advertised for sale in *The Public Advertiser* on 27 March 1760, thus anticipating the Foundling Hospital Collection by some three months (indeed, it seems more than likely that the Foundling book was produced in response to this one). Only a single copy of this little book has been located, with a price of 2 shillings added in ink at the top right corner of the title-page. It has ten pages of engraved music[63] and fourteen more of typeset hymn texts. These twenty-seven texts include all those in the 1759 and 1761 selections (see Table 5). On the last page is "A Prayer for the Use of the Magdalen Chapel."[64] However, judging by its title, the book was designed for home as much as chapel use.

Of the twenty-two tunes, nine might be described as old English, with dates of origin ranging from 1562 to 1724. Two had distinctly Methodist associations, one a German tune adapted by John Wesley for his *Foundery Collection* of 1742, the other the "debased" but attractive version of "Tallis's Canon" that is first found in that book.[65] Eleven are new—nine later claimed by Call himself, one attributed to a Mr. Prior, and one remaining anonymous; but these attained little popularity outside the Magdalen books themselves, whereas many of the older tunes were among those most often reprinted in the century. The famous Easter Hymn tune (then and now best known with the words "Jesus Christ is risen today") appeared with a relatively new Thanksgiving Hymn, "Glory be to God our king," by Dodd.

---

[63]More than one engraver was evidently involved. The F clef is stamped on pages 1-6, hand-drawn on pages 7-8, and stamped in a different style on pages 9-10. Thomas Bennett was a music engraver, seller, and publisher (Humphries and Smith, *Music Publishing*, 68).

[64]This prayer was by Thomas Secker, Archbishop of Canterbury. It was "revised and authorized" on 10 May 1759, according to the Minutes as cited in Compston, *Magdalen Hospital*, 160; and it appears in the 1759 *Rules*.

[65]For further discussion of this once hugely popular but now obsolete version of the tune, see Maurice Frost, *English & Scottish Psalm & Hymn Tunes c. 1543-1677* (London: S. P. C. K. and Geoffrey Cumberlege, Oxford University Press, 1953), 392; Nicholas Temperley, "The Adventures of a Hymn Tune, I," *The Musical Times* 112 (April 1971): 375-76.

Table 3. Organists of the Magdalen Hospital Chapel

Name	Date of Appointment According to Compston*	Other Information
Thomas Call	1758?	Described himself as organist on eds. A/a (27 March 1760) and A/c (12 June 1762)
B. Wayn	. . .	Called Smith's "Predecessor" in preface to ed. C. One Benjamin Wayne, d. 1774, was appointed organist of St. Alban, Wood Street, in 1766 (Dawe, *Organists*, p. 152).
Adam Smith	1765?	Described himself as "late organist to the Charity" on ed. C; called "late organist of the Chapel" on ed. B2/a
William Selby	1766	Called "late organist of the Chapel" on ed. B2/b. Emigrated to New England, 1773
Mrs. Smithey	1769	
Mrs. Schmedes	1772?	
Mrs. Hannah Gossyn (or Gowen)	1777	
Miss Mary Schmedes	1784	
Miss Henrietta Lockhart	1794	Daughter of Charles Lockhart, whom she assisted as organist of the Lock Hospital Chapel, 1790-97
Miss Evans	1798	
Miss Emily Dowding	1798-1841	Also a candidate at the Foundling Hospital in 1798 (see p. 16)

* *Magdalen Hospital*, p. 215. Compston states that "previous to 1777 the succession is somewhat uncertain" and that "Mr. Selby was the last of the male organists (excluding temporary substitutes)."

Table 4. Magdalen Chapel Tunebooks

Edition	Date	Compiler	Publisher	Short Title	Pagination	Exemplar
A/a	[1760]	T. Call	T. Call	Tunes As They Are Used	[2], 10, [14]	US-NH, M2136.C156+
A/b	[17622]	?	J. Phillips	A Collection of Psalm and Hymn-Tunes	12	GB-Lbl, D.620.b.
A/c	[1762]	T. Call	T. Call	Tunes & Hymns As They Are Used	[2], 16, [14]	GB-Lbl, D.577.
B1/a	[1766?]	?	H. Thorowgood	Hymns Anthems and Tunes ibid., Book I	f, [2], 42	US-Uemperley
B1/b	[1770?]		H. Thorowgood	do.	f, [2], 42	GB-Lbl, F.1120.kk.
B1/c	[1780?]		Longman & Broderip Bland & Weller	do.	f, [2], 42	GB-Lbl, E.497.nn.(1)
B1/d	[1800?]		M. Clementi & Co.	do.	f, [2], 40, [2]	GB-Lbl, E.585.a.(2)
B1/e	[1802?]		Broderip & Wilkinson	do.	[2], 42	GB-Lminet, IV/73/2/13
B1/f	[1803?]		Preston	do.	f, [2], 42	GB-Lminet, IV/73/2/14
B1/g	(wm1806)			do.	f, [2], 42	GB-Lbl, F.1120.gg.(1)
B2/a	[1770?]	W. Selby?	H. Thorowgood	Second Collection	[2], 3-22	GB-En, Cwn.650.
B2/b	[1775?]		H. Thorowgood	do.	[2], f, 111-30, [2]	GB-Lbl, E.602.y.(1)
B2/c	[1780?]		Longman & Broderip	do.	f, [2], 111-30	GB-Lbl, E.497.nn.(2)
B2/d	[1803]		Broderip & Wilkinson	Hymns Anthems and Tunes, Book 4	f, [3], '42', 111-30	GB-Lminet, IV/73/2/14
B3/a	[1773?]	?	H. Thorowgood	Third Collection	[3], 2-31	GB-Lcm, IX.E.3.
B3/b	[1775?]		H. Thorowgood	do.	[3], 42-70	GB-Lcm, B.III.5.(2)
B3/c	[1780?]		Longman & Broderip	do.	f, [3], 42-71	GB-Lbl, E.497.nn.(3)
B3/d	[1803?]		Broderip & Wilkinson	Hymns Anthems and Tunes, Book 2	f, [3], 42-73	GB-Lminet, IV/73/2/14
B4/a	[1775?]	?	H. Thorowgood	Fourth Collection	[4], 73-108	GB-Lbl, E.1498.u.
B4/b	[1780?]		Longman & Broderip	do.	f, [4], 73-108	GB-Lbl, E.497.nn.(4)
B4/c	[1803?]		Broderip & Wilkinson	Hymns Anthems and Tunes, Book 3	f, [3], '42', 75-110	GB-Lminet, IV/73/2/14

HYMN BOOKS

C	[1767?]	A. Smith	S. Hooper	*New Musical Pocket Companion*	f, [6], 59	GB-Lbl, C.16.r.
D/a	[1770]	?	C. & S. Thompson	*Hymns Anthems and Tunes*	f, [4], 37	GB-Lbl, F.1120.mm.
D/b	[1785?]		S. A. & P. Thompson	do.	4, [37]	GB-Lbl, F.1120.oo.
D/c	[1790?]		Goulding, Phipps & D'Almaine	*New Edition of the Hymns*	f, [4], 36	GB-Lbl, E.1498.w.
D/d	[1790?]	?	S. A. & P. Thompson	*Hymns, Anthems and Tunes*	f, [4], 36	GB-Lbl, F.1120.pp.
E/a	[1775?]	?	H. Thorowgood	*Companion to the Magdalen-Chapel*	f, [2], 130	GB-Lbl, F.1120.ll.
E/b	[1780?]		Longman & Broderip	do.		none located US-Cn, VM2136.B59p.1780
E/c	[1799?]		Longman, Clementi	do.	f, [1], 3, 130	GB-Lbl, F.1120.o.
E/d	(wm1807)		Clementi & Co.	do.	f, [2], 3, [1], '42', [1], 42-130	GB-Lbl, E.1498.h.
E/e	[1810?]	?	Clementi & Co.	*New Edition of the Hymns*	f, [2], 130	GB-Lbl, F.1120.xx.
F	[1790?]	?	John Preston	*Fifth Sett of Psalms and Hymns*	22	GB-Lbl, a.76.g.(5)
G	[1790?]	?	Longman & Broderip	*Hymns Anthems & Tunes . . . for the Guitar*	36	GB-Lminet, IV/73/2/15
H/a	1791	?	S. A. & P. Thompson	*Psalms & Hymns with the Ode*	f, [2], 32, f, [2], 33-62	GB-Lbl, E.1498.l.
H/b	[1800?]		Henry Thompson	do.	f, [2], 32, [2], 33-62	
H/c	[1810?]	?	C. Wheatstone	*New Edition of the Hymns*	[2], 32	US-Pu
I	[1810?]	?	Preston	*Music Performed*	125, 16	GB-Lbl, E.497.v.

Note: Lines grouped together indicate editions with identical musical contents. Library sigla follow RISM. GB-Lminet = Minet Library, Lambeth. f = frontispiece; in some cases where "f" is lacking, the frontispiece may have been removed from the copies examined. wm = watermark.

Table 5. Hymn Text Numbering in Magdalen Rules and Tunebooks

| | Numbering in Text Sources | | | | | | Numbering in Musical Sources | | | | | |
Text Incipit	Rules 1759-60	A/a,c (appdx.) 1760-2	Rules; Account 1761	Account 2d ed. 1763	Account 3d ed. 1766	Account 4th, 5th eds. 1769-70, 1776	B1 / G	C	B2	F	H
AMSAWT	1	1	1	1	1	1	1 / 1	1			1
GTTMGT	2	2	2	2	2	2	25	2	2		2
TSFOHW		3	3	3	3	Ps.19	2 / 2	3	Ps.19		Ps.19
TLMPSP		4	4	4	4	Ps.23	3 / 3	4	Ps.23		Ps.23
WRFTBO		5	5	5	5	3	4 / 4	5			3
WATMOM		6	6	6	6	4	5 / 5	6	4	4	4
GGWWAW		7	7	7	7	5	6 / 6	7nm	5		5
LOTSHO		8	8	8	8	6	7 / 7	8	6		6
MGAITT		9	9	9	9		8 / 8				
AAWNBN		10	10	10	10		9 / 9				*
HLUSOT		11	11	11	11	8	10 / 10	11	8		8
GOMLTC		12	12	12	12	9	17 / 17	12	9		9
FWTDPA		13	13	13	13	10	16 / 16	10			10
JCIRTH		14	14	14	14	11	11 / 11	*			11
CSBWAT		15	15	15	15		13 / 13	15			
GGOHAO		16	16	16	16		14 / 14				*
GBTGOK		17	17	17	17	13	26nm		13	13	13
AGGWHO		18	18	18	18	14	19 / 19	17	14	14	14
WSYLYW		19	19	19	19		27nm				*
TDOWTD		20	20	20	20		12 / 12	19			
SDTGBH		21	21	21	21		20 / 20				
IVTDNR		22	22	22	22		22 / 22				*
MGNIFS		23	23	23	23		18 / 18				*
MGWGHI		24	*	*	*		24 / 24				*

Text							
DSSAMF		25			23		
TITDTL	3	26	*		15	*	**
HMGFTS		27	*		21	*	**
TLIMSM			*			*	
(Ps.23)			*				
LTSOBL			*			*	*
("Anthem")							*
GNANBW		15	*		*	*	15
("Ode")			*		*	*	15
CSMYVR		*	*			*	
("Verse")							
HATGHD				7			
ESBWAT				12			12
ROMSTH				16			16
ALMMTI				17		17	17
FOMHOP						18	7
OGOMHM						18	18

Note: For edition designations see Table 4. Texts are abbreviated, as in the Hymn Tune Index, by the initial letters of their first six words. A number indicates a numbered hymn; an asterisk denotes that the hymn was present but unnumbered. Ps. = Psalm, nm = no music.

23

Not long afterwards, the publisher John Phillips brought out *A Collection of Psalm and Hymn Tunes As They Are Performed at the Magdalen and Foundling Chapels. Properly Set for the Organ, Harpsichord and Guittar by Several Eminent Masters* (edition A/b). This too survives in only a single copy. It has twelve pages of music with twenty-five tunes. All except one of those in Call's book are reprinted; the nine later claimed by him are attributed to him here, and there is also the one attributed to Prior. In addition, Scott's Psalm 23 and Smith's Foundling's Hymn are reprinted from the Foundling Collection, edition A/a (see Table 2). There are two novelties: a curious hymn attributed to "John Luther" that is not found anywhere else; and a garbled version of the Easter Hymn tune, replacing the correct version that Call had printed, but now with its proper text.

Call responded by reprinting his own collection (A/c), with the music expanded to sixteen pages, the title plate altered to read *The Tunes & Hymns As They Are Used . . .*, and "Price 2s." added. Pages 1-10 were reprinted from the same plates; six pages of new music were added, so that there were now settings for all but two of the hymns. The texts were printed at the end as before, though reset. On the verso of the title-page, Call had the following engraved:

The Publick is here Caution'd

To beware of those Tunes and Hymns, that have been Pirated and Reprinted, by Phillips, in St. Martins Court, they being Imperfect as there are in this Book ————— a Dozen of the most Capital Tunes, which are not Contain'd in any other Book; and whosoever shall for the Future, Pirate, or Reprint, any of the Author's Tunes in this Book shall be Prosecuted; nor can any Books of the Kind be Depended on, but what are Publish'd by the Organist of the Chapel he only Permitted.

Enter'd at Stationers Hall.[66]

He did indeed take the precaution of depositing the work at Stationers' Hall on 12 June 1762. This was unusual for musical works at this date; as David Hunter has pointed out, it afforded scant protection, since the copyright laws pertaining to verbal texts had not yet been held to apply to music.[67]

---

[66]The dash before the words "a Dozen" replaced the word "nearly," which can be faintly read. In fact, precisely twelve tunes in the book are not in edition A/a or A/b; nine of them are claimed as Call's compositions.

[67]David Hunter, "Music Copyright in Britain to 1800," *Music & Letters* 67 (July 1986): 278; D. W. Krummel, comp., *Guide for Dating Early Published Music: A Manual of Bibliographical Practices* (Hackensack, N.J.: Joseph Boonin; Kassel: Bärenreiter, 1974), 136.

The next entrepreneur in this field was Henry Thorowgood, who used Call's second edition as the basis for his own piracy,[68] *The Hymns Anthems and Tunes with the Ode Used at the Magdalen Chapel Set for the Organ Harpsichord, Voice German-Flute or Guitar* (edition B1). The earliest issue (B1/a), only one copy of which is known, evidently dates from about 1766. Humphries and Smith assign a date range of 1764 to 1767 to the Henry Thorowgood imprint without street number. A new numbering system is introduced for the hymns (not corresponding to that of any official Hospital publication: see Table 5), and the musical contents are now clearly ordered: Hymns I-XXV; Anthems I and II (both classifiable as hymns); seven psalm tunes set to psalms from the *New Version;* and the new Ode, which is not found in the official text selections until 1766 (Table 5).

The music is the same as that of edition A/c, except that the Easter Hymn is given its proper text. The only addition is the Ode, a through-composed hymn setting, or "set piece," beginning "Grateful notes, and numbers bring / While Jehovah's praise we sing," which sounds like a very direct encouragement to put money in the collection plate. Though it is scored, like all the other Magdalen music so far, for only one voice line with instrumental bass, it has sections for "1st Gallery" and "2d Gallery." The words have been assigned to Dodd,[69] but a contemporary source, compiled by Dodd himself, attributes the Ode to "the Rev. Mr. Totton."[70]

A new attraction was the frontispiece: a full-page engraved illustration of "A Magdalen in Her Uniform." This is a version of a popular print that seems to have originated as the frontispiece to Jonas Hanway's *Reflections, Essays and Meditations on Life and Religion* (London, 1761), where the young woman, in her characteristic broad-brimmed hat, with hands demurely crossed at her waist, stands in front of a building carved with the word CHAPEL; a tree in the left background has a raggedly dressed, unhappy-looking woman sitting below. In Thorowgood's version, the background is eliminated, and the Magdalen holds a book of music in her right hand.[71] This proved to be the most popular feature of the book; it appears in almost every subsequent edition, as Table 4 shows (editions designated "f" in the sixth column had some version of the frontispiece).

---

[68]To be fair, it is possible (however unlikely) that Thorowgood paid royalties to Call or to the Hospital.

[69]Julian, *Dictionary*, 450.

[70]Dodd, *Account*, 1766.

[71]For the original 1761 version, see Rodgers, *Cloak of Charity*, frontispiece. For the version on ed. B2/b, see Plate II. For the version on ed. E/a, see Frost, *Historical Companion*, facing p. 28.

25

The next issue (B1/b) is almost identical, but "Book I" has been added to the title-page plate, and a text index has been inserted at the end. Presumably it was published after Book 2 had been printed, or at least planned. The earliest known issue of Book 2 (B2/a), however, has the publisher's address, "N° 6 North Piazza, Royal Exchange," which implies 1767 or later. It also has a revised Prayer with a footnote referring to "the late" Archbishop Secker (he died in 1768), and it uses the same revised numbering system for the hymns that is found in the fourth (1769) edition of the *Account* (see Table 5). This earliest issue survives in three known copies.[72] It is paginated [2], 3-22, the last seven pages being a guitar arrangement of the accompaniments. The title is *A Second Collection of Psalms and Hymns use'd at the Magdalen Chapel: The Words by D* Watts D* Doddridge D* Dodd M* Dryden and M* Lockman The Musick Compos'd by D* Arne M* Willm Selby and M* Adam Smith Late Organists of the Chapel Set for the Organ.*[73] Most of the texts in this volume had already been set to music in Book 1. There are nine new tunes by Selby, two by Adam Smith, and one attributed to Arne.

Books 3 and 4 were also published by Thorowgood, conjecturally in about 1773 and 1775, respectively. They continued the numbered sequence of hymns started in Book 1: Hymns XXVIII-XLII in Book 3 and XLIII-LVIII in Book 4, but the immediate source of their texts is unknown. None of them appears in any edition of hymns authorized by the Hospital. The music, too, is new throughout. These books are evidently a purely commercial effort, using the name of the Hospital but having no actual connection with it or its music. The fact is covertly acknowledged in the wording of their title-pages: "Hymns for the Use of the Magdalen Chapel" rather than (as in Books 1 and 2) "Used at the Magdalen Chapel."

The title-page of Book 4 advertised the other three volumes at 2s., "Or the whole compleat, bound together" at a price of 10s. 6d. Presumably "the whole compleat" is edition E/a, *A Companion to the Magdalen-Chapel*, which has the four books in the order 1-3-4-2: Book 2, which fell outside Thorowgood's numbering system for the hymns, now has its own title-page, *An Appendix to the Magdalen Hymns &c.* A note in the Index explains: "Many of the Psalms and Hymns being reset to different Musick, by several Composers, the

---

[72]At the National Library of Scotland (Cwn.50), at Magdalen College, Oxford, and in the author's possession.

[73]The arrangement of the wording is such as to make it clear that Selby and Smith, but not Arne, were late organists of the Chapel. According to *The New Grove Dictionary of Music and Musicians*, 20 vols. (London: Macmillan, 1980), 17:117 (confirmed by Compston, *Magdalen Hospital:* see Table 3), Selby was organist from 1766 to 1769.

Publisher [Thorowgood] thinks proper to inform the Reader that he has placed them in an Appendix." Thus, the original pagination of Books 2 and 3 had to be changed; the change was made on the original plates and is found on later issues of these books when sold separately. Book 4 is found only with the pagination it has in the combined volume, which suggests that the combined volume and Book 4 appeared at the same time.

A new version of the engraved frontispiece now appeared, with an ornate frame (see Plate II). It has a background showing Great Surrey Street (now Blackfriars Road) with the Obelisk on the left and the new hospital buildings on the right. The move to this site took place in 1772,[74] and it placed the Hospital near the Asylum for Female Orphans, which had been there since its foundation in 1758. This helps to date editions B2/b, B4/b, and E/a.

Sometime between 1776 and 1781, these books were taken over by Longman & Broderip. They were advertised, both separately and in combined form, in a catalogue of 1781.[75] The separate volumes (B1/c, B2/c, B3/c, B4/b) are found with contents reengraved but in exactly the same layout as Thorowgood's. The title-pages are printed from Thorowgood's plates, with the imprint changed to "Longman & Broderip N⁰ 26 Cheapside." The same firm also published a special guitar edition of Book 1 (edition G). Later, Broderip & Wilkinson, a successor to Longman & Broderip, adapted the title-page of Book 1 for use with all four parts (with a blank after the word "Book" to be filled in by hand) and changed the imprint to "Broderip & Wilkinson," implying a date between 1798 and 1808. At this point, the former books 2, 3, and 4 were definitely renumbered 4, 2, and 3 to agree with the revised pagination, but the Prayer, with page number 42, appeared in each book.

The combined volume (E), on the other hand, seems to have followed Longman to the firm of Longman & Clementi (E/c) and eventually appeared with the imprint "Clementi & Co." (E/d) in about 1807. This firm later published a misleading *New Edition of the Hymns* (E/e): though reengraved, it had exactly the same contents and layout as before.

There is no evidence that Books 3 and 4, with their unauthorized texts, were ever used in the Hospital chapel services. Perhaps there

---

[74]See Dodd, *Account*, 5th ed. (1776); Compston, *Magdalen Hospital*, 74. The foundation stone was laid in 1769, the new hospital was completed in February 1772, and the new chapel was opened in May 1772. It was "an octangular edifice erected at one of the back corners" of the quadrangle (B. Lambert, *The History and Survey of London and Its Environs*, 4 vols. [London: T. Hughes & M. Jones, 1806], 3:175).

[75]British Library, Hirsch IV.1110.(1.).

27

was an attempt to introduce them there; at any rate, the revised bylaws of 1791 sought to regulate the position: "The psalms and hymns, which are intended to be sung on Sundays, are laid before the Committee, by the Organist, on the preceding Thursday; and nothing is permitted to be sung (unless at the Anniversary) but the psalms and hymns printed for the use of the Chapel."[76]

Three other publishers, Bland & Weller, Clementi, and John Preston, also offered editions of Book 1 (B1/d, e, g). Clementi's has a new version of the frontispiece in which the Magdalen holds the music in an extended right hand and a glove in her left, with three other girls in the background: it is signed "King sculp. 411 Strand."

Preston added *A Fifth Sett of Psalms and Hymns Used at the Magdalen Chapel* (F); it is advertised in a catalogue dated 1790.[77] Unlike Books 3 and 4, it has texts (eight psalms and five hymns) entirely chosen from the authorized hymn selection of 1769 and follows the numbering used there, obviously in the hope of adoption by the Hospital chapel. However, like Book 2, it has a guitar part at the end. The frontispiece shows the central figure with music in her left hand, although the background still shows the obelisk on the left and the hospital buildings on the right. Later, Preston combined all five books in *The Music Performed at the Magdalen Chapel Consisting of Anthems Hymns and Psalm Tunes, Composed by Handel and Other Great Masters, Arranged for the Organ Piano Forte and Voice* (edition I), which the British Library catalogue dates circa 1810. In this edition, the guitar pages of Book 2 and of the *Fifth Sett* are omitted; the order of the books is 1-3-4-2-5, and there is yet another engraving of the frontispiece.

We must now return to the 1760s. A rival edition (C) had appeared shortly after Thorowgood's, entitled *The New Musical Pocket Companion to the Magdalen Chapel, Containing All the Odes, Psalms Anthems & Hymns, With Their Several Favourite Airs Now in Use. Never Before Made Public, with a Thorough Bass for the Harpsichord or Organ: By Adam Smith, Late Organist to the Charity. To which is subjoined ye celebrated canon of Non nobis Domine* (London: Printed for S. Hooper at the East Corner of the New Church in the Strand). Smith must have held the post of organist for a short time before William Selby's appointment in 1766. The book probably

---

[76]*Bye-Laws* (1794), 27.
[77]British Library, Hirsch IV.1113.(8.).

appeared in about 1767.[78] The numbering of the hymns follows that of the 1766 *Account,* but the selection is closer to that of the 1769 *Account* (see Table 5). The frontispiece is obviously copied from B1/ a: it is the same in every detail, down to the folds of the girl's dress, but is in mirror image, with the music held in the left hand. The engraving is signed "Adam Smith delin. et sculp." The printing and layout of this edition are quite crude.

The contents do not correspond to those of any other edition. The most significant new item is called "An Anthem" but is actually a strophically repeated tune with an eight-verse hymn, "Let the solemn organ blow," extolling Queen Charlotte, "our Royal Patroness": the Queen had agreed to be patroness early in 1765.[79] Its text was in the 1766 *Account* (Table 5). The tune is elsewhere ascribed to Johann Christian Bach (1735-82), "composer to Her Majesty."[80] Also present is the Ode. Both had been published in *The Christian's Magazine* for 1765. The last page is filled up with the well-known canon *Non nobis Domine,* traditionally credited to William Byrd. As the title-page wording implies, this piece is hardly likely to have been used at the Magdalen Chapel.

Yet another edition was put forth by the firm of C. and S. Thompson, entitled *The Hymns Anthems & Tunes with the Ode Used at the Magdalen Chapel Set for the Organ, Harpsichord, Voice, German-Flute or Guitar* (edition D/a). It was advertised for sale in *The Public Advertiser* on 30 June 1770. No compiler is stated, and in fact the contents are partly based on the Phillips edition (A/b), as is revealed by the astonishing reappearance of the "garbled" Easter Hymn as well as John Christopher Smith's Foundling's Hymn, never authorized for use in the Magdalen Chapel. The anthem "Let the solemn organ blow" is taken from Adam Smith's edition, edition C. Other items are taken from B1, and there are a few entirely new pieces. The texts are essentially those of the 1769 *Account* but in a completely different order. The hymns are not numbered—another fact that makes it unlikely that the Hospital authorities had anything to do with the publication.

Thompsons used a form of the familiar frontispiece, but with a different background, showing a near view of the Hospital on the left and a tree at right. Possibly this represents the old Whitechapel

---

[78]Smith describes himself as "late organist to the charity," which sets 1766 as the earliest possible date. However, the book contains five new settings of "Old Version" (Sternhold and Hopkins) psalms and none from Tate and Brady's *New Version.* This would not be likely after the 1768 decision of the Governors to use Tate and Brady (Compston, *Magdalen Hospital,* 164).

[79]Compston, *Magdalen Hospital,* 65.

[80]*The Christian's Magazine* 6 (1765): 140.

building, as the new buildings were not yet completed in 1770. A later issue (D/b) has the imprint changed to S. A. & P. Thompson, implying a date circa 1778 to 1793, but this title-page and imprint were also used for a still later edition (D/d) in which the contents were rearranged and one item omitted. The former Thompson edition was pirated by Goulding, Phipps and D'Almaine, who had the gall to name their version *A New Edition of the Hymns, Anthems and Tunes* (D/c).

Another Thompson edition (H/a) is called *The Psalms & Hymns with the Ode or Anthem Sung at the Magdalen Chapel. Adapted for the Voice, Harpsichord, &c. A New Edition: The Words Corrected from the Chapel Edition, with Other Improvements. Part I*. It has sixty-two pages, with a second title-page after page 32 identical to the first except that *Part I* has become *Part II*. As the title claims, it adopts the official words of the Hospital hymns, with a new selection of tunes chiefly taken from editions B1, B2, and D. Some of these have texts excluded from the 1769 *Account*, and a note says that "Those Hymns which are distinguished in the above Index by an Asterisk . . . though now omitted in the Service of the Chapel, are here retain'd for the use of those who wish to perform them in private."[81] This edition was later reissued by Henry Thompson (H/b).[82] A slightly different version of Part I of this edition was issued by Charles Wheatstone (H/c), some time between 1805 and 1815; it may be a reprint of a missing Thompson edition, between D/b and H/a.

Through this maze of editions, the striking thing is that the first collection, essentially the one compiled by Thomas Call (edition A/c), remained more popular than any of the sequels. It formed the basis of edition B1, issued separately by at least six publishers, and of editions C and G, as well as the first part of the composite volumes D, H, and I. The two tunes that have survived in church use today are both by Call: PLAISTOW from edition A/a and LYNE from edition A/c. Some of the texts were widely used. They were drawn on, for example, for the hymn supplement of the 1786 "proposed" prayer book of the American Protestant Episcopal Church.[83] The Ode, or a shortened version of it, turned up in countless collections, British

---

[81]They are also marked by an asterisk in the last column of Table 5. It will be seen that these texts had been included in the *Account* up to the 1766 edition but were eliminated in 1769. They are, on the whole, the more emotional and "Methodistical" of the hymns.

[82]He was in business alone circa 1798 to 1805. The only known copy of H/b is imperfect: pages 41-44 are missing and are replaced by pages 41-44 of William Riley's *Psalms and Hymns for the Use of the Chapel of the Asylum or House Refuge for Female Orphans* (London, [1767]).

[83]See Louis F. Benson, *The English Hymn: Its Development and Use in Worship* (London: Hodder & Stoughton, 1915), 394.

and American. Some of the hymns of Books 3 and 4, which may never have been used in the chapel at all, were copied in other books.

It would be some while, however, before the Magdalen hymns would be widely used in Anglican churches. Some of the texts would not have been generally acceptable there until well after 1800. But there seems no doubt that the hymns were current in private houses: hence the enthusiasm of publishers to reprint and extend them. The evidence for domestic use is clear. Accompaniments were provided for harpsichord, guitar, flute, and later piano; some editions had texts not authorized for use in the Hospital chapel. The music must have won its way with the public partly because it was associated with the moving story of the redemption of unfortunate young women, symbolized by the ever-popular frontispiece.[84]

---

[84]I am indebted to the Governors of the Thomas Coram Foundation for permission to study the archives of the Foundling Hospital, and to the Trustees of the University of Illinois and of the British Library for allowing the reproduction of the pages in Plates I and II. I am also grateful to the staffs of the following libraries for their assistance: Greater London Record Office; Royal College of Music, London; Lambeth Palace Library; Minet Library, Lambeth; Fitzwilliam Museum, Cambridge; Magdalen College, Oxford; National Library of Scotland; National Library of Ireland; American Philosophical Society, Philadelphia; Newberry Library, Chicago; Duke University, Durham; Pittsburgh Theological Seminary; Washington State University, Pullman; University of Texas at Austin; National Library of Medicine, Bethesda, Maryland.

XI

The Lock Hospital Chapel and its Music

IT has been generally recognized that the music of the Lock Hospital chapel was an important new influence in English and American church music during the late eighteenth and early nineteenth centuries.[1] The chapel attracted fashionable congregations and thereby disseminated an elegant, theatrical type of hymnody that was far removed from the norms of church music, whether in cathedral, town church, village parish or dissenting meeting-house. Many hymn tunes first used at the Lock Hospital became enormously popular; some still remain in common use; and their style became the model for a 'school' of hymn tunes that remained in vogue for several decades.

The principal source of this music is, of course, the printed collection of tunes that was known as the 'Lock Hospital Collection': its actual title was *A Collection of Psalm and Hymn Tunes, Never Published Before . . . To Be Had at the Lock Hospital near Hyde Park Corner.* However, the details and chronology of this collection, and the musical activities of the chapel, have never been thoroughly investigated, in part because the whereabouts of the hospital records was not widely known.[2] In this article I have aimed to establish the facts and to place them in their proper historical and social context. The main sources of information are the minute books of the Lock Hospital, preserved at the Royal College of Surgeons, Lincolns Inn Fields, London; the Hymn Tune Index database;[3] and an examination of many surviving copies of the Collection and

---

I am grateful to the librarian of the Royal College of Surgeons for kindly allowing me unrestricted access to the archives of the Lock Hospital.

[1] See, for example, Louis F. Benson, *The English Hymn: Its Development and Use in Worship* (London, 1915), 329–30: *Historical Companion to Hymns Ancient & Modern*, ed. Maurice Frost (London, 1962), 100–1; Irving Lowens, *Music and Musicians in Early America* (New York, 1964), 154–5; Erik Routley, *The Music of Christian Hymns* (Chicago, 1981), 75–6 and Examples 264–6.

[2] For instance, Simon McVeigh wrote: 'Unfortunately the Minute Books . . . seem to have disappeared' ('Music and the Lock Hospital in the 18th Century', *The Musical Times*, 129 (1988), 235–40 (p. 236)). McVeigh relied on the anonymous *Short History of the London Lock Hospital and Rescue Home, 1746–1906* (London, 1906). Falconer Madan, in his exhaustive book *The Madan Family and Maddens in Ireland and England: A Historical Account* (Oxford, 1933), did not list the Lock Hospital records among the manuscript sources he used, and he, too, relied on the 1906 *Short History* for information about Martin Madan's work at the hospital. Most library catalogues assign the first edition of the Collection to the year 1769, on the basis of Madan's dedication, but in fact much of it had appeared earlier in separate numbers, as Maurice Frost realized: see his letter in the *Bulletin* of the Hymn Society of Great Britain and Ireland, 24 (July 1943), 8, and his typescript notes in his copy of edition A/e, now at the Royal College of Music, shelfmark B.III.28.

[3] The Hymn Tune Index is a computerized index of all hymn tunes associated with English-language texts found in printed sources published before the year 1821. It is housed at the University of Illinois at Urbana, Illinois, and is to be published in book form by Oxford University Press.

of the corresponding wordbook, Martin Madan's *Collection of Psalms and Hymns*.

The eighteenth century was a time when many charities were founded in Britain to deal with the social consequences of growing industrialization, urbanization and the decline of the Puritan ethic. Greater sexual promiscuity following the Restoration of Charles II in 1660 had led, it is generally agreed, to an increase in prostitution, disease and the abandonment of infants, and the affluent classes viewed these trends with growing alarm. Charity was supported on the one hand by rationalists and deists, who believed that enlightened planning, rather than divine intervention, must provide the solution to human problems, and on the other by Evangelical Christians, who saw a duty to work for the souls of carnal sinners and their victims.

Many of the new charitable institutions made great use of music, both for its efficacy in raising funds and for its power of emotional expression. The Foundling Hospital, the Asylum for Female Orphans, the Magdalen Hospital and the Lock Hospital all maintained chapels in which music played a prominent part, and most of them also organized special musical entertainments to raise money. The Foundling Hospital, founded in 1738, was famous for its performances of *Messiah* both under Handel's personal direction and after his death. It maintained a choir of children that led the singing in its chapel and published an influential collection of the music used there, of which the first issue appeared in 1760. The Asylum for Female Orphans and the Magdalen Hospital, both founded in 1758, developed girls' choirs staffed by their inmates. Although these two charities did not themselves publish music books, several commercial publishers produced collections of music sung at their chapels, which went into many editions.[4]

The Lock Hospital,[5] founded in 1746, was a place for the treatment of venereal disease. The building was soon erected on land rented for £1 per year from Lord Grosvenor, in what is now Grosvenor Place (the present Chapel Street was named after the hospital chapel); at the time it was in a park or meadow with no other buildings near it.[6] Patients were admitted either on the recommendation of a governor who subscribed five guineas per year, or by donating two guineas to the charity.[7] The hospital was founded chiefly on the initiative of William Bromfeild (1712–92), surgeon to Frederick, Prince of Wales. It quickly attracted the support of many of the nobility and gentry. Bromfeild 'used his great influence with the theatrical and musical professions, and during the first seventy years

---

[4] I discuss the music of two of these charities in some detail in my forthcoming article 'The Hymn Books of the Foundling and Magdalen Chapels'.

[5] The name simply means a place where people are locked away to prevent contagion. The medieval Lock Hospital in Southwark had been a leper house. With the decline and eventual extinction in England of leprosy it came to be used instead for venereal patients, but it was now moribund, and closed in 1760.

[6] It is already visible in John Rocque's *Plan of the Cities of London and Westminster* (1746). See Felix Barker and Peter Jackson, *The History of London in Maps* (London, 1990), 54. The first patients were admitted on 31 January 1747, according to *Short History*, 4.

[7] One guinea = 21 shillings (s.); 1 pound (£) = 20 shillings; 1 shilling = 12 pence (d.).

46

of [the hospital's] existence much assistance was granted to the Hospital by the two Garricks, Charles and David; James Lacey, Samuel Foote, John Rich, Ed. Vanbrugh and Captain Denis, George Frederick Handel, who wrote a special Oratorio for the Hospital, . . . Pelligrini, Guardini [Felice Giardini], John Beard, Charles Avison, J[ohn] Worgan the composer of the Oratorio "Manasseh", the original score of which he presented to the Hospital'.[8]

There is some apparent irony in the fact that the public theatres, generally regarded as a hotbed of prostitution, and as such condemned by Methodist and Evangelical clergy, were also a prime resource for a charity supported by these same clergy, who sought to alleviate one of prostitution's worst consequences. A possible explanation is that a number of the patients at the hospital may have been members of the theatrical and musical professions, so that their former colleagues felt a special duty to help them.

The Lock Hospital, then, was at least as well placed as its rivals for promoting oratorios and other performances to raise funds. Its activity in this direction has been well described elsewhere, chiefly on the basis of newspaper reports.[9] But chapel music was another matter. The Lock Hospital differed from the other charities in important respects. In the first place, it was a hospital in the modern as well as the eighteenth-century sense: its inmates were ill, often severely and incurably so. Secondly, they could be of differing age, sex, social background and moral persuasion, and did not necessarily have enough in common to form a coherent community. They were not, like the Foundlings, all innocent victims; nor were they, like the Magdalens, all reformed sinners. Some might, indeed, be penitent prostitutes, but others could be innocent persons who had contracted the disease by contagion; others again could be prostitutes or their customers who had every intention of returning to their activities when cured. These points are brought out in a notice that the General Committee decided to place in the daily newspapers on 15 November 1755:

On Saturday last, a Lady of Quality hearing of the Resolution of the Gov[rs] of the Lock Hospital . . . To fit up a Ward for the reception of Married Women only, Generously paid the Expences of the same A Precedent worthy to be followed by every humane Person As it is a Charity noways inferior to any other now subsisting & in many respects claims more the attention of the Public, As not only Unhappy Women injured by the Cruelty of bad Husbands are Received, But little Innocents who are frequently born with the Disease Imbibe it from their Nurses or otherwise infected by ways little suspected & hardly Credited by a virtuous Public near two Hundred of which from two to ten years old have been Cured in that Hospital that had fallen Victims to

---

[8] This passage is taken from an anonymous typescript headed 'Casual Club. Some points in the history of a London hospital' (c.1910), Royal College of Surgeons, TRACTS D-LOC, p. 13. Handel did not in fact write an oratorio for the hospital, but he gave a performance of *Judas Maccabaeus* for its benefit in 1753. 'Pelligrini' is perhaps a misapprehension of the title of Hasse's oratorio *I pellegrini*, which was performed for the hospital in 1757 (McVeigh, 'Music and the Lock Hospital', 240). Most of the others in this list of musicians, theatrical artists and entrepreneurs are mentioned in the minutes as having given their services for the hospital's benefit.

[9] McVeigh, 'Music and the Lock Hospital'.

261

Villians [*sic*] Misguided by a Vulgar Notion that by a Criminal Communication with a healthy Child a certain Cure might be obtained for themselves.[10]

The Magdalen Hospital, indeed, sent women afflicted with venereal disease for admission to the Lock Hospital, and asked if they could be accommodated in a special ward, so that they would not be exposed to the influence of unregenerate prostitutes. The Lock Hospital Committee offered general support but regretted that until sufficient funds were available 'it will not be in our power to appropriate a Ward or Wards for Penitent prostitutes only or to appoint a Chaplin to attend them an Object much to be wish'd for the Honour and Benefit of both Charities'.[11] Similarly, the Foundling Hospital in 1759 asked the Lock Hospital to accept a child suffering from venereal disease.[12]

In these circumstances the inmates of the Lock Hospital did not, like those of the other charities, offer a pool from which a chapel choir might easily be drawn. Frost and Routley assumed that the Lock, like the Foundling and Magdalen Hospitals, had a choir composed of inmates.[13] But this seems most unlikely. Many inmates were too ill to attend chapel at all, and an important and often trying part of the chaplain's duties was to visit patients in the wards at least twice a week.[14] Those who were well enough to attend chapel services could not be displayed to the congregation in pretty uniforms, as at the Foundling Hospital, or even heard singing behind canvas screens, as at the Magdalen. They were not 'respectable'. Special entrances to the chapel were constructed, one for male, the other for female patients, so that they could be present without being seen by the rest of the congregation.[15] In 1762, a few weeks after the official opening of the chapel, it was ordered 'That the Men Patients go up to Chappell a Quarter of an Hour before Divine Service is over, & that during that time the Ward Doors will be Lock't & the Key kept by the Nurse of the Mens Ward for the time being'.[16] A later description (1802) shows that patients played only a passive part in the services: 'Two

[10] Committee minutes, Board 1, 15 November 1755 (see also *The Public Advertiser*, 17 November 1755). The governing body of the hospital was the General Court, which met quarterly and sometimes for additional special meetings. The ordinary administration was carried on by the (Weekly) Committee or Board. The minutes at the Royal College of Surgeons begin in 1755; they are found in a series of books labelled 'Court 1', 'Board 1', etc. Some but not all volumes are paginated. Minutes of the General Court are partly in separate volumes and partly interspersed with the committee minutes. There are two volumes numbered 'Board 2'; the second is distinguished by a diagonal line through the '2'.

[11] Board 2, 30 September 1758. On 13 February 1762, 'A L[ett]er being received from the Magdalene House desiring the readmission of Eliz: Brown as she still has Venereal Symptoms upon her', the committee ordered that she be readmitted. But on 13 December 1764 the committee informed the Magdalen Hospital that they could accept no more patients from them, 'as this Charity is greatly in debt'.

[12] Board 2, 24 March 1759; see also Foundling Hospital records, Greater London Record Office, A/FH/A/3/2/6, 21 March 1759.

[13] Frost, *Historical Companion*, 100; Routley, *The Music of Christian Hymns*, 75.

[14] This was one of the duties laid down by the General Committee on 19 May 1780 (Board 9, p. 339). Morning and Evening Prayer were read in the wards every day; see [Martin Madan], *Every Man Our Neighbour. A Sermon Preached at the Opening of the Chapel, of the Lock Hospital . . . March 28, MDCCLXII* (London, [1762]), 26.

[15] Royal College of Surgeons, TRACTS D-LOC, 8.

[16] Board 2̸, p. 184, 25 September 1762.

48

Clergymen officiate in the Chapel annexed to the Hospital twice every Lord's day, and all the patients, who can leave the wards, are required to be present; and though they are placed out of sight, they have every advantage of hearing. They are also attended by the visiting Chaplain in their wards; who twice in the week preaches both to the men and women separately.'[17] In 1763 the nurse of the men's ward was ordered to 'lie' with her husband in the 'Mens Patients Chapel'. In 1776 the accounts record a payment 'To Mrs Roberts for papering the Wom[en]s Chapel'.[18] These were presumably separate rooms used by patients who could not attend the main chapel.

At the Lock Hospital, then, the inmates could not sing effectively on their own behalf. The congregation must sing for them.[19] This meant, in the first place, that the texts to be sung must be fairly general in nature: there could be nothing quite like the Foundling's Hymn, or the Ode in the Magdalen Collection, which put into singers' mouths direct words of appeal representing their particular situation. It meant also that the singing would not be carried out by high, young voices only, and that there was no choir on the premises that could be required to rehearse for as long as might be needed. To hire professional singers was hardly an option when all available funds were needed for running the charity. The situation was not unlike that in an ordinary parish church; or perhaps it was worse, for there were not even the 'charity children' of a parish school to rely on.

But it was obviously inadequate to set musical standards no higher than those of an ordinary parish church. New and fashionable music was to be introduced, so that the Lock Hospital might equal or surpass the other charities in the music of its chapel services, and thus attract the wealthy. Special measures were needed – measures for which there was no precedent. It would be necessary to persuade the congregation itself, or some part of it, to submit to musical training and rehearsal. The idea that a congregation should sing for itself, rather than listen to the singing of a choir, was strongly held by the Methodist movement, and more particularly by John Wesley himself. The Wesleys, and several other early Methodist leaders, were themselves highly musical, and believed in the emotional power of music to promote religious feeling. It is no accident, therefore, that Methodism was a strong force in the activities of the Lock Hospital.

The dominant personality in the development of worship in the Lock Hospital Chapel was Martin Madan (1725–90).[20] He was a formerly dissolute lawyer who had been converted by hearing John Wesley preach.

---

[17] An Account of the Lock Hospital (London, 1802), 9.

[18] Board ƶ, p. 251, 26 May 1763; Board 8, p. 291, 27 June 1776. The 1906 Short History states (p. 11) that 'The patients, both male and female, had to attend', implying that they attended the main chapel, but clearly this was true only for those who were able-bodied.

[19] This was apparently still true in 1849, when a collection of Hymns for the Use of the Congregation of the Lock Chapel, Westbourne Green, compiled by the Revd Thomas Garner, was published. The hospital had moved in 1842 to a site in Westbourne Green now occupied by part of the buildings of St Mary's Hospital, Paddington. The Grosvenor Place buildings were demolished in 1846.

[20] The name is pronounced 'Madden'. See F. Madan, The Madan Family, 10, n. 2.

On the death of his father, Colonel Martin Madan (1700–56), a wealthy country squire, equerry to the Prince of Wales and Member of Parliament, he inherited a considerable fortune.[21] Already a governor of the Foundling Hospital and ordained a priest in the Church of England in 1758, Madan in 1759 was 'so kind as to promise to Officiate as Chaplain to this Hospital, Gratis', an offer that was gratefully accepted; he was promptly made a governor 'during his performing the Duty of a Chaplain'.[22] The committee decided to adapt the South Men's Ward as a 'place for divine Worship . . . as the Board Room is too small and liable to be impaired by frequent use of it as a Chapel'. Madan offered to cover the expense.[23] This temporary chapel must have been provided with a small organ.[24] It was about this time, in the year 1760, that Madan compiled and published his hymn anthology (see Table 1), and although at first it had no ostensible connection with the hospital it was to be almost the sole source of hymns in the 'Lock Collection' tunebook. From the third edition

TABLE 1

EDITIONS OF *A COLLECTION OF PSALMS AND HYMNS, EXTRACTED FROM VARIOUS AUTHORS, AND PUBLISHED BY THE REVEREND MR. MADAN*

no.	date	pages	hymns	notes
[1]	1760	vi + 168	'170' [171]	There are two hymns numbered 73.
2	1763	vi + 192	'194' [195]	Pp. 169-92 subtitled 'An Appendix', with 24 hymns.
3	1764	viii + 192	195	Nos. 73²-194 renumbered 74-195.
4	1765	viii + 192	195	
5	1767	viii + 192	195	
6	1769	vi + 192	195	Three hymns replaced by others without disturbing the numbering.
7	1771	vi + 192	195	
8[a]	1774	viii + 192	195	
8[b]	1774 [1777?]	viii + 203	209	As 8[a] (from same typesetting) as far as p. 192.
9	1779	viii + 203	209	13 hymns replaced by others without disturbing numbering. Pp. 193-203 from same typesetting as in 8[b]. 'An Appendix' subtitle removed.
10	1783	vii + 204	210	Smaller size. One hymn (no. 210) added.
11	1787	vii + 204	211	One hymn (no. 211) added, one substituted.
12	1787	vi + 204	211	
13	1794	viii + 204	211	

Exemplars of all the above editions are held by the British Library. Editions 3–12 have the following imprint: 'Printed by Henry Cock & sold at the Lock Hospital'. For further details (though with slight inaccuracies) see F. Madan, *The Madan Family*, 275–8.

---

[21] His private income was about £1,800 a year, rising later as his estates became more profitable. *Ibid.*, 104–17.

[22] Board 2, 24 March 1759. On 21 May 1761 he was made a 'perpetual governor' in recognition of 'repeated Benefactions arising from the Chapel &cª' (Court 1, p. 268). His predecessor had been paid 20 guineas a year.

[23] Board 2A, 29 March, 5 April 1760.

[24] On 22 May 1766 the committee was informed that a Mr Peirce had purchased 'the little Organ in the Old Chapel' for 40 guineas.

50

(1764) onwards it carried on its title-page the words 'sold at the Lock Hospital'.

In 1761 the governors agreed to Madan's proposal to build a new chapel for 800 people in the garden at the back of the hospital, provided that they were not called upon for money. Madan again undertook the financial responsibility. The austerely designed chapel (see Figure 1) was opened on 28 March 1762, Madan preaching the opening sermon, which was later published (see above, note 14). On 11 October 1764 he reported 'That all the Expenses Incident to the Building and finishing the Chapel . . . were totally paid', and handed it over to the governors, 'being now clear [of debt], the moneys arising therefrom intended to be paid into the Board tow^{ds} the maintenance of the Patients of this House'.[25]

Figure 1. The Lock Hospital chapel in an engraving dated 1 December 1788 (reproduced by kind permission of the Greater London Record Office).

The first mention of an organ for the new chapel occurred on 11 July 1761, when Bromfeild proposed buying one for £200. Instead, the committee arranged to borrow an organ built by John Byfield the elder for Sir Joseph Hankey. Eventually this instrument was purchased from Hankey for £125.[26] Madan's accounts for the chapel in the years 1762–5 include amounts for 'Readers and Organists salaries', without naming the organist, and these continue in the hospital accounts until 11 May 1769, when Charles Lockhart was paid £6 5s. for playing the organ in the quarter beginning Christmas 1768.[27] Lockhart may have been the

[25] Court 2, p. 33, 11 October 1764; Board 3, p. 248, 27 December 1764.

[26] Board 2, p. 75, 6 March 1762; Court 1, p. 286, 29 May 1762; Court 2, p. 33, 11 October 1764.

[27] Court 2, pp. 44, 45, 94; Board 6, 11 May 1769.

organist from the start, though he was only 16 or 17 when the permanent chapel was opened. In any case, it seems clear that Madan himself provided the impetus as well as the financial backing for the music in the chapel, and determined the form that it would take. As both patron and chaplain he would have had complete authority, subject to the supervision of the committee. He was himself a musician of substantial abilities, as is proved by the hymn tunes he composed.[28] For a time, another noted musician, Thomas Haweis (1734–1820), was assistant chaplain.

Charles Lockhart (1745–1815), blind from birth, and later organist of several London churches, also played an important part in the development of the individual style of singing at the Lock Hospital during his first two terms as organist (see Table 2). At some point congregational rehearsals were introduced, as is shown by an exchange that took place in 1778.

TABLE 2

ORGANISTS OF THE LOCK HOSPITAL, 1768–1801

name	date commenced	date terminated	salary
Charles Lockhart	? (by 26 December 1768)	25 December 1770	£35 per annum
Richard Harris	26 December 1770	25 June 1772	£35 per annum
Charles Lockhart	26 June 1772	25 December 1778	£35 per annum
Mr Adams	26 December 1778	14 January 1779	£2 2s.
Mr Carter	14 February 1779	25 September 1779	£35 per annum
Richard Harris	26 September 1779	died 24 May 1790	£30 per annum
Thomas Costellow	23 May 1790	2 June 1790	£2 2s.
Charles Lockhart	10 June 1790	25 June 1797	£42 per annum
(Chapel closed for repairs summer 1797; Miss de Coetlogon played for services at a nearby church.)			
Charles Wesley	2 November 1797	25 March 1801	£42 per annum

On October 15 the committee ordered

> That Notice be sent to Cha⁵ Lockhart the Organist of this Chapel informing him that in case he neglects instructing the Congregation, from five to six on a Friday Evening being the usual part of his Duty, he will not be paid his next Quarters Salary, and if it is his intention not to do it in future, he will acquaint Mr [Jabez] Fisher the Secretary with his resolution, that the Genˡ Court may Elect another Organist in his room.

Lockhart replied, with some spirit,

> that as it never was his agreement to teach the Congregation at the Lock-Chapel to sing, he is determined not to do it, without an addition to his present Salary. Charles Lockhart will take care of the duty as usual till Christmas next; when the Genˡ Court may chuse another Organist.[29]

Lockhart's resignation was accepted. To clarify the matter for the future, the court ordered

> That the Organist of this Chapel in future do attend every Sunday, Morning and Evening Service; on Wednesday Evening 6. O'Clock, and on Friday Even-

[28] It is not known how he acquired his musical competence. At Oxford, to his father's annoyance, he had 'fiddled and shot partridges'.
[29] Board 9, pp. 182, 184: 15, 22 October 1778.

52

ing at 5 O'Clock, to instruct the Congregation in singing the Hymns, before the Service begins: And on all other occasional Hollidays which are usually observed in this Chapel . . . And that the stated Salary of the Organist in future, be Twenty Pounds a year, with a Gratuity not exceeding Ten Pounds; or in such proportion as the Governors may think he deserves.

Ordered that as Charles Lockhart the late Organist of this Chapel has been discharged for neglect of Duty, that Willm Bromfeild Esq: & the Rev. Mr. De Coetlogon [assistant chaplain] be requested to provide a supply till another Organist be Elected.[30]

But the next Organist was found unsatisfactory. The committee concluded that 'it is impossible for the Congregation to sing the Hymns accompany'd by Mr Carter, whose abilities as a Professor are universally allow'd, but not being conversant with the Manner in which they have been taught to sing them, occasions great confusion in that part of the Service', and asked Bromfeild to provide a more suitable person.[31] Richard Harris, who had replaced Lockhart for a short time in 1770–2, now officiated for more than ten years, but the singing declined during his tenure, and with it the chapel revenues.

The takings of the chapel from seat tickets and collections (as distinct from the proceeds of special oratorio performances in the chapel) are recorded in detail in the minute books. On 27 December 1764, as already noted, the chapel was clear of debt and the moneys arising thereafter could be devoted to the running of the hospital. The chapel account balance for 1764/5 was £407 10s. 7½d. In 1768/9 chapel receipts included £850 15s. 0d. for seat tickets, £75 6s. 5½d. for collections on communion days and £27 14s. 4d. for 'the Sale of Hymn and Music Books'. In 1789 the best years were over: the chapel committee discussed 'the great decrease of the profits arising from the Chapel for several years past it being only £222 13s. 8d. the last year'. Accordingly the General Court appointed a special committee 'To enquire into the cause of the great decrease of the profits arising from the Chapel for several years past'. Among other causes the committee mentioned 'the defect of the singing in the Chapel'.[32]

The 1780s had seen a general decline in the hospital's musical activities. The annual oratorio performances ceased after 1780.[33] Part of the trouble had nothing to do with music or the chapel. A factional struggle was raging, and there were angry arguments about the running of the hospital, climaxing in 1781. As a result, many noble and influential governors resigned. But 1780 was also the year in which Madan published his book *Thelyphthora*, in which he adduced Old Testament authority to

[30] Court 3, p. 52, 14 January 1779.
[31] Board 9, p. 270, 16 September 1779.
[32] Court 3, p. 363, 7 May 1789. In 1783 the Select Committee reported that they had ordered a practice every Wednesday evening before service, which they said was 'very well attended by the Congregation, and is likely to be productive of a considerable improvement' (Court 3, p. 148, 16 January 1783), but two years later they noted a 'very great declension in the Congregation of the Chapel' (p. 184, 27 January 1785).
[33] McVeigh, 'Music and the Lock Hospital', 237. On 22 February 1781 the committee decided to 'postpone' the usual performance of Giardini's *Ruth* and instead to have two special sermons preached by William Romaine and John Berridge, both prominent Evangelicals.

267

advocate polygamy as a preferable alternative to prostitution. A scandal erupted; Madan was attacked in print. He continued as nominal chaplain (he was, in any case, unpaid), but he lived in seclusion until his death in 1790. His successor, Charles de Coetlogon, seems to have had no musical interests or abilities. To deal with the sudden vacuum left by Madan's departure, the General Court on 17 May 1781 appointed a 'Select Committee for the Management of all the affairs of the Chapel' which met sporadically during the succeeding decades.[34] The absence of Madan, as well as that of Lockhart, probably accounts for the neglect of the singing during the 1780s.

In 1790, when Harris's death was imminent, the governors turned once again to Lockhart, who 'said he would not undertake the Organists place for less than forty Guineas per Ann[um] – for which sum his Deputy or Daughter, should attend every Sunday Morning, and either himself or Daughter should attend every Sunday Evening: And that he would make a point of attending every Wednesday Evening, himself – in order to instruct the Congregation in singing'.[35] At a Special General Court for the purpose of electing an organist, Lockhart's terms were accepted, and he was elected by 20 votes over John Ashley (5 votes) and Thomas Costellow, a former pupil of Lockhart's, who withdrew. The committee's reasons for recommending Lockhart are highly significant:

> The Committee considering that the peculiar mode of singing, so many years established in the Chapel and deem'd so highly advantageous to the collections, was for many years conducted by M[r] Lockhart to the greatest satisfaction of the Governors and the Congregation, and that the singing and Income have both greatly declined since the Organ has been in other hands, notwithstanding some of the Organists were esteem'd capital Performers; . . . are of opinion that M[r] Lockhart . . . is in every respect the most eligible candidate.[36]

It was not long before dissatisfaction with Lockhart began to surface once again. The court on 26 July 1792 drew up new rules, among them:

> 2. That the Ministers who officiate, be authorized to appoint the Hymns on all Occasions.
> 3. That if any Hymn be appointed to which there are two or more Tunes, the Organist be desired to choose that with which the Congregation is best acquainted; And that he play some customary approv'd Psalm Tune when none is appointed [i.e. when the tunebook does not provide a tune for the appointed hymn].
> 4. That Mr Lockhart be desired to practise all the Tunes which have been long in Use in the Chapel, together with the new Tunes lately presented by him to the Charity, in rotation.[37]

Later the court ordered that 'the Practice of singing on Sunday Evenings after Service, be discontinued; and that the select Committee do take into

[34] There is a gap in the Select Committee minutes from 1791 to 1800 and another from 1804 to 1806. After that the committee met only occasionally.
[35] Select Committee Book (C.1), 20 May 1790.
[36] 'Book 73', 10 June 1790.
[37] Court 4, 26 July 1792.

54

Consideration the proper Time & Mode of practising the Hymns and the instruction of the Congregation in singing'.[38] Clearly all was not well, and Lockhart, for whatever reason, had been unable to restore the pre-1780 position as the governors had hoped.

His third and final dismissal, in 1797, was due to his failure to attend regularly.[39] His successor was Charles Wesley junior (1757–1834, son of the hymn-writer Charles and elder brother of the composer Samuel). Although he agreed to attend on Wednesday evenings as well as Sunday mornings and evenings ('except during the Ancient Music Concerts'), nothing was said about instructing the congregation. The court specified only 'That the Organist be desired to attend punctually at a Quarter after Ten in the Morning, & at a Quarter before six in the Evening, at all times of public Worship in the Chapel; to play Voluntaries of solemn Music, and to receive information from the Ministers, respecting the Hymns that are to be sung'.[40] Wesley was in trouble in 1799 and 1800 for neglect of duties.[41]

At the beginning of the new century the hospital was in grave financial trouble and was selling capital reserves. In an effort to reduce expenditure, the wife of George Medley, one of the governors, offered to play the organ without pay 'during the impoverished state of the Hospitals finances, only requesting that the governors will provide a Substitute during the time it may be necessary to be in the Country, which may probably be four or six weeks annually'. This arrangement was accepted and Wesley was paid off. In 1808 Mrs Medley was succceeded by 'Mr. Bramah of Pimlico', who was also unpaid.[42]

The two chaplains, de Coetlogon and Scott, resigned in 1802, and were replaced by one, Thomas Fry, who set about making changes in the services. A new hymn selection (to be described later) was introduced in 1803. The boys of Hans Town Charity School, Knightsbridge, were brought in to lead the singing, and were taught by the organist; according to the *Short History* (p. 15) this practice also began in 1803 and continued until the chapel was pulled down in 1846. In 1807 the boys were provided with a special form to sit on.[43] In return Fry was permitted occasionally to preach a sermon in the chapel for the benefit of the charity school.[44] During these years the chapel became profitable again. Beginning at Christmas 1809 a professional organist was once more engaged, a Mrs Smith, at a salary of £21 per annum.[45] But the singing was now probably much like that of any London church, with a children's choir leading an unrehearsed congregation in unison singing.

From the 1760s to the 1790s, then, there had been a 'peculiar mode of singing' that was highly popular and had thus brought in money for the

[38] Court 4, 2 May 1793. The precise action taken by the Select [Chapel] Committee is not on record because of a ten-year gap in the minutes.
[39] Board 15, 25 May, 1 June 1797.
[40] Board 15, 6, 13 July, 2 November 1797.
[41] Board 15, 3, 10 January 1799, 9, 16, 23 October 1800.
[42] Court 4, 22 January 1801; Board 16, 12 February 1801; Board 17, 11 February 1808.
[43] Chapel Committee Book C.1, 3 April 1806; Board 17, 8 January 1807.
[44] Board 17, 26 February 1807.
[45] Board 17, 29 March 1810.

charity. No precise description of it is available. Evidently it was associated with Lockhart's organ playing and his way of teaching the congregation, and was hard to maintain in his absence, though it may well have been initiated by Madan. To gain further insight into the character and style of this singing it will be necessary to turn to the published tunebook; and before its music can be considered a bibliographical digression is necessary.

Table 3 sets out the early editions of the Lock Hospital Collection. It was a cumulative affair, at first issued in 12-page numbers and then in larger and larger portions until by 1793 it had reached its full size of 193 pages of engraved music. The earlier editions were undoubtedly compiled and edited by Madan, and were presented by him to the hospital, as recorded in the dedication of the 1769 edition (A/c), quoted below. Later portions were added by Madan and by Lockhart; the latter oversaw the 1793 edition (A/d) which carried a preface signed by the secretary of the hospital, Jabez Fisher (d. 1800).

The book, then, was published by the charity itself. It was offered for sale at the hospital, and in the early years also by Edward Dilly. After the first 'complete' edition (A/c) had appeared, Robert Bremner was authorized to sell copies, for which he received a commission of one seventh part. Later, John Preston advertised 'Lock Hymns, Vol. I, Vol. II' for sale, among music acquired from Bremner.[46] Furthermore, in 1774 Madan reported to the committee

> that he had rece'd. a Message from Mr Bremner Music Seller in the Strand, acquainting him that Henry Thoroughgood Music Seller under the Royal Exchange, was going to Print the Music of the Lock Hymns for his own benefit; as this may be a great detriment to the Hospital, the said Hymns being given for the sole use and benefit thereof . . .
>
> It was moved and seconded, That the Secretary do wait on Mr Hickey in St. Albans Street, Attorney at Law, and one of the Governors of this Charity, desireing the favour of his Opinion, whether any stop can be put to this by moving for an Injunction on the Equity of the Statute of Q. Anne or otherwise.

Counsel's opinion, however, was unfavourable, as he could find 'no words contained in any of the said Acts, which give the Property of Musick to the Inventors or Composers thereof . . . Tho your Case is peculiarly severe, I doubt of the success of an Application for an Injunction.'[47] This was in full accordance with other legal opinions of the time.[48] Nevertheless, Thorowgood seems to have thought better of his plan; perhaps the governors were able to bring some kind of pressure to bear on him.

No discussion of the earliest numbers of the Collection is to be found in the hospital minutes, probably because they were in the first instance a

[46] Board 6, p. 309, 19 July 1770; Board 8, p. 146, 8 December 1774; Board 9, p. 217, 4 March 1779; J. Preston, *Catalogue of Music*, British Library, Hirsch IV.1113.(8), dated 1790.

[47] Board 8, p. 70, 10, 24 March 1774.

[48] See David Hunter, 'Music Copyright in Great Britain to 1800', *Music and Letters*, 67 (1986), 269–82 (p. 278).

56

TABLE 3

GROWTH OF THE LOCK HOSPITAL COLLECTION, EDITION A, *c.1762–1793*

pages   sectional designations   edition, date, (title-page no.)
exemplar

pages	sectional designations			edition, date, (title-page no.) exemplar		
1–12	no. 1			A/a, [c.1762], (1) US-LAu Cage/ M2156/H993, item 3		
13–24	no. 2	no. I		[c.1763?]	A/b, [c.1765], (1) GB-Lbl F.1120.tt	
25–36	no. 3			[c.1765]		
37–48	no. 4		vol. I	[c.1766?]	A/c, (1769), (2) GB-Lbl E.1429.b.	
49–60	no. 5	no. II		[c.1766?]		
61–72	no. 6			[c.1766?]		A/d, (1792 [1793]), (6) GB-Lbl E.1429.a.
73–120	no. III (?)			[c.1767]		
121–142	no. IV (?)			[1769?]		
143–156	[no. 1?]			Madan, *Six Hymn Tunes* [1772], (3) US-LAu Cage/M2156/H993, item 1		
157–168	[no. 2?]	no. V	vol. II		[1792?]	
169–174				[Melton Mowbray] (4) [c.1775?]		
175–177				[Whitchurch & Dalston] (5) [c.1775?]		
178						
179–193		no. VI			[1793]	

Known editions are enclosed in continuous lines, conjectural ones in broken lines.

Title-page transcriptions

(1) A Collection of PSALM AND HYMN TUNES, Never Published before. PRICE 2s
To be had at the Lock Hospital near Hyde Park Corner, and of E. DILLY in the Poultry.
NB. This Collection is Published for the Benefit of the Charity.
(2) A Collection of PSALM AND HYMN TUNES, Never Published before. Price one Guinea bound.
To be had at the Lock Hospital near Hyde Park Corner.
NB. This Collection is Published for the Benefit of the Charity.
(3) SIX NEW HYMN TUNES, SET BY THE REVEREND Mr. MADAN. Price 2s. 6d.
To be had at the Lock-Hospital, near Hyde Park Corner, and at Mr. Bremner's in the Strand.
Where may be had, the First Volume compleat, Price bound, one Guinea.
(4) MELTON MOWBRAY. A HYMN for 3 Voices with a Thorough Bass for the Harpsichord,
Compos'd by Chas LOCKHART Organist of the Lock HOSPITAL CHAPEL near Hyde Park Corner,
and of St Catherine Cree Church Leaden Hall Street. Pr: 1s
(5) WHITCHURCH and DALSTON. Two HYMNS Set to Music for 3 Voices with a Thorough Bass
for the HARPSICHORD. By CHARLES LOCKHART. Pr: 1s
(6) A new, and improved Edition of the Collection of PSALM and HYMN TUNES Sung at the Chapel of
the Lock Hospital with considerable additions.
LONDON Printed for the Benefit of the Charity, and to be had at the Lock Hospital:
And at Longman and Broderip's No 26 Cheapside, or at No 13 Haymarket.

private venture by Martin Madan, though 'published for the benefit of
the charity'. Madan reported income from 'Sale of Sermons, Hymn
Books' up to 25 December 1764, and more specifically £28 10s. from
'Sale of Hymns & Musick Books' in the first quarter of 1765.[49] Maurice
Frost described a copy of the first number consisting of 12 leaves printed
on one side only.[50] This cannot now be located, but the only known copy
of this first issue (A/a), though printed on both sides of the paper, has all
page numbers at the top right corner of the page, suggesting that the
plates were indeed originally designed for printing on one side only. It has
an ornamental engraved title-page, unsigned. The first page of music has
the signature 'Engraved by J: Caulfield'.[51]

The precise date of this first number cannot be established with cer-
tainty. The texts are all drawn from the first edition of Madan's *Hymns*,
published in 1760; none are from those added to the second edition of
1763. The music is for two voice parts and figured bass, with a few short
'symphonies' for organ; as we have seen, a small organ was already
available in the temporary chapel opened in 1760. The title claims that
the tunes were 'never published before' and a careful study of the contents
provides no challenge to the truth of this statement before page 54. It
seems likely that this edition appeared in 1762 or possibly 1763.[52]

Pages 13–24 and 25–36 also probably appeared as separate numbers:
pages 13–24 have a slightly different engraving style from the others. The
next surviving edition (A/b) contains the first 36 pages together: there are
two known copies, at the British Library and at the Rowe Music Library,
King's College, Cambridge. The title-page is identical to that of A/a, including the price of 2s. (which, in fact, probably applied only to the first
number). 12 of the 24 new hymns have texts that first appeared in the second (1763) edition of Madan's *Hymns*. The fourth edition of 1765, but
not the third of 1764, carried the following advertisement:

> Twelve Hymn Tunes, revised and corrected by an eminent Master, and neatly
> printed, price 2s.
> Twenty-Four Hymn Tunes for the Use of the Hospital. Price 4s.

If, as seems likely, these referred to pages 1–12 and 13–36 respectively,
then A/b probably appeared in 1765.

It looks as if there were three more 12-page numbers after this, since
slight changes of engraving style are again consistent with the possibility.
If the first six presumed numbers (pp. 1–72) were ever issued as a single
volume, no copy of them in this form has ever been discovered. It is sug-
gestive, though, that the same Los Angeles bound volume that contains
the only known copy of edition A/a also contains a copy of pages 73–142,

[49] Court 2, pp. 44, 45.
[50] Frost, *Bulletin*, 24, p. 8. He describes this copy as being printed from 'different plates' from the 1769 edition, which is not the case with the Los Angeles exemplar of edition A/a.
[51] John Caulfield had also engraved the first edition of the Foundling Hospital hymnbook in 1760. See Temperley, 'The Hymn Books'.
[52] Frost comes to a similar conclusion (*c*.1763), although it is based on a wrong date for edition (b) of Thomas Butts's *Harmonia sacra*. See Frost, 'Harmonia sacra, by Thomas Butts', Hymn Society of Great Britain and Ireland, *Bulletin*, 61–2 (1952–3), 66–71, 73–9 (pp. 77–8).

58

without title-page.[53] This latter portion is roughly equivalent in size to the first six numbers, but it is not itself divisible into six 12-page numbers.[54]

The decisive moment came in 1769, when the whole volume of 142 pages appeared with a dedication surmounted by a line engraving of the hospital building. It is worth extensive quotation:

> To the Most Noble Peregrine, Duke of Ancaster, Perpetual President, . . . Vice-Presidents, and to the rest of the Governors of the Lock Hospital, To whom the Entire Copy of this Collection of Hymn and Psalm Tunes is presented, as a Benefaction to the Hospital, that the Profits arising from the Sale of it, may be applied for the Benefit of the Charity.
>
> My Lords and Gentlemen,
>
> I have at last, with no small Care and Trouble, completed this Book of Tunes for the Use of the Chapel, and as the Publication of them may be of Service to the Charity, I must desire your Acceptance of the Entire Copy. . . .
>
> I should be exceedingly ungrateful, was I not, upon this Occasion, to acknowledge the Obligations which the Charity lays under, to Messrs. Giardini, Vento, Alessandri, Worgan, Burney, Arnold, and the other great Masters, who have embellished the Work, by their excellent Compositions and Corrections.
>
> I should hope that all Music-Sellers and Printers will observe, that the Property of this Music is now vested in You for the Benefit of the Charity, and that the Poor Objects who are sharing your Bounty, will have no Reason to complain of their being injured by Surreptitious, and Piratical Impressions.
>
> I am,
>
> My Lords and Gentlemen,
>
> Your humble Servant,
>
> M. MADAN.
>
> Knightsbridge, August 18, 1769.

The original engraved title-page was used, but with the price altered to 'one Guinea bound' and with Dilly's name removed from the imprint. The hospital accounts begin to show income from the sale of 'Music Books'. A Mr Matthews was paid 12s. for 'binding books on acc^t of the Chapel' from 1 May to 2 August 1769, and on 31 August the secretary

---

[53] There is clear evidence that further numbers had been issued some time before the publication of edition A/c in 1769. Ten tunes, ranging from p. 44 to p. 88, are found also in a certain edition of Thomas Knibb's *The Psalm Singer's Help* and in no earlier book. All editions of Knibb's book are undated, but this one (edition c) cannot have been later than 1767: a letter from Knibb to the Revd Wheelock Prest, a missionary in New England, dated 30 March 1767, has the following postscript: 'I have cal^d a New tune, in page 72 Lebanon, out of respect to you' (Hanover, New Hampshire, Dartmouth College Archives, no. 76, 7230.1). The only edition with a tune called 'Lebanon' on p. 72 is the one in question – edition c, with 164 pages. Now it is in general more likely that Knibb copied from the Lock Collection than the reverse, because the latter has attributions to composers, whose help Madan later acknowledged. But in this case there is additional evidence to that effect. Of the ten tunes, eight have the same name in both books, but the tunes named 'Nativity' and 'Feversham' in the Lock Collection are named 'America' and 'West St' in Knibb's book. It is easy to see why Knibb would rename a tune 'America': the Dartmouth archive reveals that he was selling quantities of his books to American colonists. And in the case of 'Feversham' the change is explained by the fact that he already had another tune with that name in his book. There is no apparent reason why Madan should have renamed either tune. I conclude from this that the cumulatively printed Lock Collection must have reached at least p. 88 by early 1767. (The Dartmouth archive was brought to my attention by Dr Ruth Mack Wilson; I am grateful to her for this assistance.)

[54] By this time, some hymns were taking up more than one page, and pp. 85, 97 and 109 do not coincide with the beginning of a hymn.

reported 'that he hath rec^d of [the chapel clerk] on acct of [the chapel] for Six Dozen & 4 Hymn books, reckoning 13 to the Doz^n exclusive of what have been given away by order of . . . Mr Madan, £6. 19. 4. . . . And also for Music Books Bound (exclusive of what has been given away by order of . . . Mr Madan) £2. 11. 0.' The first sum undoubtedly refers to Madan's *Hymns* (texts only). The second sum is hard to account for at the stated price of 'one Guinea bound'. It is clear from this and later entries that the music book remained available in numbers at 2s. each.

The next component of the book was first published separately as *Six New Hymn Tunes, Set by the Reverend Mr. Madan*. It was advertised for sale in *The Public Advertiser* on 27 July 1772, and may well have been the object of one of the following account entries, more probably the second:

30 May 1771   Thos Baker for Printing Music for the Chapel to
              the 16th instant   7. 0. 0.
18 June 1772 Paid Mr Thos Baker . . . for Engraving Music, by
              order of the Rev. Mr Madan   3. 3. 0.

One copy of this publication has been found: it, too, forms part of the above-mentioned volume at Los Angeles. It has a title-page found nowhere else, and is paginated 1–26. It contains not six, but 12 hymn tunes by Madan, and the second set, beginning at p. 15, has a different size and style of page numbers, suggesting that they had been repaginated and were perhaps first published as an independent booklet of 12 pages.

Two more separate sections follow, which would later be combined with the 12 Madan hymns to form 'number V', as explained in the preface to edition A/d (quoted below). They have not been found as in-dependent entities, but they must at one time have had independent status because, in edition A/d, they still have their own half-titles and prices. They consist of elaborate tunes by Charles Lockhart, who styles himself 'Organist of the Lock Hospital Chapel'; almost certainly, their original publication dates from his second term as organist (1770–7). On the once blank page of the second of these (which would become p. 178) is printed the still well-known hymn tune 'Invocation' (now more often named 'Carlisle') with its own unique attribution: 'by Mr Lockhart'. There is good reason to think that this was added after Lockhart had been reappointed organist in 1790, when it was decided to create a second volume of the Collection.[55]

This next advance in the hymnbooks occurred in 1793, when the secretary reported to the General Court

That Mr Lockhart has compleated the new Tunes which he proposed to the select Committee to be added to the Collection for the use of the Chapel of

[55] For one thing, the separate title-page of the second added section (Table 3, title-page (5)) refers to 'Two Hymns', not three. Corroborative evidence lies in the gradual changeover from the upright lower-case 's' similar to an 'f', to the modern form. On pp. 1–42 (see Table 3) the modern 's' is used only at the ends of words, as was traditional. On pp. 143–77 it is used consistently in tune names and Italian tempo indications, but still only at the ends of words in the hymn texts. On p. 178, as on pp. 179–93, it is used everywhere, except as the first of a pair of adjacent 's's in the hymn texts. Thus it is likely that p. 178 was engraved some years after pp. 175–7, and near the time when pp. 179–93 were engraved.

60

this Hospital; that he has had the same engraved, on Twenty five Plates, and presented them, together with all the Plates, for the benefit of the Charity.[56]

Clearly this represented pages 179–93 and was the last portion to make up the complete book, issued in 1793 (edition A/d). This has its own subtitle on page 179: 'Number VI. Composed by Charles Lockhart, Organist to the Charity.' The six new 'numbers' bear no relation to the original 12-page numbers, and therefore they are represented in the third column of Table 3 by roman numerals. The matter is explained in the preface to the complete edition, signed by Jabez Fisher, the secretary, and dated 3 May 1792:

> The first four Numbers (at 5s. each) will contain the whole of the Volume which hath been hitherto sold for a Guinea [edition A/c]: – The Music published by Mr. Madan, as the first Part of a second Volume, will be included in the fifth Number, to which are added four Tunes composed by Mr. Lockhart.
> The sixth and last Number will consist intirely of new Music, which Mr. Lockhart has kindly presented to this Charity.

We do not know how the first volume was divided into four numbers, but the likely points are after pages 36, 72 and 104, which were the dividing points when edition A/f was divided into four books (see below).

Edition A/d had a new title-page, without the illustration, calling the book 'A new, and improved Edition' and adding Longman & Broderip to the imprint. This firm may well have printed the volume, for on 6 February 1794 the treasurer was 'ordered to pay Messrs Longman & Broderip £20. 6s. 6d. for printing Music, on acct. of the Chapel'.[57]

The firm's successor, Broderip & Wilkinson, issued a newly engraved edition of volume 1 (the original pp. 1–142), in four books, each with its own title-page and frontispiece, and extending to 285 pages (as a result of larger print and spacing, not additional music).[58] There is no reason to think that this was authorized by the hospital.

Another edition, appearing in 1800, used the title-page and 1769 dedication of edition A/c, and has therefore been treated as a copy of that edition in some library catalogues. But the contents are those of the complete 1793 edition (A/d), with some minor musical alterations made on the plates (notably on pp. 16, 88 and 105). Moreover, at the foot of the index on page [vi] are the words 'Printed by Watts and Bridgewaters, Queen-st., Grosv. sq.'. On 26 February 1801 the charity paid £30 7s. 'to Mess. Watts & Bridgewater for Print$ to Mich$ last'.[59] Three copies of this edition (A/e) have so far been traced.[60] The Manchester copy has watermark dates of 1800 (pp. v/vi) and 1804 (pp. 12/13). A later issue from the

---

[56] Board 14, 2 May 1793. Unfortunately, the more detailed proceedings that doubtless took place at the meeting of the Select (Chapel) Committee are unrecorded owing to a gap in book C.1.

[57] Board 14, 6 February 1794.

[58] This edition is dated c.1807 in the British Library catalogue, on unknown grounds. It is here numbered A/f. The firm Broderip & Wilkinson was in business from 1798 to 1808.

[59] Board 16, 26 February 1801.

[60] British Library, E.1429; Royal College of Music, B.III.28; Manchester Public Library.

same plates (A/g) has the price deleted from the title-page plate, lacks the Watts & Bridgewaters imprint, and has a watermark date of 1817.[61]

Finally the Collection was reissued in the United States as *The Collection of Psalm and Hymn Tunes Sung at the Chapel of the Lock Hospital. From the Last London Edition* ([Boston]: West & Blake and Manning & Loring, 1809; 198, [2] pp.; here called edition B). By way of introductory matter it contains both the 1769 dedication and the 1792 preface, plus an 'Advertisement to the American Edition' dated September 1809.[62] The only deliberate musical change from edition A/c is the rearrangement of the upper voice parts so that the voice bearing the 'tune' appears immediately above the figured bass stave.

Meanwhile the hospital had published a new official hymnbook (texts only). It was prepared by the chaplain, Thomas Fry, in consultation with John Pearson, a governor. After revision by members of the chapel committee it was printed by W. Nicholson in October 1803, in at least two sizes, one a 12mo, the other a 'pocket' 32mo.[63] Of its 331 hymns (of which 326 are numbered), little more than half (168) came from its predecessor, the last edition of Madan's *Hymns* (see Table 1). The 43 texts dropped from that book included 13 that were still in the music book. So there was a clear move away from the use of the Lock Hospital Collection just at the time when the chapel was reverting to ordinary congregational singing led by a boys' choir.

In 1807 Matthew Cooke, organist of St George, Bloomsbury, played the Lock chapel organ for three months during the absence of Mrs Medley, for which he was paid five guineas. At the same time it was recorded that 'the Board accepts the offer of M[r] Cooke's dedicating to them the Collection of Hymn Tunes he means to publish'. Later, however,

the Advertizment of a set of Hymns, dedicated to the Lock Governors, and laid this Day before the Board, by Mr Cooke, appearing to the Board as likely to injure the Charity; Resolved, that a Letter be sent to Mr Cooke to request he will not publish any Hymns agreeable to that Ad[vertisemen]t, nor make farther application for subscript[ns] under the sanction of the Lock Governors.[64]

Nevertheless, the collection was engraved and printed by Skillern and Challoner, London, and published by Cooke under the title *A Collection of Psalm and Hymn Tunes, for the Use of the Lock Hospital Chapel.*[65] All

[61] Copy: British Library, F.1122.m.

[62] Shaw-Shoemaker 17967; reproduced under that number in the American Antiquarian Society's Readex microcard series. For a full description see Allen Perdue Britton, Irving Lowens and Richard Crawford, *American Sacred Imprints 1698–1810: A Bibliography* (Worcester, Mass., 1990), 234–5.

[63] Chapel Committee Book C.1, 30 June 1803. Nicholson's printing bill for £65 4s. was submitted on 25 October 1803; the secretary was reimbursed £110 16s. 6d. for 'printing paper &c.' for 1803, compared with a normal annual expenditure on stationery of some £10–15 (Board 17, 28 June 1804). The book's title (cf. Table 1) was *A Collection of Psalms and Hymns, Extracted from Various Authors, for the Use of the Lock Chapel. A New Edition.* London: Printed by W. Nicholson, Warner Street. And sold at the Lock Hospital, near Hyde-Park-Corner. 1803 (12mo, 241 pp.: British Library, 3436.h.16; 32mo, 273 pp.: British Library, 3434.a.30.) This book was reprinted without change of content in 1810 and 1826.

[64] Board 17, 29 October 1807, 21 January 1808.

[65] Copy: British Library, B.370.g.(1).

the texts but one were chosen from the 1803 hymnbook and followed its numbering. Of the 18 tunes, 14 were completely new, and none were from the Lock Hospital Collection. Cooke had a chance to introduce these tunes when he deputized for the organist in 1808 and 1809, but there is no evidence that they came into general use at the Lock Hospital or elsewhere.

In 1810 the General Committee 'Ordered that a New Edition of the large Hymn Books be printed, under the direction of the Revd Tho' Fry and Mr Pearson'; this can only refer to the music collection. This was the year in which a paid organist was once more appointed. But nothing seems to have come of this order. No revised edition of the Lock Hospital Collection was ever published.

So the essence of the Lock Hospital music consists of the 127 tunes composed over a period of some 30 years (about 1762–92), by a number of composers, but yet bearing a strong corporate individuality and character that marks it out from almost all predecessors. A primary source of this character was Methodism. The texts of the Lock Hospital Collection leave no doubt that this book is associated with the Methodist/Evangelical movement.[66] All but three are taken directly from Madan's *Hymns*,[67] which is regarded as the first Evangelical hymnbook.[68] They are, for the most part, 'hymns of human composition', rather than metrical psalms, which were still the principal and almost exclusive fare in orthodox Anglican churches. Many of the hymns are by leading Methodists such as the Wesley brothers and John Cennick, but often in the altered forms found in George Whitefield's *Hymns for Social Worship* (1753) which was its chief source.[69] The alterations 'suited Madan better than the originals (alterations so bitterly resented by Wesley in the preface to his hymn-book of 1780)',[70] and indicate that Madan, though originally converted by hearing Wesley preach in 1750, ultimately joined the Calvinistic wing of the Methodist movement that was led by Whitefield, William Romaine and Selina, Countess of Huntingdon.[71]

---

[66] In the 1760s and 70s both groups considered themselves part of the Church of England, though they were treated with hostility by the church authorities. When the split came, those that remained in the church were predominantly though not exclusively Calvinists rather than (like Wesley) Arminians, and became generally known as Evangelicals; those who left the church became Calvinistic Methodists. Before that time, however, there was no clear distinction between Evangelicals and Methodists. (For further discussion see Temperley, *The Music of the English Parish Church*, 2 vols. (Cambridge, 1979), i, 204–7.)

[67] The three new ones are 'Our little bark on boist'rous seas' (by Zinzendorf, in an unidentified translation); 'Hail, great Immanuel' (anonymous); and 'Dear object of our strong desire' (Walter Shirley). Statistics of the authorship of the texts in Madan's *Hymns* may be found in F. Madan, *The Madan Family*, 275, 278. The most heavily represented authors are Charles Wesley, with 92 hymns; Isaac Watts, with 63; and John Cennick, with 15.

[68] George Reginald Balleine, *A History of the Evangelical Party in the Church of England* (London, 1908), 109.

[69] Benson, *The English Hymn*, 330.

[70] John Julian, *A Dictionary of Hymnology* (2nd edn, London, 1907), 332–3.

[71] Madan's conversion may have been influenced by his mother's religious views. Judith Madan (1702–81), née Cowper (she was an aunt of the poet), came under the influence of both Wesley and Lady Huntingdon in about 1749, and more so after the death of her husband in 1756. As a known Methodist, Madan had difficulty in obtaining ordination, and succeeded only through the influence

Many Methodist hymn texts were on a much higher emotional level than the metrical psalms to which Anglicans and Presbyterians were accustomed, or the hymns of Isaac Watts that formed the staple of Independent and Baptist worship at this time. Emotion was further heightened, in the religious meetings of Wesley and Whitefield, by the ardent style of congregational singing that they encouraged, with all who could standing up and taking part. A third element, tending to raise the immediacy and intensity of the hymn-singing experience, was the introduction of current styles of secular music, and even, in some cases, tunes already known as theatre music or other similar songs.

The meetings of Wesley and Whitefield, however, were popular in character, and were directed especially to the poorer classes. Many were held out of doors, or in barns and warehouses. Unaccompanied singing was the rule; anthems, fuguing tunes, and other elaborate music were denounced because they discouraged some from joining in the singing and brought in 'formality', which was anathema to Wesley. Organs were unknown in Wesleyan meeting-houses. As late as 1828 there was strong objection at the Methodist Conference to the acquisition of an organ at Brunswick Chapel, Leeds.[72] Many of the early Methodist tunebooks, however, provide for instrumental accompaniment.[73]

Madan had to provide singing that would attract the rich and fashionable and induce them to support the Lock Hospital with their charity. He himself, the rich son of a military officer and courtier, was of a higher social class than Wesley and better able to move in aristocratic circles.[74] Without sacrificing Methodist ideas and principles, he modified them to suit the Lock situation. The texts were largely Methodist, but the particular selection tended to favour the cheerful and positive rather than the fervent or anguished tone that is found in many of Charles Wesley's hymns. The music was congregational, but was such as might appeal to

of Lady Huntingdon. He was ordained deacon in 1757 (by Benjamin Hoadly, bishop of Winchester), priest in 1758. In 1757 he became domestic chaplain to the Hon. Henry Bathurst, later Earl Bathurst, another link with the court of Frederick, Prince of Wales. Between 1755 and 1768 he 'itinerated' as a Calvinistic Methodist preacher; his assistants, Haweis and later de Coetlogon, were also Calvinists. He was a close friend of Romaine. (Information from F. Madan, *The Madan Family*, and the *DNB* articles on de Coetlogon and Haweis.)

[72] See John Spencer Curwen, 'Methodist Psalmody', Curwen, *Studies in Worship-Music*, 1st ser. (London, 1880), 24–40.

[73] There are no accompaniments in John Wesley's *Collection of Tunes, Set to Music, as they are Commonly Sung at the Foundery* (London, 1742) or his *Select Hymns, with Tunes Annext* (London, 1761). But the title-page of Butts's *Harmonia sacra* says it is 'for Voice, Harpsichord and Organ' and provides figured basses; Wesley himself specifically approved this feature of the book. Knibb's *A Collection of Tunes in Three Parts* (London, [1755?]) and *The Psalm Singer's Help* (4 edns, London, [1765?]–[1775?]) have figures as well as text for the bass line, and *The Divine Musical Miscellany* (London, 1754), associated with Whitefield's *Hymns for Social Worship* (London, 1753), is scored for a single voice line with figured bass. These features may have been for home use: domestic organs were not uncommon. It is a fact, however, that organs were a feature of the Countess of Huntingdon's larger chapels by the time her Connection officially separated from the Church of England in 1782, and it is possible that the Calvinistic Methodists disagreed with the Wesleyans on this matter. I am grateful to Margo Chaney for her assistance on this point.

[74] In 1768 Madan was stigmatized by the Wesleyans as one of the 'genteel Methodists of Lady Huntingdon's connexion' (F. Madan, *The Madan Family*, 109). Wesley, though highly cultivated and a descendant of Anglican and Dissenting clergy of several generations, confessed to his brother in 1781: 'I was a little out of my element among lords and ladies. I love plain music and plain company best' (Curwen, *Studies*, 39).

64

those who had frequented the operas, oratorios and concerts of the time, and knew the latest theatre songs.[75] That is to say, it imitated modern art music.

For the first time, Italian composers were recruited to provide music for English hymnody, including one (Felice Alessandri) who was on a brief visit to London to present two *opere buffe* of his own composition. This is perhaps the clearest indication of how far Madan would go to attract the upper classes, and perhaps also theatre professionals, who, as we have seen, were strong supporters of the charity. There were models for a theatrical style of church music in the interests of charity, most notably in Italy itself. The music of the Venetian ospedali, as admiringly observed by Charles Burney, 'was of the higher sort of theatric style, though it was performed in a church'.[76]

To make an English congregation sing in the *galant* style of contemporary Italian opera was a new challenge. Madan met it resourcefully. It could be done only with an organ and with congregational rehearsal. Neither would have met with Wesley's approval, or probably Whitefield's either. But it was remarkably successful, at least for a time.

The ensemble texture that was perhaps most fashionable in the mid-eighteenth century was that of one or two relatively high melodic lines, moving largely in parallel thirds or sixths, with a figured bass. It was the texture of the trio sonata, the chamber duet, the newly fashionable accompanied sonata, the symphony, the solo song and above all the opera, where even male parts were sung by high voices (the castrati). Over 90% of the tunes in the Lock Hospital Collection are duets for two trebles, at least as far as notation goes.[77] They are scored for two voices in the G clef and a bass part with figures that is for the most part exclusively instrumental, though in a few tunes the rhythm makes it possible that the bass was also sung to the words.

* The strict Calvinist tradition had forbidden women to sing in church, and most parochial collections at this date still gave the lead to the tenors, with more-or-less optional treble and alto parts above. The G clef had been ambiguous in English tunebooks since 1677, when John Playford, in his *Whole Book of Psalms . . . Compos'd in Three Parts, Cantus, Medius, & Bassus*, had scored his cantus and medius parts in the G clef but had stated in his preface: 'All *Three Parts* may be as properly sung by Men as by Boys or Women.' But Anglican books did not much copy Playford's

---

[75] Such a practice was specifically opposed in orthodox Anglican circles. A sermon preached at the Three Choirs Festival in 1753 warned the 'sacred musician' to avoid 'levity of notes': 'Let him carefully decline the introduction of all such addresses to the passions in his notes, all such complications of sounds, as, having once been connected with words of levity, may naturally recall into light minds the remembrance of those words or their ideas again.' If church music transgressed in this regard, the hearer should try to avoid secular associations: 'Let him rather study to adapt good ideas to the sound, and thereby correct the judgment of the musician.' William Parker, *The Pleasures of Gratitude and Benevolence Improved by Church-Musick. A Sermon Preached . . . at Hereford, On Wednesday, Sept.12, 1753* (London, 1753), 24–5. See also William Riley, *Parochial Music Corrected* (London, 1762), preface.

[76] Charles Burney, *The Present State of Music in France and Italy* (2nd edn, London, 1773), 145–93; the quoted passage occurs at p. 156. One of the four ospedali, the Incurabili, founded in 1517, was for venereal patients and penitent prostitutes.

[77] 120 out of 127. There are two solos and five trios.

format. Four-part harmony, with the tune in the tenor, remained the norm in parish church books in the eighteenth century, but some placed the tenor as well as the soprano in the G clef, using the C clef only for the alto.[78] Gradually, women and children began to double the tenor tune in the higher octave, until by 1800 there was much uncertainty as to which voices should sing the tune.

Wesley and Whitefield both encouraged women to sing the hymns along with men. The format of two trebles and bass was used in two Methodist-connected books that had preceded and possibly influenced Madan's: Knibb's *A Collection of Tunes in Three Parts* and Butts's *Harmonia sacra*, both intimately related to the Lock Collection in their contents and designed use. But in both cases the tune was borne by the 'middle' voice, and the bass part, though figured, was also underlaid for singing. Madan placed the tune on the top stave and provided a purely instrumental bass. In many of the tunes, the two upper voices are nearly equal in range; if they are both sung by sopranos, the tune is often obscured and overlaid by what is harmonically a subordinate part.[79] On the other hand, if the texture is interpreted as soprano and tenor, the lower voice often goes below the bass, sometimes with disastrous effects on the harmony.[80]

Example 1 shows a passage where both problems arise. If the second voice is treated as a tenor and transposed, it goes below the instrumental bass in the second full bar, with the hideous effect of an appoggiatura below the bass resolving onto a 6-4 chord. But if it is sung at pitch as a second treble, it obscures the graceful curve of the melody in the third bar. Again, a passage like that in Example 2 is hardly credible with the lower voice transposed down, because of the string of consecutive fifths it produces. Example 3, on the other hand, has parallel fifths on the word 'Comfort' if sung by two sopranos, but produces ugly parallel 6-4 chords if sung by soprano and tenor.

Example 1

THE PENITENT   Set by W.B.

_____

[78] For a full discussion see Temperley, *The Music of the English Parish Church*, i, 184–90.

[79] In one place, however (p. 68), the second voice would be higher than the melody even when transposed down an octave.

[80] There is little possibility that this danger was avoided by means of a 'double bass' an octave below the written bass notes. Organs with independent pedals were virtually unknown in England at that time, as were 16-foot manual stops. See Nicholas Thistlethwaite, *The Making of the Victorian Organ* (Cambridge, 1990), 14–15, 105.

Example 2

Example 3

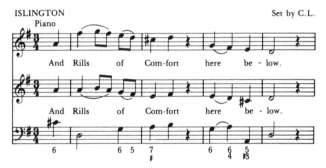

Surprising though it may appear to modern ears, the probability is that this music was intended to sound in four vocal parts, with both melodic lines sung by women at pitch and by men an octave lower, despite the occasional harmonic inversion or covering of the tune. The parallelisms in Examples 2 and 3, though still present, sound much more tolerable if sung in that way. This double texture was perhaps the 'peculiar mode of singing' that Lockhart had developed at the Lock Hospital. It was copied in many later tunebooks, particularly in Dissenting circles, and also in North America.

Two tunes in the book specify alternation between men and women,[81] and in both the second men's part goes below the instrumental bass at times. There is some reason to think that in Methodist circles whenever a line of text was repeated (which happens frequently in this book) it was sung first by women alone and then by men and women together.[82]

*   [81] Pp. 96, 134. This custom seems to have originated in 'dialogue hymns' specially written for the purpose by John Cennick, some of which were included in Whitefield's *Hymns for Social Worship*. One of the two men/women tunes in the Lock Collection is a dialogue hymn, 'Tell us, O women; we would know Whither so fast ye move?'.

        [82] See Temperley, *The Music of the English Parish Church*, i, 212; Curwen, *Studies*, 27. The custom survives in a 'repeating' tune of Catholic origin, 'Adeste fideles'. It is also possible that the dynamic mark *p* meant that women were to sing alone: Stephen Addington's *Collection of Psalm*

The music also shows subtleties usually associated with art music, which would hardly be possible without rehearsal. Trills, mordents and melismas are frequently found in the voice parts. Dynamic marks (p, f) appear occasionally in the early numbers, and in the great majority of hymns from page 37 onwards (see Table 3). Contrasts between 'solo' and 'tutti'/'chorus' sections are used in the middle portions of the book (pp. 45–177) and it is there, also, that the most elaborate settings are found, including many 'set pieces' (through-composed hymn settings). Figure 2 illustrates many of these points: Madan's 'Denbigh' was one of the most popular tunes in the collection. The last section, entirely composed by Lockhart after his return to the organistship in 1790, contains much simpler hymns again, probably because the skills of the congregation had declined during a decade of neglect; but the *piano/forte* contrasts are still present.

Figure 2. Page 63 of the 'Lock Hospital Collection'.

The melodic and harmonic idiom of these tunes is very much in accord with opera or concert music of the day, and to that extent departs equally from the plain style of the older psalm tunes, the quirky illiteracy of country psalmody and the conservative late-Baroque idiom of contemporary

Tunes (3rd edn, Market Harborough, 1780) laid down that 'where Pia. is over a line it is to be sung soft, or only in women's voices', but this book was primarily for the use of Congregationalists rather than Methodists. John Beaumont, a Wesleyan Methodist, wrote in the preface to his *Select Hymns, Odes, Poems, and Other Choice Pieces Proper to be Sung in Public Worship* (Leeds, 1800): 'Let the Women always take their Parts alone, in the Repeats', a gloss on one of Wesley's own rules.

68

cathedral music. It is expressive in its disarmingly simple harmony and its sighing appoggiaturas; it is prettily decorative in its parallel thirds and sixths, its ornaments and melismas; it is mildly theatrical in its occasional pauses and calculated contrasts. All this, indeed, was more familiar in the theatre than in the church.

However, Madan and Lockhart, unlike Whitefield, did not take their music directly from secular sources.[83] Indeed, with only a handful of exceptions (all of them in the first six numbers, pp. 1–72), the 127 tunes in the collection are newly composed, and are attributed to their composers either by name or by initials. A key to the initials is found in the following inscription, in an unknown twentieth-century hand, on a slip of paper inserted into the British Library copy of edition A/c:

Names of Composers

M.M.	Revd. Mr. Madan	F.E.	Sir Francis Isles
T.H.	Revd. Mr. Hawes	W.B.	Mr. William Bromfield
F.G.	Mr. Giardini	J.B.	Mrs. Jane Bromfield
I.W.	Mr. Worgan	I.B.	Surgeon Bromfield
C.B.	Mr. Burney	W.I.	Mr. William Jackson
M.V.	Mr. Vento	S.A.	Mr. Samuel Arnold
C.L.	Mr. Lockhart	F.A.	Mr. Francis Alessandro
Dr.H.	Dr. Heighington		

From a Manuscript copy of Madan's Psalm & Hymn Tunes, made by James Haywood in 1769–71.

The original document described here has not been traced. There is no reason to doubt its accuracy, but certain questions arise. Why 'F.E.' rather than 'F.I.'? The spellings Bromfield (for Bromfeild), Hawes (for Haweis) and Alessandro (for Alessandri) are not quite in accord with the usual practice of the time, and Alessandri's first name was actually Felice, not Francis. However, Giardini, Vento, Alessandri, Worgan, Burney and Arnold are also acknowledged in the printed dedication to edition A/c, quoted above. The identity of 'Surgeon Bromfield' is uncertain. William Bromfeild, founder of the charity, was also its official surgeon until 1770, when he was succeeded by his son Charles, described in 1776 as 'late Surgeon to the Princess Dowager of Wales'; but his tunes are labelled 'W.B.'. James Bromfeild, probably William's brother and a possible candidate for 'I.B.', was listed not as a surgeon but as a 'visiting Apothecary'; however, he had been a governor since at least 1759 and seems the most likely person.[84] Jane Bromfeild was the wife of William. All other names

---

[83] The only possible exception is the famous tune 'Helmsley', which some authorities have derived from a theatre tune; see, for instance, *The New Oxford Book of Carols*, ed. Hugh Keyte and Andrew Parrott (Oxford, 1992), 252. But the resemblance is slight, is unsupported by evidence, and is made the more unlikely by the fact that no secular source has been found for any other tune in the book.

[84] 'An Account of the Proceedings of the Governors of the Lock Hospital. 1776', Charles de Coetlogon, *A Sermon Preached on Friday, December 13, 1776* (London, 1777), 54–5. Evidence of the family relationships is to be found in Court 1, p. 247, and Court 2, p. 137. Capital I and J were still interchangeable at this date, so it is possible that all four tunes labelled 'I.B.' or 'J.B.' are by the same person.

listed are either to be found in *The New Grove Dictionary* or have already been identified in this article, with the exception of Isles, of whom nothing is known. It is likely that all except Heighington contributed their tunes expressly for the Collection.[85] Only the unattributed items may have been taken from earlier publications. One ('Brighthelmstone', p. 29) is a version of the 'Passion chorale', *Herzlich tut mich verlangen*, best known today in settings by J. S. Bach. Table 4 shows how many pieces by each composer are found in each main section of the Collection.

Considering the number of composers involved, the uniformity of style is notable. Perhaps the explanation lies in the words 'revised and corrected by an eminent Master' in the 1765 advertisement, and the word 'Corrections' found in Madan's 1769 dedication. Giardini, who was made a perpetual governor on 21 May 1761, seems the most likely candidate for the 'eminent Master'. He may have drastically 'corrected' the work of his less proficient colleagues, perhaps under Madan's general supervision, to the point where they all conformed rather closely to a 'house style' and to a minimum of musical literacy.[86] If Giardini was indeed the man, it would help to explain the flavour of Italian opera that pervades the book. The last ten tunes, where Lockhart was no longer subject to an editor, do show a somewhat different and simplified character.

Madan himself had an undoubted gift for expressive melody. His hymn tune 'Hotham' for 'Jesu, lover of my soul' was, and still remains, one of the most popular and successful of its period, and it is quite typical of the

TABLE 4

COMPOSERS OF THE LOCK HOSPITAL COLLECTION

composer		number of tunes:					
	pp:	1–36 (1762–5)	37–72 (1765–7)	73–142 (1767–9)	143–77 (1772–7)	178–93 (1790–3)	total
Martin Madan		13	11	9	12	–	45
Charles Lockhart		–	3	9	3	9	24
Charles Burney		–	5	4	–	–	9
William Bromfeild		6	3	–	–	–	9
Felice Giardini		3	3	1	–	–	7
John Worgan		1	4	1	–	–	6
Samuel Arnold		–	–	4	–	–	4
Jane Bromfeild		1	1	–	–	–	2
'Surgeon Bromfeild'		2	–	–	–	–	2
Thomas Haweis		–	2	–	–	–	2
William Jackson		–	–	2	–	–	2
Matthias Vento		–	2	–	–	–	2
Felice Alessandri		–	–	1	–	–	1
Musgrave Heighington		1	–	–	–	–	1
Francis Isles		1	–	–	–	–	1
Unattributed		8	2	–	–	–	10
Total		36	36	31	15	9	127

[85] The code 'Dr.H.' occurs only in a hymn headed 'Altered from Dr.H.'.
[86] There are occasional examples of parallel fifths or octaves, but apart from that the music conforms to professional standards of harmonic progression and voice-leading.

book with its decorative *galant* expressiveness. [87] It was surely the melody that caught on. Madan's basses are static, his harmony conventional (though certainly progressive for its period), and in his longer pieces he shows a tendency to return too often to the home key and chord. [88] Two other Madan tunes, 'Leeds' and 'Denbigh', also had very wide use for many decades, while 'Pelham' has been recently revived. Madan's reputation in the United States in the early nineteenth century, first boosted by the psalmodist and clergyman Andrew Law (1749–1821), reached extraordinary heights for a time. His set piece 'Denmark' became by far the most popular through-composed piece among the 100 sacred compositions most frequently printed in America before 1811. [89] He was regarded as a prime model for good sacred music by would-be reformers, and in the introductions to four published collections his name was actually coupled with Handel's. [90]

Lockhart tended towards the over-elaborate in melody. Interestingly, the only one of his tunes that has lasted is the simplest, 'Invocation'/ 'Carlisle', which he was obliged to confine to a single page for reasons already stated. Harmonically he was more skilled than Madan, and had no trouble in handling modulations in his longer pieces. The weaker side of his technique is his part-writing.

Of all the composers represented, Burney is the most operatic. He does not shrink from theatrical gestures or elaborate melismas approaching coloratura. Unlike most, he pays attention to the later verses of a hymn, sometimes providing alternative notes to accommodate irregular stress patterns. William Bromfeild's tunes, by contrast, are very simple, and seem congregationally conceived; he wrote no set pieces or organ 'symphonies'. Giardini also kept to a simple style and texture, even in his one set piece ('Cambridge'). He was responsible for another tune from the Collection that is in common use today, the splendid 'Hymn to the Trinity' (now called 'Moscow'). It was written for Wesley's 'Come, thou almighty King' which, in turn, had been a parody of 'God save the King'. The characteristic and powerful metre of the national anthem probably played its part in the success of Giardini's tune.

The remaining composers hardly contributed enough to make an impact on the character of the book, nor did their tunes reach particularly high levels of popularity. The other two tunes from the Collection that were hugely popular, 'Helmsley' and 'Sheldon', were both printed without attribution, and may have been from Knibb's *The Psalm Singer's*

---

[87] I discussed it in detail in *The Music of the English Parish Church*, i, 212, and reprinted it there (ii, Example 45).

[88] Three of his later set pieces, however ('Brunswick', 'Worcester', 'Alton'), are more enterprising in their treatment of musical form.

[89] *The Core Repertory of Early American Psalmody*, ed. Richard A. Crawford, Recent Researches in American Music, 12–13 (Madison, Wis., 1984), xxxiii. Three other tunes from the Lock Hospital Collection are on the list of 100, all by Madan: 'Christmas', 'Dunstan' and 'Hotham'. Only two composers, the Americans William Billings and Daniel Read, exceed Madan's total on this list.

[90] These are Andrew Law, *The Musical Primer* (Cheshire, Conn., 1793); Andrew Law, *The Art of Singing* (Cheshire, Conn., 1800); *The Beauties of Psalmody* (Baltimore, 1804); and *The Suffolk Collection of Church Musick* (Boston, 1807). The relevant passages are reproduced in Britton, Lowens and Crawford, *American Sacred Imprints*, 421, 401, 224, 571 respectively.

Help, edition (b) (*c*.1765). As this book cannot be precisely dated, priority and authorship remain uncertain.[91] Both are attractive primarily for the ornateness of their long-breathed phrases. The repeating fifth line of 'Helmsley', with its dancing dotted figure, is particularly catchy. The anonymous editor of the 1800 edition (A/e) liked this figure so much that he actually introduced it in lines 2 and 4 as well, by alteration of the plates (see Example 4). This tune represented all that the Victorians most despised about Georgian secularity, effeminacy, superficiality and so on. But it would not go away. In 1906 Ralph Vaughan Williams reharmonized it with Edwardian grandeur for *The English Hymnal*. But in its original form the effect was one of beguiling sensibility that, in truth, hardly matched the tortured ecstasy of Charles Wesley's vivid word-picture of the Crucifixion: 'With what rapture / Gaze we on those glorious scars'.

Example 4

HELMSLEY

The giving of money for charity can have a number of motives. It would be cynical to deny that one of them, perhaps the foremost, is simple compassion for the sufferings of fellow human beings; there is also the parallel concern felt by religious believers for the fate of sinners' souls. With these altruistic feelings may be associated a wish to assuage one's own feelings of guilt, whether induced by disobedience to the laws of God and man, by personal behaviour that may have contributed to the suffering of others, or merely by relative affluence. Some have been attracted to the Pelagian heresy, which holds that doing good works can assure salvation without the need for divine grace.[92]

[91] Another version of 'Helmsley' appeared, under the name 'Olivers', at about the same time in the collection entitled *Sacred Melody* attached to some copies of John Wesley's *Select Hymns with Tunes Annext* (2nd edn, 1765). I am preparing an article to sort out the origins of this famous tune, long a   *
subject of controversy; for a recent summary see *The New Oxford Book of Carols*, 256–7.

[92] The texts of some eighteenth-century charity hymns come close to suggesting that alms-giving is an investment whose profits will be reaped in the afterlife.

72

Whatever its motives, there is no doubt that charity was a powerful social force among the wealthier classes of Georgian society. Music, with its power to intensify feeling, was a natural adjunct. The traditional music of the Church of England, strong, dignified, and at its best a high art, was well suited to the corporate expression of praise. But it was too familiar, too old and too impersonal to make an immediate appeal to the more intimate emotions, particularly those of guilt and compassion. Martin Madan therefore turned to a realm of music where the expression of intimate human feeling was a professional function: the opera. Like other Methodists, he saw that the melting strains of operatic singing could be taken out of the theatre and put to use in the real world, particularly for charity. High-churchmen and Puritans might be shocked, but his object was achieved. Eventually, the styles of music and singing introduced at the Lock Hospital chapel, and many of the actual texts and tunes, would come to be widely adopted in the Church of England and in most other Protestant denominations throughout the English-speaking world, until checked by the return to ancient tradition and austerity led by the Oxford Movement. It is not surprising, in the end, that such a transformation in the style of sacred music began in an institution that depended directly on arousing emotion.

XII

Jonathan Gray and Church Music in York, 1770–1840

Jonathan Gray (1779-1837), alderman of York, solicitor, and amateur musician, was a figure of great local and some national importance in musical history, although he has never yet secured an entry in Grove's *Dictionary of Music and Musicians* or any * other standard work of musical reference. He was the grandfather of Alan Gray (1855-1935), well remembered today as a composer and as organist of Trinity College, Cambridge.[1] He was a man of extraordinary abilities. A member of a strong group of Evangelicals resident in York, he was active in promoting the reform of parish-church music — in particular, the revival of congregational singing. He not only helped to revitalize the singing of metrical psalms and hymns in the Church of England, but also played a pioneering role in the introduction of congregationally chanted psalms. In addition he published a series of letters written during a tour of the Continent in 1818, which provide some interesting information about Continental church music of the time. In this essay I propose to discuss in some detail his influence in the realm of church music, while giving brief attention to his other activities.

*   *   *   *

William Gray (1751-1845), father of Jonathan, was the son of a Hull customs officer,[2] and became a successful attorney-at-law (or, as we would call it today, solicitor) at York. In 1788 he bought the Treasurer's House by the Minster, dividing it into two halves and residing in one.[3] He was prominent in local affairs and was closely linked with several Anglican clergymen,

---

[1] [Almyra], Mrs Edwin Gray, *Papers and Diaries of a York Family, 1764-1839* (1927) is the principal source of biographical information about the Gray family in this and the following paragraphs. It includes a note on Jonathan Gray's musical activities by his grandson, Alan Gray.

[2] *Yorkshire Courant*, 4 February 1793.

[3] [Almyra], Mrs Edwin Gray, *The Mansion House of the Treasurers of York Minster* (York, 1933), p. 43. Jonathan Gray lived in the Treasurer's House from 1822 to 1837.

2

chiefly of the Evangelical party. One of these was the Reverend John Robinson (died 1793), headmaster of St Peter's school, then situated in St Andrewgate, who was a native of Cumberland. Through Robinson's influence two other clergymen came from Cumberland to York. One was William Richardson (1745-1821), who was educated at St Bees Grammar school, and who became a vicar-choral of York Minster and curate of St Michael le Belfrey in 1771. The other was John Graham (1765-1844), also from St Bees, who came to York in 1787 as usher (assistant master) of St Peter's school under Robinson, and later became incumbent of three churches in the city, and headmaster of Archbishop Holgate's school (from 1829). Both will play important parts in our story.

Robinson and William Gray married sisters, respectively Frances and Faith, daughters of Jonathan Hopwood. Gray was a close friend of both Richardson and Graham. They were associated, among other things, in the encouragement of the Sunday School movement in York. Gray and Richardson were founding members of the Sunday School Committee, instituted in 1786, and Gray was its first chairman; they were joined by Graham in 1797, shortly after his return to York.[4] From 1791 to 1796 Graham had been curate of Barwick-in-Elmet, near Leeds, and it was here that he became acquainted with William Hey, a prominent Evangelical, and thus with William Wilberforce himself, through whom he 'became permanently interested in, and influenced by, those evangelical truths which he subsequently preached with much success'.[5] In 1796, by the influence of Wilberforce (who had been elected M.P. for Yorkshire in 1784), Graham was presented simultaneously to the York livings of St Saviour, St Mary Bishophill Senior, and All Saints, North Street (he soon resigned the third).[6] For a man of his views Richardson was the obvious mentor in the city, and Graham

---

[4] J. Howard (comp.), *Historical Sketch of the Origin and Work of the York Incorporated (Church of England) Sunday School Committee, instituted 1786* (York, 1887), pp. 23, 123-5.

[5] R. Burgess, *The Faithful Steward: A Sermon occasioned by the death of the Rev. John Graham* (1844), p. 12n.

[6] *Ibid.* p. 13.

soon became closely attached to him: he preached at his funeral in 1821.[7]

This powerful circle of Evangelicals surrounding William Gray was clearly the predominant influence on his family. Another family connection would be made in 1810, when Margaret Gray, daughter of William, married Samuel Hey, son of William Hey and vicar of Ockbrook (Derbys.).[8] Jonathan Gray was born on 3 August 1779. Richardson was his godfather, and helped his father to instruct him in religious matters. He was educated at the Grammar School in St Andrewgate, at first under Robinson and Graham; and then prepared for the legal profession. 'When I was a boy', he wrote, 'I had set my mind on the Church; and I was put into the Office by my father against my will. I have since been well satisfied as things are'.[9] As a lawyer, indeed, he was able to use his knowledge, professional services, and influence to help a number of Evangelical causes, including church music. He was articled to his father in 1795, and appointed a Master Extraordinary of the High Court of Chancery in 1801. In 1804 he married Mary Homer of York.

There is no doubt of Gray's lifelong attachment to the Church of England and to the Evangelical party within that Church. We will see from his musical activities how deep was his concern for the vitality of Anglican worship. He involved himself in many religious causes and endeavours, including missionary societies; he was secretary of the York Anti-Slavery Association; he agitated for the reform of the local lunatic asylum,[10] of which he wrote a *History*. He also unfortunately shared the narrow churchmanship of many of his party. Near the end of his life he was publicly called upon to justify his imputation that the Roman Catholic church was 'superstitious, idolatrous and unscriptural'. In reply he published a pamphlet entitled *An Appeal to Protestants* (York, 1837) in which he quoted from his own 'minutes' of Catholic services he had attended on the Continent.

---

[7] J. Graham, *The Faithful Minister, Israel's Best Defence: A Sermon* (York, 1821). For a description of the circle of men surrounding Richardson, Graham and Gray, see Burgess, *op. cit.*, pp. 11-13.

[8] Mrs Gray, *Papers and Diaries*, p. 190.

[9] *Ibid.* p. 107.

[10] *Ibid.* pp. 108, 115.

4

Politically, Gray was an active supporter of Pitt and Wilberforce: at the parliamentary election of 1808, the first contested election in Yorkshire for 65 years, he strongly supported Wilberforce, though as under-sheriff he had to superintend the poll. In 1819 he founded the *Yorkshire Gazette*, which he used as a platform for his strong views on many subjects, including music. He was keenly interested in literature, architecture, and astronomy; he made meteorological observations for 25 years, and was even at one time placed in charge of the Minster clock. He was steward to several archiepiscopal manors as well as official stamp distributor for the city. He was the first treasurer of the Yorkshire Philosophical Society (from 1823), a governor of several public institutions, an elected alderman, and a magistrate. When he died on 11 December 1837 he was probably the most widely esteemed man in York.[11]

With all these activities Gray still found time for music. He was an active member of the York Musical Society from 1811, and on the foundation of the York Choral Society in 1833 he was made its first president.[12] In 1834 he played an important part in the specification and design of the new organ built for the Minster.[13] John Graham said of him:

'To music he was devotedly attached. This fascinating pursuit engaged from his earliest years much of his time. He played upon the organ with great facility of execution, and kindly gave his amateur services as organist, for a long series of years, at the Sunday evening service at St Saviour's church. For his own private use he had an organ of very considerable powers put up in his own house: this was used in assisting the devotional harmony of his own family, and of parties of religious friends. He had also some skill as a composer of music, and published a few chants for cathedral service'.[14]

It is not at all obvious where Gray's considerable musical abilities came from. But it is not surprising, given his background,

---

[11]'Obituary of Jonathan Gray, Esq.,' *York Chronicle*, 20 December 1837; Mrs Gray, *Papers and Diaries*, p. 108; J. Graham, *A Sermon . . . on the Occasion of the Death of Jonathan Gray, Alderman* (York, 1838); Borthwick Institute, CC. Ab. 5/34.

[12]R. Rose, *The York Musical Society and the York Choral Society* (York, n.d.), pp. 17, 19.

[13]He also represented the cathedral authorities in the case of *Hill v. The Dean and Chapter of York*, which was a dispute about the organ builder's charges. See *The Musical World*, vol. V (1837), p. 21.

[14]Graham, *op. cit.*

that they were channelled primarily into the field of church music. His immense curiosity on this subject is illustrated in the letters he wrote during his frequent travels, when he rarely omitted to comment on the music of the churches, great and small, in the places he visited. In 1806 he criticised Dr Joseph Milner, Dean of Carlisle (despite the fact that Milner was a prominent member of his father's Evangelical circle): 'I could not help being glad Dr Milner was not Dean of York, when one sees how negligent he is of the cathedral services etc.' [15] At Shanklin, Isle of Wight, in 1828, he criticised the singing of hymns and psalms accompanied by a clarinet and violoncello. [16]

In 1818 Gray undertook a tour of the Continent, primarily to study the administration of hospitals with a view to possible improvements in York institutions for which he was partly responsible. During this tour he wrote a remarkable series of letters for publication in the *York Chronicle*. They were later reprinted in a small booklet.[17] Amid lively comments on many sides of life in the places he visited, he gave descriptions of church music, both Catholic and Protestant, which he seems to have taken every possible opportunity of hearing. The letters form a useful source of information, hitherto unknown to musicologists, to add to those of more famous English musical travellers like Charles Burney, Vincent Novello and Edward Holmes. There are detailed descriptions of musical services at Aire, Douai, Rheims, Trier, Mainz, Cologne and Rotterdam, which are of special value because the writer was so knowledgeable about church music in general, though they are sometimes tainted with anti-Catholic prejudice. As a sample we may quote his account of services at Mainz on Sunday, 23 August 1818. He attended at least five churches on that day. 'At three, Vespers began at the Cathedral. The congregation chanted to the organ, which played long symphonies between each verse.' From there he went to

'the handsome modern Church of St Ignatius, which has a shewy organ; very splendid altars and lights, and a richly painted roof. – There was

---

[15]Mrs Gray, *Papers and Diaries*, p. 119.

[16]York City Library, MS. J.143; letter dated 6 May 1828.

[17][J. Gray], *Letters written from the Continent during a six weeks' tour in 1818* (York, 1819).

6

a very crowded Church; and the young Priests were [fully] employed. In front of the organ was a military band; and between every verse of the chant, (which was sung by the congregation in loud chorus to the organ) the military band, and the organ, alternately, played light pieces of music; one of which was 'Giovinette che fate all' amore' from Mozart's Opera of Don Giovanni; others from Haydn's Overtures [i.e. symphonies]; the whole was quite in the theatrical stile, and the symphonies were six times the length of the chant. The occasional rolling of the kettle-drums and blowing of the trumpets was quite martial'.[18]

A man of such upbringing, attainments, and experiences was unlikely to be satisfied with the style of English parish-church music inherited from the eighteenth century. Gray believed that the old-fashioned metrical psalmody, as exemplified in the parish churches of York, was totally inadequate as an expression of Evangelical religion; and his constant seeking out of religious music in the churches of England and the Continent was a part of his quest for something better. He found that there were few churches anywhere in which the music was really a fitting expression of God's praise. He turned therefore, like other thoughtful men of his time, to the revival of ancient traditions, and to the inspiration of new texts and music.

The old metrical psalms of the Old and New Versions were crude, unappealing, often even unmeaning to Gray's contemporaries. They were sometimes at variance with the meaning of the psalms as interpreted in the light of the Christian Gospels. The music to which they were sung was dull, its manner of performance uninspiring and lifeless, and often carried on by a parish clerk or a few schoolchildren instead of the congregation at large. Gray wished to reform this almost out of existence, and to introduce new kinds of music to parish churches — hymns with uplifting texts and inspiriting tunes, chanted psalms, intoned responses. But the weight of tradition was against him, and was augmented by the generally accepted view that the metrical psalms were not only divinely inspired but legally protected. Gray left the theological side of this question to the clergy, but he used his legal knowledge and historical scholarship to contest successfully the argument that the Old and New Versions were the only verses authorised for use in

---

[18]*Ibid.* pp. 69-70.

church. He also worked towards something new: the participation of the people in the chanting of psalms, a practice that
had hitherto been left entirely to trained choirs.

*   *   *   *

The story of the reform of church music in York goes back
beyond Gray's birth, to the appointment of William Mason[19]
(1725-1797) as Precentor of York in 1762. Mason, unlike most
cathedral precentors, was an accomplished musician, and had
strong progressive views about both cathedral and parochial
music. In his essay 'On Parochial Psalmody'[20] he sharply criticised the prevailing habit of leaving the choice and conduct of
metrical psalms to the parish clerk, and the music in the hands
of a self-appointed choir and band. He also condemned many of
the verse translations in use, and proposed using a 'judicious
selection' of passages from the metrical psalms. In rebuttal of
Dr Charles Burney's remarks questioning the right of all members of the congregation to take part in the singing, Mason
advocated unison singing in which all could easily join, with the
accompaniment of an organ or barrel organ; the tunes to be
sung faster than had been customary, and more rhythmically.
He was not alone in these views, but he was able to put them
into practice in his parish at Aston, near Sheffield where he
personally taught music to the choir. (He had a 'favorite blacksmith' there, whom he 'taught to sing Marcello's Psalms like an
angel').
    In 1771 Mason took a step that was to have far-reaching
consequences for church music. He appointed William Richardson
as a vicar-choral of York Minster, and recommended him to the
Dean and Chapter for presentation to the perpetual curacy of
the neighbouring church of St Michael le Belfrey. Richardson

---

[19]William Mason, friend of the poet Thomas Gray (no kin to Jonathan Gray), and
himself a poet and satirist, was a distinguished amateur musician (see *The Musical
Times*, vol. CXIV (1973), p. 894). He was a friend of Wilberforce, and was one
of the first anti-slavery agitators, preaching a sermon on the subject in York
Minster on 27 January 1788; but he does not seem to have been, in the fullest
sense, an Evangelical. See J. W. Draper, *William Mason* (New York, 1924);
B. Barr and J. Ingamells, *A Candidate for Praise* (York, 1973).

[20]W. Mason, *Essays on English Church Music* (York, 1795), no. 3; reprinted in *The
Works of William Mason* (1811), vol. 3.

8

was just the man to promote Mason's ideas about church music, for besides a fine tenor voice and general musical ability, he possessed an earnest idealism that was not usual among the clergy of his day. He was, in fact, an Evangelical – one of the first to be placed in charge of an important provincial town parish church. He soon attracted a large following, and for the next fifty years was an increasingly influential figure in the city and county. He instituted Wednesday evening 'lectures' (Evening Prayer with a sermon) at the church, which soon became famous. He is said to have 'suffered for his opinions almost as if he had been a dissenter';[21] yet he shamed many of his less ardent colleagues into action on many important social and religious issues.

An Evangelical at this period was not to be equated with a Low Churchman. A Low Churchman was a rationalist, who was content to let the Church remain what it had been in the early Georgian period: stable, patriotic, formal, unemotional, and undemanding. The Evangelicals had at first been followers of John Wesley – himself in many respects a strict High Churchman, who maintained to the last his membership of the Church of England. But when the Methodists gradually drifted away from the Church, some of their number preferred to remain and try to spread their opinions within it. These became known as Evangelicals.[22] They differed considerably among themselves on theological issues: some were, like Wesley himself (and Richardson), Arminians, in that they believed in personal salvation by conversion or rebirth in Christ; others, following George Whitefield, were Calvinists, who relied exclusively on God's grace and preordination. But all were agreed on the need for greater earnestness in Christian life and worship, particularly on the part of the clergy, who should treat the ministry as a vocation, not as a mere profession or source of income.

Evangelical Anglicans, like Methodists, abhorred formality in worship, and emphasised preaching and hymns as spontaneous expressions of religious feeling; they developed them both in new

---

[21]*Victoria History of the County of Yorkshire: City of York* (Oxford, 1961), p. 303.

[22]See G. R. Balleine, *A History of the Evangelical Party in the Church of England* (1908, rev. edn. 1951); L. E. Elliott-Binns, *The Early Evangelicals* (1953); H. Davies, *Worship and Theology in England from Watts and Wesley to Maurice* (Princeton, 1961).

directions. Charles Wesley, John Newton, and Augustus Toplady wrote some of the finest hymns in the English language, and some of these, it is not too much to say, brought Christianity home to millions of uneducated people who had hitherto known it as a mysterious rite to which they were expected to conform. They were also much concerned that these hymns should be sung in a way that would express the fervent praise of a congregation newly aroused by their preaching. To this end they introduced a new style of tune, closely based on the theatre and concert music of the time (and sometimes even adapted from an actual tune of secular origin); they banished the choirs which had previously monopolised the singing; they encouraged the whole congregation to take part, standing up; and they adopted a new, faster and livelier mode of singing. Even those conservative Evangelicals who would not admit hymns to the services of the Church[23] had similar views about the performance of metrical psalms.

But Evangelicals differed from Methodists in their strict adherence to church law and discipline, including the requirement of the Act of Uniformity that all public worship be conducted according to the Book of Common Prayer, though they also encouraged extemporary prayer in the home. They faced the problem of bringing genuine feeling into the recitation of words that had lost their freshness through constant repetition, and were archaic in idiom. Many of them realised that the solution to this problem lay in music. Traditionally the services had been read, without music, in parish churches, the only singing being in the metrical psalms or hymns added before and after the liturgy, often monopolised by a choir of schoolchildren or an unmusical parish clerk. More recently, volunteer choirs had begun to chant canticles, responses, and psalms; but to Evangelicals this was no improvement. They would not be content until they had induced the people as a body to join in the sung parts of the liturgy. Since the words were in prose, they could not be sung to ordinary hymn tunes. They must be chanted. But the chanting used in cathedrals had hitherto been regarded as the province of trained singers only. We shall see

---

[23] One such was William Romaine, the leader of the movement in London until his death in 1795. See Romaine, *An Essay on Psalmody* (1775).

10

how the group of Evangelicals in York dealt with this intractable problem.

It was a long time before the Evangelical clergy gained a secure foothold in the Church. They held few livings in the eighteenth century, and were compelled to conduct their ministry chiefly from the outer fringes of the establishment: from privately endowed lectureships in parish churches, from proprietary chapels, and from London charities such as the * Foundling and Magdalen Hospitals. In 1800 they were stronger in Yorkshire than in any other part of the country.[24] Several important parish churches had come into their hands, and many took advantage of the strong tradition of singing in that region to reform psalmody in the direction they desired. Henry Venn, vicar of Huddersfield from 1759 to 1771, already 'succeeded in inducing the people to join in the responses and singing'.[25] At Doncaster, George Hay Drummond (vicar from 1790 to 1795) collaborated with the distinguished organist, Edward Miller, in bringing out an influential new collection of metrical psalms with music, *The Psalms of David* (London, 1790), and in bringing new life to the singing in the parish church.[26] A similar result was achieved by John Crosse at Bradford parish church after his appointment in 1784,[27] resulting in a great increase in the congregation at the expense of dissenting communities.[28] In many cases the first steps to improvement were the acquisition or restoration of an organ and the appointment of an efficient organist. This was the case with Romaine at St Andrew by the Wardrobe, London, in 1774[29]; with Crosse at Bradford, in

---

[24]Balleine, *Evangelical Party*, p. 64; F. S. Popham, *A History of Christianity in Yorkshire* (Wallington, 1954), pp. 65-8.

[25]P. Ahier, *The story of the three Parish Churches of St Peter the Apostle, Huddersfield* (Huddersfield, 1948), p. 59.

[26]E. Miller, *The History and Antiquities of Doncaster* (Doncaster, 1804), pp. 88-9.

[27]W. Morgan, *The Parish Priest: portrayed in the Life, Character, and Ministry, of the Rev. John Crosse, A. M., Late Vicar of Bradford* (1841), p. 155.

[28]E. Miller, *Thoughts on the Present Performance of Psalmody in the Established Church in England* (1791), p. 12n.

[29]C. W. Pearce, *Old London City Churches* (n.d. [1910]), p. 164.

1786[30]; with Joseph Milner at Hull, in 1788[31]; with Thomas Sutton, another Evangelical, immediately after his appointment to Sheffield parish church in 1805.[32]

A similar policy was adopted by Richardson at St Michael le Belfrey. He was a staunch Churchman, and would hear of no criticism of either Church doctrines or the Prayer Book, always replying: 'My faith is exactly that of the Church of England; as far as I know, her doctrines are mine. Her forms of worship are preferred by me before any devotional services I ever heard or saw'.[33] In a memoir he told how, in early manhood, he had been content with the simple country living of Kirbymoorside, until in 1769 he was profoundly moved by hearing evensong at York Minster:

> 'The gloom of the evening, the rows of candles fixed upon the pillars in the Nave and Transept, the lighting of the Chancel, the two distant candles, glimmering like stars at a distance upon the Altar, the sound of the Organ, the voices of the Choir, raised up, with the pealing of the Organ, in the chaunts, services, and anthem, had an amazing effect upon my spirits, as I walked to and fro in the Nave . . . I was greatly affected'.[34]

It was just after this service that he met Mason in the Minster yard, and was asked whether he would like to be a vicar-choral. The decisive change in his life was induced not by theological argument, but by a romantic, sensuous and musical experience; one is reminded both of Wesley's famous conversion while hearing service at St. Paul's cathedral in 1738, and of the Oxford revival of the 1830s.

The music at St Michael le Belfrey was provided by children of the local Bluecoat school accompanied by an organ, and consisted of metrical psalms in the Old Version (Sternhold and

---

[30][W. Cudworth], *Musical Reminiscences of Bradford* (Bradford, 1885), pp. 112-6; Bradford Cathedral Library, Bradford vestry minutes and churchwardens' accounts.

[31]G. H. Smith, *A History of Hull Organs and Organists* (n.d. [1910]), p. 15.

[32]W. Odom, *Memorials of Sheffield: Its Cathedral and Parish Churches* (Sheffield, 1922), pp. 42, 56.

[33][J. Gray, (comp.)] *A Brief Memoir of the late Revd Wm Richardson, with added extracts from his private papers* (2nd edn., 1822).

[34]*Ibid.*, pp. 13-15.

Courtesy of York City Art Gallery

Lithograph of St Michael le Belfrey church by Francis Bedford, published c. 1835.

Hopkins)[35] with, no doubt, an occasional anthem, and voluntaries before, during and after the service. It was the only parish church in York that possessed an organ. John Camidge, the organist (1735-1803), was at the top of his profession, but he devoted most of his energies to the cathedral services. We can take it for granted that the music was slovenly and perfunctory. The last payment for repairs to the organ had been made in 1744.[36] The congregation would have played little or no part in the singing, not even troubling to stand while the metrical psalms went on. The pace of the tunes would have been incredibly slow by modern standards – some two or three seconds to a note[37] – and this would have killed any spark of energy or enthusiasm that might have been kindled by the old tunes. Richardson no doubt waited until his position was strong before starting to make changes. There is no way of knowing exactly when, after his appointment in 1771, he began to improve matters. Mason would certainly have been an encouraging influence. In 1782, at his suggestion, a barrel organ, made by Thomas Haxby of York, was installed in St Michael le Belfrey to try out its effect[38] – this being the earliest well-documented use of a barrel organ in an English church. Presumably the old organ was no longer serviceable. Mason was satisfied with the effect, and had the barrel organ moved to Aston, but Richardson decided to have a new organ. On 28 December 1784 the vestry authorised him to apply for a faculty to build a gallery at the west end with an organ on it. The faculty was granted and the gallery built; the organ was purchased (probably by subscription), and Camidge's salary raised

---

[35] A previous organist, Thomas Wanless (d. 1712), had compiled a published collection, *The Metre psalm-tunes, in four parts* (1702), 'compos'd for use of the Parish-Church of St Michael's of Belfrey in York', but it was never reprinted, and it is most unlikely that psalm tunes were still sung in parts at the time of Richardson's appointment.

[36] York Minster Library, St Michael le Belfrey Churchwardens' Accounts and Vestry Minutes.

[37] See, for instance, the metronome speed indications in Benjamin Jacob, *National Psalmody* (1819).

[38] York Minster Library, Mason, letter to C. Alderson dated York, 4 December 1782 (typescript copy).

13

from £5 to £10 in 1786. In the same year a new pulpit and reading-desk were erected in the middle aisle.[39]

In 1788 Richardson published *A Collection of Psalms*, in which he made a careful selection of verses from the psalms, using four different translations – those of Sternhold and Hopkins, Tate and Brady, Isaac Watts, and James Merrick. In his preface, after briefly justifying psalm singing as ordained of God, he continued:

'And yet the present state of Psalmody in our congregations, shews that this ordinance of God is fallen into neglect and contempt. Among many other things that have contributed to it, may be reckoned an improper choice of passages from the book of Psalms, and of tunes. To remedy this is the design of the following collection'.

He emphasised the importance of the way psalms are sung by laying down these simple rules, showing his concern for effect as well as intention:

'Those who possess a musical voice and ear, should learn the tunes perfectly, . . . and sing aloud . . .

Those who have a harsh voice, or an imperfect ear, should sing low . . .

Those who are totally without a voice or ear for music, should not attempt to sing, but be content to join in heart and affection.

Lastly: the whole congregation ought to stand up during the singing, as they do in reading the Psalms'.

(The last observation shows that psalm chanting was not yet practised).

Richardson also turned his attention to the tunes, recommending a particular tune by name for each psalm selection. The 24 tunes he listed included a number of plain old tunes, and some excellent new ones such as 'Darwall's 148th', but avoided the over-ornate fuguing and repeating tunes that had become popular during the preceding fifty years. He also in general avoided the 'Methodist' type of tune, adapted from or in close imitation of the theatre or concert music of the day. Matthew Camidge (1764-1844), who had probably taken his father's place at the organ for many years before he formally succeeded him in 1801, published a *Musical Companion* to the collection in about 1800. It was 'printed in a convenient size to bind up with an approved selection of Psalms used in many Churches.

---

[39]York Minster Library, St Michael le Belfrey, Vestry Minutes; Borthwick Institute, D/C Fac. 1785/1.

The Editor's intention is to make these Tunes more generally known among the Congregations where they are sung, that this pleasant part of public worship may be performed in a more lively manner; when those who sing are imperfectly acquainted with the tune they must wait for each Note from the Organ or Clerk, by which means every syllable is lengthened, and the whole exercise becomes languid and tiresome, whereas in congregations that have learnt the Tunes perfectly, we hear the Psalms sung with spirit and propriety'.[40] However, this object was not really served by binding the tunes at the end of the book of words. In the second and third editions (c. 1808 and c. 1830 respectively) the book was printed in a larger format, with the words immediately under the music. The tunebook was primarily designed for organists, and in its revised design had the advantage that Miller pointed out for his own collection: 'the organist has both the words and music of the psalm before him, and it must be his own fault if he do not make a judicious use of them, by observing the different sentiments conveyed in different stanzas'.

By 1817 Richardson's *Collection* was in use in 'at least thirty churches, in and near York'; and it had had the effect its author had desired:

'The Congregations in our Parish Churches had long been in the indolent habit of *sitting* during the singing of the Psalms, and had resigned this part of the service to the solo of the Parish Clerk. Wherever the Collection was introduced, the recommendation, contained in the preface to it, was immediately attended to . . .'[41]

It is noticeable that Richardson included no hymns in his collection, other than the *Veni Creator Spiritus* (authorised by its inclusion in the Prayer Book ordination service) and a communion hymn from *A Supplement to the New Version* of Tate and Brady (authorised by Queen Anne in 1703). As a strict (one might almost say High) Churchman, he held to the traditional view that only the inspired words of the psalms were allowed to be used in church, by both divine and legal authority. However, during his lifetime more and more hymns were being

---

[40]M. Camidge (comp.), *A Musical Companion to the Psalms used in the Church of St Michael le Belfrey, York* (York, n.d.), preface.

[41][J. Gray (comp.)] , *Hymns selected as a supplement to a collection of psalms used in several churches* (York, 1817), preface.

15

introduced into Anglican services, particularly in the north of England; and by 1817 he was willing to sanction a supplement of hymns. This was prepared by Jonathan Gray, and had already been introduced at St Saviour's.[42] Together the two portions were published as *The York Psalm and Hymn Book*, which went into many editions up to about 1850; the last editions were published in London.

It is worth pointing out that Richardson and Camidge also arranged performances of Handel selections in St Michael le Belfrey church, which eventually developed into the colossal York Festivals of the 1820s. They may also have initiated the practice of using selections from Handel's oratorios as anthems, to the scandal of some members of the Minster congregation.[43]

John Graham established at St Saviour's a second centre of Evangelicalism: and like Richardson, he was as much concerned with music as with preaching. In 1798 he was granted a faculty to erect a West gallery at his own expense, 'for the use of such persons only as are willing to Rent the same of the said John Graham so long as he continues Rector of the said parish and no longer'.[44] This sounds like an accommodation for an enlarged congregation rather than for musicians, but it is said that a small band was introduced to accompany the singing in the early years of the 19th century.[45] An organ was apparently erected in 1810; as there is no record in the church accounts of any payment for it, it was probably presented by Graham, or paid for by a subscription raised by him.

The first organist was Philip Knapton (1788-1833), who was the son of Samuel Knapton (1756-1831), York music publisher, organist, and double bass player. He was appointed in or before 1812 at a salary of £5 per year. Soon afterwards he compiled a supplementary collection of tunes to Camidge's, designed mainly for the hymn supplement to Richardson's psalm selection

[42]See M. Camidge, *24 Original Psalm and Hymn Tunes* (York, 1823), preface.

[43]A. Hamilton Thompson (ed.), *York Minster Historical Tracts 627-1927* (1927), unpaginated.

[44]Borthwick Institute, PR.Y/SAV 15, St Saviour, Churchwardens' Accounts; Fac. Bk. 3, p. 211.

[45]York City Library MS. Y942/7411, J. W. Knowles, 'Notes on the organs organists clerks and quires in York churches since the reformation' (1924) p. 176.

compiled by Gray. In the preface he deplored the neglect into which psalmody had generally fallen. As a remedy he proposed '1st. The introduction of greater variety both in the number and style of the Tunes employed; and of a more animated style of singing', more particularly mentioning the need for lively and cheerful tunes, and quoting Isaac Watts's remarks about speed of performance; and '2nd. The employment of a few persons, possessing a competent knowledge and experience in Music, to take a prominent part, so as to encourage and lead the rest.' Such a choir should not resemble the existing village choir, but should sing 'the simple Melodies of the Church in a plain, firm, and distinct manner.' Its purpose would be to lead the people, not to give performances. Women should be encouraged to join it. As a third remedy he proposed the teaching of singing in the recently established National Schools. In his selection of tunes Knapton aimed at a judicious mean between the 'gloomy style' of the traditional psalm tunes and the 'light and indecorous style sometimes heard in the Meeting-house'.[46] This book, like Camidge's before it, went into at least three editions.

Knapton's duties as organist at St Saviour's consisted only of playing at Morning Prayer on Sundays and Christmas Day. Churches in York had only one service on Sundays, and had long been known as 'forenoon' and 'afternoon' churches: the usual time for an afternoon service was three o'clock.[47] Graham took the lead in introducing a second service at both the churches of which he was incumbent. At St Saviour's this took the form of a Sunday evening 'lecture', an innovation which the Evangelicals borrowed from the Nonconformists, and which became particularly popular.

> 'Oh, it was a sacred pleasure, to join in the song of praise sung with the understanding by a thousand voices, and attuned to the organ's pealing notes, produced by the hand of one, in whose heart the genial current of holy feeling ran, but stopped alas ! too soon for us'.[48]

---

[46] P. Knapton, (comp.), *A Collection of Tunes for Psalms and Hymns, Selected as a Supplement to those now used in several Churches in York and its Vicinities* (York, 1816), preface.

[47] *V.C.H.; City of York*, pp. 250-1. Graham was the first incumbent to hold a Sunday evening service in York: see *Yorkshire Gazette*, 7 June 1902.

[48] Burgess, *The Faithful Steward*, pp. 14-15.

17

So wrote Graham's eulogist, adding a brief tribute to Jonathan Gray, the organist referred to in the above passage, who 'employed his splendid musical talents in elevating the tone of public worship in Psalms and Hymns and Spiritual Songs.' Gray had offered his services for the evening lecture because Knapton's duties were limited to playing at Morning Prayer, and the parish could not afford to pay additional fees.

*   *   *   *

Meanwhile, Gray was beginning to develop his own views about the reform of church music. As a forum he chose *The Christian Observer*, the chief organ of the Evangelicals, founded by Wilberforce and others of the Clapham Sect in 1801. Over the signature 'H. G.', Gray advocated both a new selection of metrical psalm translations and also the introduction of hymns. In a footnote he further pointed out that in some parish churches congregational chanting had been successfully introduced.[49]

This article was adapted for use in the Preface to Gray's selection, already mentioned, of hymns for use with Richardson's *Collection of Psalms*.[41] In his arrangement of hymns Gray anticipated later High Church hymn books, including *Hymns Ancient and Modern*, by giving first 33 hymns for the seasons of the Church Year From Advent to Trinity, then 32 for festivals and occasions; he followed these with 47 hymns for various states of the soul, and on subjects such as might be chosen for sermons (here following Nonconformist, and more specifically Baptist precedent). The selection naturally gave prominence to Methodist and Evangelical hymns.

Later this preface was again altered and expanded in an important and influential pamphlet.[50]

'There is . . . little hope of the general restoration of Church Music in our parochial service. Yet in the Parish Churches of many of our principal towns, the practice of that music, has, within the last thirty years, been revived and the Congregations join in chanting the *Venite*

---

[49]*The Christian Observer*, vol. XVII (1818), pp. 152-9. For the identification of 'H. G.' as Gray see vol. XXI (1822), p. 421.

[50]J. Gray, *An Inquiry into the Historical Facts relative to Parochial Psalmody, in reference to the Remarks of the . . . Bishop of Peterborough* (York, 1821).

Exultemus, the *Te Deum,* and *Jubilate,* the *Magnificat,* (or the *Cantate Domino,*) and the *Nunc Dimittis* (or the *Deus Misereatur,*) with a happy and devotional effect. In proportion as the usage of primitive ages is copied; in proportion likewise as the rites of the Church are respected, the structure of the poetry attended to, and her music duly appreciated, this mode of singing will be preferred above metrical psalmody'.[51] He continued with a learned historical investigation which showed conclusively that the metrical psalms had never been authorised by Parliament for use in the services of the Church of England, but only permitted before and after services and sermons by the Queen's Injunctions of 1559. He added a description of the recent case of *Holy and Ward v. Cotterill,* heard on 6 July 1820 in the Consistory Court of the diocese of York before Chancellor G. V. Vernon, which had determined that in practice the use of any metrical psalms or hymns in appropriate style, though strictly speaking unauthorised, would not be successfully challenged. This was a decisive victory for the Evangelical party, supporting both of their main principles in the reform of church music: the equal validity of hymns and metrical psalms, and the inferiority of both to the liturgy. It led to the virtual disappearance, within a generation or so, of both the 'Old' and the 'New' Versions of the metrical psalms, and paved the way for the development of the Victorian hymn book.[52]

In an Appendix Gray printed 'The Te Deum, pointed to be conveniently chanted in Churches', which he began as follows:

We praise – thee, – O – God: we acknowledge – thee – to – be – the – Lord.

The Te Deum was chosen because of the special difficulty of chanting the short verses, which Gray consolidated. He had arranged it, he said, 'for the Church of St Helen, Stonegate, in York', but he added:

'For the suggestion, and revision of this pointing in the Te Deum, I am indebted to my friend, Dr Camidge, organist of York Cathedral, who

---

[51]*Ibid.* p. 9.

[52] The lawsuit was occasioned by the publication of the 8th edition of Thomas Cotterill's *Selection of Hymns for Public and Private Use* (Sheffield, 1819) and its introduction by the Evangelical Cotterill at St Paul's church, Sheffield, against the wishes of many of the parishioners. The circumstances and results are discussed in J. Julian, *A Dictionary of Hymnology* (2nd edn., 1907), p. 334; and L. F. Benson, *The English Hymn* (New York, 1915), pp. 355-7.

19

has it in contemplation to apply a similar arrangement to the whole Book of Psalms'.[53]

This work never appeared; but others meanwhile were active, and in 1831 came the first fully pointed psalter, J. E. Dibb's *Key to Chanting*.[54] This is now very scarce, but there is a copy in the British Library. In his 'Address to the Reader' Dibb wrote:

'The fact is notorious, that very few, except Choristers, are able to join in this part of the public worship of Almighty God . . . Inability, on the part of the congregation to join in this service, chiefly proceeds from their not knowing how much of each verse is to be sung to the first, and how much to be left for the remaining notes of the Chant, which latter are to be sung in exact time . . . The Reformers placed a colon in the middle of each verse, to suit the ancient ecclesiastical mode of chanting; some further arrangement, however, is still required to render the practice easy and pleasant to each member of the congregation. To remedy this defect is the design of the present volume'.

He then explained his method of pointing the psalms, which simply consisted of separating and italicising the final syllables of each half-verse. Like Gray, he pointed out that the *Te Deum* presents special difficulties because of the shortness of some of its verses; he therefore gave three different solutions: one, in strict accordance with the Prayer Book; the second from 'Mr Jacob's Collection of Sacred Music'; and the third 'made by the late Mr T. Bridgewater, for the more immediate use of the con-

---

[53] J. Gray, *An Inquiry*, p. 70. The identity of 'Dr Camidge' is not clear. Matthew Camidge, organist of York Minster from 1799 to 1842 and certainly a friend of Gray's, was never a doctor and was not usually referred to as such. He was succeeded as organist by his son John, who had received the Cambridge Mus. D. in 1819.

[54] J. E. Dibb, *Key to Chanting. The Psalter . . . and Portions of the Morning and Evening Services of the Church, appointed to be sung or chanted, with a Peculiar Arrangement to Facilitate the Practice*. It was published at London by Hamilton, Adams & Co., in 1831, but was printed by Barclay & Coultas at York. It is further associated with York by its reference to St. Saviour's church (cited below) and by Gray's statement that Dibb's method of pointing was derived from the practice at York Minster. Dibb was an obscure figure. He may have been a son of William Napier Dibb, who was a member of the York Sunday School Committee from 1836 until his death in 1842 (Howard, *Historical Sketch*, p. 127). His only other known publication is *The Sub-diaconate* (London, 1866), a paper read to a meeting of the Church of England Clerical and Lay Association for the Maintenance of Evangelical Principles (Midland District) at Derby in 1866. Advertisements in this publication show that Dibb was Deputy Registrar for the West Riding and that he was then resident at Wakefield.

gregation assembling at St Saviour's Church, York'.[55] Here is a
verse from Dibb's psalter:

O come, let us sing un-*to the Lord:* let us heartily rejoice in the *strength
of our salvation.*

This publication prompted a long letter in *The Harmonicon*
for February 1832, signed 'M. H.'. The writer commended the
enterprise of Mr Dibbs (*sic*) but criticised the method as in-
sufficiently clear; and complained of gross defects of accentuation. (There was little justification for the first objection, but
plenty for the second.) He suggested that Dibb got his idea from
John Marsh, and referred to the *Gentleman's Magazine*, vol. 98,
in which he had set out his own views on chanting, which
agreed with Jacob's method.[56] The next issue carried a reply
from 'Δ', of 35 Aldwark, York, who agreed broadly with M. H.
but suggested that 'Dibbs' got his idea not from Marsh but from
Jonathan Gray, who had published the *Te Deum* fully pointed
in 1821. The mode of chanting advocated by Gray was attributed
to Camidge, and had since been adopted at St Saviour's. Who M. H.
may have been is hard to tell, but it is not difficult to identify Δ
as John Graham, rector of St Saviour's, who was at the time
resident in Aldwark, York.[57]

*   *   *   *

The 'pointing' problem was basically that of reconciling verbal
and musical accents. For the purpose of singing the prose psalms
to an Anglican chant, each verse is first divided into two parts
by a colon (so much is already provided in the Book of Common
Prayer). The first half-verse is sung to a phrase of four notes, the
first being the 'reciting note' which can accommodate any
number of syllables, while the other three are sung to one
syllable each, or possibly two. If the last three notes are strictly
assigned to the last three syllables of the half-verse, faulty

---

[55]Benjamin Jacob's *National Psalmody* (1819) is the work referred to. Thomas
Bridgewater succeeded Knapton as organist of St Saviour's about 1830; York
City Library, MS. Y942/7411 p. 176.

[56]I have been unable to trace the passage referred to in vol. 98 or any other volume
of *The Gentleman's Magazine.*

[57]See E. Baines, *History, Directory and Gazeteer of the County of York* (Leeds,
1823), vol. II, pp. 46, 85, 117.

21

accentuation may result, since musical accents occur on the second and fourth notes, while the third is weak. Similarly, the second half-verse is sung to a phrase of six notes, of which the first is the reciting note and the second, fourth and sixth carry musical accents. The 'pointing' of psalms is a way of indicating how the syllables of each verse are to be distributed among the notes of the chant. The more subtle kinds of pointing do so in such a way as to preserve the natural accents of the words, by making them coincide with musical accents; the crudest follows the 'rule of 3 and 5', simply marking off the last three syllables of the first half-verse and the last five of the second, regardless of the effect on the verbal accents.

It is perhaps worthwhile to review the facts about the introduction of pointed psalms, since it has been repeatedly asserted that Robert Janes's *Psalter*, published at Ely in 1837, was the first of its kind.[58] John Marsh (1752-1828), an amateur musician of Chichester, proposed in the preface to his *Cathedral Chant Book* (London, 1804) that the organist and choir of a cathedral should agree on the pointing of all the psalms and underline the last syllable to be sung to the reciting note in each verse. John Christmas Beckwith (1750-1809), of Norwich, became organist of Norwich Cathedral in 1808, and in the same year published *The First Verse of every Psalm of David, With an Ancient or Modern Chant in Score*. He set out the first verse of each psalm under the chant, following the strict 'rule of 3 and 5' which was apparently in use at Norwich (see below, 'Lincoln Mode') but offering no guidance for the other verses. J. Dixon, in *Canto Recitativo* (London, 1816), was the first to set out all the psalms fully pointed – but according to a 'reformed' type of chant of his own devising; his book could not be used with Anglican chants. Jacob, in *National Psalmody* (1819), laid out the canticles complete under chants, with suggestions for organ registration; they were designed for congregational chanting. Other collections in the 1820s did the same. Gray printed Camidge's pointing of the *Te Deum* in 1821.[59] Dibb's book, the next advance, appeared in 1831.

---

[58]See, for instance, P. A. Scholes (ed.), *The Oxford Companion to Music*, (9th edn. 1955), article 'Anglican Chanting'; B. Rainbow, *The Choral Revival in the Anglican Church (1839-1872)* (1970), p. 83.

[59]J. Gray, *An Inquiry*, pp. 71 ff.

Shortly afterwards, Gray produced another work on the subject: *Twenty-four Chants: to which are prefixed, Remarks on Chanting* (London and York, 1834). The chants were of his own composition. In the opening 'Remarks' he repeated once more the arguments in favour of congregational chanting. He referred to the correspondence in *The Harmonicon* and quoted some 'excellent' rules for chanting from J. A. Latrobe's *Instructions of Chenaniah* (London, 1832). He then reported that 'in the course of his visits to Cathedrals' he had

> 'remarked the different modes of chanting, used in choirs; some of these may not improbably have existed in the same Cathedrals for a long period, perhaps from the time of the Reformation, or even antecedent. to it. With respect to the method at York, it certainly has prevailed for, at least, more than half a century, having been traditionally carried down by one generation of singing-boys to another'.

Gray then proceeded to set out some verses from the psalms according to four modes of chanting, which he called the Lincoln, York, Canterbury and Bangor modes. The following is a summary, with examples (slightly altered for greater clarity), of his report, which is unique in the evidence it provides of the practice before Victorian reforms took effect. In each half-verse, the words before the first bar-line are all sung to the first or reciting note. A bar-line indicates that an accented note follows. Adjoining italicised syllables are sung to a single note. A hyphen or asterisk indicates that a new note follows.

No 1. LINCOLN MODE (used also at Norwich)

'The Lincoln practice totally disregards accentuation; and resembles the reading of a scholar in the first form, who has only been taught to spell syllables, but not to join them'. It is in fact a rigid application of the 'Rule of 3 and 5': three syllables are counted backwards from the end of the first half of each verse, and five from the end of the second half, without regard for verbal stress.

Lord, thou hast been / our * re-/ fuge: From one genera-/ tion * to / a - no-/ ther.

Thou turnest men to / des - truc-/ tion; Again thou sayest come again / ye * chil-/ dren * of / men.

23

No. 2. YORK MODE

'The York method recognises the propriety of accentuation; but its recognition ventures no further than to any one or more short syllables, which may occur at *the end* of a verse [or half verse]; and which can be consolidated on the last note'.

Lord, thou hast / been * our / *refuge:* From one gene-/ ra - tion / to * a-/ *nother.*

Thou turnest man / to * des-/ *truction:* Again thou sayest come again / ye * chil-/dren * of / men.

No. 3. CANTERBURY MODE (used also at St Paul's)

This adds the possibility of singing two syllables to a note other than the last, but never more than three syllables to a bar.

Thou shalt not be afraid for any / *terror* * by / night: Nor for the / *arrow* * that / *flieth* * by / day.

No. 4. BANGOR MODE (used also at Chester)

'This method consists in a still freer and more general appropriation of a plurality of syllables to one note, than is practised at Canterbury'. Four syllables to a bar are permitted.

O come, let us / *sing un - to the* / Lord; Let us heartily re-/ joice * *in the* / *strength of* * our sal-/ *vation.*

Gray points out that it is the second mode that is so severely criticised in *The Harmonicon*, but that Mr Dibb 'is no further accountable than for having exhibited the ancient York method of chanting'.

Gray had said in 1821 that 'in the Parish Churches of many of our principal towns' the congregational chanting of the canticles had, 'within the last thirty years', been revived. Now, in 1834, he repeated the statement, amending it carefully to 'within the last forty years'.[60] But he said elsewhere in the same preface that 'in those parts of the kingdom which are remote

---

[60] J. Gray, *Twenty-Four Chants: to which are prefixed, Remarks on Chanting* (London and York, 1834), p. 3.

from Cathedral Churches, . . . chanting has not yet been introduced into the parochial service'.[61] It would seem then that
Gray had knowledge that congregational chanting had been
introduced in parish churches in cathedral towns since the
1790s. In York it seems overwhelmingly probable that the innovation was first tried out at St Michael le Belfrey, where
Richardson was in charge and Matthew Camidge deputised
for his father at the organ, and where a choir of boys and
girls from the local school was available. The only other York
church with an organ before 1800 was All Saints, Pavement,
where a Snetzler instrument from Hazelwood Castle was erected
in 1791, and Matthew Camidge appointed organist; in 1803 he
resigned in favour of his son Thomas. It seems likely that chanting would have been tried out there also. There was certainly
chanting at St Helen, Stonegate, for Gray stated in 1821 that
he had arranged the pointed *Te Deum* for use there.[62] The
organist there was Samuel Knapton, father of Philip. St Saviour
had chanting in 1817, for Philip Knapton published *A Collection
of Chants used in the Church of St Saviour, York* in that year.
Graham, rector of St Saviour, was also incumbent of St Mary
Bishophill Senior, but there was no organ there until the 1840s.
At St Mary Bishophill Junior the organist was H. A. Beckwith,
son of Dr Beckwith of Norwich, who might well have put his
father's methods of pointing into practice. Another organist
who may have favoured chanting was a Mr Tomlinson, who
became organist at St Saviour's in 1835 and at St Helen's in
1840. His *Universal Psalmody*, which was also used at St
Cuthbert's and other churches in York, contained 50 chants.[63]
Matthew Camidge stated on the title page of a collection of
church music published in 1823: 'As chanting is becoming
general in Parish Churches the Author has subjoined Twenty
four of his own Double Chants'.[64]

* * * *

---

[61]*Ibid.* p. 1.

[62]J. Gray, *An Inquiry*, p. 9n.

[63]Information in this paragraph is compiled from the records of various churches at
the Borthwick Institute, York, and from York City Library, MS. Y942/7411.

[64]M. Camidge, *24 Original Psalm and Hymn Tunes* (1823).

25

There is little doubt, then, that there was a good deal of psalm chanting in York churches in the early decades of the 19th century, and that much of it was congregational. All this was before the Oxford Movement, which is usually credited with the revival of parochial chanting. Was York exceptional in this respect ? Or was psalm chanting more generally prevalent, as Gray and Camidge seem to imply ? A distinction should be clearly made between chanting by a parochial choir, in attempted imitation of cathedrals, and chanting by the congregation. Parish choirs had begun to appear shortly before 1700, and had soon tried to imitate cathedral practice. Chants for, at least, the canticles had been a commonplace feature of printed collections of parish-church music for a hundred years, going right back to the first edition of John Chetham's *A Book of Psalmody* (Sheffield, 1718). These were intended, however, for the groups of 'singers' or voluntary choirs that were common in eighteenth-century country churches. From Selby in 1751, for instance, Dr Richard Pococke reported:

'This town is no corporation, and has neither clergy man nor justice of the peace. They chant all their service, except the litany; and the clerk goes up to the Communion table and stands on the Epistle side to make the responses, and they sing well not only the psalms but anthems'.[65]

Selby Abbey, whatever its former splendour, was in the 18th century a poorly endowed parish church. Its chanting was accomplished by uneducated parish singers, from copies of Chetham or a similar collection, accompanied perhaps by a few wind instruments – some of which have survived and can be seen in the Abbey. Examples of this kind of chanting by choirs can be found frequently in the 18th century, less so in the early 19th century; it was more common in the West Riding and North Midlands than in other areas of the country. It seems however that *congregational* psalm chanting was found only where Evangelical influence promoted it. The earliest distinct reference to congregational chanting that I have come across dates from 1790. The writer, Dr William Vincent, describes the chanting by choirs recently introduced in certain churches and chapels in London, but points out that these choirs instead of singing alone should be leading the congregation.

[65]J. J. Cartwright (ed.), *The Travels through England of Dr. Richard Pococke*, (Camden Society, 1888), vol. I, p. 173.

313

'A common chant is easily attainable by the ear; and if the same was always used, would soon become familiar to the audience, and all be insensibly led to join in it. . . For this purpose, no chant is better calculated than that which the charity children sing at the conclusion of each psalm, at St Paul's. – It is composed by Mr Jones, and has been adopted in one congregation with success'.[66]

But the great difficulty was that congregations, unlike choirs, could not be expected to learn and rehearse the psalms of the day; nor could they chant them from the Prayer Book, since the pointing provided there was inadequate. It was for this reason that congregational chanting was at first limited to the *Gloria Patri* ('at the conclusion of each psalm') and the canticles, which could be repeated often enough for regular congregations to learn how to chant them with reasonable uniformity. It was also for this reason that Camidge, Gray and others began to devise methods of pointing that could be used for chanting even by an unrehearsed congregation. Pointed psalters were not printed for cathedral choirs, which had, after all, got along without them for nearly three centuries. The need for them arose only when congregational chanting became widespread. Gray and Camidge may have been unduly influenced by their knowledge of local practice in York when they spoke of a revival of congregational chanting in the early 1820s. But a writer in *The Bristol Mirror* in 1822, who was clearly a partisan of neither York nor Evangelicalism, gives supporting evidence. In letters signed 'Minimus' he stated, absurdly enough, that Evangelicals associated both organs and chanting with Rome; but in spite of this, he went on, the practice of chanting was 'reviving'. 'In many parochial churches the hymns [i.e. prose canticles] following the lessons are regularly chaunted, and the congregations begin to take part in the performance.' He claimed that modern chants had become too elaborate and that 'for this reason . . . chaunting is so generally and so improperly confined to the choir. It should not be. The music of a chaunt is not the proper place for the display of the agility of some voices to the discouragement of others, but should be such as

---

[66]W. Vincent, *Considerations on Parochial Music* (2nd edn. 1790), p. 10n. The reference is to the annual mass singing by the charity children of London parishes at St Paul's cathedral. This footnote is not in the first edition (1787).

27

that all might comfortably join in it'.[67] This was precisely the view of the York Evangelicals. In 1831, J. A. Latrobe made a general survey of the practice of church music. He said that chanting by choir and congregation had been adopted in 'many parochial churches', especially for the canticles; in some churches the *Gloria Patri* was chanted after each psalm, in others the introductory sentences and responses. But chanting of the *psalms* was 'generally confined to cathedrals'.[68]

It was in the same year, 1831, that the first fully pointed psalter — Dibb's — appeared in print, emanating apparently from York. It would seem then that through the efforts of Jonathan Gray and his colleagues, York churches were in the vanguard of the movement for congregational chanting. Several had chanted canticles, some perhaps before 1800; some may have had chanted psalms. It was not long before other pointed psalters appeared.[69] The pioneers of Ritualism brought a new energy and a new point of view to the cause: *Laudes Diurnae*, with the psalms pointed and set to Gregorian tones, was published by Redhead and Oakeley in 1843. The long and fruitless battle between 'Anglicans' and 'Gregorians' was beginning, as one of many fronts in the destructive war between Tractarians and Evangelicals. Both sides took up entrenched positions, and forgot what they had in common. As far as parish-church music was concerned, both had wanted the music to be more dignified, more expressive, and more congregational. Many Tractarians emerged from a strong Evangelical tradition. The early Tractarians constantly reiterated the principle that true church music was for all to sing. *The Parish Choir*, which during the five years of its existence (1846-51) was the chief forum for discussion of

---

[67]*Quarterly Musical Magazine and Review*, vol. IV (1822), p. 175 (reprinted from *The Bristol Mirror*).

[68]J. A. Latrobe, *The Music of the Church* (1831), pp. 265-76.

[69]Two anonymous collections of pointed canticles were published in London in 1835, one describing itself as 'arranged and marked for easy and distinct congregational chanting'. Janes's psalter followed (Ely, 1837); T. Harrison's (Leeds, 1839); J. L. Brownsmith's (London, 1839); Dr Farman's (London, 1840); James Stimpson's (Newcastle, 1840); R. Gray's (Bridlington, 1841); an anonymous Canterbury publication (1841); J. Butterfield's (London, 1842); S. S. Wesley's (Leeds, 1843). After that they came thick and fast.

the musical problems of the ritualist movement, had this to say about Gregorian psalm tones:

'They should be sung in unison, with an organ accompaniment. If sung in harmony, the harmonies should be sung by a few skilled voices only, whilst the mass of the people should still sing the melody'.[70]

On more than one occasion the editor, Robert Druitt, found much to admire in the music of the Methodists:

'Go to a Wesleyan or other Dissenting meeting-house; not an old established one, frequented by people well-to-do in the world; but a little rude upstart place, such as is common in the suburbs of London . . . There you hear what congregational singing is'.[71]

Evangelicals and Tractarians both wanted to draw all the people into the expression of praise, and more particularly into the chanting of psalms. Both were defeated, in the end, by a more secular, more materialistic or Low-Church view. In the eighteenth century choirs of country churches had tried to imitate the music of 'their Mother Churches, the Cathedrals'.[72] The movement gained momentum in the nineteenth century, as with increasing affluence citizens wanted to see in their parish church a material improvement reflecting the improvement in their own status. The 'fully choral service' introduced at Leeds Parish Church in 1841 was a culmination of this movement, and was duly imitated in churches all over the country.[73] No expense was spared in the adornment of new and restored churches, and the same policy was followed in providing for music: a well-paid, well-trained, and beautifully-robed choir would sing the liturgy, to the highest professional standard attainable. The cathedral service was the obvious model for their singing, and in 1875 it was *The Cathedral Psalter* that at last provided a model for uniform chanting in churches – uniformity having become an important goal since the rise of the Diocesan Festival, beginning with that at Lichfield in 1856.

---

[70]*The Parish Choir*, vol. I (1846-7), p. 87.

[71]*Ibid.*, p. 153.

[72]'The Design of this Undertaking is to better and improve this excellent and useful Part of our Service, to keep us an Uniformity in our Parish Churches, and bring them as much as may be to imitate their Mother-Churches, the Cathedrals'. From the preface to J. Chetham, *A Book of Psalmody* (Sheffield, 1718), and many later collections.

[73]Rainbow, *Choral Revival*, pp. 26-42.

29

The development of choral music in the parish church was in no sense a victory for the Oxford Movement, or indeed for any group of idealistic churchmen. Rather was it a triumph of secular materialism and snobbery over the revival of religious spirit that had marked both the Evangelical and the Tractarian movements. It was deplored by many clergymen of all shades of opinion. At the Church Congress of 1884 several speakers alluded to the rarity of good congregational singing in the Church.[74] In 1891, a speaker asserted that he knew of 'but one church in London where the whole service is joined in by the congregation without even the lead of a choir. An organist . . . leads a congregation of 2000 worshippers'.[75] The result was most inspiring. 'At another neighbouring church, principally attended by a fashionable congregation of some 1200 people, the whole of the service was "performed" by a large and efficient choir'. He cited three distinguished clergymen from the three main parties within the church in support of the view that 'choirs' professionalism had ruined congregational devotion'.

'Congregational devotion' through music had been the aim of Mason, Richardson, Graham, Gray, Dibb and their followers at York. It is perhaps ironic that one of the products of their efforts, the pointed psalter, facilitated the *choral* chanting of psalms in parish churches, which ultimately defeated one of their aims. Taking a broader historical view, however, one can see that the chances of widespread success had never been good. Although Gray believed he was merely reviving an ancient practice of the church, there is no evidence that ordinary parochial congregations had joined in the chanting of the psalms or other parts of the service, either before or after the Reformation — least of all to music in any way resembling an Anglican chant. Only in special circumstances where congregations can be rehearsed — as in monasteries, colleges, or public schools — has congregational chanting been really successful. The Archbishops' Committee reported in 1951:

---

[74] *The Official Report of the Church Congress held at Carlisle* (1844), pp. 308-32.

[75] *The Official Report of the Church Congress held at Rhyl* (1891), p. 273. The church referred to is probably St. Pancras: see a similar description in W. Spark, *Musical Reminiscences* (London and Leeds, 1892), p. 47.

'It may be a regrettable fact, but it has to be admitted that the Psalms, whether they be sung to plainsong or to Anglican chants, do not lend themselves readily to singing by the average congregation'.[76]

The other musical form that Jonathan Gray had sought to improve was the hymn. Here he was on surer ground; there were no technical difficulties to be overcome, and there was a popular tradition to build on that was older than the Reformation itself. It is, indeed, in the hymn and hymn tune that the Evangelical movement has left its lasting musical monument. The *York Psalm and Hymn Book*, with its accompanying tunes, the joint product of Richardson, Gray, Camidge and Knapton, may have been only one of a number of pioneering Evangelical hymn collections, but it was one of the most influential, lasting for more than sixty years in a period when hymn books came and went at a bewildering rate. The earlier nineteenth century was the last period of regional hymn collections: after the publication of *Hymns Ancient and Modern* in 1861, it was not long before that book had obliterated almost all traces of local competitors. Long before that time, the livelier, more earnest mode of singing that Richardson and Gray had advocated was accepted without question in all Anglican churches, so that it is now difficult to imagine the slowness and dreariness of the style that preceded it.

Jonathan Gray was able to combine musical expertise with a degree of education, social position and power of advocacy that was beyond the reach of professional musicians in his time. The combination made him the ideal agent for that reform of parish-church music which was so ardently desired by the Evangelical party; and although his success was mainly local, and even there not achieved single-handed, it also played its part in the general improvement of music in the national church.

---

[76]*Music in Church* (rev. edn., 1957), p. 34.

XIII

Organ Settings of English Psalm Tunes

Why did England not develop anything like the German organ chorale? The reason is not as simple as one might think. It is tempting to put it down to the usual scapegoats – the Puritans, because of their dislike of organs and elaborate music. It is true, of course, that the greatest flowering of chorale-based organ music took place in the Lutheran church, and that Lutheran influence was small in the Church of England before the 19th century. It is also true that the Puritans tried to get rid of church organs in England: they almost succeeded in 1562, and they did succeed in 1644. Between those dates organs in most parish churches were allowed to fall into disuse or were dismantled and sold.[1] Between 1660 and 1830, London churches and those of the larger provincial towns gradually acquired organs, though many country churches and parish churches in cathedral cities were still without them in the mid-19th century.[2]

But the situation was very similar in many of the Reformed parts of Europe. Zwingli and Calvin themselves would not allow organs in worship; organs were silenced or dismantled in Switzerland, the Palatinate, East Prussia and the Netherlands.[3] Although some Reformed churches in Germany acquired them before the end of the 16th century, their purpose at first was to provide music at secular assemblies held in church, and there was a long struggle for a hundred years or more before they were generally accepted in worship. In some Reformed areas, such as Scotland and French-speaking Switzerland, they were still outlawed in the early 19th century.

Yet the Calvinist Netherlands, as is well known, was one of the greatest centres of church organ building in the 17th century; and it was Sweelinck, in his fantasias and variations on psalm tunes, many of them from the Genevan psalter, who pointed the way to the later German development of the organ

---

[1]   See A. Smith: *The Practice of Music in English Cathedrals and Churches, and at the Court, during the Reign of Elizabeth I* (diss., U. of Birmingham, 1967), 421–9; N. Temperley: *The Music of the English Parish Church* (Cambridge, 1979), i, 51–2.

[2]   See Chapter VIII in this volume.

[3]   W. Blankenburg: 'Church Music in Reformed Europe', trans. Hans Heinsheimer, *Protestant Church Music: A History* by Friedrich Blume and others (London, 1975), 551, 570.

chorale. Several German sources, printed and manuscript, of organ works based on the Geneva psalm tunes date from before 1600.[4]

In England, by contrast, no organ settings of psalm tunes of any description are known between those in the Mulliner Book of about 1560 and the simple harmonizations in Tomkins's *Musica Deo sacra* (1668).[5] An isolated setting of OLD HUNDREDTH by John Blow, in which each line is treated as the basis of a point of imitation, survives, as does a related setting attributed to Purcell.[6] There are a number of 18th-century settings of a rudimentary kind, but little or much artistic worth until Sebastian Wesley began to emulate the Bach chorale prelude in his *Selection of Psalm Tunes* (1838).

There is no doubt that organs were played in church during the Elizabethan period, even in parish churches. William Steade, parish clerk of Holy Trinity, Hull, was accused in 1570 of playing too much during the service and taking up time that could have been used for the sermon; in his defence he replied that he only played four times at morning prayer and four times at evening prayer on Sundays and holy days.[7] A large amount of keyboard music from the period has survived,[8] including a number of pieces called 'voluntaries' or 'verses' which were presumably for church use, and a surprisingly large number based on plainsong associated with Latin texts, but virtually nothing based on psalm tunes.

It may be argued that most organ music was probably written either for domestic use or for cathedrals. But metrical psalms were immensely popular for home singing, and a whole series of polyphonic arrangements appeared, from Day's (1563) to Ravenscroft's (2/1633), for cultivated persons to sing at home, often with the accompaniment of the lute and other instruments.[9] If organs (or, for that matter, virginals) were present in many private houses, why did they not accompany the psalm singing? Or, if they did, why have no accompaniments survived? Metrical psalms were sung in cathedrals, too. In many cathedral cities people attended morning service in their parish churches, then gathered in the cathedral nave to hear the sermon, which formed part of the ante-Communion service. Metrical psalms were sung, sometimes before and usually after the sermon.[10] It is doubtful whether the organ took part in this

---

[4]   Blankenburg, 555–6.

[5]   If any reader can refute this statement, I should be most interested.

[6]   John Blow: *Complete Organ Works*, ed. Watkins Shaw (London, 1958), 64; Henry Purcell, *Works*, vi (1895), 59.

[7]   J.S. Purvis: *Tudor Parish Documents of the Diocese of York* (Cambridge, 1948), 227.

[8]   A very full list may be found in Francis Routh, *Early English Organ Music from the Middle Ages to 1837* (London, 1973), 112–26.

[9]   See P. le Huray: *Music and the Reformation in England 1549–1660* (London, 1967), 377–83.

[10]   Smith, 238–45.

proceeding, however; the choir and organist may have concluded their duties after the singing of the Responses to the Commandments.

It is remarkable that the only reference to an organ accompanying metrical psalms in Elizabeth's reign comes from Machyn's diary for 17 March 1560: 'All the people did sing the tune of Geneva, and with the bass of the organs' when a well-known Puritan divine was installed vicar of St Martin, Ludgate.[11] The organ books of the period contain all types of service music from festal psalms to verse anthems, but not metrical psalms. The only exceptions are the settings from the Mulliner Book.[12] There are only two, and they have little in common. One is a simple transcription of a mildly polyphonic four-voice setting of psalm 1 by Shepherd. The other is based on the 1561 tune[13] for Sternhold & Hopkins's *Lamentation of a Sinner* ('O Lord, turn not away thy face'). The tune is in the alto register, with a filling-in part above, and running scale passages for the left hand (Ex. 1). If it represents an improvisatory practice of the early 1560s, it is unique of its kind; and it must be pointed out that the text of this tune was an original hymn, not a metrical psalm, and hence of doubtful propriety for use in worship from the Puritan point of view.[14] Legally it could be sung before or after service, like a metrical psalm or anthem, under the terms of the royal injunctions of 1559.[15]

Ex. 1   **Mulliner Book (c1560)**

The next record of organ accompaniment of psalm tunes comes from the time of Charles I, when we read that Thomas Tomkins accompanied the psalm after the sermon at Worcester Cathedral.[16] The settings he left, published after his death, are extremely conservative by comparison

---

[11]   *The Diary of Henry Machyn*, ed. J.G. Nichols (London, 1848), 152; cited Smith, 637.

[12]   *Musica Britannica*, I, ed. D. Stevens, nos. 82, 109.

[13]   M. Frost, *English & Scottish Psalm & Hymn Tunes c. 1543–1677* (London, 1953), tune no. 10.

[14]   This tune and text were used, on the other hand, as the basis of several polyphonic choral settings which survive in cathedral sources. See R.T. Daniel and P. le Huray: *The Sources of English Church Music 1549–1660* (London, 1972), 57.

[15]   cited le Huray, 33, and on p. 4 (Chapter I) above.

[16]   I. Atkins: *The Early Occupants of the Office of Organist at Worcester* (London, 1918), 57.

4   *Organ Settings of English Psalm Tunes*

with his other keyboard music; they are awkwardly spaced, and suggest a cumbersome organ with slow-speaking pipes in a large building (Ex. 2). A few anonymous settings of the same type were also printed in the 1660s.[17]

Ex. 2   Thomas Tomkins (pub. 1668)

Then there is Thomas Mace's famous description of the psalm-singing at York Minster during the siege of York in 1644, when the royalist congregation was assisted by the choir and 'a most Excellent-large-plump-lusty-full-speaking-Organ'.[18] It seems that by the 1640s, at any rate, organ accompaniment of psalm tunes was not unusual. But the absence of either musical settings or references to the practice for the 80-year interval since 1560 suggests that the psalms were not accompanied during most of that period, even in cathedrals. It will not quite do to say that organists must have improvised their settings. Much keyboard music of all sorts was improvised, and yet English examples of other kinds of keyboard music have come down to us in quantity; and what about the many Dutch and German psalm settings from precisely the same period?

The reason for the absence of English organ settings of psalm tunes, in my opinion, was one of economics and prestige. The Church of England was a peculiar blend of Catholic and Calvinist elements, reflected in the dichotomy between cathedral and parochial services, which, though using the same liturgy, assumed entirely distinct characters through the differing use of music. Elizabeth, while allowing the Puritans to have their way in the singing of unaccompanied metrical psalms before or after the service, made it abundantly clear by the example of her Chapel Royal that she would encourage the maintenance of polyphonic traditions. She herself would probably have become a Catholic if doing so would not have undermined the legitimacy of her succession,[19] and the prevalence of music with Latin texts throughout her

---

[17]   On a double sheet (printed about 1669) bound into some copies of John Playford's *Musick's Hand-maide*, editions of 1663 and 1678; see Temperley (1979), ii, ex. 19b.

[18]   Thomas Mace: *Musick's Monument* (London, 1676/R1958 and 1966), 19.

[19]   M.M. Knappen, *Tudor Puritanism* (Chicago and London, 1939), 168.

reign (and organ music based on them) was doubtless partly due to her personal encouragement.

For church musicians there was little choice. The cathedrals and the Chapel Royal provided them with a living, and with scope for their talent; the parish churches had little to offer. All their training, all their interest, compelled them to associate themselves with the Chapel Royal and the cathedrals, and hence, in the main, with the high-church or anti-Puritan party. They would naturally show this allegiance by having nothing to do with metrical psalms, even when they were sung in the cathedral. It was a very different matter in the Netherlands or the Reformed provinces of the Empire, where there were no cathedrals, where the town churches were the central institutions for music, and where municipal authorities were willing to provide substantial funds for 'church concerts', performances of sacred music in the church with organ accompaniments.[20] Eventually, as the zeal for strict Calvinism declined, these forms of elaborate sacred music were gradually admitted to the worship service itself. But in England those who liked elaborate sacred music went to hear it at the cathedral, which had its own endowments independent of city councils, and could afford to disregard the popular forms of church music.

Many elements of this situation persisted after the Restoration and into the 18th century. Parish organists were not paid a living wage: £20 was the normal annual salary in the 18th century, and they earned it by accompanying the psalms and playing voluntaries on Sundays and Christmas Day. In the London area, a group of wealthy parishes in Westminster was typically served by musicians of the Chapel Royal and the Abbey; the poorer churches of the City and surrounding districts frequently shared an organist, or employed an obscure musician of probably third-rate abilities, or had no organ. In cathedral cities there was usually one fashionable church which employed the cathedral organist to play for its Sunday services, and the rest had no organs at all. The growing industrial and market towns sometimes secured a good organist (for instance, Burney at King's Lynn, Avison at Newcastle-on-Tyne, Miller at Doncaster), but he could make a living only by cultivating a wide practice as a private music teacher or organizing secular concerts and festivals.

Typically, an organ would be purchased by subscription in an effort by the wealthier parishioners to improve the psalm singing; but the people, who had been singing without accompaniments since time immemorial, were reluctant to change their ways. Organ settings of psalm tunes from the 18th century, therefore, are functional; they consist of elaborate 'givings-out' of the tune followed by slow, simple harmonizations, often with interludes between the

---

[20] Blankenburg, 571.

lines (Ex. 3). One such set survives in MS in John Reading's Organ Book (dated
* 1716) at Dulwich College.[21] A published set by Daniel Purcell appeared in 1718,
and another, but without givings-out, as *The Psalms by Dr. John Blow Set Full for
the Organ or Harpsichord* (London, *c*. 1731).

There is enough similarity among all these to suggest that they represent
standard procedure rather than original composition.[22] They reflect both the
unbelievably slow tempo into which the tunes had fallen during generations of

Ex. 3 (a)   **Daniel Purcell (1718)**

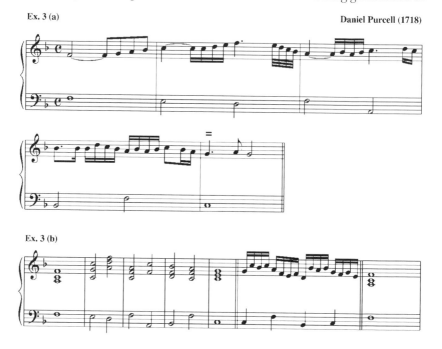

Ex. 3 (b)

unaccompanied singing, and the curious kinds of 'ornamentation' and *portamento*
that had become habitual.[23] The interludes may well have accompanied the
lining out of the words by the parish clerk, which had become a sort of chant.

---

[21] It is described by Gordon Phillips in his introduction to no. 21 in the *Tallis to Wesley* series
(London, 1962).

[22] For complete examples see M. Frost, ed.: *Historical Companion to Hymns Ancient and Modern*
(London, 1962), 90; Temperley (1979), ii, ex. 20. Later sets, with interludes between verses but not
between lines, include: *The Organist's Pocket Companion* (*c*. 1756, 2/*c*. 1767); Starling Goodwin: *The
Complete Organist's Pocket Companion* (*c*. 1775); and Francis Linley: *A Practical Introduction to the Organ*,
Op. 6, 9th edn (London, *c*. 1795).

[23] For a full description of 'the old way of singing' see Temperley (1979), i, 91–9, and
Chapter IV above.

Since the purpose of the organ was to improve the singing, any distraction by counterpoint or other ingenious resource would have been out of place. As a matter of fact, these givings-out are not unlike some Dutch and German organ chorales of the same period, also designed for actual accompaniment of congregational singing.[24]

But the more highly-developed type of organ chorale in Lutheran churches was evidently not tied down to accompanying the congregation, but was either for a 'prelude' (analogous to a giving-out) or for an independent improvisation, perhaps at the end of a service or at a sacred concert. An English organist was not apparently tempted to base his voluntaries on metrical psalm tunes, again, no doubt, for reasons of prestige. The wealthy merchants who paid his salary wanted to hear elegant music at the end of the service, in the newly fashionable style; the first published voluntaries were actually arrangements of Italian sonatas,[25] and original published voluntaries, from Roseingrave's onwards, were in one of the current styles of secular music. Many clergymen, indeed, complained that they were too secular.[26] English composers did not attempt to tackle the technical problems of reconciling the modal tunes of another age with the composing methods of their own time. This challenge was met on the Continent, supremely by Bach, because the Lutheran and even Reformed churches there had institutionalized the integration of popular music into their worship. In England the old dichotomy remained, and composers had no motivation, even if they had the skill, to combine the two traditions in organ pieces – let alone choral cantatas.

In the early 19th century many books of psalm and hymn tunes were printed with simple harmonizations for the organ, replacing the figured bass of earlier times. Some of them included interludes to play between the verses, but they were generally humdrum affairs of strictly functional character.[27] From this period, too, many barrels survive for mechanical barrel organs, with

---

[24] See, for instance, Conrad F. Hurlebusch: *De 150 Psalmen Davids* (Amsterdam, 1746). Even some of Bach's bear a superficial resemblance to English givings-out (e.g. *Wer nur den Lieben Gott*, BWV691, NBA iv/3, p. 98) or harmonizations with interludes (e.g. *Lobt Gott, ihr Christen*, BWV732a, NBA iv/3, p. 63).

[25] *Voluntarys or Fugues made on purpose for the Organ or Harpsichord by Ziani, Pollaroli, Bassani, etc.* (London, 1710).

[26] For example, Arthur Bedford: *The Great Abuse of Musick* (London, 1711/R1965), 216–17; William Mason, 'On Instrumental Church Music' (1795), *Works* (London, 1811), iii, 312–13.

[27] See, for instance, William Horsley: *A Collection of Psalms, with Interludes* (London, 1828); Cornelius Bryan: *Effusions for the Organ* (London, c1830); William Spark: *A Collection of Psalm Tunes and Chants* (London, 1847). The Horsley work was described by Frank Howes in 'The Dead Past', *Music & Letters*, xxii (1941), 257–60. As late as 1880 an interlude was sometimes played before the last verse of a hymn; see J. S. Curwen: *Studies in Worship Music* [1st series] (London, 1880), 95.

8   *Organ Settings of English Psalm Tunes*

ornamented versions of standard tunes that give a reliable idea of the practice of the time.[28] The idea of varying the harmonies of a tune from verse to verse, well known on the Continent since the 17th century, seems to have taken root in England only in the 19th; it was checked, but not arrested, by the Oxford Movement. Henry Smart in 1855 published a set of varied harmonizations for the traditional psalm tunes, together with givings-out (he used the old-fashioned term), intended as examples of an essentially improvisatory procedure (see Ex. 4).[29] Later Victorian hymn books often included a few hymns written out with different settings for each verse, such as Sullivan's for St Anne,[30] or the still familiar 'Praise, my soul, the king of heaven' by Goss (1869). The tradition was maintained in various organists' guides published in the late Victorian and

Ex. 4   Henry Smart (1855)

Edwardian periods, reaching the *ne plus ultra* in a book by Madely Richardson, organist of Southwark cathedral.[31] Richardson emphasized the almost unlimited possibilities available for organ accompaniment, which he compared with the orchestral accompaniments of oratorio choruses by Handel or Mendelssohn. He gave, by way of example, nearly a hundred different ways of accompanying the opening phrase of Webbe's tune Melcombe: two of them are shown in Ex. 5.

    The Victorian religious revival was little concerned with organs or psalm tunes, but the Bach revival stimulated a series of composers to attempt a more
* learned and artistic treatment of Anglican tunes. Wesley, in his interludes to traditional psalm tunes 'adapted expressly to the English organ with preludes', showed what he had learned from Bach.[32] He was followed later by Basil

[28]   N. Boston and L. G. Langwill: *Church and Chamber Barrel-Organs* (Edinburgh, 1967), 17

[29]   Henry Smart: *A Choral Book* (London, 1855).

[30]   For *Church Hymns* (1874), reprinted in Temperley (1979), ii, ex. 83.

[31]   A. Madely Richardson: *Modern Organ Accompaniment* (London, 1907).

[32]   S. S. Wesley: *A Selection of Psalm Tunes* (London, 1838); see Paul Chappell: *Dr S. S. Wesley* (Great Wakering, 1977), 156–7, 182.

Ex. 5 (a)　　　　　　　　　　　　　　　　　A. M. Richardson (1907)

Ex. 5 (b)

Harwood, Charles Wood, and above all Hubert Parry (two sets, 1912 and 1916),　*
who actually called his settings 'chorale preludes', though they were based
on English psalm and hymn tunes (Ex. 6). Quite clearly this was a product
imported ready-made from Germany.

Ex. 6　　　　　　　　　　　　　　　　　C. H. H. Parry (1912)

Allegro ♩ = 100

Full Sw. *p*

[Gt. cpld. to Ped.]

　　The meagreness of our heritage of organ settings of psalm tunes is due,
then, not so much to Puritanism as to the split character of the musical
tradition in the Church of England. No other religious body had the resources
to patronize art music during the critical period of the 17th and 18th centuries;
and the church used those resources to support musical institutions that were
decidedly independent of popular forms.

XIV

Ancient and Modern in the Work of Sir John Stainer

Few Victorian composers have had such a bad press as John Stainer (1840–1901). He died well respected in the musical world.[1] Yet only six years after his death, Ernest Walker passed unfavourable judgement on his music, which he lumped with that of John Bacchus Dykes (1823–76) and Joseph Barnby (1838–96) under the general stigma of 'sentimentalism'.[2] Taking his cue from Walker, Edmund Fellowes was very hard on them in his authoritative study of English cathedral music. As a leader in the revival of Elizabethan and Jacobean music, he placed what he called the 'mid-Victorians' at the other end of the scale. Though praising Stainer's choice of texts, he took the trouble to print two rather weak passages to demonstrate that the anthems were written 'too easily' – as if a composer was to be judged by his poorest work.[3] Kenneth Long, whose book *The Music of the English Church* could be called 'Fellowes plus prejudice' (even to the point of using many of the same examples), repeated Fellowes's views of Stainer in less restrained language.[4] He added a gratuitous attack on Stainer's *Crucifixion* (not, strictly, within the scope of his book), which he called 'squalid music', and he even criticised those who venture to perform it, calling them 'a hard core of organists and choirmasters who are ignorant and self-satisfied'. Recent commentators are more mildly negative. John Caldwell says that Stainer's anthems and services 'are often weakened by an enervating chromaticism and a static movement of the vocal parts'.[5]

---

1 See the many tributes quoted in Peter Charlton, *John Stainer and the Musical Life of Victorian Britain* (Newton Abbot: David & Charles, 1984), pp. 169–75.
2 Ernest Walker, *A History of Music in England* (Oxford: Clarendon Press, 1907), p. 308.
3 Edmund H. Fellowes, *English Cathedral Music from Edward VI to Edward VII* (London: Methuen & Co., Ltd., 1941), pp. 222–26. Jack Westrup made no relevant changes in this section when revising the book for the 5th edn (1969).
4 Kenneth R. Long, *The Music of the English Church* (London: Hodder & Stoughton, 1971), pp. 364–65. He also singled out for disdain a passage from Barnby's *Jubilate* in E which he had copied from Fellowes, who, in turn, had taken it from Walker.
5 John Caldwell, *The Oxford History of English Music*, vol. 2 (Oxford: Oxford University Press, 1999), p. 308.

104

The accepted twentieth-century view among critics and scholars was that Stainer was an excellent man and musician, who did much for musicology and music education, and for Magdalen College, Oxford, and St Paul's Cathedral; but as for his compositions, the less said the better. At mid-century Jack Westrup summed it up in a passage added to Walker's *History*: 'Fortunately Stainer's reputation depends not on his music but on his services to scholarship. Musicians today have no use for *The Crucifixion* but *Dufay and His Contemporaries* and the volumes of *Early Bodleian Music* are still valued.' It was almost as if Stainer were being given a consolation prize.[6]

This critical consensus had little to do with the views of the public, which knew and loved Stainer largely as a composer and arranger. *The Crucifixion* continued to be a great favourite, and still is, no matter what the critics think;[7] the services and anthems lingered on cathedral lists; and several of the hymn tunes, chants and carol harmonisations have survived both the general anti-Victorian reaction and the rediscovery of older music.[8]

Before attempting to reassess Stainer's church music, I will first discuss the perception that he was primarily an important musicologist. (I pass over his importance to music education, which is probably considerable, and his activities at St Paul's, which have been thoroughly described by Timothy Storey.[9])

In 1940, to mark the centenary of Stainer's birth, an unsigned article appeared in the *Musical Times*.[10] It had little good to say about Stainer's compositions, and reserved its enthusiasm for his scholarly work, saying that 'his book, "Dufay and His Contemporaries", is still a standard work on 15th-century music'. George Guest picked up this idea in a later issue of the same journal: 'It is probably true that as an all-round scholar and musician, Stainer was unrivalled in this country. His many papers published in the Proceedings of the (now Royal) Musical Association are proof of the former – as is his book on Dufay, which is still a classic.'[11]

In fact there is no such book. *Dufay and His Contemporaries*, published in 1898, is not a 'book on Dufay' by Stainer but an edition of selected songs from Bodleian MS Canonici misc. 213 by Stainer's son and

6 Walker, *A History of Music in England*, 3rd edn, rev. J.A. Westrup (Oxford: Oxford University Press, 1952), p. 330.
7 Long in 1971 admitted that 'each year hundreds of performances continue to be given'.
8 Fourteen of his tunes are in *Hymns Ancient and Modern Revised*, [2nd edn] ([London]: William Clowes & Sons, Ltd., 1972), and five of the most popular carols still carry his harmonies in *The New Oxford Book of Carols*, ed. Hugh Keyte and Andrew Parrott (Oxford: Oxford University Press, 1992).
9 Timothy Storey, 'The Music of St. Paul's Cathedral' (M.Mus. thesis, University of Durham, 1998), pp. 1–40.
10 'John Stainer, 1840–1901', *Musical Times*, 81 (1940), pp. 300–301.
11 George Guest, 'Counsel from the Console', *Musical Times*, 100 (1959), pp. 104–5.

daughter. The palaeographical expertise was supplied by E.W.B. Nicholson, then Bodley's Librarian. Sir John contributed only a chapter of the introduction, in which he did not discuss the manuscript or its provenance, but analysed the music. He also probably went through the musical text, adding editorial suggestions. It was much the same with the 1901 publication, *Early Bodleian Music*. In that case Stainer's contribution remained unfinished at the time of his death, but the editors acknowledged that he was responsible for the added *musica ficta* accidentals.

It is true that Stainer became interested in fifteenth-century music in the last few years of his life, apparently as a direct result of the historical lectures he organised at Oxford after his appointment as professor in 1889. The texts of these lectures are lost, but their titles and the names of the lecturers are preserved, and have been printed as an appendix to Peter Charlton's book.[12] At first Stainer spoke on such subjects as 'The present state of Music in England', 'Mendelssohn's oratorio, "Elijah"', 'Mozart's Requiem', and certain theoretical topics, leaving the early history to Hubert Parry. In 1893 he gave his first 'early music' lecture, on 'Palestrina's Mass, Aeterna Christi Munera', and in 1896 he spoke on 'The secular compositions of Dufay, with illustrations'; later he ventured into other Renaissance topics such as Morley, Hassler, and early psalm-tune harmonisations.

Some of these topics are also reflected in his addresses to the Musical Association. It is probably true that Stainer's prestige helped to arouse interest in these earlier kinds of music, a fact for which Parry expressed his gratitude in comments following Stainer's paper delivered to the Musical Association on 12 November 1895.[13] This was entitled 'A Fifteenth Century MS. Book of Vocal Music in the Bodleian Library, Oxford' and was about Canonici misc. 213. Musical illustrations were played on three or four violas, because of the difficulty of finding singers who knew how to pronounce medieval French. No doubt the lecture was essentially the same as the one to be delivered at Oxford a few months later. Stainer's introductory chapter to *Dufay and His Contemporaries*, which he dated 'Oxford, 1898', was a revised and more comprehensive version of the same material.[14]

In the Musical Association paper Stainer reacted to the music as a musician, and a modern musician at that. He was obviously fascinated by the notation and musical style of Dufay and the ways in which they differed from his own time. In one example, shown here as Ex. 5.1, from Dufay's

---

12 Charlton, *John Stainer*, pp. 205–8.
13 John Stainer, 'A Fifteenth Century MS. Book of Vocal Music in the Bodleian Library, Oxford', *Proceedings of the Musical Association*, 22 (1895–96), pp. 1–21.
14 John Stainer, 'Chapter III', in J.F.R. and C. Stainer (eds), *Dufay and His Contemporaries: Fifty Compositions* (London: Novello, 1898), pp. 27–45.

106

Ex. 5.1   Dufay's 'Belles vueillies votre mercy donner', as transcribed by Stainer

'Belles vueillies votre mercy donner', there is a glaring false relation between the two lower parts. Stainer theorised that the sharp before the bass *f* was a warning to singers *not* to sharpen the note according to the rules of *musica ficta*; in other words, it meant 'sing F natural'.[15] He offered no supporting evidence. In Heinrich Besseler's edition of the same song,[16] now considered authoritative, the sharp is retained and the alto *f'* is supplied with an editorial sharp as well, a rather awkward solution. Interestingly enough, Stainer's theory that a sharp might in some circumstances mean 'don't sharpen' has been revived much more recently, backed up by substantial evidence; but it is still controversial.[17] I cannot adjudicate the case, but I draw attention to the fact that Stainer's solution was prompted solely by his musical intuition, which, of course, was based on modern tonality.

Ex. 5.2a is also a musical example from the 1895 paper, taken from another song by Dufay, 'Bon jour, bon mois'. Stainer says of it: '[Dufay] clearly wishes in one place to make a cadence in A minor, but he diverts it thus, being clearly unable to reach the desired key. This frequent avoidance of definite cadences in keys into which he evidently would be glad to modulate is a sign of the peculiar and unsettled state of key-tonality in his time.'[18] But by 1898 he had changed his mind, probably under the influence of scholars who knew about *musica ficta*. When the song appeared in *Dufay and His Contemporaries*, editorial accidentals were supplied as in Ex. 5.2b,[19] and in his Introduction he said of this song: 'His [Dufay's] modulations are much superior to those by most of his contemporaries ... notice ... the smoothness of the modulation into *A minor*' (from G minor), with the example printed as in Ex. 5.2c.[20]

---

15 Stainer, 'A Fifteenth Century MS.', p. 5. This song is not included in *Dufay and His Contemporaries*.

16 *Guillelmi Dufay Omnia Opera*, ed. Heinrich Besseler, vol. 6 (Rome: American Institute of Musicology, 1964), p. 77.

17 See Don Harrán, 'New Evidence for Musica Ficta: the Cautionary Sign', *Journal of the American Musicological Society*, 29 (1976), pp. 77–98; Irving Godt and Don Harrán, 'Comments and Issues', *Journal of the American Musicological Society*, 31 (1978), pp. 385–95. Neither source mentions Stainer's anticipation of Harrán's theory.

18 Stainer, 'A Fifteenth Century MS.', p. 11.

19 Stainer and Stainer, *Dufay and His Contemporaries*, p. 134.

20 Stainer, 'Chapter III', p. 35. The same solution is offered by Besseler, *Guillelmi Dufay*, p. 66.

333

Ex. 5.2 Three different transcriptions of a passage from Dufay's 'Bon jour, bon mois'

Stainer's comments in these two cases are a sign that he was no musi- *
cologist, but rather a highly intelligent musician, who believed in the
excellence and permanent validity of modern, that is nineteenth-century,
harmony. He could understand early music only in teleological terms:
'the composers of the first half of the fifteenth century are still groping
after facility of modulation and contrast of keys'.[21] That was not an
unusual attitude in his time and place, and it elicited no protests in the
discussion at the Musical Association, or in reviews of the edition. But it
had certainly been overtaken by musicologists well before that time –
mostly German, but including also such British scholars as William
Chappell (1809–88), Edward Rimbault (1816–76), and the French
émigré Arnold Dolmetsch (1858–1940). The contemporary edition of
the *Fitzwilliam Virginal Book* (1899), edited jointly by John A. Fuller
Maitland (1856–1936) and William Barclay Squire (1855–1927), also
displayed a professionally musicological approach in clear contrast with
Stainer's.

If we look at Stainer's life as a whole, we see that he was instinctively a
modernist. In an address to the Church Congress at Leeds in 1872 he
made a plea for representing the best music of all periods in the choice of
music for cathedral services, including the most modern. 'There are some
ancient melodies', he said, 'which lived before *harmony* (in the modern
sense of the word) was invented, which have come down to our time in all
their original simplicity ... The so-called Ambrosian Te Deum is one of
these, and when harmonised quite simply, may claim its ... right to be
heard sometimes within our cathedral walls.' But he went on: 'I do not,
however, mean to say that modern chords should not be used.'[22]

This approach is borne out in Stainer's harmonisation of the Ambrosian
Te Deum as printed in the *Cathedral Prayer Book* (1891), part of which is

21 Stainer, 'Chapter III', p. 35.
22 [John] Stainer, untitled paper, in *Authorised Report of the Church Congress Held at
Leeds, October ... 1872* (Leeds: Thomas Ponsonby, [1872]), pp. 334–39, at p. 336. It was
reprinted in *The Choir* (26 Oct. 1872) under the title 'The Principles on which Music should
be Selected for Use in Cathedrals'.

108

Ex. 5.3   Stainer's harmonisation of the Ambrosian Te Deum

shown in Ex. 5.3. The melody is taken from John Marbeck's *Booke of Common Praier Noted* (1550), and is roughly in the Phrygian mode. Stainer began by using chords that he thought would have been acceptable in 1550. But when, at 'We believe', the same melody is reharmonised in C major, though each chord is still a common triad (or a 6–3 on D, perfectly respectable in sixteenth-century terms), the spirit as well as the theory of modality is lost, and the tempo and dynamic marks reveal a thoroughly nineteenth-century outlook. Later, Stainer finally yields to temptation and writes a 'modern' harmonic progression. As it happens, his setting of 'Day by day we magnify thee' is practically identical with the first phrase of that quintessentially Victorian tune 'Hollingside', by Dykes, often sung to the hymn 'Jesu, lover of my soul'.

But before passing hasty judgement let us look, for a moment, at what J.S. Bach did to a sixteenth-century tune in the Phrygian mode, 'Aus tiefer Not' (Ex. 5.4, from Cantata 38, last movement). The harmonies are more flagrantly anachronistic than anything Stainer did. If Bach, who can do no wrong in the prevailing view of music history, modernised modal music for his time, why shouldn't Stainer do the same for *his* time?

Having, I hope, cleared away the illusion that Stainer was primarily important as a scholar, I would like to reconsider his position as a

Ex. 5.4   J.S. Bach's harmonisation of 'Aus tiefer Not'

composer, specifically in the area of church music, which was obviously the centre of his creative effort and achievement.

Stainer's second address to the Church Congress, at Brighton in 1874, had a significant title: 'On the Progressive Character of Church Music'. Here he took to task those who imitated ancient styles in their church music, thus firmly setting himself against not only William Crotch and the other Gresham Prize judges of S.S. Wesley's time, but also his revered mentor, Sir Frederick Ouseley (1825–89), who was present and had given the previous lecture. Indeed he explicitly criticised not only the imitation of older styles, but the styles themselves, in those cases where 'counterpoint renders confused or unintelligible those sacred words on which it should be, as it were, a commentary'. He repeated his plea: 'I only ask that modern music shall have its proper place assigned to it, side by side with the old, and I only preach that those who call themselves church-composers should aim at something better than bygone styles.'[23]

Of course, modernity is relative. There is a natural tendency for the music of the church, in striving to suggest eternal truths, to resemble the general musical style of one or two generations earlier, so that the oldest worshippers present are not shocked by a sense of disruption or decay. Stainer's compositions show that his idea of modernity was founded on music of the Classical period, especially Mozart's. It is significant that he played Mozart's *Ave verum corpus*, a very Staineresque piece, as an illustration of the 1874 lecture. He was himself a master of Classical melody and harmony, to which he added decorative chromaticism from time to time – another trait for which he has been condemned with astonishing venom, although his chromaticisms can all be paralleled in Mozart's work.

---

23 [John] Stainer, 'On the Progressive Character of Church Music', in *Authorised Report of the Church Congress Held at Brighton, October … 1874* (London: William Wells Gardner, [1874]), pp. 530–38, at p. 531.

110

To a Mozartian base he added a few touches of Schubert, Mendelssohn, and Spohr, expanding, but not disrupting, the Classical tonal system to encompass keys such as the flat submediant that had become part of the normal tonal range by 1830. But Stainer did not embrace the 'Music of the Future': there are no hints of Wagner, Liszt, or even Brahms. In his inaugural address as professor at Oxford, he expressed a fear that 'a too plentiful use of that descriptive and sentimental colouring which we derive from the modern "romantic style" should tempt our church musicians into a striving after picturesque and dramatic effects not consistent with the dignity and repose of worship'.[24] He must have been thinking of Gounod, and his English disciples such as Barnby, who were willing to throw off the inhibitions of cathedral tradition.[25] He went on, 'Three centuries ago the musician, quite regardless of the meaning of the words, revelled in the intricacies of counterpoint: now, our church composers watch narrowly every shade of meaning in the words in order to represent it in a tone-picture. Is this a legitimate form of Church music?'[26]

Thus, in using terms such as 'modern' and 'progressive' in the context of church music, Stainer was taking a moderate stance. Between two undesirable extremes he forged his own style, which was based on his ability to write an attractive and singable melody and to enrich it with the full resources of early nineteenth-century harmony. Both counterpoint and word-painting were available tools, but they were used with conscious restraint, especially in his later works.

The first, and so far the only, serious and unprejudiced study of Stainer's church music is the work of an American scholar, William Gatens.[27] Americans have never suffered from the hang-up about the Victorians that afflicted British musicology and criticism for much of the twentieth century; an earlier American work is also free of this particular bias in its treatment of Stainer.[28] Gatens points out that 'Stainer obviously recognizes the pitfalls on each side of the controversy: the danger of irreverent theatricality on the one hand, and of frigid antiquarianism on the other. The tenderness and expressive understatement may be seen as a

---

[24] John Stainer, *The Present State of Music in England* (Oxford, 1889), p. 11.

[25] Walker, *Music in England* (1907, p. 308), states that Gounod was Stainer's chief model, and has been followed in this view by the later commentators. I would dispute this as regards the church music, though Gounod's theatrical manner is present in *The Crucifixion* and is occasionally found in the anthems and services. It is much more strongly evident in some of Barnby's anthems.

[26] Stainer, *The Present State of Music in England*, p. 12.

[27] William Gatens, *Victorian Cathedral Music in Theory and Practice* (Cambridge: Cambridge University Press, 1986), chap. 9.

[28] Elwyn A. Wienandt and Robert H. Young, *The Anthem in England and America* (New York: The Free Press, 1970), pp. 268–79.

possible solution.' He exonerates Stainer from the charge of easy superficiality: 'Stainer's own church music is thus an attempt to put into practice
deeply considered issues and theories exhibited in this and other essays.
His compositions are not a contradiction of his principles, as some later
critics have suggested, but a confirmation of them.'[29]

As an example of a work in which these principles were successfully
deployed, though not on a consistently high level, I have chosen the
Evening Service in B flat major.[30] It was written for use in St Paul's, but not
by the cathedral choir: it was for the London Church Choir Association, a
combination of parish church choirs of several thousand voices, at its fifth
festival in 1877. For this reason, and also no doubt with an eye to publication, it is confined mostly to four-part writing and makes no use of antiphonal effects.

In this service Stainer made his boldest step towards the 'symphonic'
type of setting later developed by Stanford. He planned it with a strong
and clearly 'modern' polarisation between the keys of B flat and D, which
he extended to the Morning Service in B flat composed a few years later.
When the combined service was published in 1884, it was conceived as a
whole. The title was *The Morning and Evening Service together with the
Office for the Holy Communion set to music in the key of B flat*. But the
Benedictus is wholly in the key of D, while the Communion Office is in F,
with one of its movements (the Sanctus) set in A. The overall key scheme
of B flat – D – F/A/F – B flat resembles that of some of Schubert's sonatas
and chamber works.

In 1877 the Evening Service had been conceived as a self-sufficient piece,
consisting, of course, of only two canticles: Magnificat and Nunc Dimittis.
But even within this smaller scheme there is a strong polarisation between B
flat and D. The Magnificat begins on a D major chord for the organ,
followed by a seven-bar thematic build-up to the choir's entrance in B flat
on a robust unison melody. There is an episode in D major with a sweeter
and more reflective melody ('and Holy is his Name'), then the organ
opening returns as a transition back to B flat, where there is a repeat of the
first tune ('He hath shewed strength'). More remarkably, the Gloria Patri
quickly moves to the key of D. When it returns to B flat, Stainer provides a
full fugue on the subject shown in Ex. 5.5a (the descending fourth is derived
from the main melody). It has exactly the same rhythm and unfortunate
word repetition as the subject of a similar fugue in Barnby's Service in E
(Ex. 5.5b), which was later ridiculed by Tovey as a 'strange theological

---

29 Gatens, *Victorian Cathedral Music*, p. 172.
30 This work was performed at a special Victorian choral evensong associated with the
conference, at Holy Trinity Church, Prince Consort Road, on Wednesday, 18 July 2001.

112

Ex. 5.5 Comparison of fugal subjects in the Gloria of (a) Stainer's Magnificat in
B flat (1877) and (b) Barnby's Magnificat in E (1864)

(a)

(b)

dogma, that of the Chorister's 40th Article of Religion'.[31] Tovey has a
point. Though this is an extreme case, Stainer too frequently weakens the
sense of the text by adhering to Classical phrase structures.

The development of the fugue is vigorous, if somewhat routine, and
leads to an exciting climax. Here Stainer, having conceded on the one side
to the 'contrapuntal' school, makes a move towards theatricality (Ex.
5.6). Then the main theme returns in the organ over a dominant pedal,
during the final repetition of 'Amen'.

Ex. 5.6 Gloria from Stainer's Magnificat in B flat

---

[31] Donald F. Tovey, *The Main Stream of Music* (London: Humphrey Milford, 1938),
reprinted in *The Main Stream of Music and Other Essays*, ed. Hubert Foss (Oxford:
Clarendon Press, 1949), pp. 330–52, at p. 339.

Fellowes said that 'the B flat service was written with special reference to the acoustic conditions of St. Paul's cathedral. It sounds ineffective and vulgar in most other buildings.'[32] Ex. 5.6 is the only passage I can find that gives any support to this sweeping statement, for it exploits the unusually long reverberation of the great cathedral.

The Nunc Dimittis begins with one of those tender melodies that Stainer wrote so well, and that clearly exemplify his 'middle way' (Ex. 5.7). Like many predecessors, he begins this Song of Simeon with male voices only. Again, as in Ex. 5.5a, he makes the phrase regular by word repetition, as Mozart often did; but in this case the repetition is harmless. The decorative chromaticism and the smooth part-writing, stretching at times to six voice parts, show Stainer at his best and most confident. A second, more ordinary melody (8 + 9 bars) is for trebles answered by the full choir, ending on the dominant; one more phrase completes the canticle text.

For the Gloria Patri Stainer could have simply repeated the one that followed the Magnificat, as most Victorians did, or written a completely different one, which was the habit of a minority of his contemporaries

Ex. 5.7   Stainer, Nunc Dimittis in B flat

32 Fellowes, *English Cathedral Music*, p. 225.

114

including George Garrett (1834–97). He did neither. The first part, modulating to D major, is the same as before; but when the theme of Ex. 5.5a enters, it is sung as a choral unison, treated as the bass of organ harmonies. There is new counterpoint, but no fugue. The final amens are shorter and less dramatic, and the whole doxology is in proportion to the shorter text and quieter character of this canticle.

These considerations show Stainer thinking on a larger scale, and using techniques derived from modern secular music to provide a broad structure. Another development from the same source, shared with many Victorian cathedral musicians, was his management and variation of texture. He used unison passages, staccato organ chords, varied spacing of chords, careful dynamic shading, and contrasts of tempo with a skill that had built up in Anglican music since the choral revival got under way in the 1840s, but in which he surpassed his rivals.

At this point I would like to examine a conversation that Stainer had with Fellowes, which has often been quoted. Dr Fellowes told the story twice in print; he also recounted it to me when I went to see him at Windsor Castle on 24 July 1951 to ask him about Victorian church music, but I took no notes. Here is the 1941 version:

> He did in fact know that he had written most of his earlier anthems too easily. Within a year of his death he confided to the present writer that he regretted deeply that so many of them had been published, adding that they had been written in response to pressure put upon him in early days by the clergy and others, who assured him that they were 'just the thing they wanted'.[33]

In 1951 Fellowes put it in this way:

> He suddenly stopped me in the Magdalen walks and said he wanted me to know that he regretted ever having published most of his compositions; that he knew very well they were 'rubbish' and feared that when he was gone his reputation might suffer because of his inferiority ... He was then a poor man and gave way to demand, and he now deeply regretted it.[34]

The most significant difference between the two printed texts is that the first refers only to 'his earlier anthems' while the second is about 'most of his compositions'. In both, however, it is clear that Stainer was looking back to the early part of his life; this is reinforced by 'early days' in the 1941 text and 'He was then a poor man' in the 1951 text. And this is in itself a remarkable fact, because most commentators, including Walker, Fellowes, Westrup, Long, Charlton and Gatens, consider that his earlier anthems are his best works. The very first to be published, 'I saw the Lord'

---

33 Ibid., p. 224.
34 Edmund H. Fellowes, 'Sir John Stainer', *English Church Music*, 21/1 (1951), pp. 4–7, at p. 7.

(1858), is the only one praised by Walker, Westrup and Long, and is 'generally considered ... Stainer's best anthem', according to Fellowes.[35] The early anthems, it is agreed, are more in the traditional form and style of cathedral music, and they have less of the 'mid-Victorian' characteristics that some find objectionable; as Gatens says, 'they follow much the same pattern as the larger anthems of Goss and Ouseley' (p. 173).

In contrast, most of the later anthems were published by Novello & Co., often as supplements to the *Musical Times*, and were evidently intended for parochial use.[36] They are short, technically undemanding, and generally sweet and melodious. One of the last is the little-noticed 'O bountiful Jesu', which appeared as a supplement to the *Musical Times* of 1 February 1900. This was near in time to the remarks Stainer made to Fellowes 'within a year of his death', which occurred on 31 March 1901. We must assume, then, that 'O bountiful Jesu' is not one of those 'early anthems' that the composer told Fellowes he considered to be 'rubbish'. On the contrary, it is a mature specimen of the style that he had long cultivated as most appropriate and edifying for church music, the style which, in my opinon, brought out his best qualities.

Always resourceful in his choice of texts, Stainer took this one from a prayer that he found in a primer of 1553:

> O bountiful Jesu, O sweet Saviour, O Christ the Son of God, have mercy upon us, mercifully hear us, and despise not our prayers. Thou hast created us of nothing; Thou hast redeemed us from the bondage of sin, death, and hell, neither with gold nor silver, but with Thy most precious body offered once upon the cross, and Thine own blood shed once for all for our ransom; therefore cast us not away, whom Thou by thy great wisdom hath made; despise us not, whom Thou hast redeemed with such a precious treasure.

Its content is not unusual, being nothing other than the central tenet of Christianity, but in the Anglican world of 1900 it was unfamiliar in diction and in image, for instance in its reference to gold and silver. It is fervent, intimate, and beautiful in form and phraseology. Stainer strove to match its quality in his setting.

The anthem is in four vocal parts throughout, and 'May be sung without accompaniment'. There is no attempt at word-painting, except for well-placed climaxes at the words 'sin, death, and hell' and 'whom Thou hast redeemed'. Instead, Stainer evokes the mood and overall

---

35 Ibid. Long loosely extended the story to embrace his nemesis, *The Crucifixion* (1887) – hardly an 'early' work or one written when Stainer was a 'poor man', and certainly not an anthem – claiming that 'Towards the end of his life Stainer bitterly regretted having published it'; *The Music of the English Church*, p. 365.
36 There is a useful list in Gatens, *Victorian Cathedral Music*, p. 185.

116

Ex. 5.8   Stainer, 'O bountiful Jesu'

feeling of the prayer. The first sentence is formed into a tender, regularly phrased 12-bar tune (Ex. 5.8), which modulates to the dominant key. The voices are mostly kept to the lower part of their range, where amateur singers can most easily modulate their tone for expression and follow the careful dynamic markings. Slightly higher notes (the alto g' in bar 2, the tenor e' in bar 3) make a disproportionate effect, and so does each dissonance, whether passing or accentual. One is made aware of the individual vocal lines, not by counterpoint, but by harmony and spacing. Even the notoriously static Victorian alto part, as in the repeated notes of bars 7–10, draws the ear's attention to itself when other parts move around it.

The sentence is then sung again, with the same music subtly transformed by different dynamics, beginning *pianissimo* (after the end of Ex. 5.8), and by a change of spacing at 'have mercy upon us', the trebles rising to e''. The repeat of bars 9–12, instead of passing through E minor to D major, passes through A minor to G major, so that a miniature sonata form is the result, followed by a little coda referring back to the opening (Ex. 5.9).

Ex. 5.9   Stainer, 'O bountiful Jesu'

Ex. 5.10   Stainer, 'O bountiful Jesu'

118

Continuing to follow late-Classical models, Stainer changes key to E flat, where the first climax takes the voices to a higher range. A modulation to the dominant of G minor prepares for the return of the first tune. It is now carefully adapted to new text, 'therefore cast us not away', requiring a double upbeat and some compression of the musical phrase. This time, after the cadence on the dominant (bar 8 in Ex. 5.8), new material (Ex. 5.10) leads quickly to the second and principal climax.

A few elements of Stainer's craft may be mentioned here: the soprano/tenor imitation during the sequential rise in bars 1–6; the climax itself, where all four voices join to sing the same text, and the trebles and basses are on their highest notes; the way the expected 6/4 chord on the first beat of bar 10 is avoided, slightly prolonging the tension; then the interrupted cadence in bar 12, as the well-spaced voices at last subside to the awaited repose on the chord of G. Then the anthem ends with a repeat of Ex. 5.9 and an Amen.

By the simplest of means Stainer has achieved a truly devotional effect. It is easy to see why this sort of anthem was welcomed by parish congregations, who looked to their choir music not for intellectual challenge but for beauty, consolation and reassurance – all of which call for a high degree of predictability, but also a high level of art. The master knew exactly when and how to provide them, deploying a kind of skill that has since eroded almost to vanishing point in 'serious' music, though it is still practised in some species of popular music. Stainer's emphasis on pleasant, regular melody and rich harmony was not due to ignorance or bad taste, still less to 'enervation' or 'effeminacy', but was a principled acceptance of the resources of Classical music as suitable for the needs of the contemporary church. Some, including Fellowes, have likened his anthems to Victorian part songs, as if this in itself placed them automatically beneath serious consideration. The parallel is apt, but the implied stigma is not.

Nobody has suggested that Stainer was a great composer, or that he made important contributions to the profound changes in musical style that were taking place in his time. I am not advancing such claims now. I do maintain that he was a consummate artist. Of course anyone may like or dislike his music as a matter of taste, but it is time to give up the sweeping and uninformed condemnations of his modernisation of plainsong, and of his secularisation of church music, as if these were crimes by definition. He should be restored to his proper place in English musical history.

ADDENDA AND CORRIGENDA

Most of these essays were printed before the *Hymn Tune Index* (*HTI*) came into existence, with its full information about psalm and hymn tunes and printed tune collections. Tunes can generally be located in the online *HTI* at hymntune.library.illinois.edu by means of a 'tune search', using the tune name or incipit. Frost tune numbers in Nos. III and V can be turned into *HTI* tune numbers by using the table in the printed *HTI* (Oxford, 1998), vol. 2, p. 583. For No. VI a special table is provided on p. 173 of this book.

III. John Playford and the Metrical Psalms

Playford's career at the Company of Stationers is recounted in my article 'John Playford and the Stationers' Company', *Music & Letters* 54 (1973), 203–12. In addition to the collections discussed here Playford had published nine of the most common psalm tunes set for the gittern, or English guitar, in *A Book of New Lessons for the Cithern and Gittern* (London, 1652), obviously for domestic use. Also, Playford included in the 1658 edition of *A Breif Introduction to the Skill of Musick*, but not in later editions, three tunes by Henry Lawes with texts by George Sandys. All these are indexed in the online *HTI*.

Though not strictly psalm tunes, Playford added three hymns to his 1677 *Whole Book of Psalms in Three Parts* (1677), each with a new tune. A communion hymn, 'All glory be to God on high', was set to Frost 199 (*HTI* 546a), under the name MARTYRS, which was later used by Elias Hall for the older communion hymn (see No. V, p. 246). The hymn *On the Divine Use of Music* ('We sing to him whose wisdom formed the ear') was set to Frost 201 (*HTI* 548) and the Benedicite to Frost 7 (*HTI* 249).

Note 68: The organs in London churches are more fully discussed in No. VII.

IV. The Old Way of Singing: Its Origins and Development

Ex. 10: The second example from Chetham's collection, complete with bass, may be found in Musica Britannica, vol. 85, no. 6.

V. The Anglican Communion Hymn

Page 134: No. 3 was printed in the 18th century with various tunes, the last being composed for it by Robert Price, assistant organist of St. Michael's,

Coventry, and printed in 1775 (*HTI* 3799). A revised and improved text of No. 4 appeared in *A Collection of Church Tunes... Used in Episcopal Congregations* (Aberdeen: Chalmers, [c.1800]) and from 1802 became popular in American collections with the tune ARUNDEL (*HTI* 5022a).

Page 135: William Tans'ur composed his own tune for No. 8 called HOLY COMMUNION, first printed in 1735 (*HTI* 1455).

Page 138: Only two of these hymns had appeared with tunes in 18th century Methodist publications: No. 14 in Thomas Butts's *Harmonia Sacra* (c.1755) and later Wesleyan books with the tune DEDICATION (*HTI* 2236), and No. 17 in Martin Madan's *Lock Hospital Collection* with Charles Lockhart's tune LOTHBURY (*HTI* 3276). Doddridge's hymn, No. 19, was included in the *Magdalen Chapel Collection*, edition A/c, with a new tune by Thomas Call (*HTI* 2795).

VI. The Origins of the Fuging Tune

In this essay, both sources and tunes are identified by codes referring to Temperley & Manns 1983 (cited on p. 172). These have since been displaced by *HTI* codes. The old source codes are resolved in Table 2 (p. 146) and on pages 148–51.

For tune codes, the table on p. 173 converts all the italic tune numbers listed in the essay to *HTI* tune numbers, allowing readers to refer to the *HTI* database for more complete information about each tune and its history. In some cases earlier sources of the tunes have been located since the essay appeared.

Sally Drage has drawn my attention to the following passage from *Remarks and Collections of Thomas Hearne*, edited by H.E. Salter, vol. 9, p. 321 (Oxford Historical Society Publications, 85 [1914]):

> June 29 [1727] (Thur.). At Wotton, near Abbington in Berks., lives one Beesly, a Farmer, who hath a son called Michael Beesly, living there also with his Father. This son (who was born at Sunningwell, where his Father then lived) is an ingenious young man, and hath learned to ingrave only by once seeing the late Michael Burghers ingrave, so that he hath composed and ingraved a book, about singing Psalms and Anthems, himself (wch he teaches in Parochial Churches), of wch there are two Editions.

This provides interesting new information about Beesly, and shows that he began publishing church music considerably earlier than was thought. The book referred to is likely to be *A Book of Psalmody* (*HTI* code BeesMBP); the earliest edition located is dated 'not later than 1740' in *HTI*. That collection, however, contains no fuging tunes, so the new information does not alter the conclusion that the rage for fuging tunes was started in about 1746 by Beesly's *A Collection of 20 New Psalm Tunes.*

VII. Organs in English Parish Churches, 1660–1830

More complete and in some cases more accurate information about organs in the City of London may be found in Donovan Dawe, *Organists of the City of London 1666–1850* (Padstow, 1983).

VIII. Organ Music in Parish Churches, 1660–1730

The earliest known comprehensive set of organ psalms published in England was *The Psalms by Dr Blow Set Full for the Organ or Harpsicord as they are Play'd in Churches or Chapels.* It appeared in Blow's lifetime, for it was advertised in *The Post Man* on 19 August 1703. A second, enlarged edition appeared in 1705. These have not survived; the earliest known exemplar dates from after Blow's death in 1708, probably from 1718, in a copy bound with Daniel Purcell's similar collection published in that year. For details see *HTI*, BlowJPSF c. For another of Daniel Purcell's settings of psalm tunes see Musica Britannica, vol. 85, no. 6. A rival, probably pirated, edition of the Purcell set appeared in 1718 as part of *The Harpsichord Master Improved* (see PurcDPSF b).

IX. Croft and the Charity Hymn

Note 4: In fact the later editions of *The Psalms and Hymns* (*HTI* #SPHW), starting in 1697, were intended for St James's only, and at first reverted to two vocal parts (Cantus and Bassus), but from the 7th edition (1708) returned to three parts (SSB). In the same year the *Supplement to the New Version of Psalms* (*TS TatB), in its 6th edition, began providing bass parts for its tunes, which had hitherto been printed as melodies only. Henry Playford's *Divine Companion* (1701) catered for parish churches with pieces for SB and SMB.

The Second Book of the Divine Companion (PearWDC2), compiled by William Pearson (who succeeded to Henry Playford's music publishing business) and published in about 1725, contained several hymns and anthems explicitly intended for charity children to sing on fund-raising days, some with lower voice parts which were no doubt sung by the members of the parish societies. These include three of Croft's four charity hymns (those numbered I, IV and VI in the list on p. 211), anticipating Barker's printings by many years.

Hymn VI, in this version, has a full SATB chorus. For an edition of Hymn I
see Temperley, *The Music of the English Parish Church*, ii, no. 24.
Note 9: This footnote set off a controversy, which is reported in my essay on
ST. ANNE in Raymond F. Glover, ed., *The Hymnal 1982 Companion* (New
York, 1994). The balance of the evidence supports Croft's authorship. He
was known as both Croft and Crofts, and the Christian name 'Philip' in the
church records could well have been an error.

XI. The Lock Hospital Chapel and its Music

Page 278: 'The strict Calvinist tradition had forbidden women to sing in church.'
This statement needs correcting, for in fact the question was debated in
Calvinist circles from the Reformation onwards. A defence of women's
voices is to be found in *Singing of Psalms a Gospel-Ordnance* (London, 1650)
by John Cotton, the English Puritan divine who became a religious leader
in New England. By 1700 women's participation in singing was accepted
in the Church of England, but their inclusion in voluntary choirs was only
beginning. According to Sally Drage it was more common in Lancashire
than elsewhere.
Page 280, n.81: For Burney's setting of the dialogue hymn 'Tell us, O women'
see Musica Britannica vol. 85, no. 81. Nos. 28 and 85 are also from the
Lock Hospital Collection.
Page 285, n. 91: The promised article never appeared. But see my essay on the
tune HELMSLEY in Raymond F. Glover, ed., *The Hymnal 1982 Companion*
(New York, 1994).

XII. Jonathan Gray and Church Music in York, 1770–1840

Page 287: I made sure that Gray was recognized in *The New Grove* (1980 and
since).
Page 296, line 9: In fact the Foundling and Magdalen collections were less
evangelical than the Lock Hospital Collection (see No. X).

XIII. Organ Settings of English Psalm Tunes

The chronology of the Dulwich MSS. is revised in No. VIII. Sebastian Wesley's
organ settings, referred to briefly here, are fully discussed, with examples,
by Peter Horton in his authoritative book, *Samuel Sebastian Wesley: A Life*
(Oxford, 2004), pp. 62–4 and 174–6. Parry's chorale preludes are treated by
Jeremy Dibble in *C. Hubert H. Parry: His Life and Music* (Oxford, 1992),
pp. 446–7 and 477–8.

XIV. Ancient and Modern in the Work of Sir John Stainer

In my anxiety to do justice to Stainer as a composer, I unfairly disparaged his achievements as a scholar. Jeremy Dibble has restored the right balance in his perceptive study *John Stainer: A Life in Music* (Woodbridge, 2007). In particular Dibble shows from primary sources that Stainer played a larger part in the two editions of Bodleian manuscript music than I suggested here (Dibble, pp. 257–63).

INDEX

Page references for main treatments are shown in italics; n = *footnote.*

INDEX

INDEX

INDEX

INDEX